RUMBLE IN THE JUNGLE

WELCOME TO THE delightfully twisted fantasy world of Blood Bowl where humans, elves, goblins and ogres work out their aggression on the football field, rather than the battlefield. *Rumble in the Jungle* is the fourth novel that follows the rags to riches career of star thrower Dunk Hoffnung and his team the Bad Bay Hackers. After winning the *Spike! Magazine* tournament final, the Hackers set sail for the fabulous land of Lustria to seek new challenges. In the hot, steamy jungles, Dunk and his friends have to fight off zombies, pygmy halflings, lizardmen and more – and that's before they face off against the Amazon team in the Tobazco Bowl!

By the same author

THE BLOOD BOWL OMNIBUS
(Contains the first three Blood Bowl novels:
Blood Bowl, *Dead Ball* and *Deathmatch*)
by Matt Forbeck

A BLOOD BOWL NOVEL

RUMBLE IN THE JUNGLE

Matt Forbeck

Dedicated to the Green Bay Packers, for filling my life with great football. Also to the people of Costa Rica, especially the desk staff at La Bahía de Los Delfines in Tambor: Pedra, Marco, and Gabriella. Many thanks for showing us around the jungle.

My gratitude, as always, to everyone at the Black Library, especially Marc Gascoigne and Christian Dunn, with special thanks to Lindsey Priestley and Nick Kyme for their undying patience.

A BLACK LIBRARY PUBLICATION

First published in Great Britain in 2007 by
BL Publishing,
Games Workshop Ltd.,
Willow Road, Nottingham,
NG7 2WS, UK

10 9 8 7 6 5 4 3 2 1

Cover illustration by Philip Sibbering

A CIP record for this book is available from the British Library.

ISBN 13: 978 1 84416 517 9
ISBN 10: 1 84416 517 5

Distributed in the US by Simon & Schuster
1230 Avenue of the Americas, New York, NY 10020.

See the Black Library on the Internet at
www.blacklibrary.com

Find out more about Games Workshop
and the world of Warhammer and Blood Bowl at
www.games-workshop.com

'Hi there, sports fans, and welcome to the Blood Bowl for tonight's contest. You join us here with a capacity crowd, packed with members of every race from across the known world, all howling like banshees in anticipation of tonight's game. Oh, and yes there are some banshees... Well, kick-off is in about two pages' time, so we've just got time to go over to your commentator for tonight, Jim Johnson, for a recap on the rules of the game before battle commences. Good evening, Jim!'

'Thank you, Bob! Well, good evening and boy, are you folks in for some great sporting entertainment. First of all though, for those of you at home who are unfamiliar with the rules, here's how the game is played.

'Blood Bowl is an epic conflict between two teams of heavily armed and quite insane warriors. Players pass, throw and run with the ball, attempting to get it to the other end of the field, the end zone. Of course, the other team must try and stop them, and recover the ball for their side. If a team gets the ball over the line into the opponents' end zone it's called a touchdown; the team that scores the most touchdowns by the end of the match wins the game. Of course, it's not always as simple as that...'

FOR THE LIFE of him, Dunk Hoffnung couldn't figure out what he was still doing on a Blood Bowl pitch. At the end of the last season, he'd led his team — the Bad Bay Hackers — all the way to the Blood Bowl championship. In the course of that, he'd found his true love, repaired his relationship with his brother, and saved the Empire from Khorne the Blood God.

To top it all off, he'd reclaimed his family's lost fortune, including the keep they'd once owned in Altdorf, the Empire's capital. He had fame, friends, and more money than he would ever need. What else did he have to prove?

Dunk had wrestled with these doubts several times over the past week, during the first round of the *Spike! Magazine* tournament. Now, though, the game demanded his full attention, as the spiked ball sailed down out of the black night and into his arms, making him the primary target for the eleven armed and armoured dark elves playing for the Darkside Cowboys.

'Hoffnung grabs the kick-off, and the final semifinal game of the tournament is underway!' Bob Buford's voice rang out across the stadium over the Preternatural Address system. The crowd roared to answer him, its lust for blood feeding the volume.

'Just listen to those fans!' Bob's partner, Jim Johnson, chipped in. 'There's nothing like a pack of people screaming at the top of their lungs!'

'Sounds like you're talking about last night's dinner,' the ogre Bob said to the vampire Jim. 'Stop it! You're making me drool!'

Dunk scanned the situation downfield. Most of his team-mates — the ones in the yellow and green uniforms with the three-sword H logos on their helmets — raced ahead of him, converging to a point, trying to form a protective wedge behind which he could run. Meanwhile, the pale skinned elves in the black and blue uniforms came charging up the field, seeking to find a way past the Hackers' linemen so they could rip Dunk's heart from his chest.

Dunk spun to the left and charged up behind his brother Dirk, pump faking a pass to the right. Only one of the Cowboys got fooled. He hesitated just long enough for Spinne to smash him to the ground, and then do a little dance on his helmet with her spiked shoes.

'Oh, that's gotta hurt!' Bob said. 'I wonder if I could get her to do that to me after the game!'

'Gee, Bob, don't you think her boyfriend, Dunk, would object?'

'Hey, if he wants to watch, he has to pay like everyone else!'

'Really?'

'Okay, I'll let him in for half price, but just this once!'

Dunk ignored the blather over the PA. He wondered if the Cowboys' coach had paid the pair to say things to distract him. It didn't strike him as something the Cowboys would do. Not that they wouldn't cheat, they just wouldn't be that subtle about it.

Unfortunately, it worked. One of the Cowboys blazed straight past McGraw — one of the Hacker linemen — with not even a whisper of protest. Dunk gaped at the oncoming dark elf for a moment: the white dreadlocks flopping out from his helmet on all sides, the snarl on his perfect face, the muscles that were far too big to naturally fit across an elf's shoulders.

The things that drew his eye the most, though, were the long, glittering blades that jutted out from the steel bracers protecting the elf's forearms. One of them was covered with fresh blood.

Dunk knew then that McGraw was dead. If he didn't move fast, he would share his team-mate's fate. He would have liked to have called the man his friend, but he barely knew him. McGraw had made the team in the pre-tournament tryouts, just as Dunk had three years ago, and the only thing he could tell anyone about McGraw was that he thought Bloodweiser was like carbonated seal piss.

'Whoa!' said Jim. 'Looks like the newest Hacker is DOA. Er-Rel Towens dropped him without even a stutter in his step!'

'I got dibs on that fountain of blood spurting from his neck!' said Bob. 'The fresh stuff is best!'

'Speaking of which, how's that corpse tattooing campaign of yours coming along?' asked Jim.

'The "Dead-On Label"?' More coaches are going for it, especially once they see how much they can get for fresh kills on the open market. They pay for those players and have to get their value out of them somehow!'

Dunk juked left again, and then raced to the right. The move faked Towens out of his left shoe, but he still kept after Dunk, snagging the green jersey with his long, thin fingers.

Dunk twisted around, hoping to wrench his jersey from the elf's grasp, but he just reeled him in instead. The Cowboy assassin slashed at Dunk with the blade stabbing from his free arm, and the Hacker thrower put up the only thing he had to block it: the ball.

The edge of the blade skittered off the ball's reinforced surface, its point gouging a long trail in the side of Dunk's helmet. Dunk raised the ball before him again to fend off another slash, then another. A quick glance up the field told him he had to do something to lose this attacker soon, or the rest of the Cowboys would tackle him under a huge pile. If that happened, he'd take more jabs than a dartboard.

Dunk took the ball in both hands and smashed it into Towens's face. The dark elf glanced up at the last second and took the point of the ball right in his faceguard.

And there it stuck.

When Dunk tried to pull the ball back, it wouldn't come. It had got wedged into the faceguard like an axe in an old oak. Try as he might, Dunk couldn't wrest the thing loose.

'Get it out!' Towens screamed. 'For the hatred of all that's unholy, get it out!'

From the blood dribbling down the elf's chest, Dunk guessed that the football was wedged in more than just the helmet. Towens let go of Dunk's shirt and began to slash at the football with his blades. They were too long for him to stab the points into the pigskin, though, and the spikes and hide repelled his attempts to saw through them.

Dunk reached for the ball again and grabbed on with both hands. He tried to plant a foot on the elf's chest for leverage, but Towens slashed at him with his blades, and he leaped back.

'Hold still, damn it, and I'll get it out,' he said.

Towens ignored Dunk's pleas and charged straight at him, following the sounds of the thrower's voice over the cheering of the crowd. Dunk stepped to the side like a matador and tripped Towens as he went by. The elf went face down into the Astrogranite, where the spike on the other end of the ball stuck.

It was about that time that the ogre showed up.

M'Grash K'Thragsh crushed one Cowboy beneath a massive boot with serrated spikes, then tossed another clear into the stands on his way over to reach Dunk. The hapless dark elf went sailing into the first few rows, fans scattering like cockroaches before a torch. Once the player crunched into the stands, though, he disappeared under a swarm of them.

Moments later, the Cowboy popped up on the upraised hands of the crowd, and Dunk saw him get body-passed straight towards the cheap seats at the top of the stadium. The sight sent a shudder through him as he remembered how the same thing had happened to him in his first game in this very stadium. The various awnings on the outside of the stadium had broken his fall, but the sausage vendor whose cart he'd crushed had beaten him hard enough to put him into a three-day coma.

Dunk put those thoughts out of his head as the ogre stormed up towards him and put a hand on his shoulder. 'Dunkel okay?' the massive, tusk-faced creature in the Hackers uniform asked.

Dunk nodded at his friend. 'Just get the ball.'

M'Grash reached down to grab Towens by the back of the helmet, and there was a sickening snap. Dunk winced as the ogre handed him the ball with the helmet and head still attached to it. He'd got what he'd asked for, but not what he'd meant.

'Oh!' Bob said. 'That's going to leave a mark!'

'Grave "marker", I think you mean!' said Jim. 'So much for Towens renegotiating his contract, unless he plans to play for the Champions of Death! Coach Tomolandry always says any other team's loss is his gain!'

'What now, Dunkel?' M'Grash started to say. The ogre had a brain the size of Dunk's fist, which was barely enough to make his body move, much less think of where to move it. He needed constant direction.

'Charge!' Dunk said, pointing down the field towards the distant end zone.

M'Grash knew the drill. He led the way in front of Dunk, tearing through any foes brave or stupid enough to challenge him, while Dunk carried the ball behind him and looked for an open catcher down-field. They'd run the same play hundreds if not thousands of times before. It was simple enough for even M'Grash to grasp it, and it worked.

As they went, Dunk wrenched the football away from the helmeted head, and got up close behind M'Grash. Shielded by the ogre, he juggled the ball up under one arm and held Towens's head out wide in his throwing hand.

Before they got twenty yards down the field, though, M'Grash fell to his knees, grabbing at his helmet and screaming as if in horrible pain.

Dunk wanted to check on his friend, but he knew that if he stopped moving the Cowboys would pulverise him. So, he scanned the pitch and spotted the team captain, a dark-skinned legend by the name of Rhett Cavre, kicking over a defender and breaking away. Unfortunately, he had two other dark elves converging on him, and a toss in that direction would be a sure interception.

Dunk cocked back his arm and hurled Towens's head in the man's direction, hoping it would buy them a few minutes. Without even looking to see if Cavre caught the helmeted remains, Dunk rushed to M'Grash's side. 'Are you all right?'

'Oh yes, my foolish friend,' M'Grash said, his voice thick with a Bretonnian accent. 'I am better than ever.'

Dunk knew instantly that something was wrong. He spun on his cleats to sprint off in the other direction. Before he could get away, though, a meaty hand reached out and grabbed him around his lower leg.

M'Grash climbed to his knees, and Dunk got a good look at his eyes. They stood vacant, but for a horrible red glow. Dunk felt like someone had poured ice into his jock strap.

The crowd cheered.

'Interception!' Bob shouted.

'You, on the other hand,' the ogre said in someone else's voice, 'are soon to be beyond all troubles.'

Dunk wanted to scream, but he knew it would do no good. He tried to shake his leg free instead, but M'Grash's grip only tightened on him as he laughed at Dunk's pathetic attempt.

'Live by the ogre, die by the ogre,' M'Grash said. 'Words to be torn to pieces by.'

Then Dunk knew what had happened. The Cowboys' team owner and wizard, the legendary liche Berry Bones, must have used some kind of spell to take over the ogre's mind. That put the undead spell slinger in the driver's seat behind M'Grash's monstrous body.

Dunk lashed out with his free boot and caught the ogre between the eyes, smashing his nose into his face. M'Grash dropped the thrower and clutched at the blood flowing from his nostrils.

'Ow!' M'Grash said. 'You'd think that ogres would be immune from pain. They must just be too stupid to feel it.'

Dunk grimaced at the mess he'd made of M'Grash's face. He never wanted to hurt his friend, but the wizard had made it clear that his only other choice was to die. As the ogre reached for him again, he did the wise thing and fled.

The crowd erupted in a cheer. 'Touchdown, Cowboys!' said Jim.

Dunk glanced up at the Jumboball, a massive crystal ball through which wizards from the Extraordinary Spellcasters Prognosticated News Network (ESPNN) broadcast images of the game, and spotted a Darkside Cowboy spiking Towens's head in the end zone.

'Wait a minute, Jim,' Bob said. 'The referee in the end zone is waving that off. Seems that's not the ball "Itchy" Mirvin had in his hands, but it looks like he's finally secured that starting position over Towens!'

The crowd roared, and Dunk didn't need to look at the Jumboball to know that every finger in the stadium was pointing at him. He brought the ball up from where he'd been trying to hide it under his arm and cradled it in a proper football hold. The roar grew louder.

Dunk could feel M'Grash's breath on his neck: hot, steamy, and smelling of the insanely spicy sauce of chimera wings. He risked a glance back and saw his friend reaching for him, the red glow still dancing alongside murder in his eyes.

Dunk put everything he had into a final burst of speed, but it wasn't enough. The ogre's legs were too long, and he pounded along too fast.

Dunk had raced against M'Grash in practice and had always beaten the ogre in a flat sprint. He'd long suspected his friend had been throwing the races to him, but then he'd realised what was going on. Dumb as he was, M'Grash didn't trust the ground under his feet. He ran slower than he could have because he wanted to make sure he didn't fall.

Whoever was in M'Grash's head now didn't share that fear. Assuming it was Bones, he had the ogre's legs pumping as hard as he could.

Dunk stuck the ball out in his left hand to fake going in that direction, then cut right. M'Grash tried to follow him, but tripped on his massive feet. As he went tumbling forward, he reached out with his humongous hands spread, and one gigantic paw closed around Dunk's leg again.

The pair somersaulted forward and flipped more times than Dunk could count. His head rattling around in his helmet almost knocked him senseless. His years of training helped him hold on to the ball despite the fact he almost lost his lunch.

They rolled to a rest at the foot of a tree, and for a moment Dunk couldn't figure out how they'd managed to find themselves outside the stadium. Then he heard Edgar's voice.

'What the bloody hell's this then?' the treeman in the Hackers uniform asked as he leaned over Dunk and M'Grash. 'Aren't you two supposed to be on the same team?'

M'Grash glared up at the treeman and roared.

Dunk waved at Edgar until he caught his wide, green eyes, and then stabbed a finger at the ogre, who still had his leg in his fist. 'Timber!' Dunk yelled.

The treeman recognised the call and executed the play perfectly. He put his branches up tall, held himself rigid, which wasn't hard as treemen don't bend well in the first place, and tipped himself over onto the ogre.

M'Grash yelped in surprise and then pain as Edgar toppled over onto him, crushing the ogre beneath the treeman's bulk. M'Grash's hand let go of Dunk as he struggled to reach back to grab Edgar and pull him from his back. The ogre's muscle-bound arms didn't stretch that way though. He was stuck.

'By all the dark gods!' M'Grash said. 'Get him off! Make it stop!'

Dunk scrambled to his feet and saw at least half of the Darkside Cowboys converging on him. After seeing how he'd tricked them into destroying the most important part of their star catcher's corpse, they were out for revenge as much as for the ball. Since he had both, he made a doubly attractive target.

Dunk decided his best bet was to halve his lure. With so many of the Cowboys coming at him, the Hackers' catchers were open. Cavre stood waving his hands in the end zone, an easy score, but Spinne jumped up and down on the opposite side of the field from Dunk. He cocked back his arm and fired a pass off at Spinne.

The Cowboys rushing towards Dunk watched the ball spiral through a perfect arc over their heads and land in Spinne's outstretched hands. She held it high and waved it at them, taunting them, then bent over and smacked the ball on her rump. The crowd erupted at the display of cockiness, and the Cowboys switched their attention from Dunk to Spinne.

'Wow!' Jim said. 'How many times do you see a Blood Bowl team pick getting the ball over sheer spite?'

'That's what makes the Cowboys one of the most profitable teams out there! Coach Bill Per-Sells' ruthless fiscal discipline drills this into his players' heads: It's not about blood! It all comes down to the bottom line!'

'Plus, Schönheit did a masterful job of making them mad at her. If you have to choose between revenge for a team-mate or revenge for yourself, there's no contest!'

For the briefest moment, Dunk feared for Spinne, but he felt the same way every time she stepped on to the pitch with him. He'd got over it, mostly. He never liked putting her in danger, but she'd made it clear she expected him to treat her like an equal. In any case, he'd needed a distraction so he could deal with M'Grash.

Dunk reached down and grabbed the doorknocker of a nose ring that hung from the ogre's nose, right where it pierced his slab of a septum. 'Let him go,' he snarled at the wizard within.

M'Grash stopped whining at the treeman and turned his attention to Dunk. He reached for him with a massive mitt, but Edgar slapped down his arm with a branch.

'That'll bloody well be enough of that,' Edgar said.

Dunk wrenched M'Grash's nose ring, and the ogre screamed in pain. Dunk had never heard such a horrible and pathetic sound escape his friend's mouth.

'Get out,' Dunk said, 'now! Or I rip your nose apart.'

The ogre froze. 'You wouldn't hurt your best friend.'

'It wouldn't bother my friend. Too stupid, right?' Dunk twisted the ring slowly until it seemed like it might pull right through the ogre's skin. 'You, though, I'll bet you're smart enough to feel every bit of it.'

M'Grash growled in frustration, loud enough to hurt Dunk's ears. Then his face went slack.

As the red light vanished from M'Grash's eyes, the ogre looked up at Dunk. 'Dunkel?' he said, his child-like innocence restored.

'Yes?' Dunk asked, relieved to have his friend back, in many, many ways.

The ogre crossed his eyes at Dunk's hands, still on the nose ring. 'Let go now?'

'Right!' Dunk let the ring loose and leapt back, waving Edgar off.

'About time,' Edgar said as he rolled off the ogre's back.

'Touchdown, Hackers!' Jim said. The crowd burst into screams of excitement.

'Wow!' Bob said. 'I haven't seen moves like that since last night's dinner. Those snotlings really didn't want to end up in your belly.'

'For all the good it did them.' Jim gave a cruel laugh.

Dunk pumped his fist at the crowd. It had been a rough start to the game, but they'd still come out of it well. If the Cowboys had already tried their worst tricks, they had the game in the bag.

'Pardon me,' Edgar said from where he'd rolled off M'Grash and on to the Astrogranite. 'Do you think the ogre I just bloody well saved might be persuaded to give me a hand up?'

'We won!' Dunk ducked as his brother Dirk poured a tankard of ale over his head. The cold, frothy liquid ran down Dunk's neck and back, making him roar in mock rage. Then he gathered the younger Hoffnung up in a bear hug and growled in his face.

'Championship game, here we come,' Dirk grinned.

Much as he wanted to, Dunk couldn't be angry with his brother. He was too happy about the victory to begrudge the man such enthusiastic joy.

Before he could say a word, though, M'Grash gathered the two men up into an even larger, lung crushing embrace. 'Hackers win!' The ogre topped off his cheer with a howl that caused everyone else in the locker room to cover their ears.

Spinne leapt up on a bench and gently pried Dunk loose from the ogre's grasp. 'Be gentle with him,' she said with a smile.

'I sorry,' M'Grash said, his toothy grin fading.

'I was talking to Dunk and Dirk,' Spinne said as she reached up to give the ogre's tender nose a pat. 'Are you feeling better yet?'

The ogre's grin returned, wide enough to swallow Spinne's head. He nodded happily at her. 'Doc help.'

'Took half a gallon of my best materials, and three yards of sutures, but he'll be fine,' said a white haired, sour faced elf with a monocle over the eye not covered with a blood-stained patch.

'Thank you, Dr Pill,' Dunk said.

The elf growled the gratitude away, just as he always did.

'How about the others?' a dazzling, dark haired woman asked, as she squirmed forward between two players. As she spoke, a glittering gold ball with a hole in one end hovered before her and off to one side. Then it spun its black eye from her towards the ill-mannered apothecary.

'I don't speak on camra,' Dr Pill said, regarding the hovering ball with suspicion.

'But I'm Lästiges Weibchen, with ESPNN, and Hackers fans everywhere are dying to know the fate of Standplatz Innen, Sicheres Gegangen and Geborenes Verurteilt.'

'If they're dying, they'll be in good company. Innen, Gegangen, and Verurteilt were all DOA. You can thank the Cowboy's "hidden" blades for that.'

Dunk's grin fell from his face, and a silence hung over the rest of the room. 'Couldn't you do anything for them?' he asked. As soon as the words left his lips, he winced, ready for one of the apothecary's biting retorts.

Instead, Dr Pill shook his head sadly. 'They left DNZ orders, "Do Not Zombify", so I, ah, rendered them useless to the vultures from the undead teams.'

'Doctor,' a low voice said from behind Dunk, 'that should very well be enough.'

Dunk turned to see Captain Pegleg Haken standing in the doorway of the coach's office. He held his yellow tricorn hat in his hands, exposing the top of his head, where Dunk saw that his long, curly, and inky locks had started to thin. A tall, stunning woman with bronzed skin and sun bleached hair stood next to him.

'We're celebrating a victory here,' the ex-pirate turned coach said, raising his hooked hand in the air as he stepped into the room on his wooden leg, 'which is why I prefer to leave the news of our fallen friends until the morning after.' He glared at Dr Pill as he spoke.

'Never weep for a Blood Bowl player,' Cavre said. Stepping between the captain and any issue took brass, and Cavre had plenty. He had been the team captain and the coach's right-hand man since long before Dunk had joined the team. If anyone could skirt Haken's wrath, it would be him.

'Aye,' the captain said, acknowledging Cavre's wisdom by jutting out his chin. 'They died doing what they loved. We should all be so lucky as to carve those words on our headstones.'

'Hear, hear,' the players murmured. The loudest of them was Rotes Hernd, the backup thrower. She sat on the bench much of the time, waiting for Dunk to get tired or hurt, but she'd been close to at least two of the dead players.

Rotes stood as tall as Spinne, but was built broader across her shoulders. She had the arms of a thrower, while Spinne had the hands of a catcher. The two made for an excellent combination during practices, although Dunk and Spinne connected better on almost every level.

'Who's your friend?' Schlechtes Getrunken, one of the backup linemen asked. With Gegangen dead, he had moved up to a starting position, something he'd been celebrating hard since the final whistle had blown to end the game.

Dunk suspected Getrunken had actually started in with his celebration well before that. Many coaches ignored a player taking an occasional nip from a bottle during a game. The alcohol helped kill the pain most players felt on the field, and the fear too.

Sometimes players went a little overboard though. Dunk recalled one game early in the previous year's Chaos Cup tournament in which the Greenfield Grasshuggers, a halfling team, had been so drunk that they'd just laid there on the field as the Laurelorn Paladins trampled over them. Being sticklers for the rules, the Paladins had insisted on playing the game as long as Grasshuggers were still on the field, whether they were conscious or not.

Getrunken clearly had celebrated a bit too hard. He leered at the statuesque blonde, who stared the tall, burly man level in the eye and sneered at him.

'I am called Enojada,' the woman said, her spicy accent tinged with disgust at Getrunken's state. 'I have business here with your Captain Haken, and possibly with your team as a whole.'

'I'm part of the team, baby,' Getrunken said, slurring his words. 'I can help you with any hole you need–'

Before the man could finish his sentence, the woman had knocked him to the floor with a sweep of her leg. Getrunken went down hard, his head cracking on the stone floor, knocking him even more senseless than he'd been. As he fell into a deep snore, she put a booted foot on his chest and leaned forward to look at the others. Her eyes dared them to retaliate, to come to their team-mate's defence.

No one moved. Getrunken had only been with the team for just over a week, and none of them had formed much of an attachment to him yet. That rarely happened, Dunk knew, until a player survived a tournament. Then he'd bond with the others on their way back to Bad Bay, aboard the team's cutter, the *Sea Chariot*. He'd then become a brother, part of the family.

Right now, they only saw a lethal woman standing over a drunken fool.

Haken cleared his throat. 'My Hackers? Allow me to introduce Miss Ay-No-Ha-Da.' He pronounced every syllable separately, as if the foreign word felt strange on his tongue. 'She hails from Lustria, across the sea.'

Lästiges gasped, and the camra over her shoulder turned on the strange woman. 'I've heard of you,' she said. 'You're an Amazon, one of the best Blood Bowl players Lustria ever produced.'

The tanned woman smiled, showing all of her glaring white teeth. 'That was a long time ago. I'm retired these days. I work for the AFL, the Amazon Football League, now.'

'What brings you all the way across the ocean?' Lästiges asked. 'The *Spike! Magazine* tournament?'

'Partially,' Enojada said. 'I watch the games on Cabalvision, of course, but there is nothing like being in the stadium.'

'Why are you really here?' Spinne asked. As she spoke, she held Dunk's hand and gripped it tightly.

The Amazon smiled at Spinne, sizing her up. Dunk wondered if she was appraising his love for a uniform or a grave.

'In Lustria, we have our own tournament. It is not so famous as your Blood Bowl championship, of course, but everyone in Lustria watches it. This year, the AFL has decided that we should reach out to our companions across the sea, the ones that brought the holy sport of Blood Bowl to us, and invite them to join our league.'

Alarm bells went off in Dunk's head, starting with the words 'holy sport'. Fanatics of any kind, religious, Blood Bowl, or otherwise, put him on edge. He remembered the priest back in Dörfchen who'd tried to sell him out to the chimera menacing that little town. That experience had capped off his opinion of organised religion. Well, that and having to save the whole of Altdorf, the seat of the Empire, from the plots of the Blood God Khorne.

Everyone in the room started to talk at once.

'We can't go,' Erhaltenes Spiel, one of the starting linemen, said. 'We have a championship to defend.'

Dirk smirked. 'A land full of gorgeous Amazons to wrestle with doesn't sound too bad to me.' He elbowed Jammernder Anfäger, a starting lineman, and the younger player laughed.

Lästiges shot daggers at Dirk with her eyes. The two of them had been dating on and off for years, but their jobs kept them apart for weeks at a time. The strain on their relationship often showed, but she was too much of a professional to attack a Blood Bowl player on camra, or so Dunk hoped.

Others chipped in with their opinions, but it all came to a halt with a horrible screech. Dunk turned to see Pegleg scratching a long furrow in the team blackboard on the far side of the locker room. He kept it up until he had everyone's attention and then scraped a little bit farther just to be cruel.

'We're not going anywhere,' Pegleg said into the merciful silence. 'The money is here in the Old World, not halfway across the planet in the bush leagues.'

Enojada scowled, her plastic demeanour cracking for just a moment before she restored her perfect smile. 'Of course,' she said, 'we expected as much. It is a pity though. The Lustrian Lusties, the team I used to play for, was very much looking forward to the honour of playing against you. Now I must face the pain of telling my team captain that you have decided she is not worth facing.'

'I'm sorry,' Spinne said, 'but I don't see how that's our problem.'

Enojada licked her lips at Spinne as if she were a fly that had just wandered into her web. 'Not you, of course, my darling.' Her gaze locked on Dunk and then Dirk. 'But she will miss seeing the men she loves so much.'

Dunk felt like he'd been disembowelled. Spinne raised an eyebrow at him, and Lästiges looked as if she might pick up a spiky bit of armour and drive it straight into Dirk's heart.

'Just who is your captain?' Dunk asked, dreading the answer. He didn't know what game this Amazon was playing, but he suspected he wouldn't like it.

'I thought you knew,' Enojada said, raising her hand to her mouth in mock shock. 'She is called Kirta Hoffnung, of course. She is your sister, no?'

Dunk didn't need to look at his younger brother to know they'd both come to the same decision. 'We're going,' Dunk and Dirk said in unison.

'Mr Hoffnung and Mr Heldmann,' Pegleg said, his whisper more menacing than any shout, 'in my office.'

The ex-pirate walked back through the door in which he'd been standing, and Dirk and Dunk stormed through it. As they strode through the shocked silence of the locker room, every eye locked on them. Dunk spared a sidelong glance for Enojada, and had to fight the urge to wipe the smirk off her face. The woman might be the only link he had to his sister, but she didn't have to be so smug about it.

Pegleg hobbled around behind his desk and said, 'Close the door.' Before Dunk could slam it shut, Enojada slipped in.

'Out,' Pegleg said. 'This is team business.'

'I believe I might be able to help.'

'I think you've done enough, miss.'

'Mizz.'

'How's that?'

'We Amazons prefer to be called "mizz", not "miss".'

Pegleg tossed his hat on the desk before him. His eyes bulged like they wanted to pop from his face. 'Get. Out. Of. My. Office.'

'She stays,' said Dirk. Enojada winked at him, and the man blushed. He recovered and backhanded Dunk on the arm. 'If she knows where Kirta is, I don't want to let her out of my sight.'

Dunk nodded. Then he looked at Pegleg, and braced himself for the man's reaction. 'She stays.'

Pegleg spat on the floor. 'Fine. She should hear this too: We're not going.'

'We are,' said Dunk.

'Now, boys,' a voice said from behind Dunk. He glanced back to see a rotund halfling, his agent, Slogo Fullbelly, peeking in through the still open door. 'Listen to reason.'

'Forget it, Slick,' Dunk said. 'If Kirta's in Lustria, that's where we're heading.'

Pegleg scowled. 'You can't leave the team. We're in the finals in two days.'

'Rotes can take my place,' said Dunk. 'She's been gunning for my spot for over a year.'

'She's not the thrower you are.' He glared at Dirk. 'And we don't have anyone to replace you either. You're both staying.'

'We don't need to leave until after the game,' Enojada said. 'That still gives us plenty of time to make it to the Tobazco Bowl.'

Dunk raised an eyebrow at the woman. 'Why do they call it that?'

'Our stadium is formed in the natural crater in the top of Mount Tobazco.'

'Crater? What caused that?'

'Well, it is a volcano.'

Dunk slapped his forehead.

'So,' Slick said, 'you boys want to run off to find your sister and play ball in the middle of an active volcano.'

'Oh,' said Enojada, 'it sleeps now.'

'You mean it's dormant?' asked Dirk. Dunk could see he was pleased with himself for having come up with the word.

'Yes, that is the word.' The Amazon smiled at Dirk.

'See,' said Dunk, 'safe as can be. It can't be any worse than playing in the Dungeonbowl.'

Pegleg slammed his hook into the top of his desk, and there it stuck. 'We have an obligation to play in the Dungeonbowl again this year. We have a contract with the Grey Wizards to represent them. We cannot back out of that.'

'The Hackers can play. You just won't have Dirk or me.'

Pegleg's nostrils flared as he spoke. 'As your little agent there can no doubt inform you, Mr Hoffnung, you have a contract with me. I plan to hold you to it.'

'I'll buy myself out of it.'

'The contract is not for sale,' Pegleg said between gritted teeth.

'Dunk and I have plenty of money,' said Dirk, 'now that we've inherited our family estate.'

'This isn't about gold,' Pegleg said.

Dunk, Dirk, and Slick gaped at him.

'That's the problem with players and their agents,' Pegleg said, 'short-term thinking. Of course it's about the gold, but not the gold I can hold in my hand.'

Dunk squinted at the ex-pirate. 'What did you do with Coach Haken?'

Pegleg waved him off. 'You don't get it, do you? Last year, we did just what we set out to do, what I've set out to do every year of my career: win the Blood Bowl championship.'

'So? You should be happy.' He stared at his coach. 'You're not happy.'

'He's never happy,' said Dirk. 'Maybe the night after a win. The next day, he's back to being cranky as ever. Coach Bombardi's the same way.'

'I get it,' said Slick, rubbing his chubby chin, 'he's after a dynasty now.'

Dunk scratched his head. 'What?'

Pegleg sat back in his chair and regarded the others. 'A dynasty: a legacy, a chance to build not just a winning team, but a legend.'

'You're getting old,' Dirk said.

Pegleg catapulted up out of his chair and lunged at Dirk. Unfortunately, his hook was still stuck in his desk from when he'd slammed it down earlier. He'd been trying to free himself the entire time without letting anyone know, but now he'd forgotten himself and almost broken his wrist for his trouble.

Dunk stepped between Pegleg and his brother before the ex-pirate went for his cutlass. He held his hands up in front of him to try to calm the enraged man down.

'What Dirk means, I think,' Dunk said, taking an instant to glare at his brother, 'is that you're starting to think not about what you're doing, but about how you'll be remembered.'

'And what in the deep blue sea is wrong with that?' Pegleg asked, still pulling at his hook.

'Nothing at all, but,' Dunk said as he stabbed a finger at his head, 'you're thinking too small.' He gestured towards Enojada. 'Just think; you could coach the first team to be the undisputed champion on two continents. Haken's Hackers would be the first team to truly be known as the best in the entire world.'

Pegleg leaned forward on his stuck hook. 'You,' he said to Dunk, 'are full of shit. Beating up on a bunch of little girls halfway around the world while we should be back here kicking the tar out of serious opponents will only make us a laughing stock.'

Enojada moved so fast that Dunk saw only a blur. One moment, the desk stood between Pegleg and him, and the next it had been smashed in half. The Amazon stepped back to where she had been standing near the door, and the coach looked down at his free hook and waggled it on the end of his wrist.

'My apologies for the "little girls" crack, mizz,' Pegleg said. He spoke in a soft, steady tone once more. 'But my point still stands. From the point of view of the Blood Bowl fan, Lustria is just another bush league. We're staying here.'

Dunk scowled, and then decided to play his trump card. 'We'll buy the Hackers from you then.'

'What?' Pegleg stuck his hook in his ear and scraped it around, pulling out a good chunk of wax. 'Could you repeat that, Mr Hoffnung? I don't think I heard you correctly.'

'Dirk and I will buy the Hackers from you. We can sell the keep and the rest of our holdings in Altdorf and have plenty of money to handle the purchase.'

'The Hackers are not for sale.' The man spoke as low as a whisper, but still growled like a mother bear defending her cubs.

Slick cleared his throat, and then spoke, softly and reverently. 'Come on now, Pegleg, everything is for sale, at the right price.

Pegleg's voice rose straight to a scream. 'You'd have a better chance putting a bid in on my thrice damned soul! Now get out of my office, now!'

AT THE BAD Water tavern down on the docks of Magritta, Sparky the dwarf bartender had a round of drinks ready before Dunk even reached the bar. The entire place erupted in cheers as Dunk, Dirk, and Spinne made their way in from the chilly night air, with Slick and Enojada in tow.

The Bad Water had become known as the Hackers' hangout while in town, and Sparky and the bouncers there did the best they could to ensure that the crowds wouldn't drive their famous patrons away. They had permanently roped off a few tables in the corner for the Hackers' to sit at, and they'd emblazoned Hacker logos and merchandise over nearly every surface in the bar.

As Dunk made his way towards the bar, a trio of Darkside Cowboys fans in black and blue face and

body paint leapt at him from out of the crowd.
'Hackers suck!' the three men said in unison.

Before Dunk could even respond, the Cowboys fans
disappeared beneath a swarm of kicking legs and
swinging arms, all wearing the Hackers' familiar green
and gold colours. A moment later, the battered men
popped up atop the arms of the crowd and were
passed straight towards the wall opposite the door.

'Hold it,' Sparky shouted, although no one but
Dunk seemed to hear him. There was nothing to do
but watch the three bodies passed straight towards the
picture window and then get tossed right through it.
Dunk heard one, two, three splashes as they tumbled
into the seawater below.

'I lose more windows that way,' Sparky said as Dunk
finally made it to the bar to collect the first round of
drinks.

Dunk tossed an extra bit of gold on the bar. 'To
make up for the destruction.'

Sparky shook his head even as he leaned over the
bar and pocketed the money. 'You don't have to do
that. We make enough off you drinking here to cover
a new window every day of the week.' The dwarf
grinned through his thick, bushy beard. 'But I do
appreciate it.'

'Three Killer Genuine Drafts and one Halfkein for
Slick,' Sparky said. He nodded his head towards Enojada. 'What about for your friend?'

'She's an Amazon.'

'I think that's clear.'

'Really, from Lustria. Got anything that might make
her feel at home?'

Sparky leapt down from the narrow walkway that ran behind the bar, and Dunk heard him rummaging around among countless bottles. A moment later he popped back up with a tall, thin, clear bottle filled with a golden liquid. He opened it and stuffed a green wedge into it, then slapped it on the bar in front of Dunk. The label read 'Corpse-Rona.'

'What is it?' Dunk asked.

'Piss water.' Sparky scowled at the bottle. 'Seal piss, I think.'

'Seriously?'

'How would I know it tastes like seal piss?' Sparky held up a thick, stubby hand. 'Wait. Don't answer that.'

'What's with the green thing?'

'It's a lime. Sailors eat them on long voyages to stave off scurvy.'

Dunk glanced at Enojada. 'You think she has scurvy?'

'Nah. The fruit just makes the piss tolerable, or so I'm told. I don't put vegetables in my own drink, and I don't trust drinks that require them.'

Dunk nodded his thanks, picked up the tray on which Sparky had set the drinks and toted it over to his table. Dirk, Spinne, and Slick each grabbed their drinks, and Dunk handed the Corpse-Rona to Enojada, who accepted it with a wide smile.

'I had no idea you could find such things here,' she said. 'This is awful.'

Dunk stared at her. She pointed at the bottle and laughed.

'In Lustria, this is the kind of swill that no one will drink, so we export most of it. In other lands, the lure

of its exotic origin sells it better than its lousy flavour
does at home.'

'Do you want something else?'

Enojada shook her head and snatched the bottle
from the tray. 'It may be the worst part of home, but
it's still home.'

Dunk sat down and decided to get right to it. 'Tell us
about Kirta.'

'You do not waste much time with pleasantries,'
Enojada said. 'I like that.'

'So?' asked Dirk.

Enojada took a sip of her beer and rolled it around
on her tongue for a moment, clearly enjoying the
attention far more than her drink. 'Kirta is alive and
well. She is our team captain, one of the best blitzers
that Lustria has ever seen. She is a natural at it. Clearly
the talents required for Blood Bowl run strong within
your family's blood.'

'But how is she alive?' asked Dunk. 'We thought
she'd died when the Guterfiends arranged for an
angry mob to storm our family keep.'

'She escaped,' Enojada said with a simple shrug.
'Alone, she found her way outside the city and made
her way down the Reik until she came to the sea. When
she reached Marienburg, she fell prey to a press gang
that captured her and sold her to a pack of pirates.'

Dunk grimaced at the thought of his sweet, little sister among a band of ruthless buccaneers. Spinne
reached out and took his hand to comfort him, and
he did not push it away.

'Some time later, she wound up sailing down the
Scorpion Coast. In the temple city of Tlaxtlan, she was

auctioned off as a slave and purchased by the Lusties' owners. It was the best deal they ever made.'

'Our sister is a slave?' Dirk asked, his temper rising along with his voice.

'No longer.' Enojada's eyes seemed a thousand miles away. 'She proved to be a natural player, and within the space of a single year she was able to demand not only her freedom but a healthy salary.'

'A born negotiator, eh?' said Slick. 'She doesn't share that with her brothers.'

The halfling noticed Dunk and Dirk staring at him. 'And thank the gods for that, sons, or you wouldn't need me.'

'Then where would we be?' Dirk said, daring Slick to answer.

'Now she's the team captain, you say?' Dunk said, trying to shift the conversation back to his sister. He ran his tongue along his lower gums. 'It's a great story. It really is. I only have one question.'

Enojada raised her thick eyebrows. 'Yes?'

'Why should we believe a word of it?'

Enojada smiled. 'Of course, you do not know me, and I come to you with the most fantastical story possible, a story too good to be true. Why should you trust me?'

'Exactly.'

'You shouldn't.'

Dunk sat back to consider this.

Enojada continued. 'I'm nobody to you; a woman who comes to you out of the blue with a wild story about a woman you know is dead. No matter how much you care about your sister, how can you possibly want to cross the ocean just to check out my story? Especially when I have a clear motive for wanting to trick you into doing just that?'

Dunk glanced at Dirk, and then looked straight into Enojada's eyes. 'That about sums it up.'

'Kirta said you would be like that. She hoped you'd be at least that canny.'

Dunk felt ill. He'd stood up to his coach over a thin hope bound up in a web of flimsy lies. He knew he'd never forget this. Pegleg wouldn't let him.

'So she told me to tell you this one word, to confirm my story, to let you know that it's all true.'

Dunk waited in silence, but Dirk couldn't take it. 'What is it?' he demanded.

Enojada pursed her lips and spat out a single word. 'Nunya.'

Dunk almost fell off his chair. Spinne grabbed him by the arm and straightened him back up. Dirk wasn't so lucky and slipped off his seat to the floor.

'What's it mean?' Slick asked. 'Is that someone's name?'

Dunk nodded. 'Sort of. It's what she called her doll. She had it since she could talk.'

Spinne frowned. 'That's an unusual name for a little girl to give a doll. What does it mean?'

'None of your business.'

Spinne glared at Dunk. 'I was just asking. If you don't feel we're close enough for you to share such information–'

'No!' said Dunk. 'That's not what I meant at all. The doll's name is Nunya. N-U-N-Y-A. Nunya Bidness.'

Dunk burst into Pegleg's office. 'We need to talk.'

'It's customary to knock, Mr Hoffnung.' The coach peered up at Dunk over a pair of half-moon glasses he'd been using to read a sheaf of papers scattered on the desk in front of him.

Dunk reached out and knocked on the new desk's surface. 'We need to talk now.'

Pegleg put down the papers. 'Today is your day off. Can't this wait until tomorrow?'

'We play tomorrow.'

'Then after that.'

Dunk shook his head. 'We need to deal with this now. I'm going to Lustria, and Dirk's coming with me.'

Pegleg removed his glasses and set them on the desk. 'You don't say? How about Spinne?'

'She's coming too.' Dunk thought she would, at least.

'You're going to undertake a long and perilous ocean voyage to find your sister's ghost on the say-so of a damsel, pardon me: Amazon, you know nothing about.'

'Enojada is telling the truth.'

'You seem sure.'

'I am.'

'So, there's no way that a wizard could have stolen a memory from you or your brother or one of dozens of souls who once worked in your family's keep to fabricate this "proof" you seem to think you have?'

Dunk stopped and thought about this for a moment. 'It's possible, sure.'

'But you're going anyhow.'

'I am.'

Pegleg rubbed his goatee with his good hand. More grey shot through the black than when Dunk had first met the man three years before.

'You know, Mr Hoffnung, coaching a Blood Bowl team is one of the more thankless jobs around. If your team loses, everyone blames it on you, from the announcers to the fans to even the owners, should there be others than yourself. If your team wins, the players get all the credit, at least the star players do. Players like you.'

'I'll come back. We all will.'

Pegleg raised an eyebrow. 'And how would that work? As soon as anyone leaves the team, under his own steam, or feet first, I have to replace him.'

'Openings develop after almost every game,' said Dunk.

Pegleg nodded. 'You're not leaving. I won't let you out of your contract.'

'But Coach–'

'Don't give me that, Mr Hoffnung. Where will I be able to find three seasoned athletes who play together as well as you, your brother, and your woman? And you know that if you leave, M'Grash will be useless for months.'

'We're going anyhow.'

Pegleg went entirely cold. Dunk had seen the man rage at people before, tearing into them with his hook as well as his furious words. This terrified him far more.

'If you leave, I'll sue you for breach of contract. I'll have the Game Wizards track you down and use their magic to compel you to fulfil the terms to which you agreed.'

Dunk stared at the man. 'You wouldn't dare. You can't.'

'Try me, Mr Hoffnung.'

'Can he do that?'

Dunk turned to the door, and Slick appeared a moment later. The halfling nodded at Pegleg and swallowed hard. 'I'm afraid so. The contract is clear about this. Every Blood Bowl contract has such clauses. They stop the players from wandering off after their first pay day and only coming back after blowing every last copper of it.'

'And you let me sign that?'

Slick shrugged. 'It's standard, son. There are all sorts of clauses that protect you too. That's why we call it a deal rather than slavery.'

'I never would have–'

'Can you read, son?'

Dunk didn't like where this was heading. 'I read the contract.'

'And you understood what you were signing.'

Dunk nodded. When he turned back to look at Pegleg, the man grinned at him.

'I'm so pleased to know that you can see it my way, Mr Hoffnung. I hope this incident illustrates to you just what a treasured member of our team you are.'

Pegleg stood and offered his hand to Dunk, as if the meeting were over. Dunk ignored it.

'Isn't there any way out of this?' Dunk asked. 'Can't I just refuse to work?'

Pegleg chuckled. 'Unless you're physically unable, Mr Hoffnung, you're required to take to the field when I order it. Or I can have the Game Wizards make you.'

'Would you really do that?' Dunk stared into Pegleg's dark eyes. 'You'd have those idiots wave me around the field like a puppet on their strings? They'd get me killed before half-time.'

Pegleg dropped his hand. 'I'd rather not, truth be told. I… Back in my pirate days, I had just such a spell used on me. I hated every second of it. I swore that I'd do whatever I could to get away from there as soon as I could, and kill everyone I could on my way overboard.'

'Yet you'd do that to me.'

Pegleg spat on the floor. 'You don't seem to be leaving me much of a choice. It's that or lose the *Spike! Magazine* championship.'

Dunk shook his head. 'And the money that goes with it. That's all you give a damn about.'

Pegleg opened his mouth to speak, but stopped. After a moment, he tried again. 'The money is important, true. You and your team-mates like to get paid, as do the referees I have to bribe, and Dr Pill, and all the other staffers that help us out around here, but that's not why I do this.'

Pegleg shook his head. 'I like to win, Mr Hoffnung. I live to win, to be part of a team that is better than all the rest, and to lead that team to be the best that it can possibly be.

'You want to run off to find your sister. Your family is important to you. I understand that, believe it or not.

'I don't have a family of my own. I don't have a woman to hold.' He glared at his hook. 'The Hackers are my family, my cause, my purpose, and I won't let you or anyone else mess that up.'

The man's speech, his passion, reverberated with Dunk. He understood just what he was talking about, and he felt shame for having thought that only money meant anything to his coach. But, it wasn't enough to stop him from doing what he had to do.

'Are you done?'

Pegleg sat back down in his chair and gestured for Dunk to say his piece.

'I feel just horrible.'

Pegleg allowed himself a little smile. 'Apology accepted,' he said, waving off Dunk's words. 'No need to say anything more.'

'No,' Dunk said, clearing his throat, and then coughing hard. 'I feel horrible, sick that is, ill.'

He sat down hard in one of the chairs in front of Pegleg's desk. He could smell the varnish on it, but he pretended his nose was so stuffed that a full clove of garlic wouldn't have got through it.

'I don't know where I must have picked it up. Some kind of virus.' He pounded on his chest and gave up a few more coughs. Then he laid the back of his hand across his forehead. 'I feel faint, feverish, too, I think.'

'You're going to play sick?' Pegleg sat forward in his chair. 'You wouldn't dare.'

'Play? Sick?' Dunk lolled his head on his shoulders as if it had become too heavy to lift. 'Sorry, coach. I don't think I could play sick. I might be contagious. What if it's the plague?'

'If it is the plague, you'll get off easy compared to what I'll do to you.' The cold menace had gone. Pegleg had reverted to rage. 'You won't get away with this.'

'What's my contract say about that, Slick?' Dunk asked, letting his head fall back so he could stare at his agent with blank eyes.

Slick edged his way back out of the door as he spoke. 'It's pretty clear. The "Illness and Injury Clause", also known as "IIC" or "Ick", states that a coach cannot force an injured or ill player to take the field, period.'

'It's a sham!' Pegleg stood up and slammed his hook into the top of the desk. 'You're healthier than me, you scurvy dog.'

'Really?' Dunk said. 'Maybe you should see someone about that, coach? Dr Pill could probably get you fixed right up.'

The man started to come around the desk to grab Dunk and haul him to his feet, but his hook was stuck once more. 'I'll take you to Dr Pill. Gah! I order you to report to him for an evaluation and treatment. He'll put an end to this poppycock.'

'Oh, I would,' Dunk said, 'but as I recall, difficult as it is in my fevered condition, the contract clearly states that we have to use a third party doctor on which we can both agree. Team physicians are just too easily pressured by their employers.'

'He's right,' Slick said. 'That got put in back when coaches kept forcing their players to take to the field in the second half against Nurgle's Rotters, no matter how many quarts of vomit they produced.'

'You're playing tomorrow,' Pegleg said, 'if I have to kick your rump out onto that field with my wooden leg!'

Dunk stood up, cleared his throat and stared Pegleg in the eye. He'd allowed the man to terrify him for as long as he'd been a player. That was a time honoured part of the player/coach relationship in Blood Bowl, and he'd abided by it. The fact that Pegleg could intimidate the Emperor made that easier, but with one foot already out of the door, Dunk found that the man no longer had such a hold over him.

'Try it,' Dunk said, 'and you'll be wearing two of those pegs.'

Pegleg stopped cold in the middle of taking a breath to start a new rant. He choked the air back and glared at Dunk. Before the coach could say a word, Dunk spoke.

'I'm not playing tomorrow. I'm not playing the day after that. I'm not playing until you release me from my contract.'

He gave a gentle cough into his fist as he turned to leave. 'As soon as you come to your senses, I think I can arrange to come to mine.'

'You REALLY THINK I should still play?' Spinne asked as she adjusted the chinstrap on her helmet. She and the other Hackers stood in the Hackers' dugout on one side of the field, making last-minute preparations before the game.

'If I happened to catch whatever "illness" it is you seem to have, I think people might understand how that could happen.'

'Get out there,' Dunk said. He clapped his brother on the arm. 'You too. I can make my point on my own. No need for the rest of you to suffer with me.'

Dirk cast a wary gaze towards the dugout on the opposite side of the field. 'We'll be out there playing while you sit here safe on the sidelines, far away from Khorne's Killers. Tell me again who's suffering here.'

'It's too late for Pegleg to replace you. If you don't play, the others will probably get killed.'

'So tell me again why you're shamming sickness so you can stay out of the game if you're so concerned about our health.'

'I have to do something to break Pegleg's will.'

Dirk put a hand on his brother's shoulder. 'Can't you find another way? We're going to miss you out there, painfully.'

'Don't you want to find Kirta?'

Dirk winced at this. 'Of course I do, if she's really there. This seems like an awful risk to take on some Amazon's say-so, even if she did know about Nunya.'

'I don't trust her either,' said Dunk. 'After all, she's basically working as an agent for the Amazons, and most agents are slime.'

'Hey!' Slick said.

'Present company excepted, of course.'

'Son,' Slick said, 'you've got it wrong. All *good* agents are slime. It goes with the territory.'

Dunk did a double take, and then decided that the halfling was serious. Sometimes he wondered how he'd ended up with such a person in his life, and why he would trust his agent with not only his money but his life. So far, though, despite his bluster, Slick had never steered him wrong.

Something screeched into the sky and exploded over the field.

'There's the signal for the start of the game!' Bob said. 'Welcome to the finals of the *Spike! Magazine* tournament, pitting the world champions, Bad Bay Hackers against the bad boys of the Chaos Circuit, Khorne's Killers!'

Dirk patted Dunk on the back while Spinne mimed a kiss at him through her helmet. Then they followed the others as they charged out into their positions on the field.

Dunk's heart sank as he watched them go. He'd faced similar dangers with them countless times. Khorne's Killers couldn't be worse than the Chaos All-Stars they'd faced in the Blood Bowl finals last year, right? But this time he'd be watching from the sidelines, unable to help.

'Hard, isn't it?' Pegleg said right behind him.

Dunk almost jumped out of his shoes. He spun around and put a few, judicious feet between him and his coach. Pegleg ignored him, keeping his eyes focused on the Hackers as they took the field.

'Being left behind while the people you care most about in the world go off to play the game, to risk their lives, to grab the glory. It's hard.'

'Don't you do that every game?' Dunk asked.

Pegleg nodded. 'Aye, Mr Hoffnung, and that's why I'm tougher than you. You won't break me over this. You might as well give up and get out on that field right now. That way you can avoid the heartache of watching your friends get torn to pieces while you sit here on the sidelines, nursing your damned cause.'

The coach's words stung Dunk more than he would let on. He'd been up most of the night struggling with this question, but as dawn had broken over the horizon he'd known he'd made the right choice.

'You're only concerned about your team,' Dunk said. 'I'm doing this for my baby sister.'

With that, he sat down on the far end of the bleacher from Pegleg. The other players stared at him. Dr Pill sneered for a moment, and then strode over and perched next to Dunk.

'You should get your lazy, wimpy ass out there,' the apothecary said.

'I'm making a point.'

'You made your point. Now you're just making me look bad.'

Dunk raised an eyebrow at the old elf.

'You're "sick". I'm the team apothecary. It's my job to fix you up. You're not fixed. I must not be doing my job.'

'Everyone knows that's not true.'

Out on the field, the Killers kicked off the ball, and the Hackers scrambled into position to grab it. The ball sailed right towards Rotes Hernd, who'd started in Dunk's place.

'I'm sure the Game Wizards would be happy to hear that.'

Dunk froze. 'They're right behind me, aren't they?' He could not bring himself to turn around.

Dr Pill snorted. 'I'm not that clever. Besides, as pissed off as I am at you, I respect what you're doing.'

'You do?'

'Family comes first, even over Blood Bowl, especially over Blood Bowl.'

'But you wish it didn't make you look bad.'

'Precisely. But that's the least of your worries, I'm sure.'

The old elf clapped Dunk on the back and stood up to greet the stretcher coming off the field. A pair of thick armed dwarfs carried it from either end, and Getrunken sprawled across it, his helmet dangling from one limp hand.

'What happened?' Dr Pill asked. 'I didn't see the injury.'

Pegleg came over, caught the front of Getrunken's jersey with his hook, and pulled Getrunken to a sitting position. The man's head lolled forward on a limp neck, and his eyes rolled open, bloodshot and vacant. When he exhaled, Dunk could smell the rotgut on his breath, even from where he sat.

Pegleg put a hand over his face and growled in disgust. 'It was self-inflicted, before the game began. He's three sheets, maybe four.'

Dr Pill shook his head and sneered. 'The wimp asked me for something to kill the pain, and then does this.'

'What pain?' asked Dunk.

'Emotional.' Dr Pill rolled his eyes. 'Couldn't take the stress of starting the game, he said.'

Pegleg slapped Getrunken across the face with his fleshy hand. 'Get on your feet, you dog. Get up, or the next slap will be from my hook!'

Getrunken's eyes snapped to focus on the hook still holding him upright. He started to say something, and then brought up his helmet, inverted like a bowl, and bent over it. Pegleg snatched back his hook as the man retched into his helmet.

'Get him out of here,' Pegleg said to the dwarfs. He shot a glare at Dr Pill. 'Get him sober for the second half. He's starting again whether he's ready or not.'

'They'd kill him in a state like that,' said Dunk.

'Better to die on the field than in the locker room.'

Pegleg stabbed his hook out towards a burly young man sitting in the dugout's far corner. 'You!' he said.

'Yes, coach.' The young player charged up to the ex-pirate and snapped off a sharp salute. 'Nicht Bereit reporting for duty, coach.'

'This is a Blood Bowl team, not the army, Mr Bereit.' Pegleg stared at the young man's vacant gaze, and shrugged, giving up on explaining the differences. 'You're in. Take that sot's place in the line.'

Bereit quivered with excitement. 'Yes, coach. Right away, coach.' With that, he charged out onto the field.

Pegleg glowered at Dunk. 'I've been reduced to this,' he hissed, and marched off.

Dunk shrugged. As the team took losses during the game, his position only grew stronger. He couldn't root for his team-mates to get hurt, but he wasn't above taking advantage of it.

Dunk watched as Hernd connected with Spinne on a long pass. Before Spinne's feet even touched the ground, one of the Chaos players, a ram headed creature with glowing eyes, wrapped a tentacle around her waist and tossed her to the ground. Dunk gasped, but when the ball rolled free, the Killer went after it instead of Spinne, and a moment later the woman sprang back to her feet.

'It's not easy to sit here and watch, is it?' a soft voice said next to him.

Dunk turned to see a fair-skinned Estalian beauty sitting next to him, her flowing, black hair spilling over the back of her Hackers uniform as her wide, dark eyes glittered at him. 'Camisa Roja,' she said, pointing at herself.

'You just joined the team?'

She nodded with a grin. 'This is my first game. I feel so blessed to have made the cut with such a great team. I can't wait until I get to play.'

Dunk gave her a smile that barely touched his lips.

'It's so sad that you're too sick to play,' she said, putting a sympathetic hand on his arm. Then she snatched it away. 'Hope it's not contagious.'

'I'm fine,' he said, waving off her concern.

'Oh? Then why aren't you out there on the field?' She stared at him as if he'd started to drool.

'It's complicated.'

Dunk didn't mind talking to the woman, but he didn't know her. Dr Pill's offhand threat to turn him over to the Game Wizards had made him cautious about trusting anyone, especially when it came to new faces. Her smile returned, more guarded this time.

'I see. It's just that I'd give just about anything to be able to be out there with the ball in my hands.'

'Funny,' Dunk said, more to himself than her. 'I've never felt that way about it.'

'HELDMANN IS DOWN! I repeat, Heldmann is down!'

Dunk leapt to his feet and stared out at the field. A huge pile of people and creatures had formed on the far side of the field. Legs, arms, horns, tails, and tentacles thrashed about, and Dunk couldn't make a bit of sense of it.

He jumped out of the dugout and stared up at the Jumboball. The image on the humongous crystal ball showed exactly what Dunk saw: a huge mess. Green and gold jerseys struggled with black and blue ones in a massive scrum that showed no signs of breaking up.

'Did you see that hit?' Bob said. 'I haven't seen anyone that brutalised since the end of the last season when you finally came home to your wife after six solid months on the road.'

'True enough,' Jim said. 'The little lady packs a heck of a wallop. I spent a week in the infirmary recovering after that!'

A flash of black and white stripes caught Dunk's eye, and for a moment he hoped that a referee had appeared to help break things up. He knew that Dirk had to be somewhere in that pile up, as were Spinne and the rest of his friends, but he couldn't get a glimpse of him. Then he saw that the ref's shirt was empty, shredded, and covered with glowing, green blood.

'What happened to the ref?' Jim asked. 'He's supposed to step in when it gets like this!'

'You missed his transformation? We've gotta see an instant replay for that!'

The image on the Jumboball jumped, and a high-blooded elf appeared in the centre of the crystal, wearing a referee's striped shirt. It seemed to be a break between plays, and the elf reached out and grabbed a water bottle from a bench for a quick drink. As he poured the liquid from the bottle, it began to glow with a sickly, green light.

The referee wiped his mouth with the back of his hand, and then stared at the green glow there. A moment later, he fell to his knees, clutching at his throat. As he writhed on the edge of the field, his skin began to turn a bright red, and blades made of bone emerged from his wrists. He used them to tear off his shirt, slicing through the fabric and into his skin.

A line of long, wispy tentacles rose from the referee's spine as he bent his back. A beak sprouted from his face. Feathers sprang from his legs.

'I don't know about you,' Bob said, 'but that's the ugliest chicken I've ever seen.'

'Wonder how those legs would taste,' said Jim. 'What? They all look the same once they've spent a good hour in a barbecue pit!'

Without warning, the referee launched into the game, his eyes glowing with hatred and the greenish taint of Chaos. A moment later, Dirk appeared on the screen, sprinting along the field, the ball tucked under his arm. The referee leapt at him, his mutated arms spread wide as he flapped into the air on his bent, feathered legs.

Dirk's free fist smashed into the referee, but it wasn't enough to knock the mad creature away. He went down beneath the referee in a flurry of tentacles and feathers.

'Does that count as too many creatures on the field for the Killers?' Bob asked.

'I don't know,' said Jim, 'but who's going to call the penalty?'

'If those remains in M'Grash's fists are any indication, the Killers are already a player or three short!'

'Stay here,' Pegleg shouted.

Dunk glanced back to see him facing down the others, holding his hook high and daring them to try to get past him. 'I will not have my team start a bench clearing brawl!'

Dunk stared across the field to see the Killers' coach, Pike PcCarthy, a burly, fish faced fiend with whips for arms, lashing his players back towards the bench. Until he'd seen PcCarthy in action, Dunk had wondered how anyone could keep a pack of monsters like the players of Khorne's Killers under control. Then he'd seen PcCarthy disembowel a water carrier for supplying water that was too pure.

Still, even PcCarthy didn't want to be seen instigating an all-out brawl in the *Spike! Magazine* championship game. He knew that if he let his players loose, he might never get them back.

'If you wish to keep your jobs,' Pegleg said, 'you will remain with the seat of your breeches scraping for splinters on those thrice damned benches!'

Dunk launched himself out of the dugout and sprinted across the field, straight for the pile up. He ignored his coach's pleas for him to stop. Dunk wanted to lose his job, and if he could help his brother out in the meantime, then all the better.

The players in the pile didn't see him coming. They were too busy tearing each other to pieces to worry about outside threats. The Killers in the opposing dugout, though, saw Dunk coming and pointed his advance out to Coach PcCarthy.

Howling in rage, the fish-man called his players to their feet, and sent them sprinting, galloping, slithering, and slurping off to show Dunk and the rest of the Hackers a lesson. Dunk had a good head start on them, though, and knew he would reach the pile first. He glanced back and saw that Pegleg had finally relented. The rest of the Hackers had followed him on to the field.

When Dunk neared the pile up, he took a flying leap into the air and came down hard on the first Killer he saw. As he reached the zenith of his arc, Dunk realised he'd made one big mistake. He'd rushed onto the field without his armour.

That not only meant he had no protection, but neither did he have spikes or blades to use against his foes. At the moment, there was little he could do about it. He brought his legs forward and came down with the best-protected part of his body: his feet.

Dunk's boot stomped the back of the helmet of a Killer in front of him into the Astrogranite so hard that the spikes on the front of the helmet stuck there in the synthetic stone. The creature, jersey number 616, squealed like a pig that'd just learned the big secret of the slaughterhouse as it flailed about helplessly.

Dunk reached out and grabbed the faceguard of another player's helmet. Reptilian eyes stared back at him when he wrenched the player's head around, and a forked tongue flickered out to caress the back of his hand. The creature hissed at him as it arched its neck back to strike with its venomous fangs.

Dunk pulled down on the helmet hard, putting all his weight into it. The move bent his foe in half. Thankfully, the snakeman didn't have any arms to flail at Dunk, and for a split-second he felt safe.

That came to an abrupt end as he saw the creature's scorpion's tail arch up behind it. Dunk knew he'd have to let the beast go or suffer its lethal sting.

'Quake "The Plumber" doesn't look too happy about his new Hacker hood ornament!' Bob said.

'That's right!' said Jim. 'He's about to give Hoffnung a piece of his, um, tail!'

'Ya gonna sssuffer sssucker,' the creature hissed.

Dunk reached out with his free hand and pulled at the buttons on the side of the Killer's chinstrap. Just as the tail started to come down, the chinstrap gave way, and the snake-scorpion-man stumbled backward onto its raised tail. Dunk looked down at the spiked helmet in his hand. Now, at least, he had a weapon.

Then he spotted his brother Dirk. He lay on the bottom of the pile up, not moving. A stomping hoof glanced off his helmet, and he did not protest.

Dunk swung the helmet hard at the bull-headed creature who'd just stepped on Dirk, and its spikes bit hard into the minotaur's arm. The creature reared back its head to unleash an angry cry, which still sounded to Dunk like a 'Moo'. Then it spun on him and tried to gore him with the five horns that sprang from each edge of the pentacle branded on its forehead.

'That's Dunk Hoffnung in there, without a shred of armour!' said Bob.

'I've seen a lot of dumb in this game, but that's plain stupid! That's Nilla Likker, number 43, he's facing off against there!'

'Hackers fans may remember when Hoffnung killed Nilla's cousin, Schlitz "Malty" Likker of the Chaos All-Stars, during the Chaos Cup half-time presentation almost three years back!'

'Hoffnung always maintained that he'd saved the star player from being controlled by the evil wizard Schlechter Zauberer, who'd called Khorne the Blood God down to possess the legendary player's body!'

'Looks like Khorne's going to get his due today!'

Dunk ducked around Nilla's horns, smashing them aside with the spiked helmet. He'd been in enough of a fight before Bob and Jim had started blabbing on and on about his history with Nilla's family. Now the mutant minotaur was madder than ever.

Nilla snorted a noxious cloud of green poison from his wide, red-rimmed nostrils, from which dangled a thick, slimy hoop of gold. Dunk took in a double lungful of the stuff. It burned his throat and sent him into spasms of coughing and wheezing. He hurled himself towards his brother, hoping to protect Dirk with his body, but a meaty fist closed around the back of his neck and hauled him back.

Dunk dangled from the end of Nilla's arm, kicking like a man in a noose. His boots glanced off the minotaur's armour, not even leaving a scratch. He tried to pry the creature's hand from his throat, but it was like trying to tear apart steel with his bare fingers.

'Killed Mmmmooo-alty!' The minotaur roared into Dunk's face. The scent of rotting flesh on its breath was almost worse than the greenish poison still searing Dunk's lungs. 'Mmmooo-ust die!'

The minotaur shook Dunk by the neck, and the thrower wondered how long it would take for his spine to give way. If his body fell from his neck, would he be conscious long enough to watch it hit the ground? Even the vaunted Dr Pill wouldn't be able to help him with that kind of injury.

Dunk gave up on getting Nilla's fingers from around his throat, and he lashed out with his fists. The minotaur's horns made it impossible for the creature to wear a helmet, but the way it shrugged off Dunk's blows, it obviously didn't need one.

Dunk kept smashing at the minotaur's head, hoping one blow might finally hurt the creature more than it hurt him. He couldn't breathe, though, and his arms began to tire. He knew he wouldn't last much longer.

Dunk wondered where his friends were. Dirk was out cold, but how about M'Grash? Or Edgar? Or Cavre, or any of the other Hackers? What about Spinne?

Thoughts of Spinne flashed through his head as the world started to fall away down a tunnel. Desperate to survive, to get back to her, he lashed out again, too weak to form a fist. His fingers fell around something thick and metallic, warm and curved in his hand.

He twisted it as hard as he could.

Nilla let out a horrific howl of pain and dropped Dunk to protect the nose ring he'd grabbed. This proved a terrible mistake, as it left Dunk hanging from the ring with all his weight.

Still struggling to regain his breath, Dunk clutched the ring for all he was worth, swinging back and forth. Nilla smashed into his ribs with a massive fist, and the breath left Dunk's body again. He hung on despite this, knowing that as soon as he let go, the creature would be on him once more.

The force of Nilla's blow pulled harder on the ring, and the creature howled in frustration and pain. Heartened by this, Dunk swung his feet up and planted them on the minotaur's chest. Then he yanked on the ring with all his might.

Nilla's scream threatened to burst Dunk's eardrums. Dunk used the pain in his head to drive his determination. He pulled harder and harder until he felt something give.

Dunk landed hard on the Astrogranite. He stared at the ring, still in his hands, but now free of its owner's face. Greenish-black blood glistened on it and covered Dunk's fingers.

'Yowch!' Bob said. 'That's going to leave a lot more than a mark.'

A giant scorpion's tail smacked down and knocked the ring from Dunk's hand, the stinger catching on the metal rather than Dunk's flesh. Dunk scrambled backward on his rump, stopping only when he ran into a tree.

Surprised to feel his back against a tree that someone had planted in the middle of the field, he craned his head back and spied Edgar looming over him.

'That's about bloody well enough of this nonsense,' the treeman said. He gathered Dunk up in his branches and held the man high over his head, out of the reach of even the minotaur.

From this vantage point, Dunk could see that the game had devolved into nothing more than a brawl. Bodies lay scattered about the pitch, both in Hacker and Killer uniforms, and blood, sweat, and ichor covered those few players still standing. Dirk still lay unconscious, with Bereit, Roja, and Reyes collapsed nearby.

There had to be a way to end this, but Dunk couldn't see how.

Carve squared off against a rat-faced, bat-winged beast. A trio of worm armed, lamprey-faced creatures wrapped themselves around M'Grash, who was trying to tear them into fishing bait. Spiel and Anfäger bashed away at a crab bodied creature that sported someone's severed arm in one of its massive claws.

Not seeing Spinne anywhere, Dunk cast his gaze wider. He spotted her standing alone in the end zone, waving her arms wildly. With all the carnage going on around him, Dunk breathed easier knowing that Spinne wasn't in the middle of it.

Then Dunk spotted the ball still tucked in Dirk's arms. Everyone else around him was too busy fighting each other to pay any attention to it. If he could reach it, he might be able to put an end to this.

Nilla smashed into Edgar's trunk from one side, and Quake's tail stabbed into his bark from the other. The treeman tottered for a moment, but did not fall.

'I've had enough of this bloody bullshit,' Edgar roared as he swung his lower branches at the minotaur.

Seeing his chance, Dunk leapt from Edgar's upper branches, straight towards Dirk. He rolled as he hit the Astrogranite, and came to a halt right next to his brother's body. Fighting the urge to check if Dirk still breathed, he snatched the spiked ball from his brother's limp arms.

Cocking back his arm, Dunk's thrower instincts kicked in. He scanned downfield to see Spinne still open, but his ears detected the pounding of hooves behind him. He didn't need to have eyes in the back of his head, like the ones he now saw on the crab-beast battling Spiel and Anfäger, to know that Nilla was bearing down on him.

Dunk held his breath and waited. If he moved too soon, the minotaur would change course and catch him on its horns. He had to time this just right.

When every nerve in his body told him to move, he spun to the left, hoping that he hadn't guessed wrong, knowing that his life would be forfeit.

As Nilla blasted past him, like a bull charging past a matador, Dunk let out that breath and hurled the ball downfield. He stood and watched as it arced through the clear, Estalian sky and hung at its zenith for a heart-stopping moment before spiralling down into Spinne's outstretched arms.

'Touchdown!' Jim's voice said. 'Touchdown! Hackers score!'

'So we won?' Dirk said. His bloodshot eyes had fluttered open as Lästiges had leant over to kiss his battered forehead, and he stared up at her, Spinne, and Dunk in pain and wonder.

Dunk grinned down at his brother lying in a bed in the infirmary. Although beaten close to death, the fight that had raged around Dirk had kept any of Khorne's Killers from taking the time to execute him. He bore more bruises than a sack of bongo bashing bananas, but he would live to play again.

'We scored the only touchdown before the game had to be called for a lack of players on each side.'

'How many were left?'

Spinne stepped up to answer. 'The Killers had just four players conscious after the fight. We only had six.'

Dirk tried to frown, but stopped when it hurt too much. 'I've seen games played with less,' he said.

'We were ready to keep playing to the last player, but PcCarthy was so angry with his team for letting us score that he whipped the ones still standing half to death.' Dunk grinned. 'When it came time for the kick-off, none of them could make it onto the field.'

'I'll bet Pegleg's happy.' Dirk tried to smile, but gave up on that too.

'You'd be wrong there, Mr Heldmann,' the ex-pirate said as he burst into the room. Dunk could see from the scowl on the man's face that he wasn't joking.

'Why not?' Dirk said. 'We won the tournament. The team earned a huge purse, and you have another trophy for the *Sea Chariot*'s cabin.'

'And we've lost our sponsorship for the Dungeon-bowl.'

Dunk's stomach fell. 'What? Why?'

Lästiges held up her hand. 'I can answer that.' She reached into her bag and pulled out a white sphere the size of her fist. She set it on a table, and a trio of green tentacles sprouted from the bottom of it. It spun around, and fixed a wide pupil on the sports reporter.

'What's that?' asked Dunk.

'Eye-Pod,' Lästiges said. 'Latest thing from Grapple. It plays Magical Projection Three and Four files.'

'MP3s and MP4s?' Spinne said.

Lästiges nodded. 'Watch.'

An image blinked to life inside the large, black spot of the pupil. It showed Dunk in a post-game interview.

'Does this mean you're back?' Lästiges said from somewhere off-camra.

In the image, Dunk flushed, and then coughed. 'I'm still not feeling too well. If it hadn't been for that brawl, I'd still be lying down on the bench.'

At a wave of Lästiges's hand, the image froze.

'So?' Dunk said, trying to keep his frustration from his voice.

He knew he'd blown his strike. As soon as there had been any real danger to his friends, he'd charged back out onto the field. Now that Pegleg had seen that happen, he'd be able to use it against him every damn game. After all, when was there ever a Blood Bowl game in which the players weren't in mortal peril?

'The Grey Wizards believed you, Mr Hoffnung, even if I didn't,' said Pegleg. 'Worse yet, the game showed them that we couldn't win without you.'

'But that's not true,' Dunk said. He liked the idea of being indispensable, but he knew that others could step up to take his place. 'We're a team. I couldn't have made that play without Spinne or Edgar, or any of the others.'

Dirk scowled, but said nothing.

'Be that as it may,' Pegleg said, 'the Grey Wizards decided to pull their sponsorship and return it to the Reikland Reavers once more.'

'That's not fair,' Dunk said.

Pegleg gave him a pitying look. 'How long have you been playing this game, Mr Hoffnung? And you still use words like "fair"?'

Pegleg scowled. 'Anyhow, it's back to Bad Bay for us.'

'I'm not going.'

Everyone in the room turned to look at Dirk.

'You'll be fine soon, honey,' Lästiges said, stroking Dirk's brow. 'We can follow them when you're better.'

Dirk shook his head. 'Dunk's right. He's been right all along. If Kirta's alive, if there's even a chance, we have to find her.'

Dunk's heart leapt. 'We can leave as soon as you're ready.'

'Wait,' said Pegleg.

'If you're going, I'm going with you,' Spinne said.

Dunk started to tell her not to worry, but thought better of it. Instead, he put an arm around her waist, drew her close, and said, 'Thanks.'

'Wait,' Pegleg said.

'I'll go too,' said Lästiges. She framed her hands together in a circle, as if around a crystal ball. 'I'll get the network to sign off on it as a documentary following the famous Hoffnung brothers on their daring quest into the deepest, darkest jungles to rescue their long-lost little sister!'

'Wait!'

Pegleg stood before them, trembling with anger.

'You don't get it, do you?' he said. 'This is *my* team, *mine*! And you are *my* players. You have contracts, and you're not going anywhere.'

Dunk stared at the man. He'd forgotten about the Game Wizards and how they could compel both him and Dirk to play for the Hackers, no matter their wishes. The horror of that meant they'd have to come up with another way.

One easy solution crept into his skull. He could kill Pegleg right here and now. By the time anyone could do anything about it, he and Dirk, and Spinne and Lästiges could hire a ship and be out to sea, beyond the Game Wizards' reach.

Dunk had killed before, and he knew he'd do so again. That was a Blood Bowl player's lot, but could he bring himself to murder his coach? Right here in cold blood?

'If you don't, Dunk, I will.'

Dunk glanced at Dirk and saw that his brother had been thinking the exact same thing.

'If I wasn't stuck in this bed, I'd have done it already.'

Pegleg went pale. 'Now, gentlemen,' he said, backing towards the door, 'let's not do anything we'll all regret.'

'I won't regret it,' Dirk said as Dunk moved forward, 'not for a second.'

Pegleg raised his hook, holding it between Dunk and himself. 'I won't go easily, Mr Hoffnung. I may not be able to take you all, but I'll cut as many throats as I can before I go down.'

Dunk put his hands up to calm the ex-pirate down. 'This is getting out of hand,' he said. 'No one here wants to hurt anyone.' He glanced at Dirk, who scowled at him. 'Well, not everyone. At least I don't.'

Pegleg snorted. 'You want to run off after ghosts from your past on a fool's errand. I won't allow that. Something has to give.' He spat on the ground as if daring Dunk to get nearer. 'It won't be me.'

Someone knocked on the door. Everyone froze. Might it be the Game Wizards, come to check on Dirk or Dunk? Or maybe M'Grash had shown up for a visit. If so, Dunk knew he could get the ogre to side with him.

Enojada's voice filtered through from outside. 'Can I come in?'

'We are engaged in a private conversation, madam,' Pegleg said.

Enojada giggled. 'Not so private that everyone in the hall could not hear it. If you like privacy, maybe you should learn to speak softer, no?'

'Let her in,' said Dunk.

'Forget it,' said Pegleg, menace edging his voice. 'She started all this mutinous bilge.'

'I believe I may have a solution for your problem,' she said in a singsong voice.

Dunk stepped forward carefully, and Pegleg raised his hook to strike. Dunk did his best to ignore it and reached out to open the door.

Enojada flung the door wide, shoving Pegleg aside. The ex-pirate spun away from her, keeping his hook held high.

'Hello, my friends,' Enojada said. 'Why all the long faces?' She surveyed each of them in turn, ending with Pegleg. She wagged a finger at him, and then curled it around his hook. The gesture surprised him so much that he did not pull away.

'Now, I have heard the horrible news about how the Grey Wizards do not require your incredible services any longer, and I can understand how that might dampen your spirits. However,' she said, stopping to flash a wide smile that glowed against her tanned cheeks, 'I have a cure for your woes.'

Pegleg yanked his hook back. 'I do not care for anything you have to say. I know a con artist when I see one, and I see right through you, madam.'

Enojada's smile didn't waver. 'How can I be a con artist when I tell you only the truth? Not only that, I come with both money and proof?'

'Proof?' said Dunk.

'Money?' said Pegleg.

'Yes, yes, yes, for you both.'

Enojada reached into her pocket and produced a diamond the size of her fist, shot through with streaks of red. 'This is the Eye of the Daemon,' she said, holding it out before Pegleg. 'I am authorised to offer this to you as a fee for travelling to Lustria to take part in our tournament. Should you win the tournament, you will receive its match.'

Pegleg had to wipe the drool from his lips. 'Is that the purse then?'

Enojada flashed a tight smile as she shook her head. 'That's the bonus you'll get, over and above the purse, if you win.'

Pegleg reached for the gem with his good hand, but Enojada pulled it away, clucking her tongue. 'That is only yours, if you agree to join us in Lustria for the Tobazco Bowl. I do hope you find it in your heart to do so.'

'What about the proof?' Dunk asked, stepping in before Pegleg could give the woman an answer. 'What do you have for us?'

With a twinkle in her eye, Enojada produced an Eye-Pod of her own. She set it down on the table next to Dirk's bed, and it produced its own set of tentacles, wobbling over to stand next to the other one.

'You have these in Lustria now too?' Lästiges said with a gasp.

Enojada shrugged. 'But of course. Grapple is everywhere. Their DieTunes music player is very popular.'

An image flickered to life in the Eye-Pod's pupil, and Dunk felt his breath catch in his chest. The same thing happened to Dirk, and the man groaned in pain.

There, in the centre of the image, sat a beautiful, young woman with long, blonde hair swept back from her regal face. Her blue eyes sparkled, and a wry grin played across her red lips. She was taller, tanner, older, than Dunk remembered her, but he knew her right away.

'Kirta.' Without a doubt, this was his sister.

'Hello, Dunk and Dirk,' the image said. For a moment Dunk wondered if Kirta had heard him speak, but he had to remind himself that the Eye-Pod could only play images it had already recorded.

'If all has gone well, Enojada, my emissary, has found you and relayed our proposal to you. I do hope that you can find a way to take her up on it. I would like nothing more than to see you once more.

'I had long thought that you had perished at the hands of the mob that destroyed our family and our keep. It wasn't until I saw the Blood Bowl championship game last year that I discovered I was wrong. We do not have many Old World games on our Cabalvision networks here, but I always watch the big match.

'I was so delighted to see Dunk playing for the Hackers. Then to learn that my brother Dirk is none other than star player Dirk Heldmann, my heart nearly burst.

'I have so many questions for you, as I suppose you do for me. I am well, living here among the Amazons. They took me in when I was most desperate and have proved good and stalwart friends. I captain our Blood Bowl team, and I look forward to testing my mettle against...'

Kirta's voice trailed off, and tears welled in her eyes. She tried to speak again, but emotion choked off her words. She bowed her head for a moment, and when she raised her eyes again they burned with determination.

'I do hope that Enojada finds you and brings you to me. I cannot wait to see you again. You are all the family I have left in the world. Please come as quickly as you can.'

With that, the Eye-Pod's pupil went dark. Dunk reached out for the device, but it scampered away on its tentacles and leapt into Enojada's open hands. 'I'd like to have that,' Dunk said.

Enojada gave him a wink and held the Eye-Pod before her like a serpent with forbidden fruit. Then she flipped it towards him, and he caught it in the air. It felt warm, but not so slimy as he had feared. The tentacles on it retracted, and he put it in a shirt pocket.

'Consider it a down payment for your fees,' she said with a knowing grin.

'That's not his decision to make,' Pegleg said with a snarl, 'it's mine.'

Every set of eyes in the room focused on the coach. He squirmed under their gazes and doffed his yellow, tricorn hat. Dunk noticed more grey hairs atop his head then he'd seen before.

'Just how long is this affair of yours going to take?' he asked. 'Lustria's not just around the corner.'

'It is a journey of several weeks, of course, but it is not as far as you might fear.'

'When is this tournament of yours?'

'It is held at the height of the summer solstice.'

Pegleg nodded. 'Then forget it.'

He turned to leave, but Dunk slammed the door shut.

'Why?' Dunk couldn't understand what was going through his coach's head. 'We're not going to be in the Dungeonbowl anyhow. They're offering you a fortune just to show up, and another fortune if we win.'

'"If"?' said Dirk from his bed. 'You mean "when". How can a bunch of semi-pros with delusions of grandeur have a hope against the reigning Blood Bowl champs?'

He glanced at Enojada. 'No offence.'

She gave him a wooden smile. 'None taken.'

'There's the Chaos Cup as well,' Pegleg said. 'Suppose we don't make it back in time for that. Ocean voyages are never a sure means of travel.' He caressed his hook with his good hand. 'That's one thing I know.'

'The Eyes of the Daemon are worth more than the Chaos Cup purse,' said Spinne.

'Either one of them would be,' Enojada said, her smile gone.

'It might even delay us past the Blood Bowl,' Pegleg said. 'Defending champs lost somewhere on the other side of the world, how would that look?'

'It is not that far way,' Enojada said. 'The Blood Bowl tournament is not for nine months.'

'What's this really about?' Dunk asked. He stood in the pirate's face. From here, he knew, the man could gut him with his hook before Dunk could move, but he was ready to take that risk if it meant putting an end to this.

Pegleg ran his tongue over his gums, but did not say a word.

'You've always been about winning and money,' Dunk said. 'This has both. It should be an easy game, and the purse is enough to fund the Hackers for years.'

He leaned in closer. 'What are you afraid of?'

Pegleg swallowed, and then coughed on a throat gone dry. When he spoke, his voice was barely more than a whisper.

'You don't get it, Mr Hoffnung. You never have. We have everything we want. We have money. We have fame. We are champions.

'There's only one way to go from here.'

Dunk snorted. 'Everyone loses sometimes. We've lost plenty. We'll lose again.'

Pegleg nodded. 'Aye, we will, but to top-level competitors, not to a pack of ladies playing in their little garden on the other side of the world.'

Dunk stepped back. 'You're afraid we'll lose.'

Pegleg pointed his hook at Enojada. 'People don't just come to town and offer you a king's ransom so you can come back home with them and slaughter them in their beds. We know nothing about these people or this place, or about what's really going on in that jungle she calls home.'

Dunk started to speak, but Pegleg turned his hook on him.

'I realise it's your little sister out there, but, they have nothing to lose in a game like this. Everyone expects us to beat the tar from them, and if we don't do exactly that, who's the laughing stock then?'

He stabbed his hook at his chest. 'Me!'

The ex-pirate made a feeble noise and looked down at what he had done.

'Erp.'

Blood welled up from the point at which he'd plunged his hook through his skin. It spilled down his front, staining his shirt a dark crimson. He took one step forward and said, 'Damn hook,' before he collapsed to the floor.

Dunk peered out at the ocean sparkling in the midday sun as the *Sea Chariot* chased the blazing orb across the sea. They hadn't seen a single ship since they'd reached the open sea. While merchants did travel between the Old World and Lustria, it was a long and perilous journey and a large ocean.

Dunk had never felt so small in his life. It seemed a miracle of courage that he and the team had managed to get the ship ready to sail in such a short time. He attributed it to the number of times the Hackers had been run out of town in the past. That had mostly happened in the days before he'd joined the team, but Cavre and Pegleg had told him plenty of harrowing tales of such times.

At the same time, with the wind whipping through his hair and cracking at the edges of the sails, he'd rarely felt so free. They had left the Old World and all of its baggage behind them as they sailed off towards a new and different frontier that none of them, except for Enojada, of course, had ever seen. While they had a game ahead of them, it felt like a lifetime away. For now, the rise and fall of the waves would be all they would know.

'The captain will have your head when he wakes up,' Dr Pill said as he joined Dunk on the bridge.

'So you've said many times. When do you think that might be?'

The old elf shrugged. 'Could be any minute, might never happen.'

'Really?'

The apothecary snorted. 'No. I gave him something. He'll be up soon. Even from a human view of time, and then you'll be dead.'

'Better to beg forgiveness than ask permission,' Slick said as he rolled up the stairs from the main deck.

'It's not your head on the block, is it?' said Dr Pill.

Slick flashed a broad smile. 'All the better.'

'I could keep him unconscious until we reach Lustria,' the elf said to Dunk. 'That would give you more space to run. There's nowhere to go on this ship.'

'That's an awful long time for him to be asleep.'

'He could, ah, die, in his sleep.'

Dunk goggled at the elf, who blushed just a bit.

'Wouldn't take much. Wouldn't feel a thing.'

'Are you saying you'd murder the coach?'

'I'd never *say* such a thing.'

Dunk turned to look straight into the elf's good eye. 'I thought you and Pegleg went way back.'

'That we do.' Dr Pill pursed his lips. 'That's how I would find the strength to tolerate such a terrible misfortune, should it suddenly, unexpectedly, untraceably happen.'

Dunk gave the elf a sidelong look. 'Let's do what we can to keep that from happening.'

Dr Pill shrugged. 'Just trying to simplify your life.'

Despite the heat of the day, Dunk shuddered. He waved to Spinne and Lästiges where they sat near the prow, on either side of Dirk.

Dunk's brother had recovered well under Dr Pill's care and would be as fit as ever in a matter of days.

Since the death of their father in the last Blood Bowl championship, Dunk and Dirk had gone back to being the only family they had, or so Dunk had thought until Enojada had arrived with news of their long-lost sister. The thought of losing Dirk shook Dunk up almost as much as his excitement at finding Kirta.

Before he'd started playing Blood Bowl just over three years ago, Dunk had been alone in the world. He'd lost his family, their fortune, and everything that went with them. He'd known that Dirk had joined the Reikland Reavers, but the two hadn't talked for years at that point.

At the time, Dunk hadn't thought that he'd missed any of it. Looking back, he could see how his failed attempt to become a dragonslayer had been little more than a death wish for a man with a sick and heavy heart.

Now that he'd got his brother back, he was determined never to lose him again.

That same sentiment drove his quest for his sister. He would have killed Pegleg if he'd thought that it would get him closer to Kirta, if he'd had no other choice. But he'd thought he'd seen another way and had taken that instead.

He only hoped he wouldn't regret it.

'Hoffnung!'

The captain's voice bellowed from his cabin. Dunk could hear it through the boards beneath his feet. He tapped Reyes, who had the ship's wheel, on the shoulder, and the man scurried away.

As Dunk took the wheel, Dr Pill and Slick slunk off, following Reyes towards the ship's outer railing. Everyone else on the deck did the same thing, giving the path between the captain's quarters and the bridge a wide and open berth.

The door to the captain's quarters smashed open, and Pegleg stormed out of the dark room, shading his eyes against the sunlight.

'By all that's holy or not, we'd better be on our way back to Bad Bay. If not, there's going to be hell to pay.'

Dunk felt his hands grow sweaty on the ship's polished wheel. Pegleg spun on the tip of his wooden leg and hobbled up the stairs to the bridge.

'Mr Hoffnung!' The coach's skin was a deep red, despite the fact that he hadn't seen the sun in days.

'Ahoy, coach.'

While Pegleg had been unconscious, Dunk had found plenty of time to think about how to handle this. The instant he saw the fury blazing in the man's eyes, though, all his plans fled from his head. He tightened his grip on the wheel and wondered if he should have taken Dr Pill up on his offer.

'Don't you ahoy me.' He stormed to the top of the stairs and stopped there, his hand shaking, his leg weak. 'What's our heading?'

'South-west, coach.'

Pegleg swept his gaze around behind Dunk and spotted nothing but empty sea. Dunk knew what had to be running through his head. They had to leave Magritta by the south-west, but not for long, and there would be no reason to take the cutter out into the open sea, if they were heading for home.

'Destination?'

'Amazon Island, coach, off the coast of Lustria.'

Dunk waited for the explosion, but it never came. Pegleg walked slowly over to stand next to Dunk. He hissed his words through his teeth.

'Under whose authority?'

'Mine, coach.'

Dunk felt like his heart might burst from his chest. He looked down and saw Dirk and Spinne standing on the other side of the wheel, worry etched on their faces. Slick and Lästiges peered from behind them, the reporter's hovering camra staring over their shoulders. M'Grash lumbered up from the rear, picking his nose as he tried to figure out what all the ruckus meant.

He knew Dirk and Spinne could cut Pegleg down in an instant, but they wouldn't be able to move fast enough to save him too.

'So, it's mutiny then, is it?' Pegleg brought up his hook and spotted a cork stuck onto the tip of it. His eyes bulged as he stared at it.

'After what happened, we wanted to make sure you didn't hurt yourself in your sleep,' Dunk said.

Pegleg felt for the wound with the wrong hand and smacked the cork into his chest. Dunk could see the memories of what had happened come flooding back. Stunned, Pegleg brought his other hand up and felt the stitches sticking up under his shirt.

'You nearly died,' Dunk said. 'If we hadn't called for Dr Pill right away, you would have.'

Pegleg pulled open his grimy shirt, stained with sweat instead of blood, and exposed the angry wound over his heart. Then he took the cork off his hook, and looked at Dunk.

'For that you have my undying gratitude, Mr Hoffnung.' He brought his hook up to Dunk's face. 'Now give me back my ship.'

'You mean "our" ship,' Dunk said. He squinted out at the dazzling sea, not wanting to know what would happen next. If Pegleg meant to kill him, at least the blinding sun would make sure he would not see it coming.

Pegleg's hook flinched, but did not scratch Dunk's skin. Instead, the ex-pirate reached out with the bend of the hook and pulled Dunk's chin until the thrower faced him. Dunk searched the man's eyes for murderous intent and found it swaying there like a cobra ready to strike. 'Pardon me, Mr Hoffnung, but I don't think I could possibly have heard you right.'

Dunk stuck out his hand for Pegleg to shake. 'I'm part owner of the Hackers now. Glad to have you back, partner.'

The last word hit Pegleg like a troll lineman. He shook his head and looked up at the sky, and then at the sea around him. 'I died, didn't I? This is Hell. I tried to live a good life, to do right by people. I barely ever cheated my players, but I guess you can't make up for a misspent youth. I'm in Hell.'

He stared at Dunk, and then slashed at him with his hook. Dunk ducked behind the wheel, and the hook bit deep into the polished wood, sending off splinters.

Dunk pushed away from the wheel before Pegleg could attack again. As he did, the wheel began to spin, slowly at first, but then picking up speed. As the sails overhead began to flag, Pegleg jumped forward and grabbed the wheel.

Pegleg set the wheel straight and then tied it down so it would hold a straight heading, cursing the entire time. When he finished his work, he spun on Dunk, brandishing his hook once more.

'Explain this,' Pegleg snarled at Dunk. 'This is *my* ship, mine! No one else owns it.'

Cavre stepped up behind the captain, keeping well out of the man's reach. 'Now, captain, you know that's not entirely true.'

Pegleg went as cold as a week-old corpse. He turned to stare at Cavre and nodded. 'So,' he said, 'it's come to this. I was out, and you took over.'

'Just as you asked me to, captain. That's why you sold me part of the team and made me the team's general manager.'

'And first mate aboard ship.' Pegleg slapped the blunt end of his hook against his forehead. 'Has everything gone so wrong?'

Cavre shook his head. 'You were near death. Dunk showed me that he had a plan, and I thought it was a good one. He made an extremely generous offer for a part of the team, and I sold it to him.'

Pegleg pulled at his beard with his good hand. 'How much did you sell him?'

'Half.'

Pegleg almost choked.

'Of the whole team?'

Cavre shook his head. 'Of your shares.'

Pegleg nodded in understanding. 'So, he and I are equal partners. As long as we agree, there are no problems.'

'And when you don't?'

'You use your shares to break all stalemates.'

Cavre smiled, his white teeth gleaming bright inside the frame of his dark skin.

Pegleg reached out and clapped Cavre on the back. 'Well played, old friend.'

Dunk laughed, as did everyone else. The tension seemed to melt away from the bridge, and then from the rest of the deck. Pegleg and Cavre started to laugh as well, and for a moment Dunk thought everything would be all right.

'Just one thing,' Pegleg said, still chortling. 'Did you come up with this idea yourself?'

'No,' Cavre said, wiping the tears from his face. 'It was all Mr Fullbelly's idea.'

Down on the deck, Slick froze.

Pegleg vaulted over the wheel, straight at the halfling. Slick took off as if someone had mentioned that the last donut was still sitting in a box on the prow. Still, with his roly-poly belly and thick, stubby legs, he didn't have a prayer.

Even though Pegleg only had one good leg, he'd catch up with the agent soon enough. He was fast, and there were only so many places to hide on a ship.

'M'Grash!' Dunk said as he scrambled after the coach.

The ogre reached out and plucked Slick from the deck, and then held him high over his head, out of reach of Pegleg's swinging hook. Slick squealed in terror at first, but then clung to the ogre's hand as if it were a lifeline tossed to a drowning man.

'Mr K'Thragsh, put that bilge rat down so I can spear him on my hook like the rodent he is.'

M'Grash began to lower the halfling to the deck.

'Don't put me down,' Slick said, begging the ogre. He rose into the air once more.

'I am your coach and captain! You will follow my orders.'

Slick came down towards the deck once more. He tried climbing his way up the ogre's massive arm, but it was too wide around for him to get a proper grip on it with his tiny arms.

'Belay that!' Dunk said, coming up behind the captain. 'Don't let coach harm a hair on Slick's head.'

'Mr M'Grash, I am your employer, and I am giving you a direct order.'

'I am your best friend, *and* your employer, and I say, leave him where he is.'

M'Grash's massive eyeballs shuddered back and forth between Dunk and Pegleg for half a minute. Then his monstrous lower lip pouted out and started to tremble. A moment later, the ogre collapsed to the deck and began to sob, cradling the halfling protectively in his arms, keeping anyone from touching him for good or bad.

Dunk stepped up to M'Grash and put his arm around one of the monster's shoulders. 'Come on,' he said soothingly, 'it's not that bad.'

'The hell it's not!' said Pegleg. 'Let loose that miserable butterball of a turkey, or I'll lay you open with my hook.'

M'Grash's sobs only grew stronger.

'Stop it!' Dunk said to Pegleg. 'Can't you see what you're doing to him?'

'Why is he sobbing like that?' Lästiges said. 'He's big enough to toss them both overboard any time he likes.'

'I've seen this before,' Dirk said. 'Dunk used to do this once upon a time too.'

'Why's that?'

'Look at him,' Dirk said, pointing at the weeping ogre. 'He hates it when Mum and Dad fight.'

'Shut up!' Dunk and Pegleg said to Dirk in unison.

The two men looked at each other and had to laugh. They started out slow, but ended up bent over cackling, tears streaming down their cheeks.

M'Grash reached out with a massive, tentative hand and patted both of the men on the back at the same time. 'It's okay,' he said. 'M'Grash be better ogre now.'

They turned to look at him, and then burst into deep-hearted laughter once more. Seeing the concern on the ogre's face, Dunk soon straightened up and clapped his friend on the shoulder. 'It's all right,' he said. 'You did great. We'll be fine.'

M'Grash offered a tentative smile.

'Buck up, you big baby,' Pegleg said. 'We can't afford the nappies for a child your size.'

M'Grash froze and gaped at the ex-pirate. Dunk wondered if the ogre might finally snap and hurl their coach overboard. The creature reached out towards the ex-pirate with a massive mitt, and tousled Pegleg's hair.

Pegleg patted the ogre's hand affectionately. 'It's all right, big boy. Dunk and I need to finish our discussion, but we'll be all right. Don't you worry about it.'

M'Grash grinned, opening his mouth wide enough to swallow Slick whole. Instead, the halfling scampered out of his arms and scurried behind the ogre's protective bulk. He peeked back around M'Grash's shoulder at Pegleg, but the coach had already turned to escort Dunk back to the bridge.

'We need to make this work,' Pegleg said, 'for the ogre's sake.'

'You're really afraid of hurting his feelings?'

Pegleg shook his head. 'Of being hurt by him. In many ways, Mr K'Thragsh is still an extremely large child. If we make him mad, he may forget who his friends are.' He looked at Dunk meaningfully. 'All of his friends.'

Dunk nodded. 'So we need to work this out.'

'At least until we can get off this ship.' As they reached the bridge, Pegleg unlashed the wheel and started to turn it about. Dunk slapped a hand on it and pulled it back to where it had been.

'What do you think you're doing?' he asked the ex-pirate.

'This foolishness is over, Mr Hoffnung. Team owner or not, you're still one of my players, and we're going home.'

'I don't think so,' said Dunk. He glanced over his shoulder and saw M'Grash watching them. 'We're fitted for the trip to Lustria, and we're already on our way. That's our destination, and I can tell you right now that Cavre agrees with me. You're outvoted.'

As pleasantly as possible, Pegleg said to Dunk, 'You can't vote against me if you're dead.'

'You know the rules against that,' Dunk said. 'If an owner is convicted of killing another owner, he automatically loses his part of the franchise.'

'Yes,' Pegleg said. 'The Game Wizards put that into place after the six owners of the Chaos All-Stars spent most of a Chaos Cup tournament trying to kill each other off. That's a fairly obscure piece of knowledge for a player to have, Mr Hoffnung. Might I guess that Mr Fullbelly educated you about that particular protection?'

'Slick has been a great help. As my agent, my official representative to the team, he's protected by that ruling as well. Otherwise, I'm told Dodger Badall will teleport in here and turn anyone flaunting the rules to a crisp.'

'Badall? The lead Game Wizard? He's part of that new crew trying to revive NAF, isn't he? That league's been dead for decades.'

'So has Badall. He just hasn't noticed yet, but he can still fry your heart in your chest should you try anything.'

'This isn't over,' Pegleg said between his teeth, keeping up his lousy smile for the ogre's sake. 'We'll turn this boat around if I have anything to say about it.'

'If you try, I'll hogtie you, and let Dr Pill feed you whatever he wants.'

Pegleg sneered, and then put his hook on Dunk's shoulder. 'I should kill you right here and now.'

'You wouldn't dare.'

As the words left his mouth, Dunk knew how untrue they were. All he could think of was getting to Lustria. Before he could respond, though, Rotes's voice sounded down from the crow's nest high above.

'Ahoy!' Rotes said. 'Ship ahoy! Off the starboard bow. Ahoy! She's flying the black flag, the Jolly Roger.'

DUNK RACED TO the front of the ship, Pegleg limping after him. He shielded his eyes with his hand and stared out at the horizon, while the ex-pirate pulled a collapsible spyglass from his coat and trained it in the same direction.

'I don't see a thing,' said Dunk. Rotes had pointed almost directly west, but all he spied was the sun glittering on the water and a few clouds gathering near the horizon.

'That's because you're looking for a ship,' Pegleg said. His spyglass locked onto something at the edge of the world.

'As opposed to what?' Dunk hated it when Pegleg talked to him like a child. After three years working with him, he should have been used to it, but now that they were business partners, he found it grated more than ever.

Of course, Pegleg probably didn't think of them as partners yet. Perhaps that would come later, or never.

'A mast.' Pegleg handed the spyglass to Dunk, keeping his eyes fixed on whatever it was he'd spotted. 'From up there, Miss Hernd can see farther over the horizon than we can. When she spots a whole boat, we can only find its tip.'

Dunk brought the spyglass up to his eye and trained it on the horizon. There, right where Pegleg had been looking, he spied two slivers of black barely stabbing up out of the dark blue waters. A black rectangle spattered with bits of white fluttered from the top of one of them.

'Can we outrun her?' Dunk asked. He handed the spyglass back to Pegleg, who pocketed it once more.

The pirate craned his neck back and hollered up at Rotes. 'What sort of ship is she?'

The woman lowered her spyglass and peered down over the side of the crow's nest. 'It's a ship, a big one.'

'What kind?'

'I'm a Blood Bowl player, not a sailor. How should I know?'

Pegleg glanced around to shout an order, but stopped when he spotted Cavre already halfway up the mast. Rotes clambered out of the tiny crow's nest and slipped down to the deck as the first mate replaced her, grumbling as she went. 'There's nothing in my job description about spotting pirates,' she said.

Pegleg ignored her. He gave Cavre a moment to survey the situation through the spyglass that Rotes had left behind. 'Report, Mr Cavre.'

'She's a galleon, captain, four masts.'

Dunk watched Pegleg for his reaction. The man went white.

'Can we outrun her?' Dunk asked.

The captain didn't answer. He turned and stared out at the slivers on the horizon, as if the gates of hell might burst open from that direction.

'If they're gunning for us, not a chance,' Pegleg said, 'but we're damned well going to try.'

The captain turned back to his ship and bellowed out his orders. 'To your stations! Mr Reyes, take the wheel and bring her full about.'

The Estalian lineman gave the captain a sharp nod and dashed off to fulfil his orders. Dunk had rarely seen the man move so fast, even on the Blood Bowl field.

'Mr Cavre, report on any changes.'

'Aye-aye, captain.'

People scrambled around the ship to prepare for the change in heading. While Dunk had no desire to head back to the Old World, he knew he'd rather delay his reunion with Kirta a bit longer than face a pirate raid.

Last year, Dunk had nearly drowned in an oceanic encounter with the daemon-crewed *Seas of Hate*, the ship on which Pegleg had once been enslaved. He didn't care to repeat the experience.

'Any chance you have some more of those enchanted cannonballs in the hold?' Dunk asked. M'Grash had hurled them by hand at the *Seas of Hate*, sinking the ship of damned souls.

'Perhaps a few,' Pegleg said. 'I intended to restock in Magritta after the tournament. I don't suppose you or Mr Cavre, or Mr Fullbelly thought about that when you took over for me, did you?'

Dunk's stomach flipped. He'd suspected that he'd got in over his head with all these business manoeuvres. Now he knew for sure.

Pegleg stood tall and surveyed his crew, as the players worked the sails and managed to bring the ship about, putting their backs to the wind. He'd trained every one of those people as both Blood Bowl players and sailors, and in either environment they worked like a well-oiled machine. His chest puffed out with pride as he watched.

'So, Mr Hoffnung,' Pegleg said, 'just how much did you pay for part of my team?'

Dunk blushed. 'Um, just about everything I have. Dirk and I even put up the family keep in Altdorf against it.'

Pegleg stroked his beard. 'Really? Imagine that. Mr Cavre drove you a hard bargain. He must have known how desperate you were. That's not a good position from which to negotiate.'

Dunk sighed. 'I didn't want to do it at all. Slick and Cavre convinced me that this was the only way, and since you'd been so stubborn about it, I believed them.'

Pegleg said nothing. He watched the sails swell with wind, and a wry smile played on his lips.

'I'd be happy to sell my shares back to you, once we get back from Lustria, of course.'

Pegleg looked back over his shoulder at the ship chasing them across the sea. Dunk could see all four masts now, even without a spyglass's aid.

'Now, Mr Hoffnung,' the ex-pirate said, 'why would I want to take you up on that?'

Dunk did a double-take. 'Are you serious? I thought for sure you'd want the whole team back.'

Pegleg arched his eyebrows. 'I'm sure that once this foolishness is all over, Mr Cavre will once again see things my way, and I'll get to keep all your loot.' He scratched his chin. 'A keep in Altdorf, you say? I always fancied living the noble life.'

Dunk blanched.

Pegleg clapped him on the back with his good hand. 'Don't you worry about that, Mr Hoffnung. If we don't escape that ship, the chances are neither one of us will ever see Altdorf again.'

The *Sea Chariot* picked up speed on its new heading, and Dunk watched the water slip away beneath them as the cutter sliced through the waves. They moved as fast as he'd ever seen the ship go, and hope surged in his heart that they might have a chance.

Then he glanced back over his shoulder, beyond the ship's aft gunwale. He could see the whole of the pirate ship, from the tip of its mast to the waterline of its hull. It had gained on them as they came about, and it seemed to be getting closer still.

'We're not going to outrace her, are we?' Lästiges said as she made her way onto the bridge, the ever-present globe of her camra floating over her shoulder.

'That's why you're the reporter and we're the team,' Pegleg said as he gave the wheel a small correction. 'Players have to believe in themselves. Reporters don't believe in a damn thing.'

Lästiges furrowed her wide and seamless brow at him. 'You do realise you just avoided the question?'

Pegleg smiled. 'Turn that camra behind us, miss, and you can answer your own question.'

Dunk turned and saw that the ship still gained on them. 'Can we turn and fight?' he asked.

'Against a galleon like that?' Pegleg asked. 'She has around three score guns on her to our none, zilch, zero. Even if we could get inside her range, what would we do, board her? They must have a couple of hundred men aboard at least, maybe twice that.'

'But we have to have a few of those cannonballs left, and we have M'Grash and Edgar.'

'Even Mr K'Thragsh can't stand against that many. Edgar? They'd turn him into timber, maybe make him into their new figurehead. And those cannonballs? If we had a score or two of them, we might have a chance.'

'But they worked so well against the *Seas of Hate*.' Dunk remembered how the rune covered balls of iron with the three finger holes in them had run right through the decks of that damned ship like a spear through a rotting corpse.

'They were blessed, and that ship was damned, and packed with daemons. Whoever's following us, they're flesh and blood on a wooden ship. Blessings don't work so well against the living.'

'Isn't there anything we can do?'

'We're running, Mr Hoffnung. Pray for a freak wind.'

Dunk reached into the captain's coat pocket and withdrew the spyglass without a word of protest from Pegleg. He looked through it at the ship following them.

It already loomed large enough in the lens for him to be able to pick out the faces of individual men peering out over the gunwales, waving their arms and pounding their fists against the ship. They bore wide grins on their faces, instead of the greed or bloodlust that Dunk had expected, and their cheery look made him shudder.

'Does she have a name?' said Pegleg.

'Who?' Dunk asked. 'Spinne?'

'The ship bearing down on us, about to destroy us, Mr Hoffnung, does she have a name?'

Blushing, Dunk swept the spyglass over the ship's hull. He found the figurehead, which had been carved to resemble a Blood Bowl catcher diving for a ball just beyond his fingers. Dunk couldn't see a face inside the spiked helmet, but he supposed the carving wasn't supposed to be of a particular player.

Then he spotted the ship's name, emblazoned on the side of the stem in blood-red letters limned with gold.

'It's the *Fanatic*,' Dunk said.

'You're kidding.'

Dunk lowered the spyglass to look at the captain. The man gave him a lopsided grin. 'What's so funny?' asked Dunk.

Slick, who'd made his way onto the bridge, spoke up. 'The *Fanatic* is the largest of the ships that follow the Blood Bowl tournaments around the Old World.'

'People do that? I thought they mostly watched the games on Cabalvision.'

'The wealthy can do what they want, and mostly they like to follow Blood Bowl. The *Fanatic* is the most notorious of the so-called "party barges". It ferries the fans and their vices anywhere they want to go.

'Their captain is an orc named Mad Jonnen. He hasn't missed one of the majors since before you were born. He used to coach the Orcland Raiders before he was fired. He was one of the best the game ever saw.'

'Why'd they fire him then?'

'He ate three of his players, on the field.'

Dunk instantly felt seasick for the first time since climbing aboard the boat.

'Okay, he didn't eat them, just took a few chunks out of them with his teeth, during the middle of a game.'

'Why?' Dunk glanced at Pegleg, hoping the conversation didn't give the ex-pirate any ideas.

'He'd bet on the game, and they'd caused him to lose thousands of crowns by not following his orders.'

'He bet against his team?'

Slick smiled. 'No, he bet on the Raiders, but the players, who'd set up bets of their own, didn't beat the spread.'

'So why's he chasing us?'

'Two possibilities, Mr Hoffnung,' Pegleg said.

Slick pointed up at the sky. Dunk craned back his head and spied the crow's next above. The Hackers' flag snapped in the breeze above, its free end pointing in the direction they were going.

Dunk looked back down at the halfling and shrugged.

'They're fans looking for autographs,' Slick said. 'The *Fanatic* is packed to the sails with some of the top fans in the sport, and the Hackers have a lot of loyal admirers these days.'

'What's the second option?' Dunk said.

'We somehow lost them a lot of money, and they're here to collect it from our hides.'

'So why are they flying a black flag?'

'Jonnen used to coach the Raiders, son.'

Dunk nodded. 'And their colours are silver on black.'

He raised the spyglass to his eye once more. There on the flag flapping high above the *Fanatic*, he spotted not a skull and crossbones but a silver helmet with a crest of spikes.

Breathing a sigh of relief, Dunk brought the spyglass down to survey the people massed at the gunwales. He expected to see the same joyful expressions they'd worn before, although he had no idea if they'd been cheering for the Hackers or for their deaths.

Each and every one of the people on the *Fanatic* wore a look of absolute terror. They waved at the *Sea Chariot*, some trying to get its attention, others using both arms to call it back. Some screamed in horror.

Dunk lowered the spyglass and grabbed Pegleg by the shoulder. 'Something's wrong.'

The ex-pirate handed Dunk the wheel and took the spyglass from him. As Dunk took control of the ship, he noticed that the *Fanatic* wasn't chasing straight after them any longer. It had started to peel away.

'It doesn't make sense,' Pegleg said. 'They had us. They were after us, and we had no way to escape. What in the seven seas could have stopped them?'

A commotion erupted at the fore of the *Sea Chariot*. Dirk and Spinne stood peering out past the bowsprit, shading their eyes with their hands. M'Grash, who stood behind them, closer to the bridge, turned and howled in fear, his face twisted into a terrified grimace.

Dunk's stomach twisted into a knot. He'd known M'Grash to overreact before. The ogre could be sent into shuddering fits by the right kind of cockroach. But anything that could honestly scare him, not just give him the heebie-jeebies, had to be truly horrible.

'What in Nuffle's balls is that?' Pegleg said as his spyglass leaned in over Dunk's shoulder.

Dunk followed the spyglass's angle and spotted a jet of water spraying into the sky, just barely to the port side of the *Sea Chariot*'s bow. At first, Dunk feared that they might have found a reef in the middle of the sea, as unlikely as that seemed. A reef, though, would have thrown up plume after plume as the waves crashed against it. This just sent up water constantly, never waning.

Spinne turned at the bow, and cupped her hands to her face. She shouted something, but Dunk couldn't hear it over the roar from whatever was spraying the water into the sky.

'Hard to starboard, Mr Hoffnung,' Pegleg said, 'now!'

Dunk spun the wheel to the right, over and over again, until it could go no farther. As he did, the ship began to turn, but too slowly. Despite changing its facing, though, the ship kept moving straight towards the plume.

Dirk shouted at Dunk too, but the roar had only got louder. Dunk couldn't hear a thing Dirk said. He shrugged at him, and started to make his way down the stairs and across the deck. That's when M'Grash came charging at him.

'Whirlpool!' The ogre's deep voice cracked in panic. 'Whirlpool, Dunkel! Whirlpool!'

Pegleg cursed. 'Lean hard on that wheel, Mr Hoffnung.'

Dunk put everything he had into it, but the wheel wouldn't turn any farther. 'I don't think it's doing any good.'

Pegleg ignored Dunk, and reached into a long, low chest built into the aft of the bridge. He pulled out a massive harpoon with a wicked, barbed tip. It was big enough to be used for hunting whales.

The coach wrestled the harpoon out of its box and handed it to M'Grash. Dunk noticed it had a large coil of rope tied to its back end.

Pegleg handed the harpoon to M'Grash and pointed at the *Fanatic*. 'There's your target, Mr K'Thragsh! Let her fly!'

M'Grash leaned back with the harpoon in his hand, his arm cocked back even farther. It wavered in his hand, bending under its own weight, and Dunk feared it might snap in half in the ogre's hand. Then M'Grash stepped forward and hurled the harpoon into the air.

The harpoon zipped through the air, too fast, as Dunk soon spotted. Years of being a thrower for a Blood Bowl team had honed his sense of a throw to a razor's edge. He knew, as the missile left M'Grash's mitt that the ogre had put too much arm into it, and not enough finesse.

A few yards past the gunwale, the harpoon went into a slow, flat turn, spinning like a dagger thrown sideways through the air. The winds caught it and buffeted it about so that it barely reached the *Fanatic*'s hull.

When it did, the side of the harpoon's shaft, rather than its tip, smacked into the ship, and it bounced off into the sea.

'Haul it back,' Pegleg shouted.

M'Grash complied, pulling the harpoon in with a series of short, sharp yanks that nearly snapped the weapon to splinters with each tug. Spinne came charging onto the bridge, and Dunk handed her the wheel. She leaned into it with all her might, moving it a few inches more than even Dunk had managed.

Dunk gave Spinne a quick, tender kiss, hoping it wouldn't be their last. Then he turned towards the ogre to lend a hand. As he did, the harpoon leapt out of the waves and stabbed point first into the deck, juddering right between Dunk's legs.

10

'AGAIN, MR K'THRAGSH!' Pegleg shouted, barely audible over the whirlpool's thunderous roar.

Dunk grabbed the ogre's arm, and M'Grash stopped in his tracks. He glanced back to see Dunk standing next to him, his hands stretched out for the harpoon. He looked to Pegleg for guidance.

The coach shook his head. 'Mr K'Thragsh, make that throw!'

'He can't do it!' Dunk said. 'Let me try.'

'I'm still the coach of this team, Mr Hoffnung. Do not defy my orders!'

Dunk stared at the man, trying to see if he'd finally gone insane. 'M'Grash is a blitzer, not a thrower. He'll never spear that ship.'

'That's none of your concern. I'm in charge here, and you will abide by my decisions.' Pegleg nodded at M'Grash, who hefted the harpoon for another throw.

Before he could let it loose, though, Dunk stopped him with a hand on his arm.

'This isn't a game,' Dunk said. 'If we blow this, we all die!'

Pegleg laughed humourlessly. 'You think it's any different in a game? Every time you step on the pitch, it's a matter of life and death. That's what makes the game so great.'

Dunk reached out to take Pegleg by the lapels, but thought better of it. He balled his fists at his sides instead.

'Don't do this,' he said. He glanced towards the bow, and saw a massive hole that had opened up in the surface of the sea before them. It looked like someone had pulled the plug from the bottom of the ocean and was letting all the water flow down the drain. A dolphin arced up out of the opposite wall of water, hung there in the sun for a spectacular instant, framed in a rainbow formed by the sun in the spray, and then disappeared into the vertical waters once more.

'You're a better coach than that,' Dunk said to Pegleg. 'You're mad at me. I get that, but don't let it cloud your judgment. Don't let it kill us all.'

Pegleg opened his mouth to snarl a riposte, but he stopped and bit his lip instead. He scanned Dunk's eyes, and nodded.

'All right,' he said, in a 'don't make me regret this' tone. He waved at M'Grash to hand the harpoon to Dunk. 'Mr Hoffnung? You're up.'

Dunk nodded his thanks, and took the harpoon from M'Grash's grasp.

'Sorry, Dunkel,' M'Grash said in a pained voice.

'Don't sweat it, big guy,' Dunk said, keeping as upbeat as he could. 'Just hold on to something and take care of Spinne.'

Dunk didn't spare a moment to watch M'Grash respond. He simply cocked back his arm and took aim at the *Fanatic*'s hull. The suction of the whirlpool had started to spin the *Sea Chariot*'s bow about to port, and Dunk had to aim past the port gunwale at the galleon. The deck of the ship bounced madly with the whirling water trying to tear it apart, making it hard for Dunk to find a clear shot. He knew that he only had time for one shot, but with the deck bucking, he had just as much chance of putting the harpoon in the sea as into the *Fanatic*.

Dunk waited for a moment, trying to gauge the bounce, to better time his throw. It felt like waiting for a receiver to get open as a pack of ogres stampeded towards him. The right moment might never happen, but he had to wait for it, or he'd waste whatever chance he might have. Making a bad throw would be just as bad, worse even, than making no throw at all.

'Throw it!' Pegleg shouted. 'Throw it now, or we're all doomed!'

Dunk held on to the harpoon for a moment longer. He wondered if Pegleg might stab him with his hook and take the harpoon from him if he held onto it for too long. He flexed his throwing arm, keeping it loose, but kept waiting for the right moment to present itself.

'We're going in!' Spinne said. 'Hold on to something!'

The ship began to nose in over the whirlpool's edge. It tottered there for a moment, hanging between one fate and the other, and it was then that Dunk saw his chance. He hurled the harpoon at the other ship.

Dunk's aim was true, and the harpoon arced through the air in a perfect spiral, the rope playing out behind it. The barbed tip slammed into the deck of the galleon and stabbed right through it, catching in the strong, solid wood.

Despite this, the ship continued its long slide over the whirlpool's edge. The deck tilted at a crazy angle, and Dunk had to grab the gunwale in front of him to keep his balance.

Dunk glanced back, and saw Spinne still clutching the wheel, Slick's arms wrapped around one of her legs as if he feared she might try to kick him away. Beyond her, people in the middle of the boat began to slide towards the railings, scrabbling to find any handhold at all to stop their descent. One man, the new back-up blitzer, by the name of Tom Linson, tipped right over the edge of the ship and out of sight.

Edgar, who always stood next to the mast, had tipped over and got his limbs tangled in the ship's rigging. The sails were useless now anyhow, and the ropes that held them in place seemed like the only thing that had kept the treeman from toppling over the ship's edge. He'd taken advantage of this to gather Guillermo and Spiel in his free branches, where they clung to him for their lives.

At the far side, Dirk had a good hold on the gunwale, and was starting to use it to climb back towards the bridge, which teetered high above him. As he struggled upward, Enojada came tumbling down. He reached out with one hand and caught her just as she was about to cartwheel into the ocean's hungry maw, which widened beneath them, ready to suck them down.

M'Grash had a death grip on the gunwale beside Dunk, and he'd already gathered Lästiges safely in his free arm. Pegleg hung from the railing by his hook, staring at the line as it played out between him and Dunk, zipping fast enough over the gunwale to make the wood smoke.

Then the line went taut.

The entire ship shuddered from stem to stern. Far below, someone screamed. Dunk hated himself for giving thanks that it didn't sound like Dirk.

The rope and the ship creaked with the strain of holding onto each other, but neither one gave. Dunk glanced back and saw the stern swinging back and forth in the rushing water, like bait on a hook trawling behind a speeding boat.

Dunk knew that this couldn't last long. Either the *Fanatic* would tow them out of the maelstrom, or they would haul it down along with them.

Dunk could still see the *Fanatic* from his vantage point at the aft gunwale. The ship had already begun to turn aside from the whirlpool when he'd harpooned it. Now, it struggled to complete a full about turn, but a ship the size of a galleon was simply too big to turn about on its keel.

The weight of the *Sea Chariot* pulling on the *Fanatic* must have given Captain Mad Jonnen and his crew fits. Despite that, it seemed like the *Fanatic* was starting to make some headway in its efforts to leave the

whirlpool behind. Dunk laughed in relief, hope that
they might yet survive, rising in him.

Then the screams below grew louder and more
numerous. He looked back, hoping he wouldn't hate
what he saw. He was horribly disappointed.

Something green and slimy had wrapped around
the middle of the cutter. It had to be at least six feet
thick, maybe more, and it slithered up, over, and
down around the deck like a living lasso, like the
world serpent from the Norsca legends that Dunk had
learned as a child. It squirmed, writhed, and slid forward without any sign of which end of it was which.

Then it tightened around the ship, bringing its full
weight to bear on the hull. The *Sea Chariot* stopped
sliding back and forth in the unforgiving current,
which was more like a waterfall, but instead of waver-
ing from side to side it started to creep down.

'No!' Pegleg shouted. 'Don't do it! No!'

Dunk looked to see what the man was shouting at,
and he saw the captain waving his fleshy fist in the
direction of the *Fanatic*. There, next to where the harpoon had buried itself in the galleon's deck, stood a
man with a glittering axe.

Dunk opened his mouth to join Pegleg in begging
for mercy, even though he knew it was useless. If the
Sea Chariot had to go down, as it seemed it would,
there was no reason for the *Fanatic* to go with her. If
he'd been standing on the deck of the *Fanatic*, the axe
would probably have already fallen.

Before Dunk could say anything, a horrific howl
drowned out every other sound. He whipped his head
back around to see the head of a massive sea monster

having breached the whirlpool's foaming walls. The thing tossed back its head and screeched again. It arched back its long, sinuous neck to strike.

Then something next to Dunk snapped with a loud, sickening twang, and the *Sea Chariot* tumbled backward into the raging maelstrom. The sea creature screamed as it went down with it.

DUNK AWOKE TO the smell of the sea, the sound of the whirlpool still roaring in his ears. He wondered if all those stories people told about the afterlife were wrong. Perhaps he was doomed to wander the earth as a detached soul, trapped in that single moment and place in which he perished.

Just about every part of Dunk hurt. He stank of saltwater. He could taste it in his mouth, and it stung his sinuses and his eyes.

He remembered the *Sea Chariot* tumbling back into the maelstrom. As much as he'd tried to keep a grip on the ship, it wasn't easy to do when the whole thing was coming apart all around you. He'd reached for Spinne at the last second, hoping that they could at least die in each other's arms, but the waters had torn them apart instantly.

If he was dead, though, it felt nothing like what he expected. His ears roared with the sound of the ocean, as if someone had strapped a massive seashell to each of his ears. He could feel the air in his lungs and the sun beating mercilessly on his face. He'd long assumed that death would be an end to pain rather than the start of it, but, either way, he hoped it would go away.

Dunk opened his eyes and saw the silvery tail of a large fish flopped on the sand beside him. He wondered if the poor creature had died next to him. Did dead fish need to breathe water?

Then the tail flipped up and down, which got Dunk's attention. He scrambled to his feet, kicking up sand everywhere. He looked down at the fish and found that the top of it looked a hell of a lot like a gorgeous, topless woman with long, blue-green hair.

'Good morning,' the fishwoman said, for a fishwoman it had to be. Dunk had never met such a creature before, although he'd heard countless stories about them. Some considered them mere legends, but in a world filled with camras and ogres, and steam-powered chainsaws, Dunk had long ago learned to rarely discount legends.

Dunk glanced around and saw that he was in part of a ship's hull that had been involved in a fatal encounter with the bottom of the sea, which was strangely bone dry. The hull surrounded Dunk on three sides, but instead of a fourth wall, where he suspected a deck should have stood, he saw a vertical span of spinning water.

Sunlight streamed in from the open end of the hull above him, as well as through various cracks and outright holes scattered throughout the hull. A beam fell on the fishwoman, and she smiled at him and flipped her hair back from her face. Despite the bluish tint to her pale skin, or perhaps because of it, she was a stunning beauty.

Then she smiled at him, revealing a set of sharp, pointy, double-rowed teeth. Dunk wondered if she'd saved him out of kindness, or for her lunch.

'Good morning,' the fishwoman said again. She cocked her head at him, and seawater poured from her lowered ear.

Dunk pulled a strand of seaweed from his hair and flicked it to the ground.

'Hello,' he said. He nearly choked on the word, and had to clear his throat before he could speak again. 'What's happening here?'

'You fell into the maelstrom,' the fishwoman said, flopping closer to him on her tail. Although Dunk was sure she could swim like a dolphin, on dry land, he knew he could run circles around her.

'I thought I was dead.'

The fishwoman smiled, again showing those shark's teeth. 'We saved you,' she said, spreading her arms wide. Dunk found it difficult not to stare at her breasts, but he did his best. His thoughts naturally turned to Spinne, and then he gasped.

'The others,' he said. 'The people I was with, what about them?'

'Some of them survived the fall into the heart of the maelstrom. Others, the ocean swallowed whole. She does not give up such treasures so easily.'

The walls of the hull seemed like they might collapse on Dunk at any moment, either trapping him beneath them or knocking him into the spinning wall of water. Either way, Dunk knew he had to get out of there. He strode over to the nearest fractured part of the hull and gave it a solid kick.

The hull around him creaked and tottered at the impact. The fishwoman squealed like a dolphin.

'That may not be wise,' she said in a strained voice. As she spoke, she flopped her way closer to the rushing water.

'I can't stay in here,' Dunk said. He pointed towards the water. 'And I can't go in there.'

He studied the wall quickly, and found a cracked portion that looked more likely to cooperate with him. He aimed a thick-soled boot at it and lashed out. The crack widened as the whole hull shook.

'Please stop.' The fishwoman folded her hands together to plead with Dunk, and he backed off from the hull.

Then he heard someone scream: Spinne.

Dunk planted his feet, lowered his shoulder, and charged straight into the crack that he'd widened. The impact hurt his unarmoured arm, but the wood gave, if only just a little. He stepped back and smashed into the hull again and again.

As Dunk hammered against the hull, he felt it shake and quiver. At first, he thought that it was about to give way. Then he realised that all he'd done was start to dislodge the hull from the sand in which it had landed. The water that ran into and past the fragment of the hull tugged at it harder due to his efforts, but it didn't seem to be moving.

'Spinne!' he shouted. 'I'm coming.'

Dunk heard a roar on the other side of the hull, a sound that could only have come from M'Grash's throat. An instant later, heavy footfalls thudded across the sand towards Dunk, and a set of sausage-sized fingers appeared under one jagged edge of the hull.

Dunk felt a hand tug on his arm, and saw the fishwoman pulling at him, trying to get him to follow her into the water. Her touch surprised him with its warmth. He supposed it would have been as cold and clammy as that of a corpse.

'It's all right,' he said. 'He's my friend.'

Then it got dark inside the hull. Dunk looked up to see the hull tipping back towards the water, blocking out the sun. He cheered, but the noise caught in his throat as he realised the problem with M'Grash's plan, if the ogre could be said to have one.

As the hull tipped backward, more of it caught in the edge of the maelstrom, and the water started to pull it backward... straight backward. Dunk edged back as the hull began to pull free from where it had become embedded in the sand. Heartened by his movement, the fishwoman yanked on his arm harder, trying to pull him into the water.

'Stop!' Dunk shouted, although he knew the ogre wouldn't be able to hear him through the wood and over the roar of the water. 'M'Grash, stop!'

The hull kept coming at him. If Dunk had felt confined before, he was now becoming claustrophobic.

Dunk watched the spinning wall of water, polluted with the flotsam and jetsam of countless wrecked ships whirring past at high speed. A bleached skull whipped by, followed by various parts of a dismembered skeleton, and Dunk knew that to enter the water would mean his death, no matter how well meaning the fishwoman might be.

The wall of wood coming towards him didn't look like it wanted to give him much of a choice in the matter. Dunk considered hunkering down against the wall of water and hoping that the hull might tip over enough to scrape over his head, but as he watched the hull drag nearer to him, he knew he couldn't rely on that happening. Instead, he drew a bead on the section of wood he'd battered and decided to give it one last shot.

Dunk got down into a three-point stance, just the way Pegleg had taught him to before every kick-off. Many players said a prayer to Nuffle, the god of Blood Bowl, as they entered the sacred stance, but Dunk had long since realised that there were solid, athletic, secular reasons to use it as well. It put him in the perfect position from which to launch a hit or tackle, and he intended to use it here for the same purpose.

Dunk lowered his head, and then launched at the oncoming wood, legs pumping him forward faster with every stride. He smashed into it with everything he had, heedless of how much it might hurt. Smashing against the hull seemed a better bet than letting it drag him to a watery doom, so he did it, hard.

The planks gave way under his vicious assault. He smashed straight through them and found himself on the other side, face down in the sand with splinters of wood all around him, the sun beating down on him again.

Dunk's skull hurt from the impact, but he felt so thrilled to be alive that he barely noticed it. He shook his head to clear it, but before he could even look up, something large and powerful gathered him up into its arms and hauled him into the air.

'Dunkel!' M'Grash shouted. 'Dunkel is alive! M'Grash saved Dunkel!'

Dunk grinned despite himself. The ogre's unconditional enthusiasm always felt contagious, and with Dunk having narrowly avoided death, he found it impossible to avoid being swept up in it. He cheered alongside the ogre and gave him a huge hug around his trunk-sized neck.

'Dunk!'

He recognised Spinne's voice instantly, and struggled to get the ogre to let him go. 'Put me down, M'Grash,' he said, still overjoyed, but determined to get free. 'I have to see Spinne.'

The ogre tossed him free, and Dunk made a running landing on his feet, dashing across the sand. He looked up and saw Spinne right there before him. She planted her feet to greet him and caught him like he was an opposing blitzer.

Dunk wrapped Spinne up in his arms and drew her close. He planted a long, lingering kiss on her delicious lips. He knew that as long as she was with him, there was nothing he couldn't do, no challenge they couldn't take, no game they couldn't win together.

'I thought you were dead,' Spinne said.

'I thought I was dead too. I thought we were all dead.' He held her close and finally opened his eyes to peer over her shoulder.

The whirlpool stretched farther across than he would have thought possible, almost as wide as a Blood Bowl field. The rotting hulks of several ships, and the shattered remains of countless others, lay strewn among the jagged rocks and across wide stretches of otherwise empty, white sand. A green and gold Hacker flag flapped from the end of a mast that had stuck like a spear in the ground, but the rest of the *Sea Chariot* seemed to be in splinters, or to have washed away, trapped in the maelstrom.

A few damp souls wandered around the wood. Dirk knelt, digging under a chunk of hull, using a broken plank as a shovel, Reyes helping him with a battered oar. Cavre wandered about the place, turning over loose bits and pieces, looking for any signs of life. Hernd sat over to the west, holding Spiel's head in her lap. The man looked half-drowned, but he still lived. Getrunken lay unmoving just a few yards beyond.

'Where are the others?'

Spinne didn't say a thing.

Dunk pulled back so he could see her face. 'Pegleg? Edgar? Anfäger?'

Spinne just shook her head. She couldn't meet his eyes. 'Gone,' she said, her voice broken and raw. 'Roja, Bereit, Anima, Ciotola, and Linson too.'

'What about Enojada?'

As Dunk spoke, the Amazon appeared atop a massive rock, and shaded her eyes as she surveyed the area. She seemed untouched by the carnage around her. But for her wet hair and her dripping clothes, he might have suspected she hadn't had a terribly rotten day.

Dunk knew someone else was missing, but he couldn't say who. He went down the roster in his head, but came up empty. Only members of the team had been aboard: the Hackers and Enojada. Who could it be?

Dunk felt sick. Not one name had come to his mind, but two.

'Lästiges?' he whispered into Spinne's ear. 'Slick?'

She raised her eyes, and he saw that she had been weeping. She shook her head. 'No sign anywhere.'

Dunk let Spinne loose and stared at the land around them, from the rock on which Enojada stood to the maelstrom's upper edge, where the raging waters of the ocean spilled down for a moment before being swept away.

'You thought I was dead too,' Dunk said, holding Spinne with one arm. 'There's still hope.'

Dunk took to running towards the large rock in the centre of the whirlpool. Spinne raced along beside him. As he passed Dirk, Dunk clapped him on the shoulder.

'Hey,' Dirk said, annoyed. He stood up to see who'd smacked him. 'Hey!'

Dunk stopped at the base of the rock, Spinne hauling up beside him. As Dunk caught his breath, something hit him from behind and smashed him into the rock. He spun about in its grasp and saw that Dirk had tackled him.

'You son of a bitch!' Dirk said. Dunk had thought his brother would be happy to see him, but the man was anything but.

'Don't talk about our mother that way,' Dunk said. 'Besides, what would that make you?'

'Just shut up.' Dirk wagged a finger in his brother's face. 'By Nuffle's leathery balls, don't you ever pull something like that again!'

'Like what? Getting sucked into a whirlpool and then rescued by a fishwoman? I'll try to avoid it.'

'Fishwoman?' Spinne said.

'Just don't do it!'

'What? You got pulled in here with the rest of us, with everyone else on the ship. What could I have done about that? What is it you don't want me to do?'

Dirk stabbed his finger into Dunk's chest for emphasis on every word. 'Don't *scare* me that way, you bastard.'

Dirk spun away and marched off, mad.

'Again with the comments about our mother.' said Dunk. 'She must be spinning in her grave.'

Spinne put a hand on Dunk. 'Take it easy on him,' she said. 'Lästiges is still missing.'

Dunk had been about to follow Dirk and have more words with him, but the fight went right out of him. He knew how upset he'd be if he thought Spinne was dead, how upset he'd been just minutes before when he'd thought they were all dead. He could give his brother a little space.

Dunk waved up at Enojada. 'See anything?' he asked.

The Amazon shook her head. 'Did you say something about fishwomen?'

Dunk glanced at Spinne, who glared at him. 'Uh, yeah. When I came to in that hull, a fishwoman was leaning over me. I think she saved me.' He glanced between Spinne and Enojada. 'You didn't see any fishwomen?'

The women both shook their heads. Enojada arched an eyebrow at him in amusement, while Spinne scowled at him.

Dunk shrugged at them. 'She disappeared when M'Grash tipped the hull into the waves. He must have scared her off.'

'Good riddance,' said Spinne.

'I wouldn't be so quick to dismiss her,' said Dunk, looking around. 'We're trapped down here. Finding anyone who can get in and out of here on their own power is a good thing, right?'

Spinne gave him an annoyed shrug. Enojada pursed her lips and spoke. 'These fishwomen, they do not think the way we do. They are predators, and they cannot be trusted.'

'Have you seen any before?'

Enojada smiled. 'Yes. They followed in the wake of our ship as we travelled from Lustria to Magritta. They constantly tempted the men to leap in after them. A few of them did, and we never heard from them again.'

'You didn't sail over on a ship full of Amazons?' asked Dunk.

'Did you not wonder why I did not travel back with such a ship?' Enojada laughed. 'We enjoy our privacy and do not have much contact with the outside world, other than for Blood Bowl. We have few ocean-worthy ships. I booked passage on a merchant ship instead.'

Dunk nodded, but he wasn't listening any longer. The pod of fishwomen that had just swum through the maelstrom's wall had captured his attention.

Dunk followed Spinne and Enojada to where the fishwomen waited for them, sunning themselves on a rock that stood just inside the spinning wall of water. The other survivors all got there before Dunk, but the newcomers waited to speak until everyone was ready to listen.

Spiel stood uneasily, an arm draped over Rotes's shoulders. Cavre, Dirk and Reyes each bore blades that they'd scrounged up from somewhere, all of which were rusty enough to fall to pieces at the first swing.

Getrunken staggered up alongside Dunk, drunk as ever. Dunk wondered if the man had been so intoxicated before they hit the whirlpool, or if he'd managed to find a source of alcohol somewhere in the heart of the maelstrom.

Dunk surveyed the fishwomen. Every last one of them was breathtakingly beautiful, with the exception of their teeth, which matched those of the fishwoman who'd been leaning over him as he awakened. She stood on the far left of the line of fishwomen, staring at Dunk with her wide, striking eyes.

The fishwoman in the centre of the line, who sat highest on the rock, spoke when all of the others had arrived. 'Welcome, men of the land, to the Orange Bowl. In your tongue, my name is Nixe.' She flung her arms wide. 'This is my family, and this is our home.'

Dunk thought of the rusty hue of the rocks that littered the bottom of the whirlpool, and he understood the name. None of the others seemed particularly eager to answer the woman. With Pegleg gone, the Hackers had no appointed leader. Dunk looked to Cavre, the team captain, and the man sighed and took a reluctant step forward.

'We apologise for intruding upon your land, fair ladies. We had no choice.'

The fishwomen tittered with laughter. Nixe flashed a restrained smile. 'Of course you didn't.'

'Are you saying you drew us here?' asked Spinne. The hostility rolled off her in waves as she glared up at Nixe.

The fishwoman shook her head patiently, while the others scowled at Spinne. Dunk took a protective step towards her, but the scowls only deepened.

'Not at all,' said Nixe. 'Any ship that passes too close to the Orange Bowl gets sucked right in, whether they want to be or not. That's what makes this such a perfect place for us.'

Spinne narrowed her brow at the fishwoman. 'What do fishwomen need with a place like this? Can't you breathe water?'

Nixe blushed. 'Of course we can, but we need a place like this so that we can, well, meet men.'

Dunk's eyes grew large at this, as did those of every other Hacker.

'You're that hard up for companionship?' Spinne asked.

Enojada stepped forward, a knowing smile on her face. 'Do not judge them too harshly,' she said. 'As an Amazon, I know what it's like to live without men. Despite the benefits, it's not easy.'

Her gaze slid up and down Dirk as she spoke. He noticed the attention, and his skin flushed a bright pink.

Dunk slapped his head to knock the last bits of water out of his ear. 'Wait. I can't possibly be hearing you right. You… you hang out here hoping for a date?'

Nixe shrugged. 'It's harder to meet men than you might think, especially for fishwomen who live in the middle of the ocean. We don't want to just toss ourselves on the nearest shore like some fish-legged hussies. We might as well just jump into a fisherman's net.'

'So you wait here until someone falls into your trap.' Spinne looked like she might charge up the rock and start tossing the fishwomen back into the maelstrom at any moment.

'It's not like we made it,' the girl who'd saved Dunk said. 'We just take advantage of what's already here.'

'So you're scavengers, taking advantage of ship-wrecks.' Spinne looked around the sandy expanse. 'Where are the other survivors then? I don't see any.'

Nixe grimaced. 'It has been ages since we've had any new visitors, and honestly, I was starting to have my doubts. After all, once you get too old, you know what they say, right maids?' She looked at her compatriots, who all giggled. 'Better chance of being eaten by a giant squid.'

Then it dawned on Dunk. 'You're... you're talking about breeding.'

Nixe affected a look of mock shock. 'I suppose you're right about that.'

Getrunken stepped forward, howling. 'Well, all right, let's get it on, fair fishwomen. Which one of you lucky ladies, fish, whatever, wants to get it on first?'

The fishwomen looked at each other, disgust warring on their faces alongside mirth.

'Come on, girls, don't be shy. There's enough of Getrunken to go around, aaalll the way around, if you know what I mean.'

'How cute,' said Nixe. 'He thinks we want to breed with him.'

The other fishwomen issued a collective 'Eeewww!'

'Hey!' Getrunken said, truly offended. 'I may have put on a few pounds around the middle, but I can still pound away with the best of them.'

Nixe winced. 'I think you're missing the point. There's no way for us to breed like humans do. We're just not built that way. We lay eggs, you see...' She blushed demurely.

Getrunken's eyes got bigger with every word Nixe said. 'You're kidding me, right? Where's the fun in that?'

'It's not about fun,' said Nixe. 'It's about survival. If we don't do this, eventually we all die off. We need some young fishwomen to join us, and we need your help to make them.'

Dunk had to interrupt. 'Don't you have any fish*men* who can help you with that?'

The fishwomen all scoffed at that. 'Do you see any fishmen around here?' Nixe asked. 'Have you ever seen a fishman? Even just a single one? If you have, be sure to let us know, because we've never seen one.'

'Hey,' Getrunken said, 'you want my help, ladies, you can have it. You just have to help yourself.'

Nixe shuddered, and the other fishwomen turned away. 'That's not how it works around here. We show up with our eggs. You fertilise them. We take them away and raise them without your aid.'

'This is sounding better all the time. Line those eggs up, fishwomen, and let's get started.'

'You fertilise them alone,' Nixe said, 'without help of any kind.'

'Aw, where's the fun in that?' Getrunken threw himself down on the sand. A few moments later, the man began to snore.

Dunk glanced at Spinne. He had known times in his life when being a sex tool for a pod of fishwomen would have been the ultimate achievement of his dreams, but not like this, never like this.

He scanned the faces of the other men and found unanimous agreement. 'Forget it,' he said to Nixe. 'Much as we'd like to help you, our team has a strict policy against fathering untold numbers of inhuman children.'

Nixe smirked. 'If you do not help us, then you will die.'

'You're threatening us?'

Nixe shook her head. 'You are trapped here. As long as you cooperate with us, we will bring you fresh food and water. Otherwise, you will be on your own.'

'You'd just let us all die down here,' said Spinne. 'I never knew fishwomen were so cold blooded.'

'It's a chilly sea,' Nixe said. 'We're doing what we have to for the survival of our kind. We're not asking for much.'

'How long?' Dirk asked.

Nixe raised an eyebrow at the man.

'How long would you leave us down here? Or, say, how many times would you require a "donation" to your cause?'

Dunk couldn't believe his brother would even consider this. They needed to stick together, or they'd never have a chance to get out.

'As many times as you can manage,' Nixe said, leaving it at that.

'So you'd never let us leave?'

'We don't get visitors down here as often as we'd like. If another group comes, we might be convinced that we could do without you.'

'How often does that happen?'

'On average? About once every few years, maybe.'

'Forget it,' said Dunk. The others murmured in agreement with him. 'We can make it without your help.'

Nixe rolled her eyes. 'We'll see how you feel when you've gone without fresh water for a few days.'

With a synchronised flip of their tails, the fish-women disappeared. They flung themselves back into the wall of water, and it swept them away.

'How come we can't do that?' Guillermo asked.

'Perhaps because we need to breathe,' Enojada said.

Guillermo smirked as he looked at the wreckage all around them. 'I don't need to breathe that bad. I'd rather die of drowning than of thirst.'

Dirk toed the snoring Getrunken. 'I think he feels the same way.'

Dunk stared up at the wall of whirling water that encircled them. He scanned it as far around as he could see, from foot to rim. He knew there had to be a way, he just had to find it.

If they could work quickly, maybe they could build a catapult out of the wreckage on the whirlpool's floor. Then they could fling themselves up over the rim. Landing in the water wouldn't hurt too badly, but then they'd have to deal with the great, sucking problem that had got them into this trouble in the first place: the maelstrom.

Dunk stared at the whirlpool's walls until his eyes ran dry. All sorts of junk spun about in the zooming water: oars, bits of masts, planks from various parts of a ship, barrels that still looked whole. If they could figure out a way to knock a few of those barrels onto dry land, they might find something that could give them a couple more days at least.

Then Dunk spotted something strange. One of the largest pieces of jetsam, something he'd mistaken for a hunk of a mast, seemed to be hanging in one place rather than getting swept along with the rest. Other bits of wreckage glanced off it from time to time, but it stayed right where it was, swaying about, but only in place.

'What is it?' asked Spinne.

Dunk strode over to the chunk of wood, keeping his eyes on it the entire time. As he walked, he clapped M'Grash on the back, and the ogre got up from where he'd been picking his nose and fell in step behind Spinne and Dunk.

As Dunk neared the piece of wood, he noticed it had a length of rope tied around it in a massive, solid knot. That had to be what was keeping the thing in place. What could it be attached to, though, for that to happen, Dunk wondered.

Then Dunk heard something coming from the wood. At first, he thought it was a trick of the whirlpool, the noise the random bits of crud made as they bounced off what now clearly resembled a tree. Then Dunk finally made out some words in the noise.

'Damn this bloody whirlpool to hell! I've had more than enough bloody water for one life.'

'Edgar!' Dunk said. He turned and shouted back over his shoulder at the other surviving Hackers. 'It's Edgar!'

Dunk sprinted towards the treeman, with Spinne close behind. M'Grash overtook the thrower in a few long strides and started shouting the treeman's name over and over again. 'Edgar! Edgar! Edgar!'

The treeman had clearly been trapped in the currents. They just needed to find a way to get him free. Dunk set his mind to figuring the problem out.

First, they'd have to see if Edgar was hurt. Then, they'd have to know how he'd ended up with that rope around his trunk. It might take them a while to assess the situation, but it would mean the least amount of trauma for Edgar.

M'Grash had other ideas. The ogre ran straight up to the treeman, still shouting 'Ed-gar! Ed-gar!'

When M'Grash reached Edgar, he reached into the water and wrapped his massive hands around the treeman's trunk. Then he leaned back and pulled.

Edgar's face leapt out of the water. 'Get me damn well out of this bloody thing!' he said.

M'Grash reached for the rope tying Edgar down, but the treeman head butted him away. 'Don't you bloody touch that!' he said. 'That's the only thing keeping me from being sucked away.'

'Pull with me,' Dunk said to M'Grash, who'd almost left off helping entirely, after Edgar's assault. The ogre joined him with only the barest of pressure.

Together with Spinne, they yanked on Edgar, but they could only get him about halfway out of the water before he was sucked back in. As the others made their way to where Edgar hung suspended in the water, they lent their strength to the cause. Every survivor was soon pulling on some part of the treeman, and together they made good progress. It still wasn't enough.

Dunk figured it out first. They were having trouble because every member of the team was pulling in a different direction at different times. They needed to work as a team, to get everyone to pull in the same direction at once.

'On my count,' Dunk shouted. 'We all pull to the right.'

Dunk grabbed Edgar as tightly as he could. The waters of the ocean seemed colder down here than on the surface, and Dunk knew it wouldn't be long before his fingers became useless. In the meantime, he had a job to do.

'On three!' he said. 'One, two, three!'

Everyone pulled at once, and Edgar popped from the water like a cork from a bottle. The others all tumbled backward under his weight, and several Hackers, including Dunk, would have been crushed if not for M'Grash. The ogre caught the treeman in both hands and strained under his team-mate's dripping wet weight. Then he tipped over to one side and set M'Grash on his feet.

'Thanks,' Edgar said down at the ogre from his vantage point. Dunk wondered if he could see beyond the whirlpool's rim from up there, or if someone in the treeman's upper reaches might.

Spinne threw her arms around the tree and gave him a hug. 'We thought we'd lost you,' she said.

'Not going to be that bloody lucky yet,' said Edgar. 'I've got more than a few rings left in my heartwood. I could be playing Blood Bowl long after you're dead.

'We might be closer to that death than you think,' said Dunk.

'Balderdash,' said Edgar. 'You can't be dead yet. I was sent here to rescue you, and I'm not going to quit until you are all safe.

'Sent?' asked Dunk. 'By who?'

'Mad Jonnen, of bloody course. Where do you think I got this rope?'

Dunk reached out and touched the rope, still bound around the treeman's trunk. 'You mean this is attached to the *Fanatic*?'

'The other end of it, at bloody least,' said Edgar. 'All you have to do is climb right back along it, and you should be fine.'

'We would have to be awfully strong swimmers to make that happen,' said Guillermo. 'I used to dive for pearls as a child, but I do not think I can force my way through a maelstrom.'

'Bloody cowards,' Edgar said. 'Give it a bloody shot. What have you to lose? A miserable death?'

Enojada laughed. 'I'll try it,' she said.

'You're out of your mind,' said Spinne. 'You'll be swept right back here in a waterlogged mess.'

The Amazon took that as a challenge. She put a hand on the rope still hanging taut from Edgar's waist and ran it along the line as she charged headlong into the water.

Enojada disappeared into the vertical waves, which grabbed her and sucked her away as if she were a child that had decided to go for a ride on a stampeding ogre's back. Her grip on the rope around Edgar hadn't held at all. Dunk followed her progress along the wall for about forty yards before she disappeared behind a rock. When she reappeared, she had fallen lower than before, and a moment later the maelstrom spat her back out onto the sand, soggy and exhausted.

Guillermo ran to check on the Amazon. A moment later, a thumbs-up from him indicated that, while she might feel awful now, she would be fine.

'I told her,' said Spinne. 'We can't afford to lose any more people.'

'I agree,' said Dunk. He spoke to Edgar. 'How far away is the *Fanatic*?'

The treeman scratched the bark under his wide and craggy mouth. 'She's anchored about fifty yards out. If we'd been smart, we'd have done the bloody same, although I suppose a tiny ship like ours might have been doomed anyhow.'

Dunk raised an eyebrow at M'Grash. 'What do you say, buddy?'

'No,' Spinne said, 'it's too dangerous. It's not like getting spun out of the whirlpool's face. You try that, and it'll suck you all the way down.'

'I survived it once.'

'And how many of us didn't?' Spinne put her hands together to plead with Dunk. 'It's insane. Don't do it.'

Dunk took her by the hand. 'If I had a better idea, if any of us did, don't you think I'd try that first? Besides, we've done this in games before, and we're still here.'

'You're not immortal, or invulnerable.'

Dunk gave her a lopsided grin, and started to strip to his shorts. 'I know. I have the scars to prove it.'

'Let me go instead,' she said. 'I'm lighter.'

Dunk considered this for a moment. 'I'm the stronger swimmer. I have the best chance of making it.'

'Can't someone else go?'

Dunk scanned the faces of the others. He'd been through hell, literally, with most of them. Outside of the rookies, whom he simply didn't know that well, they would all have risked their lives for him. He was ready to do the same.

'With Pegleg gone, I'm the majority owner of the Hackers. It should be me.'

Spinne blinked back tears and leaned forward to give Dunk a kiss. Naked, but for his shorts, he let it linger as long as he dared, and then turned and walked up to the ogre and the treeman.

EDGAR AND M'GRASH had already made a basket for Dunk between their branches and hands, and lowered it for him to step in. He climbed into the basket and gave his two giant friends a nod. They lifted him up and held him between them for a moment.

'You ready?'

'As I'll ever be. Let's give it a shot.'

'Pegleg's fine, by the way. He's waiting on the bloody ship.'

Dunk stared at the treeman. 'You might have mentioned that beforehand. How about the others?'

Edgar craned his head around for a last look. 'Assuming you have everyone here, I count a total of thirteen of us, including that bloody reporter and the halfling.'

'Slick and Lästiges are alive?' Dunk shouted, as if the words would only be true if he said them loud enough.

A whoop went up from below. Dunk didn't have to look down to know it came from Dirk.

Dunk had counted nine in the maelstrom before Edgar had arrived. With the treeman, Pegleg, Lästiges and Slick, that made thirteen. That meant Anima, Roja, Bereit, Ciotola, Linson, and Anfäger were gone, six good people drowned and dead, plus, Dr Pill, one cranky, old elf.

Dunk's grief tempered his joy at finding four of their number still alive. They were down to only nine players, short of what they needed to field a proper Blood Bowl team. They'd been in such straights before, but they'd rarely seemed so desperate.

'You got something in your bloody eye?'

Dunk wiped his face and shook his head. 'No, why?'

'That's what you humans always say when you start bloody leaking from your face over something.'

'I'm ready,' he said. 'Let's do this.'

'On three,' said Edgar. He stared into M'Grash's eyes. 'Got that?'

'One, three!' said the ogre.

'No, it's one, two, three. Got that?'

'Three! Three, three, three, three, three!'

Edgar shook his head. 'Close e-bloody-nough.'

Dunk caught Spinne's eye. 'I'll signal you when I'm on board the ship.'

'And if we don't hear from you, or see your... you?'

Dunk shrugged. 'Then I'll trust your judgement, because mine will have failed.'

Edgar and M'Grash swung Dunk back once, twice. On the third swing, Edgar yelled, 'Three!' And the two of them hurled Dunk high into the sky, up over the edge of the whirlpool.

From his vantage point, Dunk could see the *Fanatic* in the distance, but not too far away. Then he reached the zenith of his arc through the air, and the swirling waters rushed up at him from below.

Dunk hollered like a maniac as he sailed through the air, and he flailed his arms and legs all over the place. He wanted to give the people on the *Fanatic* as much of a chance as possible to see him.

He hit the water hard, as if diving from a cliff. It smacked into him and made every bit of exposed skin sting.

Dunk had gasped a large breath before he landed, and he resisted the urge to let the impact knock it all out of him. Instead, he fought towards the surface as hard and fast as he could, crawling his way through the water.

The current tried to pull him back and under every step of the way, and his lungs felt like they might burst if he didn't breathe soon. Still he fought on, unwilling to surrender, no matter how much easier, and tempting, that might have been.

As his head broke the surface, Dunk gasped for air. He kept swimming as hard as he could, though, knowing that he couldn't relax while he remained trapped in the relentless current. He shouted for help as soon as he could, and the people gathered at the *Fanatic*'s gunwales waved at him in acknowledgement.

A moment later, someone tossed a length of rope from the ship. Dunk knew that if he failed to grab this lifeline, he was as good as dead, and he swam for it hard.

Try as he might, the rope remained out of reach. He could hear the people on the galleon cheering him on, but he couldn't reach them. He swam as hard and fast as he could, but it was no use.

As a Blood Bowl player, Dunk was in the best shape of his life, better than almost anyone he knew who didn't play the game. Still, he struggled just to keep his head above water, and he could feel himself being slowly pulled backward by the unforgiving current. The roar of the whirlpool grew louder, not softer, as he tried to swim away from it, and the end of the rope grew farther away.

More than anything else, Dunk needed a moment to catch his breath, although he knew he'd never get it. He wondered how much longer he could hold out. Should he keep at it, hoping for a crosscurrent to give him the break he needed? Or should he give up while he still had some strength and try to navigate his way to the bottom of the maelstrom once more?

Dunk knew he had no good choices, and he couldn't pick one of the bad ones. If he didn't do something soon, the choice would be made for him, and perhaps in a way he wouldn't survive.

Just as he decided to give up and take his chances with the whirlpool, while he still had the strength to hold his breath, Dunk felt something brush against his leg. It was slick and cold as the sea, and it had scales.

Aboard the *Sea Chariot*, he and the others had often traded stories about monsters from the deep: giant squid, man-eating sharks, giant jellyfish called man o' wars, and worse. He hadn't given them much credence until he'd seen the gigantic sea serpent help pull the *Sea Chariot* down into the maelstrom. He'd pushed any thoughts of that creature, or any of its murderous cousins, out of his mind when he'd volunteered to try to reach the *Fanatic*.

Now, they all came rushing back at him. Panic gripped his heart, and he renewed his efforts to reach the rope that represented safety, at least from the creatures of the deep that he couldn't see. He thought about swimming towards the whirlpool, but that would put him underwater for sure, and closer to the creature below.

Then a pair of arms slipped around him from behind. Dunk would have screamed if he hadn't forced his face forward in surprise and taken in a lungful of seawater instead. He thrust his head back up and started to cough it out, all the while trying to struggle against whatever it was that had him in its grasp.

As he expelled the water in his chest, he realised the arms that held him were pushing him up out of the water, not pulling him down. He looked down and saw that they were slender and tipped with delicate hands. Then, when he felt naked breasts against his bare back, he knew what had happened.

'Hold still,' the fishwoman said into his ear, the rows of teeth behind those beautiful lips just inches from his flesh. 'You're slippery.'

Dunk stopped fighting, and the fishwoman wrapped her arms around him tighter. 'All right,' he said. 'I give up. Bring me back.'

He heard an amused laugh. 'Is that what you want? You seemed so determined to reach that ship.'

Dunk blinked, confused. He coughed the last of the water from his lungs. 'No. I mean, yes. I do want to get to the ship, but I thought–'

'That I would drag you back down in the maelstrom?'

'Well, yes.'

'I considered it. That's what Nixe would want me to do.'

'You don't always do what Nixe wants?'

'I'm a fishwoman, not a soldier, silly man.'

Dunk peered over his shoulder, and her gorgeous face was right there. All he could think of was Spinne and how much she wouldn't like to see him like this. On the other hand, he was sure she wouldn't want him to drown either.

'Where are the others?' he asked.

'They followed Nixe back to our home. She said she wanted to give you and the other men some time to consider your situation. They all left before the walking tree showed up.'

'But you stayed behind?'

'Uh-huh.' She held him tighter. 'I was watching you.'

The rope drifted closer, almost in reach now.

'Ah. Thanks.'

'You're in love with her, aren't you?'

Dunk stiffened in the fishwoman's arms. If he denied it, he might anger her with such a clear lie. If he admitted to it, she might decide to drown him.

'You don't have to answer,' the fishwoman said, disappointment rising in her voice. 'It's obvious.'

Dunk relaxed and reached for the rope. As his hand closed on it, the fishwoman let him go. The people on board the *Fanatic* cheered.

'I'm sorry,' Dunk said as he turned to look back at the fishwoman. 'But thank you.'

She swam there in the water, using her tail to push forward against the current, keeping her easily in place. Her eyes sparkled at him.

'How could I let you die?' she asked, a half-smile on her full lips. 'I saved you once. I wouldn't want all that effort to go to waste.'

'Thanks again.' Dunk pulled at the rope. The current was still strong and he'd have to work hard at it, but he knew he could make it to the ship from here.

'If it doesn't work out with her, you let me know.'

Dunk smiled ruefully. 'I don't even know your name.'

'Vonderluft.' She giggled and let the current pull her away. 'In your tongue, at least.'

With a flip of her tail, she disappeared beneath the waves. Dunk turned back to the ship and began the long haul to its deck.

He could hear Slick and Lästiges cheering as the sailors aboard the *Fanatic* hauled him over the gunwale to collapse on the main deck. She was a beauty of a ship, and huge. Dunk had never been on a four-masted craft, and the size staggered him.

His strength had all but given up as he reached the ship. He could still cling to the rope, but he couldn't pull himself up. Fresh from the locker room, he would have practically vaulted up it. As it was, he could barely move his arms.

The sailors had gamely hauled him up to the deck. The entire time, he'd wondered how long it would take, and every time he thought he'd almost made it to safety he looked up to see he still had yards ahead of him.

Now that he'd made it, he could hardly breathe. He rolled on his back and struggled to fill his lungs with air as his chilly arms hung limp at his sides. He closed his eyes to shade them from the sun, as he couldn't force his hands to that duty.

A moment later, Lästiges and Slick landed on him in a massive hug that nearly knocked the last bit of air out of him. As he gasped his excitement at seeing them, he heard a familiar voice ring out.

'Get off the lad, you two.' Pegleg's voice held steady, but Dunk could detect a raw undertone to it. 'He didn't haul himself all the way up here so you could kill him.'

The pair pushed themselves off Dunk, but knelt close to him. Shaded by their bodies, he looked up and nodded his thanks, still not enough air in his lungs for him to speak.

'So good to see you, son,' Slick said. 'I thought for sure we'd lost you!'

'And your other top clients too?' Dunk rasped.

Slick gave him a 'you know it's not like that' tap on the shoulder. 'Just glad you're safe.'

'How are the others?' Lästiges asked.

'Dirk's fine,' Dunk said. He tried to put a hand on her arm, but she'd raised her hands to cover her face. Dunk noticed the camra floating over her head, recording everything.

'Edgar made it down in one piece. He and M'Grash threw me up here. Spinne's fine too, as are Cavre, Reyes, Spiel, Hernd and Getrunken. The Amazon is alive too.'

Pegleg's good leg trembled so hard Dunk could feel it through the deck. 'So many gone, and the *Sea Chariot* too.'

'A fishwoman saved me. She defied her leader to do it. The rest of them wanted to keep us there forever.'

'Why would they do that?' asked Lästiges. 'What could they want?'

Dunk blushed, and winced as he saw the camra again. Fortunately, a set of heavy footfalls interrupted the conversation before Lästiges could force an answer.

'Is this your man?' a voice asked. It carried the weight of command in its depths.

'Aye,' said Pegleg. 'Dunkel Hoffnung, number 7, Bad Bay Hackers.'

Lästiges helped Dunk up into a sitting position, and he found enough feeling had come back to his arms for him to lean on them. He peered up at the large shape standing over him. This could be none other than Captain Mad Jonnen.

Jonnen towered over Dunk, a massive orc with green skin made ruddy by both the sun and excessive drink. Despite this, his whitish, thinning hair and startling blue eyes sparkled in his pig face. He reached down a meaty hand to help Dunk up, and for that moment Dunk felt like a child being dusted off after falling down on a playground.

'Welcome to my ship,' Jonnen said, grunting as he spoke. 'We was following you along when – boom! –

you went down that big, damn hole. We fished your friends here out of the drink, but we figured the rest of you were goners. If the Big Suck didn't get you, the Sea Snake would.'

Jonnen pursed his lips around his one remaining tusk. 'Good to have you aboard. Have a turkey leg.'

He fished a greasy specimen out of his pocket and handed it to Dunk. The thrower looked at it suspiciously. Then he noticed that Jonnen, and everyone else on the ship, was watching him. He hadn't fought his way onto the *Fanatic* to die of food poisoning, but he didn't want to offend his large host, with his army of sailors and Blood Bowl fans behind him. Throwing caution to the wind, he stuffed the turkey leg between his teeth and ripped off a bite.

'Good man,' Jonnen said, clapping Dunk on the back. The entire ship seemed to unclench with this pronouncement.

'Now,' Jonnen said, turning to his crew, 'get the dinghy down and roped up tight. We got some players to save.'

A cheer went up from the ship's forecastle, which pointed away from the whirlpool. Dunk glanced over to see the large, railed-off area packed with dozens of people.

They hailed from all races, and came in all shapes and sizes. Their faces, hair, and beards were painted and dyed in a rainbow of colours, both vibrant and dark. They each wore a Blood Bowl jersey coordinated to the colours of their skin.

Some bore ill-fitting helmets on their heads. Others had piercings or tattoos that showed their allegiances to their favourite players or teams. One dwarf had even had his head shaved, painted brown, and fitted with rows of spike to resemble a football.

They were fans. Not just any fans, but the most fanatic of fans, the people who dedicated nearly every waking moment of their lives to thinking about, talking about, and essentially worshipping their chosen teams.

'Hackers rock!' a troll said from the back of the forecastle. A good chunk of the fans joined in with him. 'Rock, rock, rock!'

A massive orc near the railing turned around and pointed at the troll. 'Hackers suck!' he shouted.

'Suck, suck, suck!' another chunk of the fans shouted. Few, if any, seemed to be without a solid, vocal, screaming opinion on the matter.

'Rock!'

'Suck!'

'*Rock!*'

'*Suck!*'

'**ROCK!**'

'**SUCK!**'

The argument devolved into a general brawl with proponents on either side poking at each other with their flabby fists. While some egos and arms might have been bruised, no one was seriously hurt.

'Fans,' said Pegleg. 'Can't live with them. Can't pay your salaries without them.'

A yowl cut through the air. Back towards the whirlpool, a windmilling Dirk arced high over the surface of the sea before falling down well short of the rope, which still drifted in the current.

'After him!' Jonnen said, encouraging the crewmen who'd just managed to get a dinghy into the water. They set to their oars ferociously, and soon managed to collect Dirk.

As the crew in the dinghy pulled Dirk aboard, Spinne appeared high in the afternoon sky. She sailed straight over the dinghy before splashing down. She only had to ride the currents back to it, rather than try to fight towards it with every ounce of her strength.

Over the next hour, the Hackers and their friends stuck down in the maelstrom were hurled up into the air over the sea, where they came to a splashy landing and were then collected. One by one, the crew rowed out and hauled them into the dinghy. Eventually, everyone had managed to make it to the top, except for Edgar and M'Grash.

Dunk swore. 'I hadn't thought of that. How are those two going to get out of there? I never should have left them.'

'If you don't leave, you stay,' Jonnen said, 'and where do you end up then? Right where you started.'

'Uh,' Dunk said, unsure of how to respond, 'thanks.'

He went to the gunwale to wait for Spinne, Dirk, and the rest to make their way up on to the ship. They climbed up a rope ladder tossed down to make the process easier. As they did, something large came surging to the surface towards the aft of the ship.

A scream went up from the fans at the forecastle, and they immediately ended their bickering. Dunk stared at the thing that had erupted from beneath the vicious current, wondering if the sea serpent had come back. Instead of something long and green, though, he saw the head of his friend M'Grash breaking the surface.

The ogre pulled himself straight up a rope attached to the anchor chain. When Dunk had seen it as he'd been hauled on to the ship, he'd ignored it. Now, he realised that it had to be the rope tied to Edgar, who was still down in the maelstrom.

Dunk cheered as M'Grash pulled himself straight up to the anchor chain and then to the aft of the ship. Once there, he turned around, reached down, and immediately began pulling on the rope.

Using his superhuman strength, M'Grash made quick headway. After only a few pulls, the rope went slack in his hands, though, and Dunk's stomach landed in his boots.

Then Edgar popped out of the water, about twenty yards off, cursing and yelling the entire time. While the treeman easily floated to the surface, it wouldn't take much for him to be sucked under the waves once more.

Fortunately, M'Grash wasn't about to let that happen. The sight of the treeman seemed to fill M'Grash with renewed strength, and he hauled on the line harder than ever. Within scant minutes, all of the surviving passengers of the *Sea Chariot* stood gathered together on the deck of the *Fanatic*.

'Amazing!' said Jonnen as he shook hands with everyone, 'just amazing. It's an honour to have you here. It truly is.' He grinned, showing all of his broken, blackened teeth.

'So,' Jonnen said, 'give us a minute and we'll get underway. I'll bet you can't wait to get back to Bad Bay.'

'But we're headed for Lustria,' Dunk said. 'We can't go back to the Old World.'

'That's too bad, because that's where we're heading.'

'BUT WE HAVE to go to Lustria. My sister's there!'

Jonnen shook his head. 'An awful shame, that's what that is. But the people I have on board didn't book a trans-ocean trip. They wanted to go to Magritta, and we did that. Now we need to get them home before they start wondering aloud why they paid us so damn much.'

Dunk looked to Pegleg, who shrugged. The man had never wanted to go to Lustria in the first place. He was hardly going to help Dunk out of this tight spot.

'We can pay you,' Dunk said. 'We can pay them too. We have the money.'

'On you?'

Dunk sighed. 'No, of course not, but I can write you a letter of credit, and you can make good on it once we get back.'

'If we take this trip, we'll miss the Dungeonbowl for sure. My passengers won't go for that.'

Dunk beckoned for Enojada to join them. The woman strode over, still dripping wet. 'How can I help?' she asked.

'This woman,' Dunk said to Jonnen, holding Enojada before him by the shoulders. 'She's the agent for a team of Amazons who invited us out to play in their championship tournament, the Tobazco Bowl. If the Hackers win the game, we'll be the only undisputed champions on two continents. Surely that's something a real Blood Bowl fan might be interested in.'

As he said this, Dunk turned towards the forecastle and raised his voice. When he got to the words 'real Blood Bowl fan,' the people there erupted into howling cheers. They took pride in the fact that they were the best fans in the world, and Dunk saw that he could use that.

Jonnen was on to him though. 'Play to the gallery all you want, Hoffnung, but I'm the captain of this ship. She goes where I say she goes.'

'Of course,' said Dunk, trying to placate the orc, who was built like a boulder. 'I never meant to try to undermine your authority. How could I, right? You run a tight ship, I can see that.'

Jonnen grunted suspiciously and gestured for Dunk to go on.

'I just think there could be a real opportunity for you here. Think of it: a chartered voyage, with the Blood Bowl tournament champion Bad Bay Hackers, to watch them play in the first ever tournament for the championship of the entire world. What true fan wouldn't want to see that?'

Dunk resisted the urge to turn towards the forecastle again, but he spoke clearly, and loudly enough for everyone to hear him. A glance out of the corner of his eye told him that they were hanging on every word of the conversation.

Jonnen sized up Dunk the way a wild boar sized up a meal. Insanity danced in the orc's eyes, and Dunk had no doubts why the ex-coach's only known first name was 'Mad.'

'All right.' Jonnen nodded at Dunk. 'You make good points, but I have to sell an idea like this to my customers.'

The fans in the forecastle roared their support. Jonnen waved them down.

'They're an excitable lot. Right now, they love the idea, but we're talking about many more weeks away from home for them, plus extra fees.'

The roaring subsided at the mention of additional money that might be owed.

'I'll pay for their passage,' said Dunk. 'I'll charter the whole boat.'

The crowd roared once more and broke into a spontaneous cheer. 'Hoff-nung! Hoff-nung! Hoff-nung!'

Jonnen waved them silent. He rubbed his chin and stared down at Dunk. Despite the orc's simple ways, Dunk could see a cold cunning in him, and he couldn't guess what the captain had brewing in his head.

'I got a deal for you, a proposition.'

Dunk looked to Pegleg for approval.

'You got us into this, "partner". Let's see you get us out of it.'

Pegleg normally wouldn't let anyone else make arrangements for the team, outside of Cavre fulfilling his orders. Having him stand off like this made Dunk nervous. He hadn't negotiated many deals in his life, and he felt like a tightrope walker performing without a net.

'I'll handle this, son,' Slick said, sliding up between him and the orc.

Jonnen stared down at the halfling and laughed. 'All right, Fullbelly,' he said. He pulled another greasy drumstick out of his pocket and handed it to Slick. 'Let's talk turkey.'

'We'll offer you a fair price for chartering your ship to Lustria,' Slick said. 'Otherwise, you'll end up taking everyone home and waiting for the next big tournament to start. Only eight teams make it into the Dungeonbowl, so that had to be your least profitable major of the year.'

'How do you figure that?'

'Am I wrong?'

'Not saying that. Just want to know how you figure it.'

Slick smiled and pointed to the forecastle. 'You, sir, have fans from a couple of dozen teams gathered up there. Sure, there are more for the Reikland Reavers than for the Greenfield Grasshuggers, but the fact is, you cater to as broad an audience as you can.

'With the limited number of teams in the Dungeonbowl, you only get the fans of those teams willing to pay your prices. If my team's not going to be there, why should I pay to come along on your trip? I'll save my money for the Chaos Cup or, better yet, the Blood Bowl tournament.

'Of all the majors to miss, the Dungeonbowl is the one to pick. It's the one you make the least money from. Going to Lustria instead could be a gold mine for you. You establish yourself as the first and only charter operation offering a service to the inaugural World Championship, and you play that up for years to come. It's a no-brainer.'

Jonnen scratched his head. 'You didn't just call me stupid, did you?'

Dunk froze. If the orc went for Slick, he'd have to jump between them. On a good day, he was sure he could take down the aging captain, but this had not been a good day for him.

'You're too smart for that,' Slick said. 'Don't insult us both.'

Jonnen stared at the halfling for a moment, while Dunk hunted for vulnerable parts of his anatomy to attack. Then the orc threw back his head and laughed.

'Sharp as ever, Fullbelly. I always liked you.'

'Everyone does,' Slick said with a grin.

Jonnen cut off his laugh. 'Here's the deal,' he said. 'I'm all for this idea of yours, but I need to sell it to my customers. I know just what will convince them that they need to spend several more weeks aboard my ship.'

Something in the orc's tone raised Dunk's hackles.

'And what might that be, sir?' asked Slick.

Jonnen's wide grin showed all his broken teeth. 'An exhibition game.'

Dunk narrowed his eyes at the orc. 'Against who?'

'Your Hackers,' Jonnen said, 'against my fans.' He swept his arm towards the forecastle, and the people there went nuts.

'We! Got! Game!' they shouted. 'We! Got! Game! We! Got! Game!'

'You're kidding,' Dunk said to the ex-coach.

'Not one bit. The fans on my ship eat, sleep, and breathe Blood Bowl. Most of them tried out for a team or twelve. Some actually played. They love the game, and they'd love to play it against the champs.

'We only have ten players. That's not enough for a full team.'

'We'll play six on six.'

'Where?'

'Right here.'

'Aboard this ship?' Dunk looked around. The galleon might be huge, but there wasn't enough space on it for a proper Blood Bowl pitch.

'Sure.' Jonnen pulled a drumstick out of his pocket, said, 'Whoops,' and put it back. He reached into another pocket and produced a short, white wand.

Holding it in his hand like a piece of chalk, he began to draw in the air. White lines appeared where he drew, and they hung there in space as if he'd inscribed them on a sheet of glass.

'Here's the ship,' Jonnen said, sketching out a diagram that resembled the top deck of the *Fanatic*. He placed the four masts in their places and outlined the space between the forecastle and the bridge.

'We play here. To score a touchdown, you just have to touch the wall or the stairs leading up to the forecastle or the bridge. Six players on a side fits well. We play with those numbers all the time.'

'What about the rigging?' Pegleg said, 'and the masts? Are they in play?'

Dunk stared at the ex-pirate. Jonnen's proposal intrigued him enough to draw him out of his funk, but Dunk couldn't believe he was actually going to consider it.

'Anything above the main deck is in play. We seal off the lower decks to prevent problems. We used to let the game move into there if the ball fell through, but we called that off after nearly sinking the ship.'

'You still have to touch the wall to score, though, so getting too high in the air doesn't help much.' Pegleg scratched his beard as he talked. 'This could work.'

'It does,' said Jonnen. 'We play it on every voyage.'

'What about gear?' Dunk asked. 'Armour, pads?'

'They're for wimps,' Jonnen said in disgust. 'We play *real* Blood Bowl. The ball's the only thing with spikes on it, and your bodies are your weapons.'

'How many of your customers do you lose doing this?' asked Slick.

Jonnen waved off the halfling's concern. 'Everyone pays in advance. For a few extra coins, we tell their next of kin they died scoring a touchdown.'

Slick grunted, impressed.

'What happens if someone falls overboard?' asked Dunk.

Jonnen grinned voraciously. 'The sea serpent usually gets them.'

'That beast follows you all around the seas?' asked Pegleg.

Jonnen laughed. 'Enough fans fall off to keep him well fed. It puts him on our side in any battle.'

'Or chase,' Dunk said, remembering how the creature had pulled them into the maelstrom.

'Do we play to points or to the clock?' asked Cavre.

The orc looked at the man, impressed. 'Points. First to make two scores more than the other wins.'

'That's not a lot of margin for error,' said Dunk.

'It's a hard game, and we play it short-handed. We used to try for two full halves, but we never finished a game. Every one of them called for a lack of players on the field.'

'Sounds like you all suck.'

All eyes turned to Dirk, who'd given voice to the insult. The man shrugged. 'What? We're talking about a bunch of out-of-shape wannabes with delusions of competency. Let's play. They won't survive the first series.'

'You're insulting our host, Mr Heldmann,' said Pegleg. His tone left no room for doubt as to his disapproval.

Dunk knew what Dirk was doing. He hoped to get Jonnen and his team angry, so they'd do something stupid. Dunk winced at the thought.

Jonnen glared at Dirk. Then he threw back his head and said in a calm and exacting voice, 'You are a guest on my ship, Heldmann, so I will let that comment slide. Much as the Reavers' coach let you slide every time your precious Hackers beat you silly. If I'd been your coach, I'd have disembowelled you as an example to the others after the shoddy performances you turned in.'

'You wouldn't have the guts,' Dirk said. He pointed at his belly and ran a finger along it, as if opening it up with a blade. 'Guts. Disembowelment. Get it?'

Dirk said all this without a smile, and no one else laughed either.

When Jonnen spoke again, he was all business. 'You play this game, and we'll get you to Lustria. That's the bargain.'

Dunk hesitated for a moment. It seemed insane to risk the team on a gambit like this, but it couldn't be worse than a regular game, right? Unless he wanted to go all the way back to the Old World and charter another ship, there didn't seem to be a better way.

Jonnen leaned in over Dunk and whispered menacingly in his ear. 'It's either that, or the lot of you walk the plank.'

Dunk stuck out his hand, and Jonnen shook it. 'Then it's a deal,' Dunk said. 'Game on!'

'THEY'RE JUST A bunch of fans,' Dunk said. 'We can take them.'

Pegleg smirked. 'This is their home field, Mr Hoffnung, and it's an unusual one. That gives them more of an advantage than you might think.'

'Jonnen wasn't kidding about his clientele,' said Dirk. 'I recognise at least half a dozen retired players in the stands. You can bet he'll put out an all-ringers team.'

Dunk scowled. 'The decision's been made. This gets us what we want, despite the risks. Let's take advantage of it.'

'Plus, there's the threat of death hanging over our heads,' said Spinne.

Dunk stared at her. He hadn't mentioned Jonnen's murderous comment to anyone. 'How did you know about that?'

'He threatens everyone, all the time,' said Cavre. 'He's promised to kill me half a dozen times.'

'And you're still here.'

'He was serious at the time, every time. There's a reason he's called "Mad", you know.'

'Who's playing?' Dunk asked, turning to Pegleg.

'Oh, you're going to let me do my job now, are you, Mr Hoffnung? How very kind of you.'

Dunk grimaced. He hadn't wanted to step on Pegleg's toes, but he knew the man would have negotiated their passage home and left it at that. Still, he had no desire to supplant Pegleg as coach. He knew that the job was beyond him, and he needed the man's expertise. If anyone knew more about football and sailing ships than Pegleg, except perhaps Jonnen, Dunk didn't know of him.

'I'm sorry,' Dunk said, in as heartfelt a tone as he could manage, and left it at that. Pegleg had never been much for sentimentality.

Pegleg nodded his acceptance, and got to work. 'Hoffnung, Heldmann, Schönheit, Edgar, K'Thragsh, and Cavre, you're in. The rest of you, sit tight with me on the bridge. We might need you at a moment's notice, and I'll need every set of eyes I have to watch for more of Jonnen's treachery.'

He stuck his hook out. The players each stacked a hand on it. Dunk slapped his on last.

Pegleg looked at each of the Hackers in turn. 'This is no ordinary game,' he said. 'If we lose, the chances are good that the survivors will get fed to Jonnen's sea serpent. We win, and we'll establish a dominance that will force the orc to keep his part of the bargain.

'Play like your lives depend on it. They do.'

He paused for a moment. 'One, two, three.'

The entire team shouted as one: 'Go Hackers!'

'We have the home-field advantage,' Jonnen said generously. 'We'll kick-off.'

Dunk knew better than to think that the orc would do them any favours, but he assented with a nod. A wide dwarf dressed in nothing more than a kilt and boots, and a gallon of yellow and blue paint, held the ball in his hands and booted it high into the sky.

Dunk instantly saw the problem. First, with so little field available, the kicker could hang the ball high enough for the rest of his team to rush under it before it hit the deck. Second, the rigging made it almost impossible for the ball not to get caught in something, keeping it stuck in the air even longer.

By the time the ball came down, the fans would be able to attack each of the Hackers several times. Since the ball would be deep on the Hackers' side of the field when it came down, they had to keep an eye on it. If it fell into a fan's hands, it would be an easy few steps to score a touchdown.

As Dunk had predicted, the ball got tangled in one of the sails on the mizzenmast, and he had to wait for it to come down to him. While waiting, he saw a barrel-chested Norscan wearing a horned helmet bearing down on him. M'Grash made to intercept the man, but he whirled around the ogre with the grace of a barbarian warrior. He would be on Dunk long before the ball arrived.

Dunk feinted to the left, and then charged to the right, all the way over to the gunwale. The Norscan gave chase, his beard, braided in separately dyed blue and silver strands, flapping in the breeze as he charged forward.

'You're going down, Hoffnung!' the man shouted as he dived straight at Dunk, his arms outstretched in a classic tackling pose.

Dunk spun about and hammered the man in the throat. As the Norscan gasped for breath, he hauled him up by his official Lapland Lions jersey and tossed him overboard. The man howled all the way down, until a distant splash cut him off.

A moment later, the sea serpent burst from the water's surface, the Norscan clamped in his monstrous jaws. The man was already dead, blood seeping from his mouth and the dozen fresh holes punctured by the serpent's teeth.

The sight made Dunk want to vomit, but he didn't have the time for that. He had to get back to the game, or he and his friends would share the Norscan's fate.

Dunk turned and saw the ball tumble out of a sail just above the mizzenmast. A ratman in a Skaven Scramblers uniform leapt up and plucked it out of the air. Edgar swatted at the creature with his branches, but he only succeeded in knocking the skaven closer to his goal.

The skaven squealed in triumph as he tucked the ball under his arm and dashed the last few feet towards the bridge. Dunk charged at him, but it was too late. The creature slapped his dirty paw against the wall under the bridge, and somewhere a whistle blew.

The fans in the forecastle went wild. 'Hac-kers suck! Hac-kers suck! Hac-kers suck!'

Although a sizeable number of the fans wore Hackers gear and colours, none of them stood up to the others. In fact, most of them joined in their nasty cheer.

Dunk scowled as they set up for the next kick-off. Since the fans had scored, the Hackers would receive again.

Pegleg roared at them from the bridge, where he stood with the rest of the Hackers and their friends. 'You are down one to nothing, you scurvy dogs! You must score the next point. If you do not, you lose.'

'You lose, you die!' the fans at the forecastle chanted. 'You lose, you die!'

The dwarf in the Dwarf Giants body paint held up the football again and gave it another mighty boot. It sailed up into the rigging, where it stuck. The spikes on the ball had jammed through the sail on the main mast and were wedged there.

Dunk and the rest of the Hackers stared at it for a moment, wondering if it would work itself loose in the breeze, and fall down. Then Dunk spotted the skaven fan clambering up the rigging, and he realised that this had all been part of the fans' plan.

Dunk charged over to M'Grash, who still stood gaping up at the ball. He tugged on the ogre's elbow and shouted his name, but it did no good. He was too focused on the ball for any of Dunk's efforts to get through to him.

Finally, Dunk punched his friend in the arm.

'Ow!' M'Grash said, staring down at his best friend with a hurt look. 'Why Dunkel hurt me?'

'I'm sorry, M'Grash,' Dunk said, pleading with his friend for understanding. 'So sorry, but if we don't get up there to get that ball, we're going to lose.'

M'Grash followed Dunk's finger up to spy the skaven getting closer and closer to the ball. Cavre had started to scramble up another part of the rigging, but the skaven had too much of a head start. He'd clearly get to the ball first.

M'Grash nodded. 'Need throw?'

Dunk clapped his friend on the shoulder. He'd thought of that first too, but he didn't trust the ogre's accuracy. He'd get Dunk close enough to grab the ball, for sure, but after that he'd probably come crashing down onto, or maybe through, the deck.

Instead, Dunk pointed at the main mast and said, 'Shake that thing as if its an apple tree.'

A glint showed in M'Grash's eyes, and the ogre stepped over and wrapped his mighty arms around the mast. He swayed back and forth with it for a moment, getting the feel for it. The fans in the forecastle started to laugh.

Then M'Grash put his back into it and gave the mast a good shake. The entire ship vibrated with his efforts, and the laughter stopped. The mast shook like a reed in a hurricane, and the ball came tumbling down.

The skaven came right after it, involuntarily. M'Grash's move had knocked the creature from the rigging, and he fell to the deck with a sickening crunch. Cavre, knowing how M'Grash treated an apple tree when he was hungry, had stopped climbing around for long enough to hold on for his life. He had managed to keep his grip, barely.

As the ball tumbled to the deck, Dunk stretched up and snagged it out of the air. He scanned down the deck and saw a ragged elf wearing an Elfheim Eagles replica helmet trying to knock Spinne off her feet. Since she'd been watching the ball instead of the elf, he'd got in a cheap shot that had sliced open a shoulder. Like the professional she was, though, she still scrambled to get open.

Dunk spied a clear angle beneath the sails, and he fired off a bullet of a pass. It zipped just over the outstretched fingers of a pair of the fan players and fell into Spinne's good arm. Then she spun around and stabbed the spike on the end of the ball at her opponent's helmet. It jabbed right through the cheap material and into the elf's brain.

The elf shuddered his life away as Spinne yanked back the ball and made a mad rush for the forecastle. She reached it and stabbed the ball into the wood, where it stuck.

The fans went nuts. A handful of them reached down from the forecastle and pulled Spinne up to their level. Chanting, 'Pass her back! Pass her back!' they body-passed her towards the bowsprit.

As they did, the sea serpent jabbed up through the water in front of the ship. The beast curled its neck in anticipation of its next meal, which the fans were about to deliver.

Dunk launched forward, determined to save Spinne. She'd realised what was about to happen and had started to fight against it. Although she could have taken on any five of the fans in even an unfair fight, many times that number shared the forecastle with her. Even M'Grash might have a hard time defending himself against them.

Dunk refused to just let the fans toss the woman he loved overboard to her death. He stiff-armed a pair of red-and-black-painted humans that tried to get in his way, and then used the dwarf kicker as a stepladder to vault over the railing and onto the forecastle's deck. As he stood at the edge of the crowd, though, he could see he would be too late.

'No!' he shouted. 'NOOOO!!!'

The fans cackled at his dismay, and Spinne was pulled right up to the bowsprit. He could not reach her in time.

Instead of trying, Dunk reached down and snatched the football from where it still stuck out of the wood below him. Then he turned and shouted at Jonnen.

The orc stood on the gunwale near where the fans were about to throw Spinne off the ship. He held on to the rigging with one hand and egged the fans on with the other, lending his howl to theirs. Red faced as he was, he looked like he'd never had so much fun in his life.

'Make them let her loose!' Dunk shouted.

The old orc indulged in a massive belly laugh. 'Why would I do that? This is what they came for: blood, danger, death! This is Blood Bowl at its finest.'

Another moment, and Spinne would be tossed to her doom. There was no more time for talk.

Dunk cocked back his arm and fired the ball straight at Mad Jonnen. 'Would you look at that?' were all but the last word to come out of the orc's mouth.

The ball caught the orc right in the chest like a shot from a cannon. The impact knocked him back off the railing, and he went tumbling into the sea. As he fell, he said one last word, 'Boom!'

Every one of the fans on the deck froze. The sea serpent, which had been drooling over the prospect of fresh Spinne for dinner, dived after the turkey-leg laden Jonnen instead.

Before Dunk could say a word, and he had plenty of time but none came to mind, M'Grash leapt up onto the forecastle next to him. The ogre slapped away everyone within arm's reach, and then bellowed, 'Put Spinne down!'

The crowd between M'Grash and the bowsprit parted, and the fistful of fans still holding Spinne up near the railing set her down gently and respectfully. They dusted her off as they put her down, stepped away and motioned for her to go to Dunk before the ogre killed them all.

Dunk ran to Spinne, who tottered on her feet. She'd lost a lot of blood from her shoulder wound, and her skin looked white where it was not covered in crimson. She leaned into him as he gathered her in his arms, doing everything she could to not collapse entirely.

'What about the game?' one of the fans asked.

'The game is over,' Dunk said, his tone as sharp as a blade. 'We win. I claim this ship in the name of the Bad Bay Hackers.'

'What if we don't care to go along with that?' a surly man said in a Bretonnian accent.

Dunk looked at M'Grash and jerked his head at the man. The ogre reached out and swatted the Bretonnian overboard.

'Any other questions?' Dunk asked.

'When's lunch?'

Dunk looked at M'Grash, but the ogre just shrugged.

'Soon,' Dunk said. Then he cradled Spinne in his arms and carried her off the deck atop the forecastle. When he reached the main deck, he stopped. Spinne's breathing was shallow, and she'd started to shiver. He'd seen people like this before, and he knew he'd lose her if he didn't do something soon.

'Is there an apothecary in the house?' he shouted. He bent to his knees and laid Spinne down on the deck. Then he yanked off his shirt and set about tearing it into strips to bind her wound. 'Anyone?' he said.

'Quit your whining,' a familiar voice said. 'I just had to get my bag.'

'Dr Pill?' Dunk said, goggling at the elf. 'How? You're supposed to be dead.'

'Thanks for noticing.' The apothecary knelt next to Spinne and opened his black bag. 'That's more than the rest of the team seems to have done.'

'I thought you went down with the ship.'

Dr Pill opened a bottle and poured some of its brackish contents onto a dirty rag. Then he used the soaking rag to clean Spinne's wound.

'Apparently not. Give me a couple more rags.'

Dunk tried to hand him the strips of his uniform, but the elf pushed them away in disgust.

'Not that filthy crap. Get the clean ones out of my bag. You want to kill her?'

Dunk reached into the bag and found the rags the apothecary wanted. As he looked into the bag, he saw that it was larger on the inside than it seemed on the outside, a lot larger.

'Did anyone else survive with you?' Dunk asked.

'Not one.'

'How did you make it?' Dunk asked.

'I had M'Grash help me. I climbed into my bag, and he threw it onto this ship.'

Dunk almost stopped pulling out rags to gape at the elf. Dr Pill took the rags from him and nodded for him to shut the bag. 'Thank Nuffle I landed on the bridge instead of the forecastle.'

'How?' Dunk stopped. That wasn't the question he wanted an answer to. 'Why? You're a doctor. Why didn't you save anyone else?'

Dr Pill grimaced, but he did not look up from binding Spinne's wounds.

'As magical as that bag is, it's a miracle I fit into it. I couldn't have fit your agent in there with me.'

Dunk sighed in amazement. Stunned as he was, he was thrilled to have the old elf around to work on Spinne. He'd seen the apothecary work miracles with players dragged off Blood Bowl fields, looking like little more than a person-shaped puddle. Spinne couldn't have been in better hands.

'Why can't you just give her one of your potions?' Dunk asked. He wanted Spinne to be entirely better, right now.

'First rule when someone's leaking their life all over the place is to stop the leaking. I could give her a potion, but if I don't bind her wounds first she'll just end up bleeding all that goodness right out of her again.'

'What can I do to help?'

'Don't you think you did enough by getting her into this game? Against a bunch of amateurs? Without armour?'

Dunk started to snap at the elf, but he realised he needed him too much to make him angry. 'I just want to help.'

'Take care of that man behind you,' Dr Pill said, not looking up from his work on Spinne. 'That would help.'

Dunk turned around to see a short, thin man standing over him, waiting for him expectantly. As Dunk stood, the man's hand stabbed out in greeting. Dunk reflexively took and shook it.

'The name is Coward Hosell,' the man said in a sing-song way. 'I am the first mate on this particular ship on which you find yourself today. I have not had the opportunity to welcome you and your fellows aboard. Please allow me the pleasure of taking care of that duty right now.'

'You're kidding,' Dunk said, confused. 'I just killed your captain.'

'Be that as it may,' Coward said, 'it is as clear to me now as it was during his tenure, just who is in charge of this ship. I am prepared to offer my services and those of my crew to you in exchange for our worthless and measly lives.'

Dunk blinked. 'What?'

'All we ask for, sir, is a chance to prove ourselves, to be the kind of contenders we can be, to show you that we can crew this ship perhaps better than any other crew on the seven or more seas.'

'Um,' Dunk said, 'all right.'

He'd been prepared for a fight, to pit the Hackers against everyone else aboard the ship. Now, the first mate had capitulated to him without even a request for surrender.

'I just have to ask,' Dunk said, trying to bite his lip as he spoke. This was too easy. He had to know, even if it spoiled everything. 'Don't you have any concern over Mad Jonnen?'

Coward shook his head, and a wide, easy grin spread on his face. 'Not really, sir. He served his purpose, it's true, but now that he's gone we're just as happy with someone else in his position. Happier perhaps.'

'And what position was that?'

Coward gave Dunk a 'you really don't know?' look. 'Why, figurehead, of course. Mr Jonnen was a fine, fine coach, and he brought a lot of passengers on to this ship, but it's not an exclusive talent. Others can do that just as well, maybe better, the reigning champions, the Bad Bay Hackers, for instance.'

Dunk narrowed his eyes at the little man. 'Who really owns this ship?'

Coward's smile grew wider, something Dunk would have bet was impossible. 'Why that's neither here nor there now, sir. As far as I am concerned, if there are any real bosses on this ship, they are our customers, the fans who purchase passage here and allow us to keep our wonderful enterprises afloat, so to speak. Everyone else just works to make them happy.'

'But in the meantime, who's in charge? I mean, who sets the ship's course? Who gets to choose where it goes?'

Coward's face seemed like it might split in half and flip over backward from his widening smile. 'Why, sir, I thought you understood. Tradition on the *Fanatic* holds that the most famous ballplayer aboard at the time the previous figurehead surrenders his position, or is forced to abdicate it, is the first in line for the position.

'That, sir, would be you.'

16

'LAND HO!'

Dunk spun out of bed at the shout that had gone up on the main deck. He'd been waiting for just such a call for days on end, and he'd started to get cranky about it. Dirk had spotted this right away and had taken to asking his brother one horrible question every time they crossed paths.

'Are we there yet?'

Dunk kissed Spinne, who still lay sleeping in the bed they shared in the captain's quarters, jumped into a pair of breeches, tossed on a shirt, and then charged out of the door.

Dunk made his way up on to the bridge. The crew, fans and Hackers lined the starboard gunwale, staring out into the distance, hunting for something that none of them could yet see. Pegleg stood at the wheel, ignoring them and keeping a steady course.

Dunk craned his head back and spied Guillermo up in the crow's nest, waving down at him. 'Land ho!' the man shouted again. Dunk could see his grin shining down from all the way up there.

'What's the situation, coach?' Dunk asked as he reached the wheel.

Pegleg had continued to be surly with Dunk since they'd taken over the *Fanatic*, but the captain had come around after Dunk had granted him command over the ship. The only choice he would not relinquish to the man was their destination.

'Once we're done in Lustria, you can have that too,' Dunk had said.

'Your generosity knows no bounds, Mr Hoffnung,' Pegleg had said, his words dripping with sarcasm. Despite this, he'd been barely able to disguise his glee, and his attitude towards Dunk had warmed considerably over the weeks.

Dunk realised one day that this had to do with the fact that Pegleg loved running a ship, but hated being the one in charge of it. 'Keeping her in shape, getting her to where we want her to go, taking care of the crew and passengers, these are worthy challenges,' he'd said to Dunk one night over a late shot of rum served in a pair of tin cups. 'Dealing with their whining and complaints is the price the man in charge must pay.'

In their current arrangement, Pegleg ran the ship, with Coward's help, while Dunk took the blame for everything that went wrong. On a ship this large, things went wrong all the time, and it was up to someone to have to deal with it. That duty fell to Dunk.

Dealing with such things didn't bother Dunk too much. He had to listen to the complaint, assure the complainant that it would be taken care of, and then report it to Pegleg and Coward, taking care to remove as much of the whining from the initial complaint as he could manage.

As a management trio, they worked well together. Dunk had what Coward generously called 'people skills,' whereas the others had know-how and experience to fall back on. Dunk pointed out more than once that 'people skills' often came down to not hating everyone else, but there seemed to be no way to get the others to change their ways on that subject, so he soldiered on.

'Mr Reyes reports sighting land on our present course,' Pegleg said. 'If it is, in fact, Lustria, it should become visible from the bridge soon.'

Dirk hailed Dunk from the far side of the bridge. 'Hey,' he said with a grin, 'it looks like we're there.'

Dunk couldn't help but smile. It had taken a lot to get here, and privately he knew that the ship's supplies were running low. The *Fanatic* had been outfitted for a long, sumptuous trip around the Old World, not across the open sea. Cutting back on the all-you-can eat feasts, to once a week, had helped stretch things out a bit, as had the death of Mad Jonnen.

'That orc went through a turkey a day,' Coward said. 'I have never, in all my years aboard a ship, seen anyone eat so much, so fast. I once asked him what his secret was.'

Dunk waited for the man to continue, but soon realised that he was expected to prompt Coward for the answer.

'And what would that be?'

'The more he ate, the less anyone else could have, and that's the way he liked it.'

With the promise of dry land and fresh food, Dunk could at least let that worry slip by. Now all he had to think about was him and Dirk reuniting with their sister. He wondered where in Lustria they'd make landfall, and how far it might be to Amazon Island from there.

'We are not far away at all,' Enojada said, as if reading Dunk's thoughts. 'I have kept track of our position by the stars. I am not an expert navigator, but I have some skill in this area. Once we reach land, I should be able to orient us in the right direction and get us to my home in no time.'

'Thanks,' said Dunk.

The rising sun burnt the low lying mist off the ocean, gradually revealing more of what lay hidden inside it. Soon, Dunk could make out the horizon, along with the barest hint of dry land along it. It appeared as a dark, thin stripe separating the sky from the sea. A wide smile broke out on his suntanned face.

As the land grew closer, more and more of the crew arose and found their way to the main deck. Soon, hundreds of people lined the gunwales as the ship tacked back to the northwest under Pegleg's orders.

The dark stripe grew to a white strip of sun-bleached sand stretching out before a deep, thick jungle that seemed to roll back from the shoreline forever. Dolphins breached the surface near where the waves broke, and as the *Fanatic* grew closer, they came to swim alongside the gigantic ship, playing in its wake.

As they neared the shore, the land that they'd seen first seemed to break away from the lands around it. The sprawling fields farther in the distance, sweeping away to the south, featured wide swaths of wind-swept savannah rather than the jungle of what Dunk now saw was either an island or the tip of a peninsula.

Enojada pointed to the emerald island before them. 'Our navigation has been nearly perfect. That is Columbo's Island. That land to the south is the Scorpion Coast. The lizardmen live there and have long been at war with invaders from the New World, many from dark elf cults that worship Chaos in its more decadent forms. We have no business there, and the lizardmen and the slann usually give plenty of distance to the islands of the River Amaxon delta, which is where we will find our final destination.'

'Columbo? The captain who discovered the New World? They named an island after him?'

'He named it. He formed a colony there shortly after landing, claiming the land in the name of his nation. That was long ago, though, and the city that once prospered has long since returned to the jungle.'

'I hear he was a little man with a preoccupation with shoes,' said Dirk, 'a detective as well as an explorer.'

'That's what they engraved on his tombstone, wasn't it?' asked Spinne, who'd just joined them. '"What did you pay for those shoes?"'

'I never did understand that,' said Dunk.

'You're too young to appreciate history, Mr Hoffnung,' Pegleg said. 'Someday, you'll realise that one man's trivia is another's obsession.'

Dunk didn't understand Pegleg either, but he guessed that confessing that would only make the coach's point.

'We'll stop there to resupply,' Pegleg said, pointing to Columbo's Island. 'If it's as deserted as you say, it should be safe enough, and we could use some fresh food and drink.'

'I didn't say it was deserted.' Enojada stared out at the approaching island. 'Just that it was no longer as civilised as it once was.'

'Tell me, ma'am,' Coward said, standing at the very rear of the bridge, 'just what does that mean? Are we putting ourselves, our people, our customers, in horrible danger?'

'Civilisation is overrated.' Enojada scoffed. 'On Amazon Island, we barely bother with clothes. People from your world might call that primitive. We think of it as freeing.'

'Bring it on!' Getrunken said as he staggered up towards the bridge. 'Freedom! FREEEEEE-DOM!'

The fans standing atop the forecastle instinctively echoed his cry. 'Free-dom! Free-dom! Free-dom!'

Dunk turned to Spinne and held her in his arms. 'Looks like freedom it is,' he said with a grin.

17

'I THOUGHT YOU said they'd greet us with flowers and drinks,' Dunk said as he helped row the dinghy out to the island.

'Once we reach Amazon Island, you will find our hospitality to be the finest in the land. Here though, I can make no such guarantees.'

'Haven't you ever been here before?' asked Spinne.

Enojada shook her head. 'On Amazon Island, we tend to keep to ourselves. Our ancestors were not native to this land. We descended from the female survivors of a Norscan settlement that once shared Columbo's Island, but abandoned it after the conflagration that destroyed the town.'

'Humans aren't native to this land?' Lästiges asked, her camra floating towards Enojada to record the answer.

The Amazon shook her head. Here, beneath her native sun, she looked more beautiful than before, more comfortable with her surroundings. Dunk hadn't noticed before how tightly wound she had been in the Old Word. Now that she was in Lustria, she was clearly at home.

'The slann and the lizardmen have been here since long before anyone can remember, including them. The lizardmen built amazing cities, the whole of which comprise of temples to their mysterious gods. Some of them were abandoned and have fallen into ruins for reasons no one understands. The ones that still stand, however, are breathtaking monuments to the greatness their people once had.'

'Do you mean that now they suck?' asked Dirk. He continued to work the oars with Dunk, pulling them closer to the island's shore.

'Language, Mr Heldmann,' said Pegleg.

Dirk stared at the man with a disbelieving look.

'There are ladies present.'

'That's never stopped you from cursing up a storm in the locker room.'

'That's his point, son,' Slick said. 'We're not in a locker room now. We're strangers about to land on a strange shore, and we should be careful to treat our prospective hosts with as much respect as we can muster. There's no telling what they might take offence to.'

Dirk rolled his eyes, which Dunk took to mean he'd capitulated to the argument, even if he didn't agree with it, for now, at least.

'Maybe we should have left our escorts behind,' said Dirk. 'Having an ogre and a treeman show up on your doorstep might be enough to set some people off.'

'They'll be fine,' said Dunk. 'I don't think I could have kept M'Grash on the ship with an army.'

'How about you, Edgar?' Dirk called. 'How you doing?'

The treeman answered from where he floated in the water behind the dinghy, M'Grash clutching tight to him. The ogre was using him as a float while propelling them both through the water with his powerful kicks.

'How am I doing?' Edgar shouted. 'I'm bloody humiliated, that's how I'm doing. I'm a treeman, not a personal flotation device.'

'Do trees float because they're full of hot air?' asked Dirk. 'Or is that just treemen?'

'You're bloody fortunate I can't stand up right now.'

'I'm sorry we had to do this, but you and M'Grash can't fit in the dinghy,' said Dunk, 'and this beat trying to tow you into shore.'

'It'll be worth it to feel some soil around my roots again,' Edgar said. 'You people packed bloody nothing for a treeman to eat. I can't live on sunshine alone, you know.'

Dunk smacked Dirk on the back of the head to silence his younger brother's snickering. If Edgar threw a tantrum on the way to the island, M'Grash might panic and drown. Dunk put a finger to his lips. Dirk rolled his eyes, but kept silent.

'Look,' Spinne said, pointing towards the shore, 'we have a welcoming committee.'

Dunk glanced over his shoulder and saw a group of people standing on the shore, waiting for the boat to come in. When they saw that they had been noticed, some of them waved.

Most of the score or so of people wore short breeches or skirts and brightly coloured shirts in floral prints. Off to one side, a band played music with a strangely relaxing yet engaging beat. One of the musicians beat on something Dunk could only describe as a steel drum, while the others pounded on large bongos, or strummed guitars.

The man in the front of the band, who wore the most colourful shirt of all, sang melodiously at the top of his lungs. As far as Dunk could tell the song had something to do with a desperate search for something lost. It sounded like a 'shaker of salt,' but he couldn't see how that could be.

A tall, tanned man stood before the rest of the crowd, dressed in an immaculate white suit. Beside him stood a person that made Slick look like a giant, a tiny, tanned person dressed in a suit identical to the larger man's.

The people on the shore waited patiently as Dunk and Dirk rowed the dinghy in through the breakers, with Edgar and M'Grash close behind them. The brothers leapt out of the boat as it scraped bottom on the sand, and pulled it in the rest of the way. At the same time, M'Grash got his footing, and then tipped Edgar back on to his roots. Then the two bigger players strode ashore.

The two figures in the dazzling white suits stepped forward, and the band wrapped up its latest song with a flourish. 'Hello,' the larger man said in a charming, well-mannered tone. 'My name is Mr Doarke, and this is my assistant, Tat II. Welcome to Columbo's Island.'

The band behind Doarke struck up a tune that had something to do with drinking and sex. Dunk did his best to ignore it, although he saw Spinne blush. Lästiges turned her camra on the band, recording it, 'for the fans back home.'

'I am Captain Haken of the free ship *Fanatic*,' Pegleg said. 'We sail for Amazon Island, but hope to take advantage of your hospitality to stretch our legs and restock our supplies.'

'But of course,' Doarke said. 'We are at your service.' His grin seemed warm and friendly, stunningly white against his bronzed skin, but underneath it Dunk thought he sensed something of the shark. He felt like they were being sized up for a meal.

Dunk left Pegleg and Cavre to handle the negotiations. When he heard the ex-pirate cry in dismay at Doarke's prices, he knew why he'd felt like a fresh roast tossed in front of a pack of starving dogs.

The singer finished up the band's latest tune with a flourish. 'Take five, boys,' he said. 'Hell, take fifty.'

When the rest of the band groaned in protest, the singer winked at them. 'Always leave them wanting more, boys. We'll have a big show tonight.'

Placated, the band members tossed themselves down on the sand to watch the surf roll in. Edgar strode off towards the line of trees beyond the beach, grumbling about finding somewhere to shoot roots for a while. M'Grash followed him, a hopeful look on his face.

'What's good to eat?' the ogre asked. It had been a long journey, and even at triple rations he never had enough to eat.

'Eat?' The treeman growled, indignant. 'You think I'm going to give you bloody pointers on which of my cousins you should dismember to fill your stomach?'

M'Grash whimpered and rubbed his empty belly. Even from such a monstrous figure, the sound was pitiful.

Edgar sighed and put a branch around the ogre's shoulder. 'You're nothing but a big, bloody baby,' he said. 'We'll find you some food. I never did like this branch of the family tree much anyhow. Bananas and coconuts? Give me a good hardwood any day.'

The singer strode up to Dunk, Spinne, Slick, Dirk, and Lästiges and stuck out his hand for shakes and introductions all around. 'Name's Buffay, Jiminy Buffay,' he said. 'We're the Moral Reefers.'

'That's an unusual name for a band,' Lästiges said, her camra focused on the man, looking for his reaction.

Jiminy grinned right into the camra's lens. 'We're the shoals on which all ships of morality founder, and we are like rocks in the steadfastness of our debauchery.'

'We should have brought Getrunken along,' said Spinne.

Dunk held her hand and spoke to Jiminy. 'It's been a long trip,' he said. 'We just want to stretch our legs and get the lay of the land.'

Jiminy raised an eyebrow, with a sidelong glance at Spinne. 'Looks to me like you already have that at your side, friend.'

Dunk wasn't sure if he should laugh or knock the man into the sand. A giggle from Spinne told him to not worry about it, for now.

'We have just the thing to help unloosen legs of all kinds,' Jiminy said. Behind him, one of the Moral Reefers lugged up a small, wooden cask. A tap had already been driven into one end.

'What's that?' Dirk asked. He'd been silent until now, watching, absorbing, gathering it all in. The mystery of the cask had finally inspired him to speak.

Jiminy cocked his head at Dirk, a twinkle in his eye. 'An island treat like no other, my friends. A delight to all those who sample it, and a boon to all who partake.'

As he spoke, another of the Moral Reefers opened the tap and poured a clear liquid from the cask into a set of cups that had been carved from the shells of split coconuts.

'What's it called?' asked Dunk.

'Ever heard tell of *rum*?'

As DUSK FELL, Pegleg and Cavre re-joined Dunk and the others, who'd been sampling Jiminy's rum all day long. Doarke and Tat II strolled up behind them, pleased looks twinned on their faces.

'We've stocked the dinghy with supplies,' Cavre said. 'We're going to take them back to the ship.'

Dunk groaned in dismay, and the others, including the Moral Reefers, all joined in. 'Aw, coach,' he said, struggling not to slur his words, 'do we have to?'

Dunk held a puppy-dog look on his face for as long as he could, and then fell against the others, laughing. Cavre and Pegleg stood over them, not saying a word, until their merriment petered out.

'We'll go on without you, Mr Hoffnung,' said Pegleg, failing to entirely keep the disgust from his voice. 'You lot sleep off whatever it is you've polluted your bodies with. We'll be back for you in the morning.'

Dunk leapt to his feet and then fell back down again. The world had started to tilt as soon as he'd got his head away from the planet, so he decided to hug its face again.

'Gotta watch out for those gravity storms,' Jiminy said. 'They're as unreasonable as hurricane season, and come with the rum.'

'The boat is full,' Cavre said. 'We don't have the room for anyone but me and the captain anyhow.'

'We could ride Edgar back,' said Dirk, giggling as he spoke. 'We could all just pile on his side and let M'Grash push us all the way home.'

Edgar's voice called out from the treeline. 'I heard that, you bloody sot! I've shot roots here, and I'm not leaving until it's time to rip them out!'

'Stay,' Pegleg said, sneering at them all, 'please.'

He spun on his wooden leg and stormed off towards the dinghy. Cavre hustled off behind him. As he went, the catcher called back, 'We'll return in the morning.'

'I'm coming with you,' said Enojada.

'You don't have to,' said Cavre. 'We will be fine.'

'He is going to hold onto the oars with his hook?'

Cavre glanced to see if the captain had heard, but the man was already halfway to the dinghy. Cavre scowled at the woman, and said, 'Fine. Then let's move.'

Doarke and Tat II waved at the two as they made for the dinghy. Then Doarke grinned down at his drunken guests. 'I see you have decided to make yourselves welcome.'

Dunk looked up at the man, but the world spun around him as he did. 'Sorry 'bout that,' he said. 'This rum of his is great.' He pointed to Jiminy, who cackled at the implied accusation.

'No worries, my friends,' said Doarke. 'We on Columbo's Island have made an excellent deal with your captain, and are inclined to celebrate such good fortune with any who care to join us.'

One of the Moral Reefers passed a cup full of rum to both Doarke and Tat II, who accepted graciously. Doarke dipped his finger into the rum, and turned to Tat II, who had produced a tiny torch. The tiny man lit Doarke's finger, and the larger man held his hand in the air above him.

'Here's to new friends,' Doarke said, raising his cup. 'May they someday become old friends. To the law of living free!'

The man slammed back the contents of his cup, and extinguished his flaming finger in his mouth.

Dunk and his friends erupted into a round of applause. Within minutes, each of them, except for Edgar and M'Grash, had duplicated Doarke's feat.

M'Grash dipped his finger into the giant-sized cup the Moral Reefers had supplied him with, fashioned from an old cask cut in half. He even managed to hold still long enough for Tat II to ignite the rum. Then, however, he could not help but run screaming for the ocean to douse the fire.

'Set myself on bloody fire?' Edgar said, his branches shaking at the thought. 'You're mad. You're all bloody mad.'

'To the law of living free!' Spinne said as she completed the ritual.

'What's all that about?' Dunk asked. He looked around and saw that Doarke had disappeared.

Tat II answered. 'The boss invented that years ago when he took over. He calls it the Statute of Liberty.'

'What does living free have to do with burning rum?'

The little man shrugged. 'You can't have liberty without some shots being fired.'

'How come you're so short?' Slick asked, not slurring his words as much as Dunk had. Normally, the halfling wouldn't be so direct, but the rum had loosened him up too.

Tat II grinned. 'You should see my sister.'

'Seriously, these other fellows are clearly men. You're clearly not.'

'My tribe is native to this land. We have lived here for centuries, surviving by being too small for the bigger creatures to notice, or at least bother with.'

Slick narrowed his eyes at Tat II. 'Are you some kind of halfling?'

'When Columbo came to our land, he had already travelled throughout your hemisphere. In the Southland, he met a people who he said reminded him of us. He named us after them.'

'And they were?'

'Pygmies.'

Slick stopped cold. 'You're pygmy halflings.' He clapped a hand over his face. 'I thought I'd seen it all.'

'Don't complain,' Dirk said. 'You finally have someone who can look up to you.'

Slick and Tat II looked at each other, and then turned and kicked sand in Dirk's face. The blitzer spluttered in protest and made to get up and chase after them. He slipped in the sand again, though, and by the time he'd recovered, they had disappeared, cackling into the darkness.

'Which way'd they go?' he asked, but not even Lästiges would stop laughing long enough to tell him.

Dunk allowed himself to spill over backward onto the sand, and lay there staring up at the stars. They were different from the ones he'd grown up looking at. He recognised a few constellations in the northern part of the sky, but most of the arrangements of the stars seemed entirely new.

'What's that one?' he asked, pointing up into the sky.

'Your hand's wobbling too much, friend,' said Jiminy. 'I can't be sure what your meaning is.'

'That one.' Dunk stabbed at the sky once more, but his once-blazing finger seemed to wander with a mind of its own. 'The one that looks like a football.'

'That's no football,' said Lästiges. 'It's a camra.'

'A cake,' said Slick.

'A trophy,' said Dirk.

'You're all blind,' said Spinne. 'It's an ogre's head.'

M'Grash whined.

'Just kidding,' Spinne said.

'Dunk, my friend, you have sharp eyes,' said Jiminy. 'That there is none other than the Football. Folks around here believe that Nuffle put those little lanterns up there for everyone to see. If it shines over your head, you're sure to be a winner.'

'We can't see it from the Old World,' said Dunk, 'at least I never have.' The others from the *Fanatic* all murmured their agreement.

'So, what's that tell you?' Jiminy grinned baring all his white teeth.

'That we're a bunch of losers,' said Dirk. Dunk smacked him on the arm with the back of his hand.

'That's, true,' said Jiminy, 'but what else?'

Dunk and his friends all shrugged.

Jiminy smiled. 'It tells you that it's a hokey legend. Of course it doesn't work that way. It hangs up there over almost every game. If it was real, everyone would be blessed to win, and then where would we be?'

'Wouldn't we all win?' asked Dunk.

'Not much of a game then, is it, my friend?'

Dunk had to concede the point.

'Personally, I think Nuffle put it up there as an advertisement for his favourite game. Without it, well, let's just say games aren't as frequent here as they are where you come from. Leave something alone that long, and people are liable to forget about it.'

'So the constellation is a gigantic billboard?'

'If you want to look at it that way, sure.'

Dunk glanced around. 'It doesn't look like it's working too well.'

'How do you figure that?'

'How many Blood Bowl teams do you see around here? Besides us?'

DUNK'S HEAD POUNDED like the inside of a steel drum when he awoke the next day. Unaware of how or when he'd gone to bed, the horrible taste in his mouth drove him from sleep. Fully prepared to find himself lying in the beach's chilly, sea-sprayed sand, he discovered that he was warm and dry, and that for the first time in a long while no deck swayed below him.

Dunk opened his eyes. He lay on an overstuffed mattress beneath ivory white linens, a canopy of thin netting hanging over the frame that surrounded his bed. Sunlight streamed in through a wide bay window set across the white-walled room from the bed.

In normal circumstances, Dunk would have been delighted to have found himself in such a place, and in Spinne's supple arms to boot. As it was, the light stabbed at him, the sheets felt scratchy, and he wondered where he might find a convenient place to throw up. If none presented itself soon, he might have to make do with whatever he could find.

'Awake already?' Spinne asked, turning to face him. He groaned in protest, but she kept right on talking. 'I wasn't sure you'd ever come back to me as drunk as you were last night.'

Dunk held his head together with his hands, hoping that the parts of his skull that wanted to leave him would stay on. 'I'd never get that drunk, honest.'

To tell the truth, Dunk didn't remember much of last night after Pegleg, Cavre, and Enojada had left for the ship. It seemed like he'd had fun, although he couldn't say for sure exactly how. Now, however, his head felt determined to keep torturing him until he could recall every last detail of how he had damaged it.

'Did you mean what you said?' Spinne asked, snuggling into his embrace, her head resting on his chest.

Dunk froze. 'Um, sure.'

'I'm so happy,' she said. 'I just can't wait!'

'Me neither,' said Dunk, hoping that she would drop him some kind of hint about what it was that would make them both so happy.

'Oh, and the way you did it, out there in the sand, under the stars. It was just perfect.'

This confused Dunk even more. A moment ago, she'd been talking about something she couldn't wait for. Now she was going on about something he did last night, and apparently did well.

'Of course, getting sick in the fire pit put a bit of a damper on it, but I can overlook that. I certainly won't include that part when I tell my sister all about it.'

'Good,' said Dunk, rubbing his belly. It growled back at him. No wonder he felt so hungry.

Spinne flipped up onto her knees and gave him a hard look. She stared deep into his eyes, and then scowled.

'You don't remember a damn thing about last night do you?'

Dunk considered lying, trying to fake his way through the conversation, but it was clear that she'd caught him. Besides, it was nearly impossible to lie about an event that he didn't know anything about, despite the fact they'd both been there.

'Fine,' she said, not waiting for a response from him. She jumped out of the bed, bare naked, and slipped back into her clothes. 'You don't have to if you don't want to.'

'What?' Dunk said, getting up out of bed. 'What are talking about?'

Spinne gave Dunk a look that could have peeled paint off a wall.

Before Dunk could get to the bottom of what had happened, a knock came at the door. Slick didn't even give Dunk a chance to respond before shouting through the door. 'Son, are you in there? I need to talk to you, now!'

'Can it wait?' said Dunk. 'I'm right in the middle of something here.'

'It's a disaster!' Slick said. 'A complete and total, and utter disaster.'

The halfling wasn't known to inflate problems. Sure, as an agent, he lied all the time, and well, but that usu-ally meant making things sound better than they were. He wouldn't kid around about something as horrible as this sounded.

Spinne opened the door as Dunk slipped into his clothes. 'What is it?' she asked. Her anger with Dunk had faded away in the face of Slick's terrible tone.

'It's the *Fanatic*! They're gone!'

Dunk cursed. 'I should have known it. Pegleg was still angry with me. The first chance he got, he ditched us all and left his problems behind.'

'No, son,' Slick said, 'that's not it at all. The ship's still there, floating right where it anchored. It's just everyone on it… they're gone.'

Dunk goggled at the halfling. 'What do you mean "gone"?'

'Gone, as in "not there any longer", "having vacated the premises", and "nowhere to be found".'

'How do you know that?' asked Spinne. 'You haven't been back there already, have you?'

Slick shook his head. 'M'Grash got eager to get back to the ship, so he swam out to the *Fanatic* earlier this morning. When he got there, he said no one was aboard.'

Dunk raised an eyebrow. M'Grash was a wonderful ogre and a great friend, but he wasn't the sharpest sword in the weapons rack. Dunk didn't know how the ogre could have missed the entire crew and passengers aboard the *Fanatic*, but he apparently had.

'I know what you're thinking, son, but the big guy seems serious.'

'I don't doubt that he is,' said Dunk. 'Being serious and being right aren't always the same thing though.'

Dirk and Lästiges appeared in the doorway. 'What's going on?' the reporter asked, her ears pricking up.

'It seems everyone aboard the *Fanatic* has decided to abandon the ship,' said Dunk.

'They just want the rum,' said Dirk. 'Can't say I blame them. I'll bet Getrunken led the attack.'

'It doesn't seem like that at all,' said Slick. His belief in the ogre's story hadn't wavered.

'All right,' Dunk said, 'let's check this out.'

Moments later, the five of them were out on the beach, staring at the ship. 'How are we supposed to get back there without the dinghy?' Lästiges asked. 'I'm not that good a swimmer.'

'But Dunk and I are,' said Dirk. He started stripping to his shorts. Dunk did the same.

'I'm coming too,' said Spinne.

Dunk shook his head. 'We need you to stay behind with Lästiges. She can't defend herself like you can.'

'Hey!' said Lästiges. 'I'm a big girl. I can handle myself.'

'Don't forget me,' said Slick. 'I'm a lousy swimmer.'

Spinne rolled her eyes. 'All right,' she said to Dunk, 'but hurry back.' She leaned in and gave him a kiss.

Right then, Dunk knew that, whatever he'd done last night and however he'd screwed it up this morning, he and Spinne would be all right.

Dunk and Dirk dived into the surf and crawled their way through the salty water to the *Fanatic*. It was a long and tiring haul, and more than once, Dunk thought that it would have been better to go back. Instead, he kept pushing on, neither Dirk nor him wanting to be the first to suggest giving up.

Dunk wondered where Edgar and M'Grash could have got to. As he and Dirk reached the ship, he spied

Edgar standing at the bow, a branch raised to shade his eyes as he looked out over the deep blue sea to the mainland beyond the island. Of M'Grash, though, he saw no clue.

Dunk and Dirk finally made it to the rope ladder that they'd descended into the dinghy just the day before. Dunk pulled himself up it first with Dirk close behind.

As he clambered over the gunwale, Dunk spotted M'Grash sitting in the centre of the main deck, his knees curled tight to his chest, his back to the ladder. The massive ogre's body shook with silent sobs.

'M'Grash,' Dunk called tentatively, 'are you all right?'

The ogre looked up from where he'd buried his head in his arms. His face was red and puffy, and his arms were soaked with tears.

'All gone, Dunkel. All gone!'

Dunk scanned the deck as he approached the ogre and put a comforting hand on his shoulder. If there was anyone on the ship besides Dunk, Dirk, M'Grash, and Edgar, he was an excellent sneak.

The ship should have been bustling with activity. The crew should have been getting the rigging ready for the ship to start moving again. The Hackers, what was left of them, should have been training on the main deck. The fans should have been making drunken fools of themselves.

Instead, the deck stood empty, and the sails flagged in the faltering wind.

'What happened?' asked Dunk. He pointed to Dirk and then the hatch that led to the below decks. The man took off running.

Dirk went to the empty bridge. As he did, he stepped over a bunch of what looked to be red-tipped toothpicks. He stared around the boat. No one was there, not even the unlucky soul who'd been stuck in the crow's nest.

The ship had been abandoned, and he and the others were alone.

'WE CAN'T TURN around and go home,' Dunk said.

'Why not?' asked Lästiges. 'Is it because of your darling sister? If she wanted to see you so badly, she should have come to Altdorf or Bad Bay, or even Magritta, to see you. You and Dirk are superstars. It's not as if you're hard to find.'

'No,' Dunk said.

'Is it because you can't leave the others behind? Anything that could take every one of them away and not leave a trace of a struggle isn't something the seven of us could stand up against. It's a lost cause. Hear me? Lost cause.'

'She's got you there,' said Dirk. 'We found dinner plates still sitting on the table in the mess, half filled with food. Anything that can pry the ship's crew, much less the fans, away from food, we don't stand a chance against.'

'No,' said Dunk, 'it's not any of that.'

'Then what?' Lästiges said. 'It's because it's not the "heroic" thing to do, running off with your tail between your legs? No one has to know. I'll shut off my camra and destroy its memory.'

The camra squealed, but Lästiges backed the floating globe into a corner with a dirty look.

'No,' said Dunk, 'it's because seven people can't sail a ship this size. We wouldn't be able to keep her underway, no matter how badly we might want to go home.'

'Leave it to you to come up with whatever excuse you can find,' said Lästiges. 'Leave it to your brother and me. We'll be back in the Old World soon, and you'll be warming the inside of a man-sized pot somewhere in the jungle.'

'You're welcome to try and sail the ship back,' Spinne said, stepping into Lästiges's face. 'You'll get just as far with the *Fanatic* as you have with your career: nowhere.'

'Hey, now,' said Dirk, 'you can't talk to my woman like that.'

'But she can do the same to my man?'

'That's different,' said Dirk, 'Dunk's my brother, family. You can pick on family all you want.'

'Then I'll pick on you. How about you learn how to pick a woman who's not such a complete idiot?'

Dunk stepped in between Dirk and Spinne. 'Stop it,' he said. 'We don't have the time to fight each other. We need to figure out what happened, and fast.'

'So you can sweep in and be the big hero, just like always?' said Lästiges.

'So we can keep the same thing from happening to us.'

Lästiges blanched and fell silent. 'That couldn't…' She turned away, and Dirk went to her, collecting her in his arms.

'Humans,' Edgar said to M'Grash. The treeman stood next to the ogre, the surf lapping at his roots and M'Grash's feet. 'I'll never understand all their blather.'

The ogre looked up at the treeman and gave him an understanding nod. Slick chimed in with a deep sigh.

'You'd think someone had asked them to build a stadium with their bare hands,' the halfling said. 'It's not that tough. Just go to Mr Doarke and explain what's happened. He'll have answers.'

'What if he's behind it all?' asked Lästiges.

'You should stick to reporting the news rather than getting involved in it,' Slick said as kindly as he could. 'Doarke couldn't have been involved in this.' He raised a hand to cut her off. 'Nor could have Jiminy or any of the Moral Reefers.'

'How can you be so sure?' Lästiges asked.

'We slept in Doarke's mansion last night, all of us twisted with spirits. If he'd wanted to remove us, he could have done so while we slept, and none of us could have stopped him.'

That shut Lästiges up for the moment.

'You're right,' said Dunk. 'Let's go talk to Doarke.'

When they reached the whitewashed mansion, Doarke and Tat II were standing on the front porch, waiting for them. 'How can I help you, my friends?' Doarke wore a wide, toothy, yet relaxed grin.

'Our captain and his crew,' said Dunk, 'they're gone.'

Doarke pursed his lips at this. 'Ah, how unfortunate. I never guessed that they would be so bold as to take on such a large and vital ship as yours.'

'You know who did this,' said Dirk.

'Allow me to explain.'

'No, boss,' Tat II said softly, 'allow me to explain.'

'What was that last word?'

'Explain! Explain!' the little man shouted.

Dunk shrugged and gestured for Tat II to go ahead.

'My people, the pygmy halflings, they tired of losing the Tobazco Bowl every year.'

'You mean, tired of getting slaughtered playing in the tournament,' Jiminy said, joining the group on the mansion's wide and lovely porch. He sat back in a wide, white, wicker chair and strummed his guitar. 'Did your shrinky-dink people ever win a game?'

'Never.'

'But they keep trying.'

'They do not give up easily.'

'Or learn lessons well.'

Tat II scoffed. 'They managed to abduct the entire crew of a galleon. They're doing something right.'

Jiminy played a few bars of 'What Do You Do With a Drunken Sailor?'

Tat II started to say something to the man, but Doarke stepped in to set things right. 'I'm afraid your friends are all in vile danger. If you are to keep them alive, you should listen to what Tat II has to say. No one knows more about the pygmy halflings than he does.'

'He's one of them,' Lästiges said. 'How can we trust him?'

'He has been in my service since I saved his life over ten years ago. He has never once betrayed me. He bears no love for his people, as they would not have him.'

Tat II basked in Doarke's praise and then spoke. 'My people wish to increase their strength for the next game. To their way of thinking, the best way to do this is to devour their foes.'

'You mean metaphorically,' Dunk said, 'right?'

Tat II shook his head. 'No, literally.'

Dunk stopped cold. 'They're cannibals?'

'That's such a harsh term. They prefer to be thought of as "not terribly picky eaters".'

When Tat II saw Dunk staring at him, he continued, 'Have you ever eaten man flesh? It's awful. Stringy and fatty at the same time.' He noticed the revulsion growing on the humans' faces and tried to make up for it in his own way. 'At least the stuff we get around here. A Blood Bowl player from the Old World might be a lot tastier.'

'That's disgusting,' said Spinne.

'Our people only believe in eating creatures they personally best in combat. We end up chewing on a lot of pineapple, coconuts too.'

Slick stepped forward, rubbing his belly. 'Now listen to me, son. A lot of the people on your friends' menu are friends of ours, so I have one question, and one question only. How can we stop this?'

Tat II smiled. Then he frowned. 'I don't know.'

Dunk leaned down and picked up the little man by the back of his collar. He held him dangling in front of him, his feet kicking like those of a hanged man. 'You're going to have to do better than that.'

'Please, Mr Hoffnung,' said Doarke, 'you are our guests. There is no reason to treat my associate so.'

'Where I come from, we don't offer up our guests for somebody else's dinner. We call that murder and betrayal, and we deal with it accordingly.'

Tat II stopped struggling, and his feet hung still. He forced a smile and spoke. 'Why, they are on the Island of Sacrifices, of course. That's where all of the pygmy halflings live, except for me.'

Dunk winced at the name of the place. He held Tat II closer to his face. 'And where is that?' he asked.

'It's the next island up the chain towards Amazon Island. After that there's Tobazco, Xocibiki, and then Amazon Island in the mouth of the Amaxon River. Past that, you get to Lustria.'

Dunk put Tat II down gently on his feet. He stared past the little man at Doarke. 'How can we get there?'

'A boat is the best way.' The suave man smiled nervously, his facade beginning to crack.

'We don't have a boat,' Dunk said evenly.

Doarke clapped his hands, eager to finally have a problem he could solve. 'We have a boat we will lend you. We can even send Tat II along as a guide.'

'We can't trust him,' said Dirk.

Dunk considered this. Although Tat II didn't seem like much of a threat, his people did. The Hackers, or those that remained free, had been taken without a fight, and Dunk would never have believed that possible if he hadn't seen it with his own eyes.

'You're taking us,' he said to Doarke.

'Ah, but I cannot. I have too many duties here.'

'I'll do it,' said Jiminy, a sparkle in his eye. 'I'm always game for a little adventure.'

All eyes focused on the man with the guitar.

'What's in it for you?' asked Slick.

'The story.' Jiminy's grin grew wider. 'What else is there?'

DOARKE'S BOAT WASN'T much larger than the *Fanatic*'s dinghy. 'She's got a sail,' Jiminy said, pointing at the single mast, which stood bare, 'but we're heading into the wind and rough seas. Better to put our backs into it for such a short voyage.'

'Whose backs?' Dunk asked. Jiminy pointed to the four oars hanging from the side of the boat, and grinned.

Dunk, Spinne, Dirk and Lästiges sat in the middle, working the oars. Slick sat up front, along with Jiminy, who beat out a time for the rowers on the front of his guitar, and then used the rhythm to segue into a cheery song about boat drinks adorned with tiny umbrellas.

Edgar floated along behind the craft. M'Grash used him like a gigantic kickboard, propelling them both through the water.

The Island of Sacrifices seemed much like Columbo's Island, save for the greeting party. Instead of Mr Doarke, Tat II, and their band, a sole pygmy halfling with a tubby belly and bronzed skin stood on the shore, waiting for the boat to arrive. He wore a grass skirt that reached below his knees, and nothing else.

Edgar and M'Grash hit the beach first. The ogre helped tip the treeman upright again, and then went back to haul the boat clear onto dry land. The people inside had to hold on for their lives. Jiminy hadn't been quite ready for the big tug, and he went tumbling off into the surf. He arose a moment later, holding the guitar aloft like a trophy, a bewildered crab hanging from the strings.

'That's some arm you got there,' Jiminy said to M'Grash. 'You can crew my boat any time.'

Seeing that the singer was all right, Dunk turned to the tiny halfling, who had stood silent and still as a statue through their arrival. He strode up to the pygmy halfling and knelt before him, crouching over farther to be able to face him eye to eye.

'I'm told you have our friends,' Dunk said, 'the people from the big ship.'

The pygmy halfling nodded.

'We would like you to set them free.'

The pygmy halfling shook his head.

Dunk thrust his thumb over his shoulder at M'Grash. 'Then give me one good reason why I shouldn't have my friend dropkick you onto the next island.'

The pygmy halfling craned his neck back to stare up the full height of the ogre. He giggled nervously.

'Then you will never see your friends.'

'Have you already eaten them?'

The pygmy halfling pursed his lips. 'We wanted to, but they are still sleeping. They taste better if they're scared when they go into the pot.'

Dunk waved M'Grash over.

'What's your name?' he asked the pygmy halfling.

'Big Richard.'

'Thanks for coming out to say hello, Richard,' Dunk said. 'Goodbye.'

As the ogre reached down for the pygmy halfling, the little man squealed. 'Wait! We don't have to eat your friends. We don't *want* to eat your friends.'

Dunk signalled for M'Grash to stop, but not until after the ogre had grabbed Big Richard by the scruff of his well-tanned neck.

'Explain,' Dunk said.

'We just want to live.'

Dunk squinted at Big Richard. He brought down his hand, and M'Grash set the little man down.

'Then you should start explaining yourself better,' said Dunk.

Big Richard stammered for a moment before finding his footing, and then began. 'Every year, our chief insists on us playing in the Tobazco Bowl, and every year we get slaughtered.'

'What do you expect?' asked Dirk. 'It would be like playing against a team of three-year-olds.'

'I don't mean we get beat,' said Big Richard. 'I mean we get *slaughtered*. We're lucky if the other teams beat us into the turf and leave us for dead. Then we might have a chance to survive. The Amazons are sometimes that kind.

'The lizardmen skin us and eat us, sometimes while we're still kicking.'

'You mean they eat you alive?' asked Spinne, aghast.

'That too, but I meant during the opening kick-off. The only time our team managed to make it to half-time was against the Jaxonville Werejaguars.'

'Really?' said Lästiges. 'They sound like a tough enough team.'

'They are. They just like to play with their food before they eat it. They wanted to make us last for the whole game, but they got hungry during halftime and finished the last of us off.'

'Why do you keep playing?' asked Edgar. 'Watch the game from the bloody sidelines.'

'We'd like to, but our coach, Hoody Wayes, insists on putting up a team every year, even though we get killed. We have a lottery just before each tournament, and the "winners" are compelled to join the team.'

'Compelled?'

'You play or have your still-beating heart torn from your chest on the Altar of Sacrifices.' He leaned in confidentially. 'We're big on sacrifices here, if you hadn't noticed.'

'Isn't there any way out of it?' asked Dunk.

'One,' said Big Richard. 'You just have to find someone else to take your place.'

'Ah,' Slick said, reaching out and patting the little halfling on the shoulder. 'So that's what this is all about.'

Big Richard nodded. 'We figured who would be better to take our place than a world-champion team of Blood Bowl players?' He looked up at the others with wide, pleading eyes. 'You'd survive for sure. You might even win.'

Dunk looked at the others. Dirk fidgeted on his feet. Spinne had clearly already made up her mind to play for the pygmy halflings. Lästiges shrugged. 'I'm not playing for anyone,' she said.

'Let them bloody die,' Edgar said. 'They're rude little pests without a bloody whit of manners.'

Big Richard started to protest, but Dunk shut him up with a sharp gesture.

'You're right,' Dunk said to the treeman. 'It's one thing to ask for help, but something else entirely to kidnap most of the team and hold them hostage.'

'Hostage is such an ugly word,' Big Richard said, wincing. 'How about "bargaining point"?'

A thick, sharp knife appeared in Dirk's hand, and he brought it up between him and the pygmy dwarf. 'I've got another point I'd be happy to bargain with.'

Big Richard folded his tiny arms over his chest. 'You don't scare me. I was chosen to be captain of this year's team. What can you do to me that's worse than what the Werejaguars have in store?'

Dirk loomed over the little man. 'I'm willing to find out.'

Dunk put a hand on his brother's chest. He felt Dirk lean into it for a moment, and then back off reluctantly, the knife still at his side.

'Let our friends go, and we'll discuss this,' Dunk said to Big Richard.

'I don't think you understand just how desperate we are. We paddled out to your gigantic ship and drugged everyone with poison darts. Then we dragged them

out to a secret location on the island. When we
realised we'd missed you, I set up here to greet you
when you came looking for us.'

'How did you know we'd come after you?'

Big Richard scowled. 'Tat II is nothing if not predictable in his treachery.'

'They've killed them already,' Dirk said. 'Let's toss
this joker into the sea and figure out a way home.'

'That doesn't add up, son,' Slick said. 'Why send this
little guy out to chat us up if they did? If they captured
the rest of the crew, they could take us down too.'

'They got the others in their sleep,' Lästiges said.
'We're wide awake and ready for them.'

'Really,' Big Richard said, 'we don't want to hurt anyone. We don't want to eat anyone. If we did, we'd have
snatched the ogre in the middle of the night. We could
have fed the whole tribe on his flesh for a week.'

M'Grash recoiled in horror from the tiny man.

'We'll do it,' said Dunk.

'You have to be kidding,' said Dirk.

'Why not? We're not playing for anyone else. Think
of the pygmy halflings as our sponsor.'

'You can't give in to kidnappers.'

'We're not giving in. We're helping them. In
exchange, they'll help us scout out the opposition and
give us a better chance to win. We'll do it.' Dunk
looked at Big Richard. 'But if we win, we keep the
purse.'

The little man broke out in a grin that seemed to be
bigger than he was. 'All right.' he said. 'I can't wait to
tell the others! Keep the money. We're only interested
in breathing.'

'Will you let the others go?' Spinne asked.

Big Richard's smile fell. 'I'm afraid we need some way to ensure you'll help us. We will treat them like kings and bring them to the game in perfect condition. Better than that even!'

This made Dunk nervous, but he decided to go along with it. 'Just tell us who we're playing for this time out.'

'The other teams just swat us like flies, so that's the name we took, from the Island of Sacrifice, of course. Welcome to the Sacrifice Flies!'

'I DON'T LIKE this,' Dirk said as he helped to row the boat away from the Island of Sacrifices and towards Tobazco Island, 'not one damned bit.'

'With Pegleg in the Flies' custody, I'm the one in charge,' Dunk said, working another oar. 'It's my call.'

'You made a bad one.'

Dunk put up his oar for a moment. The others stopped rowing. 'You had a better idea?'

'Sure. Wade into the island and kill them all.'

'That's barbaric.'

'You're talking to a Blood Bowl player. Hell, you *are* a Blood Bowl player.'

'We don't kill unless we have to.'

'I think having most of the team kidnapped qualifies for that.'

'I don't.'

Dirk stood up and stabbed a finger into Dunk's face. Before he could say anything, though, Jiminy grabbed the sides of the boat and gave it a good rocking. Dirk tumbled backward into his seat once more.

'Boys, boys, boys,' said Jiminy. 'I can see your parents had a double handful between you two.'

Dirk started to stand up again, but Jiminy sat him down with a grin. 'I can also see you ain't spent much time on a boat if you're dumb enough to stand up in one. Try it again, and you may find yourself taking a swim.'

Once Dirk had taken his seat again, Jiminy continued. 'Tell me, boys, just why are you here?'

'You mean in the larger sense?' asked Lästiges. 'I've been wrestling with that a lot myself lately, and…' Her voice trailed off as she realised everyone was staring at her. 'Sorry.'

Jiminy's grin washed Lästiges's embarrassment away. 'I mean, why are you here in Lustria? Sightseeing? Fortune hunting? Vacation? On the run from the law?'

'No,' Dunk said, 'nothing like that.'

'We're here to play Blood Bowl,' Spinne said.

'Really?' Jiminy arched an eyebrow at the woman. 'They don't have other teams back where you come from?'

'Actually,' said Dunk, 'we're here to find our sister.'

Jiminy stared at Dunk and Spinne. 'You two are brother and sister? The way you were going at it the other night, I had you figured for something a little less, ah, close, relatively speaking.'

Dunk blushed and pointed to Dirk. '*Our* sister; we lost track of her and our mother and father back when an angry mob ran our family out of its keep in Alt-dorf.'

'You boys really know how to make friends.' Jiminy's good-natured grin kept Dunk's ire down. 'I thought you resembled each other in a family way, but if you have the same parents how come one of you's a Hoff-nung and the other's a Heldmann?'

'It's complicated,' said Dunk, putting his back into the rowing.

'What in life ain't? Anyhow, the point here is that if you're looking for your sister, do that. Don't worry about the game so much, unless that's why you're actually here.'

Sitting next to the singer in the front of the boat, Slick clapped Jiminy on the back. 'The man has a point, sons. It's a simple matter of priorities. Of course, there's the purse for winning the tournament, and that's nothing to pish-posh either.'

'No.' Dunk shook his head. 'The Tobazco Bowl is only a tissue-thin pretence. We're here for Kirta.'

Slick shrugged. 'Just doing my job as your agent, telling you not to ignore your professional commit-ments. As your friend, though, I wholeheartedly approve.'

'Can't we do both?' asked Spinne. 'Look for Kirta and play the game?'

'Sure,' Dunk said, leaning close to her for a kiss as they stroked the oars again. He looked up at Jiminy. 'How long do we have before the game?'

Jiminy shaded his eyes and stared at the top of the volcano that occupied most of Tobazco Island, which grew closer with every stroke. 'They usually wait until she's just about ready to blow,' he said. 'They think the lava flows add to the drama.'

'How often does that happen?' Lästiges asked, shivering despite the tropical heat.

"Bout once a year,' he said, 'right about the same time. That's how we've known it's tournament time. Some say Tobazco, the God of Heat, chooses the date to fit him so he can watch the game in his favourite chilli bowl.'

'I thought the lava would make it hot,' said Dunk.

'Hot enough to melt the nails in your boots.'

'Then why is the bowl chilly?'

Jiminy laughed. 'Chilli's a food, not a temperature, my friend, and the hotter, the better.'

'Why do they call it chilly then?'

Jiminy scratched at his chin. 'I suppose it's something like why you call a fat man "Slim", or a pygmy halfling "Big Richard".'

Dunk nodded, understanding how this worked, but not why.

'Not worth wasting brain sweat over,' Jiminy said. 'We'll get you a bowl sometime, and you can make up your own mind about it. In the meantime, from the way that crater at the top of the volcano's started to smoke, I suspect we have three, maybe four days before the games begin.'

'So we have some time to look for Kirta first.'

'I'd say so.'

Dunk jerked his chin at the volcano. 'Then we're going to skip Tobazco Island for now. We'll go straight to Amazon Island instead, and see if we can find Kirta before this whole mess begins.'

'I DON'T LIKE the way this place smells,' Slick said, wrinkling his nose at the wind as they sat resting on the beach.

'It's not much worse than the sulphur spewing from the volcano,' Dunk said. He had to agree, though, he'd been holding his breath for most of the time since they'd landed.

'We all needed a rest,' Lästiges said, inspecting the blisters rising on the palms of her hands.

'What's Xocibiki mean, anyhow?' Slick asked.

'Bloody nasty!' said Edgar. M'Grash, who sat next to the treeman, shrugged. His nose ring often cut off his sense of smell, and for the first time Dunk saw how that could be a good thing.

Jiminy squinted into the sun for a moment. 'I think it's got something to do with voodoo, but I don't know for sure.'

'What's voodoo?' Dunk asked.

'An island flavoured hodgepodge of all sorts of different religions tossed into one. It involves evil priests, walking dead – they call them zombies – and formless spirits that ride their worshippers like a man rides a horse.'

'How do you know so much about it?' Dirk asked, his voice soaked in suspicion.

"Cause Xocibiki is the home of voodoo in these parts, maybe any parts at all.'

Lästiges shot to her feet. 'Then what are we doing here? Aren't we tempting fate by even landing here?' She shuddered and stared around at where the beach ended in a long line of untamed jungle, which somehow seemed both closer and darker now.

Jiminy waved off her concerns. 'Zombies can't stand salt water,' he said. 'Pour a little bit of salt on them, and they shrivel up like slugs. That's how come they never get off the island. Long as we stay on the beach, we should be just fine.'

'Who's the voodoo priest in charge around here?' Slick asked, his eyes growing wide.

'Baron Somebody,' said Jiminy.

'You don't know his name?' asked Dirk.

'That is his name: Somebody. Baron Somebody. Sometimes he goes by Mr Big instead.'

'Is that something like calling a fat man "Slim"?' asked Dunk.

'No, this is more of a what-you-hear-is-what-you-get thing. Somebody who's about as fat as they come.'

'A dark-skinned man who runs around without a shirt and wears his hair in long clumps?' asked Slick.

'They call those dreadlocks,' said Jiminy.

'Dreadlocks, right, through which he sticks bits of people's bones?'

'Right.' Jiminy laughed. 'He's even got one of a pygmy halfling.'

'That he wears right smack in the middle of his fat forehead?'

Jiminy stopped laughing. 'That's right. Too right.'

'How do you know about Baron Somebody?' Dunk asked.

Slick, who'd been staring out at the jungle the entire time he'd been talking, raised his hand and pointed straight into the thickest, darkest part. 'Because he's standing right there.'

The others leapt to their feet, kicking sand everywhere. There, right before them, Dunk could see a dark, round shape coalescing under the shelter of the jungle's thick, green canopy. Then the shape came towards them, moving like a landed whale.

Baron Somebody, for that was the only person that this could be, looked exactly how Slick and Jiminy had described them. As he grew closer, though, Dunk saw that they had omitted a few salient details, like the way madness danced in his oak-coloured eyes.

'Greetings, strangers!' Baron Somebody's voice boomed as if his words had been beaten out on a wide, low drum. 'I would like to know if you have accepted Death as your personal saviour.'

Dunk stopped, stunned. He looked to the others. They all shrugged at him, confused.

'Ah, no,' said Dunk. 'Should we have?'

'It is the only way to salvation! Without Death, we wander cold and lonely through life! How much better to embrace the senseless existence of Death.'

'Ain't the grave supposed to be cold?' Jiminy said.

'But of course!' Baron Somebody said. 'But when you are gathered in Death's arms, you can't feel it. You can't feel a thing!'

'And that's good?' asked Dunk.

The voodoo priest's face fell into a look of grim determination. 'Think of the struggles of life! Think about all the troubles it brings. Imagine if you never had to feel hungry or thirsty again; if you never had to feel pain, or emotions of any kind.'

Dunk frowned. 'But you couldn't feel warmth, or love, or a human touch again either.'

'A small sacrifice to make for immunity from all else. Death can save us all! It knows no prejudice. It accepts us each as we are.'

'If it's so bloody wonderful,' said Edgar, 'how come you're still breathing?'

'As a bokor, a voodoo priest, it's my solemn duty to spread the gospel of Death to all that can hear it. Sadly, I cannot do that if I am dead. Although I long for Death's release, I will delay that day so that I might serve both Death and my fellow living creatures, guiding them towards the darkness.'

'We can arrange to send you off to your master straight away,' Dirk said as he stepped up next to Dunk.

'That is not necessary, stranger, although I appreciate your kind offer. I will find my way to Death when Death wills it! In the meantime, I offer Death to all who will listen!'

'What about those who don't? Who refuse to listen to your message?' asked Spinne.

Baron Somebody smiled, revealing a set of shark teeth filed to sharp points. 'All listen in time, stranger! No matter how deaf their ears may be, Death comes for them all.'

'We're busy,' Dunk said. 'We have to find our sister on Amazon Island. We can't mess around with Death right now.'

'But you are Blood Bowl players, are you not? The Hackers? I see you on my Cabalvision. You are great servants of Death! You kill more people in an hour than most folks do in a lifetime!'

Dunk blushed. The fact that he made a living playing such a violent game bothered him sometimes, although he rarely talked about it. 'We win games by points scored, not opponents killed.'

'But Death cheers from the sidelines of every game! No matter who plays in the game, Death wins! Your Nuffle is only another aspect of Death. You already worship Death! Make it official. Cut out the middleman. Go straight for Death!'

'Blood Bowl's not about death,' Dunk said. 'It's about victory, and the ultimate victory is survival. To endure a Blood Bowl game, to come out of it not only alive but intact, there's little better in this life.'

'But it's the risk of Death that makes it so sweet! Without it, Blood Bowl would be just a bunch of people scrambling around after a ball on a patch of Astroturf. Who would pay to watch something as boring as that?'

'It's not boring!' Everyone turned around to stare at the voice that had shouted these words. It belonged to Slick.

'I make a living at Blood Bowl, but I'm no player. I could make better money running the family business back in Greenfield, but I spend my days devoted to this game, and the people who play the game.

'I love Blood Bowl for the game, not the violence. It has action, drama, pathos, triumph, and more. It's real life turned up all the way.

'Blood Bowl is more than a game. It's a metaphor for the humanoid condition. It represents the best and the worst of who we are and who we can be. You can't get better than that, especially not on a Sunday afternoon.'

When Slick stopped speaking, everyone blinked at him for a moment. Then Baron Somebody spoke up. 'Death conquers all! It's one of the best ways to win a game of Blood Bowl, by killing off the other team. Give me Death, or give me Death!

'Sooner or later, we all die! Why not come along now?'

Growing tired of the bokor's rants, Dunk stepped forward, ready to order an attack. While they weren't in their armour, every one of them besides Slick and Jiminy were Blood Bowl players. That put them among the best fighters in the world, and Dunk was ready to test their mettle against whatever the baron had to throw at them.

The baron watched the players fan out along the beach. They looked ready to take him apart. As they moved, his bulging belly began to rumble. Soon it shook like an avalanche of lard, and his laughter resounded along the beach.

'You are fools,' he said. 'There is no escape from my army of the undead.'

'Army?' Dunk said looking around. The beach stood empty in either direction as far as the eye could see. The waters lapped softly at the sand, but Jiminy had been clear that the zombies could not be found there. If they were in the jungle, fine, but the players could just run into the water. That's why Dunk felt so confident when he said, 'What army?'

'Boom! Boom! Boom!' Baron Somebody said.

As he spoke, the sands around the players and their friends shifted. Rotting arms reached up from beneath the beach, followed by decaying bodies. Human figures pulled themselves from shallow graves all around, sending sand sliding away in every direction.

'So that's why this place smells like hell,' Slick said, a waver in his voice.

'Brains!' the zombies said. 'Brains! Brains! Brains!'

'Kind of a one-track mind,' Dunk said as he and the others closed ranks, forming a defensive circle around Edgar and M'Grash. The two big guys stood back to back, allowing them to cover the others in every direction with their extra-long arms. Meanwhile, Dunk, Dirk, Spinne, and Lästiges could defend them against any attacks that managed to get through their defences. Jiminy stood between Dunk and Dirk, ready to lend a hand, while Slick clambered up Edgar's bark covered side and sat in the safety of the treeman's upper branches.

'Zombies don't have much in the way of brains, minds, or anything else between their rotting ears,' Jiminy said. 'They're dead, and they only care about two things. The first of those is following their bokor's orders.'

'And the second?' asked Dunk.

'Slaking their unholy hunger by feasting on the flesh of the living.'

'Glad I asked.'

'Give in to Death!' Baron Somebody said. He cackled viciously as his undead minions stumbled forward at their breathing targets. 'Death forgives all! It puts you beyond caring about your sins.'

One of Edgar's branches slashed out at the bokor, but the man ducked beneath it. He proved far faster and nimbler than Dunk would have believed, given the man's bulk.

A zombie grabbed the branch and bit into it. In return, he got a mouth full of splinters. Edgar flicked the creature off his arm and tossed him into the sea.

The zombie landed in the water with a splash that instantly transformed into a hiss. The water all around it burst into steam, and it howled with an unearthly pain that Dunk didn't think could apply to breathing creatures. He couldn't have replicated the zombie's cry if he'd tried. It would have torn his throat apart.

'Salt water still destroys them,' Jiminy said. 'They just buried themselves in dry sand.'

'So, all we need to do is fight our way through them to the sea, and we should be free and clear?' Dunk said.

'An excellent strategy,' Baron Somebody said. 'You should try it. Bang! Bang! Bang!'

As the bokor spoke, the beach between the players and the surf erupted once more. This time, Dunk could not see the waves for all the sand thrown up into the air before him. When it started to settle, he could see the zombies listing about between him and the salt water.

They stood at least five deep, and there had to be hundreds of them. This batch looked even more rotten than the first, as if they'd been buried under the sand for far longer, with what little clothes they wore even more damaged and tattered. Crabs of all shapes and sizes scurried in and out of their bodies, wondering why their homes had decided to get up and start moving around after offering them shelter for so long. Snails tumbled from positions to which they had thought they were rooted. Dead fish peeled away and tumbled to the ground, some of them flopping about as if stuck out of water, despite the fact they'd stopped breathing long, long ago.

'I don't think getting to the sea is any longer an option,' Slick said from above.

Dunk had to agree with the halfling. While they might be able to battle their way through the undead horde, they'd be sure to lose one or more of them in the process. Dunk thought of having M'Grash toss everyone else over the zombies' heads to land in the sea, but that struck him as both bad for the ogre, who would be left behind, and horribly dangerous for everyone else.

'Play Gamma Sutra!' Dunk called out. 'South! Hike!'

The Hacker players with him burst into action. They'd drilled this play over and over, just like they did with all their plays, until performing it had become second nature.

As a game, Blood Bowl didn't allow for much in the way of plays. It was too chaotic, too violent. The players often found themselves scrambling to survive rather than somehow get into position to pull off a set play. Still, sometimes they managed it, and when it worked it was a thing of beauty.

'Gamma sutra' was one of the easiest plays to run. In it, the smaller players lined up behind the bigger ones and charged forward, punching a hole through the opposing line. The tag 'south' meant that the team should head in the opposite direction to which they would normally go.

On the Blood Bowl pitch, 'north' meant straight ahead towards the end zone you wanted to reach. This held true no matter which direction you were geographically heading in. South was back towards the end zone you meant to defend. Most plays were called north, north-west, north-east, or some variant of those directions. South or any variation on it meant retreat, and few teams liked to go backward, even when it was the smart thing to do.

Right now, it seemed like it was the only thing to do.

Spinne dragged Lästiges around from where they'd stood on the opposite side of Edgar and M'Grash from Dunk and joined him, Dirk, and Jiminy. Then, as Baron Somebody grinned at what looked to him like a desperate attempt to press towards the sea, the biggest Hackers spun on their heels and charged into the jungle.

M'Grash and Edgar shoved aside the few zombies that stood between them and the plant cluttered green beyond. Dunk saw the creatures spill over and then pull themselves back to their feet a moment later, shrugging off blows that would have maimed living men. He shivered despite the tropical heat.

'Where are we going?' Dirk shouted as they plunged into the thick undergrowth, shoving their way through the dense mixture of vines, trees, ferns, and other plants, as the denizens of the jungle darted out of their thunderous way.

'Away from the zombies,' said Dunk.

'Don't you think we might need a better plan than that?'

'We follow Edgar and M'Grash until they run into something that won't move, or they run out of steam. Then we figure it out from there.'

'Some plan!'

'It beats Plan A.'

'Which was?'

'Hard to say, but every variant on it seemed to end up with us getting torn to pieces before we reached the sea.'

'Good point,' said Dirk. 'Keep running.'

The plants and trees gave way before the ogre and treeman's incredible onslaught, crunching and crashing down like hapless tackling dummies placed in their way. Dunk risked a glance backward and saw the zombies chasing after them. The creatures barely kept pace with them, despite the obstacles M'Grash and Edgar had to overcome. Although they were slower, they seemed to be growing in numbers as they moved along. The line of them spread out wider and wider, but never seemed to lose any depth.

'Are there more of them?' Spinne said. 'It seems like they're picking up more zombies as they go.'

'How many people have died on this island?'
Lästiges asked.

'Well,' Jiminy said, his grin not quite as easy and natural now, 'I hear tell this used to be called the Island
of the Damned, but that was back before.'

'Before what?' asked Slick, still bouncing along in
Edgar's upper branches.

'Before the zombies killed everyone who called it that.'

The halfling shook his head. 'Now that's what I call
controlling the message.'

'Any idea where we might be heading?' Dunk asked.

Jiminy grimaced. 'I don't really get over to this part
of the islands as much as you might think.'

'Probably has something to do with all the walking
dead around here.'

'You'd be surprised how fast the mere sight of such
creatures can ruin your whole day.'

'Getting chased around the jungle by them's not
doing much for my attitude either.'

'Knock off the bloody banter and figure us a way out
of here,' Edgar said. 'My bloody branches feel like
they're about to crack off.'

'Tired!' M'Grash said. 'So tired!'

Dunk knew he only had minutes before the ogre
and treeman's incredible strength gave out. Before
that happened, he had to come up with a way out of
this. Unfortunately, nothing seemed to leap out at
him. They were barging through a treacherous land-
scape that their foes knew far better than they ever
could. The only thing he could think of was to keep
running in the vain hopes they'd run into some kind
of a saltlick.

That's when Dunk saw something poke out of the top of the jungle canopy. 'South-south-west!' Dunk said.

'Is that thinking of the direction we're facing as south, or should we be thinking of the way we're going as north?' Edgar asked.

'We're going south. Veer right!'

Dunk pointed at the top of a triangular structure just poking out over the top of the canopy. It couldn't be too far away. 'Veer towards that!'

'What is it?' asked Spinne.

'I don't know,' said Dunk, 'but we'd all better hope it's something that could save our lives!'

As the top of the structure grew closer, Dunk saw that it was not a triangle but a pyramid formed by a series of stepped levels that grew smaller the closer they were to the top. Enojada had regaled them with tales of such massive buildings on their voyage. They'd supposedly been built by the lizardmen or the slann, a bloated race of elder beings older than even the elves, or so Enojada claimed.

Great birds circled in the air high above the pyramid, which the jungle had nearly claimed. Vines reached up from the lower sections, like long, ancient tendrils striving to pull the great stones down and reduce the pyramid to a pile of moss-covered rubble.

Dunk wondered how many such pyramids lay out in the larger jungle, and if any of them were still occupied by their builders. Visions of scale-covered men floated in his head as he charged through the jungle behind the two massive Hackers. If any such creatures remained near this pyramid, they'd no doubt hear the Hackers coming from several miles away.

Edgar and M'Grash weren't being subtle, but that was a luxury they didn't have. A quick glance backward informed Dunk that the zombies were still on their trail and closing ever so slowly. It wasn't that the creatures were getting faster, but the jungle had got thicker, and M'Grash and Edgar were starting to tire.

'Go for the pyramid!' Dunk said.

'We don't know what's bloody there,' said Edgar. 'Could be full of dragons, or fire-breathing lizards of some other bloody kind.'

'If we don't figure something out soon, the zombies will run us down. They never get tired. How about you?'

Edgar couldn't turn back to glare at Dunk. To do so would have required him to stop moving, which he could not do. Still, Dunk could feel the treeman's frustration rolling off him.

'Bloody fine,' he said. 'You want to hide like rats, go right ahead. I don't have anything to bloody fear from these bits of rotting meat.'

With that, Edgar veered off to the left, in the direction of the pyramid. M'Grash turned with him, like a pair of oxen yoked to the same cart. The jungle, it seemed to Dunk, started to thin a bit.

Within minutes, the jungle gave way to a clearing around the pyramid, and they were out from under the canopy formed by the ancient trees. The land around the pyramid had once been cleared of vegetation, Dunk guessed, but a thick circle of fast-growing palm trees bearing bright-yellow coconuts now surrounded the place. Mossy vines ran from their trunks all about the place, and strange creatures greeted the strangers with horrible howls from the darkened shelter of the trees' fronds.

'There has to be a way in,' Dunk said.

'I don't want to go in there.' said Lästiges. 'You don't know what's in there!'

'Can it be worse than an army of hungry zombies?'

'Good point,' Dirk said. He grabbed Lästiges by her hand and hauled her after him. He'd bickered a lot with Dunk about this trip, but in the clutch he was just the kind of man that Dunk could count on. Dunk felt proud to be able to call Dirk his brother.

'Up there!' Spinne said, pointing towards the top of the pyramid. 'I see a door!'

Dunk followed her gaze and spotted the black hole that gaped in the middle of the gigantic block that made up the top level of the pyramid. There was no way to know where it might lead, or even if it led anywhere, but he didn't see any other options. If they tried to make a stand on the side of the pyramid, they might be able to hold off the zombies for a while, but they'd be much better off if they could find some sort of fortifications behind which they could make a stand.

Dunk had no desire to be devoured by an army of the dead in some strange land, thousands of miles from the place of his birth. He wanted to die old, in his bed in the family keep, with his helmet off and Spinne by his side. Of those details, he only had Spinne. Should the worst happen, he knew that would be enough.

He reached out and took Spinne's hand, and they ran.

In the middle of the wall of the pyramid facing them, Dunk spied a long staircase that led straight up the side of the structure. It stood tall, cracked and crumbling from one end to the other, but scrambling up it would have to prove easier than trying to haul themselves up the sides of the massive blocks that made up the sides of the pyramid.

As they reached the base of the pyramid, M'Grash and Edgar slid to a muddy stop. They stared up at the top of the pyramid as if the heavens had opened up and started firing angry godlings down at them.

'Go!' Dunk said. 'Go! What are you waiting for?'

'Well, it's a bloody long way up there, innit?' said Edgar uneasily.

'Hole too small,' M'Grash said, pointing up at the gaping entrance at the pyramid's top.

Dunk smacked himself in the face. 'I-I forgot. I didn't think about how big you two are.' He glanced back at the zombies, who were closing on them fast. 'We'll try something else.' His voice fell. 'I just don't know what.'

'Go,' M'Grash said. He put a massive hand on Dunk and Spinne, and pushed them in front of him. Then he reached back and did the same for Jiminy.

Dunk had almost forgotten about the singer, who'd been bringing up the rear the entire time. He puffed and wheezed, bent over and holding his knees. 'Whew!' he said. 'I thought I was in decent shape, but you Blood Bowl players put me to shame. Where'd y'all learn to run like that?'

'The threat of death is a fine teacher,' said Spinne as she helped him stand up and catch his breath. 'In our line of work, we have to run, or be run over.' She glanced over his shoulder at the zombies getting closer. 'Kind of like now.'

Edgar pushed Dirk and Lästiges in front of him and then set Slick down on the stairs above them.

'The ogre's bloody right,' he said. 'Go. Without you lot slowing us down, we should be able to get away from that bloody lot.'

'You use "bloody" as if it's a comma,' said Dunk.

The treeman shrugged the best he could. 'It's not?' Then he swung a branch to point straight up the stairs. 'Get your bloody arses up there,' he said. 'Don't you worry about the ogre and me. We'll be fine.'

'You can't know that,' said Lästiges.

Edgar laughed, a low rumble from deep in his trunk. 'Of course, I bloody can! I'm bark and sap, no good to zombies of any kind. As for the ogre, you hear what those bloody blighters keep moaning.'

Dunk cocked his ear for a moment to be able to make out the words. He realised then that the zombies had been chanting a single word the entire time they'd been chasing them through the jungle. The pounding of his heartbeat in his ears had drowned it out.

'Brains! Brains! Brains, Brains, Brains!

'Brains! Brains! Brains, Brains, Brains!

'Brains! Brains! Brains, Brains, Brains!'

The treeman thumbed a twig at M'Grash with a smile. 'The big, bloody ogre ain't got any. He's safe.'

Dunk laughed despite himself, and then realised how near the zombies were. He clapped M'Grash on the arm and said, 'Take care of Edgar for me, M'Grash. We'll meet you on the other side of the island, on the beach facing Amazon Island.'

'Bye, Dunkel.' The ogre looked scared, as if he might cry. Dunk knew that M'Grash had no fear for himself, but it terrified the ogre to think that Dunk and the others might be killed. If Dunk asked him, M'Grash would turn and fight the zombies, giving the others plenty of time to get away. But if he did that, the ogre would die.

'Don't you worry a moment about us, big guy,' Dunk said, Spinne already pulling him up the steps after Lästiges and Dirk, who'd bounded up into the lead. 'We'll see you on the other side.'

Dunk turned and raced after the others, pausing only long enough to scoop up Slick and toss him into the piggyback position before giving it all he had. As he reached the top of the pyramid behind the others, he turned back to see Edgar pulling M'Grash along behind him, moving off to the pyramid's south.

The mass of the zombie horde ignored the two massive creatures. They reached the bottom of the pyramid, and began clambering over each other to reach their warm-blooded prey, which now stood closer to them than they had since the hunt had begun.

Dunk looked up at the darkened doorway through which the others had already disappeared. 'Ready?' he asked Slick.

'If it's zombies or the unknown, put me down for the unknown, son.'

Dunk charged forward into the darkness. 'The unknown it is.'

'Shut the door,' Dirk roared.

Dunk whirled about. 'What door?' He spied a slab of stone that stood to one side of the open doorway, and Dirk and Spinne were already working to slide it into place. Dunk moved to lend a hand and put his shoulder into moving the thing.

The massive hunk of stone ground forward slowly, but it went. As it did, Dunk could hear the zombies outside, scrambling up the long, crumbling steps.

'Brains! Brains! Brains, Brains, Brains!

'Brains! Brains! Brains, Brains, Brains!

'Brains! Brains! Brains, Brains, Brains!'

'That's the worst damned tune I've ever heard,' Jiminy said as he slipped in next to Dunk and helped push against the door.

'Let's just hope it's not the last one you ever hear,' said Lästiges. Dunk glanced over his shoulder to see her standing back to record the entire incident. A blazing light sprang from the top of her camra, zipping back and forth on a glowing piece of thin metal that arced over the top.

'What the heck is that?' Slick asked as he clambered down from Dunk's back after realising that he wasn't helping with the door any.

'Firewire,' the reporter said. 'All the latest daemonic camras have it. Check out the interface.'

Lästiges poked the camra with her fingers, and the opening on the front grew larger. 'Wide-angle shots,' she said, 'for the latest HD crystal ball formats.'

'HD?'

'High Density; they weigh twice as much as a normal crystal ball, but the image clarity is stunning.'

'Push!' Dunk shouted. 'Push!'

'Brains! Brains! Brains, Brains, Brains!'

Dunk growled in frustration as he bent his back to his task and gave it every last bit of energy he had. Dirk, Spinne, and Jiminy did the same, and the door moved faster. The voices of the zombies seemed closer than ever.

The door only had inches to go before it would slam shut. 'One more push!' Dunk said. 'On three. One! Two!'

Before he could reach 'Three!' a rotting arm shot through the opening. Dunk staggered back, the arm's ragged fingers missing his face by a feather's width.

'Run!' he said, scrambling in the other direction. The arm clawed at the open air where he'd just been standing, hoping for purchase on something fleshy and warm, he had no doubt.

'Hold it!' said Dirk.

Dunk froze. The arm was stuck there, flailing about. Although it strove for purchase, it found none, and the heavy door refused to move under the zombie's weight.

'They can't move it,' Dirk said. 'We're safe.'

A horrible moaning sound issued from somewhere deep inside the pyramid's black bowels.

'I wouldn't go there quite yet, son,' Slick said, a waver in his voice.

'We can't just stay here,' Dunk said.

'Why not?' asked Jiminy.

Another arm shot through the gap between the door and its frame, as if in response; then another, another, and another. Soon it seemed as if the door had grown a dozen different arms so that it could grab anything that tried to push against it. Thankfully, Dunk noted, it hadn't grown any feet.

Dirk reached out and snatched one of the arms in an iron grip. Then he set his foot against the broadside of the door and pulled. With a sickening crack, the arm came free of its owner, and Dirk tumbled backward on the floor.

Dirk scrambled to his feet, and the arm flopped off him to land by his boots. It lay there, still, even more lifeless than it had been before.

Two more arms stabbed into the gap where the first had been.

'We need to find a way out of here,' Dunk said. 'That door won't stop them forever. Lästiges, bring that camra over here.'

Dunk walked to the far wall of the pyramid. As he neared it, the light from the camra fell upon a waist-high table of stone. The top of it had been carved away to fit the body of someone smaller than Dunk, perhaps Pegleg's size. This depression bore dark stains that Dunk instantly recognised as blood, as did the system of thin gutters designed to drain the blood from the table. The thin gutters ran together into a larger one on the floor that ran back between Dunk's feet and towards the door.

'Human sacrifices,' Jiminy said, an uncharacteristically reverend tone in his voice. 'In the old days, the lizardmen used to hunt people around these parts and offer them up on this altar to their dark gods. I hear tell they would rip the heart out of a screaming man's chest and wolf it down whole before the thing even stopped beating.'

'What happened to them?' Dunk asked.

'They moved on, I guess.' Jiminy motioned towards the doorway with his head. 'As you might imagine, I don't get out this way all that often. Don't suspect anyone else does either.

'The continent's lousy with lizardmen, slann, skaven, and far, far worse. Out here on the islands, we have a far easier life.'

'Why's that?' Dunk asked, as he motioned for Lästiges to keep exploring by her camra's light.

'Most of these bastards can't swim worth a damn.' Jiminy smiled, back to his usual, jovial self. 'A man with a boat can make his own destiny around these parts, and he can escape it too.'

As the musician spoke, the scratching and moaning at the door suddenly stopped. Dunk turned in time to see the grasping arms all pull back out of sight.

All eyes in the room stared at the door. No one said a word. After a moment, Dunk realised that they were all holding their breath too, including him.

A booming knock came at the door, followed by a booming voice. 'Fantastic!' said Baron Somebody. 'You have found the Ancient Temple of Gloom!'

'Fantastic isn't the word I would have used,' Slick muttered.

'I'm sorry,' Dunk said. 'You'll have to come back later. We're doing the dishes.'

'Ha! Ha! Ha!' the baron boomed. 'You tickle my funny bone, stranger!'

'Shove off,' Dirk said. 'We're safe in here. Your zombies are too weak to move that door.'

'Oh, that's where you are wrong, stranger. Perhaps one zombie could not move the door. Maybe not five or even a dozen! I, however, have hundreds of zombies, perhaps thousands! If I wish the door moved, it will be moved!'

'If that's so, then why hasn't the door moved yet?' asked Dunk.

'Because I have a proposition for you, strangers! I would not have thought about this on the beach, but who knew you would be so foolish as to try to escape me in the Temple of Gloom? Far better that you be torn to pieces by my zombies than have to face the horrors you may find inside.'

'He's bluffing,' said Slick. 'What's not to like about this place? It's dry, the stone absorbs a good deal of that oppressive jungle heat, and it's refreshingly free of zombies.'

An ear wrenching groan shook the pyramid from its foundations, vibrating up through its every stone, and even through the bones of those who stood upon it.

'Maybe we'd be better off with the zombies,' said Lästiges.

'What do you want?' Dunk shouted at the door and the fat bokor beyond.

'The Temple of Gloom is also the home of the Lizard's Claw, an artefact of unparalleled mystical power. Legend says it is buried deep within the temple's bowels. Only the bravest and most worthy have a prayer of finding it.'

'That's us out then,' said Slick. Spinne shushed him.

'If you return to me with the Lizard's Claw I will set you free!' Baron Somebody said. 'I will personally escort you to your boat, stock you with supplies, and send you on your way. I will even have my zombies hum a little departure tune for you. Nothing special, just a little something I made up.'

'And if we refuse?'

'Come, strangers. You are not so foolish!'

Dunk turned to whisper with the others. 'I say we go for it,' he said softly. 'Between certain death and likely death, I'll go with likely every time.'

'I don't know,' said Dirk. 'I'm all for cracking some zombie heads and then racing off into the jungle. You and I can fight a delaying action while Jiminy and Slick help the ladies get a head start.'

'No.'

Dunk had to look around to see who had spoken. Eventually his gaze landed on Lästiges. She had her hand on Dirk's shoulder, and she was squeezing hard.

'You are not sacrificing yourself for me, and I am not running off into that jungle without you. We may die in here.' The pyramid shuddered and howled once more. 'We will *probably* die in here, but we'll do it together.'

Dunk reached out and held Spinne's hand as Lästiges spoke. The two of them didn't have to say a word to each other. They both knew they felt exactly the same way.

Dunk wondered if Dirk would put his foot down. Would he insist on sacrificing himself to save the life of the woman he loved? Or would he swallow his pride, his sense of what a man should do, and comply with her wishes?

Dirk reached up and held Lästiges's hand. He gazed into her eyes, and said, 'All right. We stand together. We live or die as one.'

Jiminy cleared his throat. 'Or as six,' said Dirk, 'whatever.'

Before Dunk could turn to answer the bokor's request, he noticed that the room was getting darker. Then he heard the stone moving, and he spun around to see the door closing, fitting perfectly into the doorframe that surrounded it on four sides.

As the door scraped into its ancient home, the noise from below reverberated throughout the temple. Somewhere, someone screamed. Dunk wished he could be sure it hadn't been him.

'IT LOOKS LIKE the only way out of here is down,' Dunk said, pointing at the narrow stairwell Lästiges had found with the light on her camra. The altar had hidden the top of it from view until the reporter had gone down on her hands and knees to really look.

'It looks dangerous,' said Spinne. 'You go first.'

Dunk smirked at her attempt at humour, and then lowered himself down the steps. He only got a few feet before he stopped.

'I can't see a thing,' he said. 'Any chance I can get a light down here?'

'Lästiges is *not* leading this little adventuring party of yours,' said Dirk.

'Party?' said Jiminy. 'I knew I should have brought my guitar, or a margarita, or both.'

'What's a margarita?' asked Lästiges.

Jiminy grinned. 'A magical concoction, a peerless potion, an incredible elixir. Or, as we like to make it: rum, orange liqueur, and a healthy dose of the drink of the Lustrian gods: tequila.'

'Sounds horrible.'

'Only in the most delicious and debilitating way.'

'Can you give me the camra?' Dunk asked Lästiges. 'Unless you want me to carry you down here piggyback.'

'I wouldn't want to take Slick's place.'

The reporter reached out and tapped the camra three times in different places, faster than Dunk could follow. The camra fell into her hand, and she caught it neatly. She then reached out and tapped it on Dunk's shoulder while giving it a clockwise twist.

The camra leapt to life again and hovered over Dunk's shoulder. When he looked at it, it looked at him. Otherwise, it stared over his shoulder at whatever happened to be in front of him. He noticed that it followed his gaze wherever it could manage it, even switching from one shoulder to the other if necessary.

At first, Dunk found this distracting, having something always hovering near one ear or the other. He'd learnt to ignore the fact that Lästiges had it around her all the time. As a Blood Bowl star, he'd seen far more camras than he could count, and he'd been on Cabalvision so often he sometimes didn't recognise the mirror in his bathroom as not being a crystal ball showing his image. Still, he'd never been on this end of a camra before, and it took a little getting used to.

Dunk looked down into the hole in the floor, and the camra looked right after him, shining its light before him. The beam spilled down the musty steps, casting their edges in sharp shadows. Its strength faded before Dunk could see an end to the passage. He took a deep breath, and then continued downward without a word.

The stairwell was only wide enough for one of them to pass at a time. Dunk came first with Spinne right behind him. Jiminy came next, peering around two sets of shoulders in case he could help as a guide. Slick trotted after him, making sure his short legs kept up with the steady pace that Dunk set. Then came Lästiges, grumbling about the loss of control of her camra and how Dunk had better get her some great shots and let her take the credit for them. Dirk brought up the rear, carefully scanning the darkness that lay behind him for any sign of trouble.

After a long while, the stairwell turned at a right angle to the left and continued down. It did so again and again, and soon Dunk realised they were spinning their way down into the bottom of the pyramid by the longest, straightest route possible, other than a direct drop, which he kept on guard against at all times.

The horrible rumbling from below kept sounding, increasing in both frequency and volume. The vibrations shook dust from the tight-fitted brick walls, and loose stones from the ceiling.

Other than that, everything seemed to be going well, right up until they hit the first trap.

Dunk put his foot down, and felt the flagstone beneath it give just a bit and then click. He wanted to jump straight out of his skin, but instead he froze right in his tracks.

Spinne avoided bumping into him, but just barely. Slick tripped over Jiminy, and the two ended up in a pile right behind Spinne. Dirk had to reach out to catch Lästiges when she almost tripped over the pair.

'What's the big–' Lästiges only got a few words out before Dirk clapped a hand over her mouth. She started to protest, but she stopped at a glare from Dirk.

'How bad is it?' Dirk said softly to Dunk.

Dunk sucked at his teeth. 'I can't tell,' he said. 'I stepped on a trigger plate, but I don't know what it's attached to.'

He twisted around to look at Spinne, being careful to keep his foot planted, and his full weight upon it. 'Back off,' he said. 'Take the others with you.'

'I'm not losing you to a damned booby-trap,' she said, her jaw set firm. 'Not after all we've been through.'

'I hope you won't, but there's no sense in all of us risking our lives against whatever this is. Back up. Please.'

Spinne stared at Dunk like a rock. Only a slight quiver in her eyes told him how disturbed she really was. She might break down about this later, when they had time for such a luxury. Right now, she was as strong as tempered steel.

She leaned forward and put her hands on Dunk's shoulders, kissing him tenderly. After a too-short moment, she pushed away and hustled the others a dozen yards back up the stairs.

At first, Dunk was relieved to be alone. Then he realised he'd finally have to deal with whatever it was he'd got himself into.

'Jump back,' Dirk called from the darkness. 'The trapper expects you to move forward.'

You cannot beat a trap, Lehrer's voice said in Dunk's head. *You can only avoid it.*

Dunk had long thought the man to be his family's most loyal retainer, until he'd found out that it had been Lehrer who'd betrayed them all. Lehrer's treachery had blown the entire family apart and ruined their fortunes. Dirk had left before it happened, but Dunk remembered it all too clearly.

That fateful night, he thought he'd lost his father, mother, and sister. Years later, he and Dirk had found their father again, but he'd been killed during the last Blood Bowl championship game, helping his sons save all of Altdorf from being trapped in the Realms of Chaos forever. At least Lehrer had gone with him.

Despite his treachery, Lehrer had been a good teacher, as sharp a man as Dunk had ever known. He'd have to have been, to fool every one of the Hoffnungs for so long.

Dunk knew that as soon as he pulled his foot from the trigger plate something horrible would happen. He could try to leave something heavy on the plate to keep it from ever coming back up and triggering the trap. He'd need something that weighed at least a hundred pounds, though, and he knew that the only things like that around here were his friends.

The ceiling above him looked solid. He stood no chance of shaking a large enough piece of it, or the walls, loose to take his place on the block. Trying to do so might trigger the trap, and if he somehow succeeded, his efforts might crush him, hurting him as badly as any trap.

If he tried to throw himself backward, he might be able to make it a few steps upward. The steps proved the biggest barrier to that though. He'd only be able to get a few feet away before stumbling on them.

Dunk steeled himself, and then lowered his body onto his haunches. He knew he'd only get one chance at this. As soon as his feet left the trigger plate, the trap would go off. He had to make this count.

With a roar, Dunk dived straight down the stairs, headfirst, his arms stretched out before him. Just before he hit the steps, he rolled up into a ball and let his momentum haul him down several more steps, dinging different parts of his body against the stone edges as he went.

When Dunk finally hit one step too hard, it laid him out flat, struggling to get his breath back and wondering if he'd broken a rib. Even panicked and hurt as he was, he turned around as fast as he could to see what had happened. The camra's beam followed his gaze, shining back up the stairwell.

His friends stood on the steps behind where he had stepped on the trap, whooping and hollering for him. Jiminy stuck his fingers in his mouth and gave a gleeful whistle that might have shattered glass.

Dunk stood up and grinned. His smile only grew wider when he saw the large hole that had opened in the steps, right behind where he'd been standing. If he'd thrown himself backward, he'd have fallen into that black pit for sure.

Dunk let out a whoop that felt as if it shook the walls. He was thrilled just to be alive. Now they just needed to figure out how to get everyone safely across the pit, and they could continue on.

That's when the steps of the stairs above the pit collapsed flat, turning the stairwell into a slide. Spinne slipped forward first and disappeared into the blackness before she could manage to scream. Jiminy and Slick slid right after her, just as Dunk launched himself back up the stairs.

By the time Dunk reached the edge of the pit. Lästiges had fallen in, and Dirk was on his way down. Dunk's younger brother had thrown himself to the slide rather than trying to fight gravity with his boots. Then he clawed at the smooth surfaces, hoping to find some kind of handhold or foothold before he joined the others. So far, he'd had little luck.

Dunk reached the edge of the pit just as Dirk finally slipped over the far side of it. His hand stabbed out to grab Dirk's outstretched fingers, but only brushed them before Dirk disappeared into the blackness.

Dunk scrambled up higher and peered down into the pit. In his head, he screamed out the names of all his missing friends. He started and ended with Spinne.

By the time the camra came up and peered down over his shoulder, the pit, which seemed bottomless, stood empty. Dunk grabbed his head with both hands and cursed. Should he jump in after them? They might need him, but if they were dead, there was no point in dying too.

'Spinne!' he shouted. If there was any way to do it, she'd answer him. Before that could happen, though, the missing stairs swung up from the far side of the pit and clicked into place, blocking off the pit from any further conversation or exploration.

Dunk hammered away at the replaced steps, but they would not give. He walked over and stomped on the trigger plate, but it didn't budge. Perhaps it needed to be reset by hand.

Dunk sat down on the steps. He'd avoided the trap, but at what cost? He was alive, but alone, trapped in the heart of an ancient lizardman temple, surrounded by brain-hungry zombies. He couldn't see how things could get worse.

Then he heard the rumbling, howling noise again, closer than ever.

Dunk turned and looked down the stairs, the camra's beam of light following his gaze. At least he still had Lästiges's device to count on. He wondered what had happened to her and the others.

He suspected they were still alive. If the creators of the temple had wanted to kill someone with that trap, it would have been far easier to just drop them into a pit filled with spikes. Instead, they'd been taken somewhere, although for what purpose Dunk couldn't begin to guess.

Then he thought of the altar high above him, and he had an idea about why the priests of this place might have wanted live captives.

He started straight down the stairs. This time, he was more careful than before. He only touched every third step, and he prodded them with his foot before stepping on them. It seemed ridiculous and took forever, but it paid off.

He found two other trigger plates set into steps. Then he reached the third. When he tested the step, he felt the subtle wobble of an untriggered plate.

Dunk tried the step in front of that one. It wobbled too. He went a step beyond. It wobbled too. Every step in front of him that he could reach wobbled.

The temple's builders had been canny. They'd known that experienced intruders would figure out about the trigger plates soon enough, so they'd installed a long line of trigger plates that stretched at least as far as Dunk's reach, and perhaps far beyond.

Dunk suspected that not all of the trigger plates were attached to something. That would have made it difficult for the legitimate travellers in the tunnel to get through. It was likely that only one or two of the plates would activate anything. The trouble was that Dunk had no way of knowing which ones they might be.

Dunk rubbed the stubble on his chin and thought about it. He soon concluded that, since he had no way to know what to do, he had to guess. He could turn around and go back, maybe try his luck with the zombies. Just one man, on his own, and a Blood Bowl player to boot, might be able to punch a hole through the zombies' line and find daylight.

But his woman, his brother, his agent, his brother's woman, and his new friend were all trapped somewhere down in the depths of the temple. He couldn't leave them all behind. He couldn't leave any of them behind.

Dunk steeled himself and jumped. This time, instead of rolling into a ball, he stopped on the step on which he landed. He wanted to touch as few steps as he could, in the hope that the temple's builders had been stingy with the traps. If so, he might get lucky and avoid them all.

The step he landed on clicked under his weight, but Dunk had expected that. He told himself that it didn't mean that he'd activated a trap, just that he'd stepped on a trigger plate. The chances were good that it was a dummy, or so he told himself.

Not all traps waited for the victim to move off the plate. Some activated right away, shooting spikes, spilling burning oil or unleashing poison gas. Dunk held still until he was sure he hadn't landed on one of those.

He made ready for another leap, and then sprang into the air. As he fell towards the next step he'd selected as a target, the light of the floating camra came with him and illuminated his way.

Dunk saw a wire strung across the passageway at about chest height. He knew instantly that he could not avoid it, and that trying to do so might cause him to injure himself when landing. Instead of avoiding the wire, he reached out and grabbed it.

The wire turned out to be as thin as a spider's web, although far stronger. It snapped in Dunk's grasp, each half zipping apart and disappearing into tiny holes set into the passage's opposite walls.

Dunk landed on the step he'd chosen and stopped. He held his breath, listening for anything to tip him off to what horrors he might have unleashed.

For a long moment, nothing happened, and Dunk blew out a long sigh. Then the horrible noise from below rumbled through the entire place again, and something large and heavy smacked down where Dunk had been.

He spun around and saw a tall, thin strip of something metallic that had landed behind him. It stood as tall as him, but was thinner than his thumb. He had to lean to the side to see that it was actually a gigantic metal disc fastened to the ceiling by a triangular rigging.

The wheel had vicious teeth cut into its outer edge, giving it a vicious, hungry look. Dunk wondered what it was meant to eat. Then it started to spin.

At first, the motion only confused Dunk. Then, as the disc began to spin faster, he grew concerned. The disc spun up to a high-pitched buzzing noise that sounded sharper than a sword, and then it started to move forward.

Dunk didn't want to run down the passageway in front of the buzzing disc, but he didn't want to be sliced in half by it either. So, he threw himself against the nearest wall and hugged it tight.

Although the stairwell was narrow, he guessed that he would be able to avoid the blade by an inch or more. If he was wrong, he knew he would pay a bloody and painful price.

As the disc spun closer, it sped up, and the buzzing of the blade seemed to reach a howl. Dunk was tempted to try to cover his ears, but he didn't want to risk losing his elbows. He felt a strong urge to close his eyes, but when the next blade popped out of the wall, this time perpendicular to the first disc, he felt glad he hadn't given into the urge.

The second blade spun up as fast as the first and slipped in right behind its partner, almost close enough for their savage teeth to act like those of interlocking gears. Dunk could see that even a halfling might have trouble avoiding the combination of the two, especially squeezing past the first. One of the pygmy halflings might have made it past, but Dunk guessed the people behind the Temple of Gloom wouldn't think of such creatures as threats, more like snacks.

Dunk couldn't see how he could manage to avoid both spinning blades. His only choice seemed to be to race farther down the stairs, but he knew that's just what the trappers who'd tricked out this place wanted him to do.

He hesitated for a moment, and the blades leapt forward, cutting off any hope of retreat. Dunk exhaled to fit closer to the wall, and the edge of the first blade spun past him. He still had the other blade to deal with, though, the one that would cut him in half at the waist.

For a moment, panic entered Dunk's head and wouldn't get out. The blades had trapped him. The temple's keepers had outwitted him. He would be killed in a horrible, painful way, and die here in this forsaken, forgotten hallway, all alone. What's more, the damned camra would record the whole thing.

Dunk refused to let it happen. He knew he only had seconds to act, if that, but he resolved to go down fighting. If he died, his last moments would not be filled with fear, but with hope.

Dunk shoved against the wall before him as hard as he could. His back smacked into the spinning blade behind him, catching it on the flat, unserrated part. It slowed as he pressed against it harder, but the friction from the spinning began to heat up the back of his shirt, and tiny imperfections in the blade tore at the fabric and his skin beneath.

With enough room to put his feet against the wall, Dunk planted both boots, as high up as he could, and shoved with all his might. His muscles bulged, and the tendons in his legs threatened to burst out of his skin. With a mighty roar, he pushed one last time, and the blade behind him gave.

The disc smashed into the far wall with a horrible clang that Dunk thought might be the best thing he'd ever heard. As the larger disc broke away from its mooring, the smaller one jumped forward, just as angry and deadly as its bigger partner.

Dunk kept his boots planted against one wall and his shoulders against the other. As the smaller blade spun at him, he arched his belly up as high as it would go, and the spinning disc cut through the air beneath him.

Sweating with the effort, and from the heat of the friction from the first blade, Dunk felt his joy turn to terror as his grip on the wall behind his shoulders slipped and he fell towards the buzzing blade below.

25

DUNK PULLED HIMSELF into a ball as he fell, hoping to pull any appendages away from the edges of the spinning disc as he landed on it. He crashed into it hard, knocking the blade right from its mounting, and it went spinning down the stairs at high speed with Dunk still on it.

Dunk's sudden landing didn't seem to stop the disc's spinning much, if at all. Lying atop it, its momentum sent him spinning too, and the world around him became a blur of walls and open passageways as the disc began its long slide down the stairwell.

The spinning left Dunk so disoriented he didn't realise he was sliding down the stairwell until the disc careened off one of the walls. The screeching sound he heard didn't come from his throat, but from the metal scraping along the front edges of the steps as the disc zoomed down the stairs. The knocking against the walls slowed down the disc's rotation, but did nothing at all to halt its descent.

As Dunk and the disc went, they tripped off every other trap along the way. Because they moved so fast, though, they were by and gone before the deadly devices could harm them. Dunk caught glimpses of stabbing spears, flying darts, gaping pits, dropping blocks, jetting flames, buzzing blades coming from every angle, billowing clouds of poison gas; and even more horrible devices of death that he couldn't identify in the small glimpses he got as he and his blade-sled whizzed past.

Dunk held on to the disc for his life. He'd sliced his fingers by reflexively grabbing at the disc's edges, but he'd discovered that he could slip his fingers into the gaps between the teeth without losing his digits. This also served for the teeth to protect his fingers when the disc bounced off one wall or the other, instead of crushing them to bits.

Still, Dunk felt like every impact with a wall or even rough contact with the next step, and there were countless such bangs and dings, might send him careening off on his own. If he was lucky, he'd fall backward, and the blade would spin on ahead of him. Then, if he managed not to trigger another trap with his landing, he might survive, or he might fall off the front end of the disc and have it slice him in two.

The corners were the worst. As Dunk slid deeper and deeper under the temple, they grew farther and farther apart, but every time the disc slammed into one it took everything he had not to give up and let himself fall off.

After what seemed like forever, Dunk realised that the darkness he, the camra and the disc were spinning through was getting brighter. The camra had given up on trying to keep up with Dunk's acrobatic changes of perspective. Instead, it had opted to hover just behind him, keeping low to avoid the various traps the disc had set off.

The camra had nearly been crushed, cracked or destroyed countless times, but it had just barely slipped past each incident with a tenacity that gave Dunk hope for his own situation. At the speed they moved, though, it did little to illuminate what lay ahead of them. By the time Dunk could see something ahead of him and understand what it was, it was already behind him.

The light did an admirable job of lighting up the horrors that Dunk had barely avoided. This, however, did little to make him feel better. It only confirmed that he was in the worst position he'd ever been in, and he despaired of ever finding a way out.

At that moment, he was sure that the people who'd fallen into the first pit and disappeared had been the fortunate ones.

When the light started to grow at the bottom of the stairs, Dunk thought that perhaps he'd finally taken one blow too many to the head, and the stars he often saw at such moments would never stop. Then he wondered if the lower levels of the pyramid were on fire. He'd heard tales that the centre of the world, towards which he'd been skidding and bouncing at a bone-shaking rate, was a ball of molten lava, the stuff that volcanoes expelled when they got angry enough to erupt.

With all the volcanic activity in the area, Dunk wondered if he might be heading for an all-too-close encounter with such scorching materials. Or perhaps he was heading for a fiery pit of hell, which he'd been told was somewhere beneath the surface of the world. His trip to Khorne's section of the Realms of Chaos last year had disintegrated any remaining shreds of belief he might have still had from his childhood, but he couldn't discount the possibility entirely. After all, he'd seen far stranger things since he'd started playing Blood Bowl.

Dunk decided that if the disc managed to make it into the open, he'd hurl himself off it, just in case. As the thought crept into his head, the opportunity arose.

The walls that had hugged and battered him on both sides for so long gave way in an instant. He found himself skidding through an open chamber, heading right for what could only be a moat filled with lava, which ran along the far side of the chamber.

The glowing red light from the lava illuminated the entire chamber, which was filled from one end to the other with lizardmen of all different types. Dunk had never considered that there might be more than one kind of lizardman, but upon reflection it made sense. After all, there were countless different kinds of lizards. It stood to reason that there might be lots of humanoids that resembled them.

Actually, it made no sense at all, but in a universe that held treemen, orcs, elves, dwarfs and so on, a little variety on the lizard side didn't faze Dunk in the least.

Dunk saw many things all at once, and taking them in kept him from leaping from his skidding wheel of doom. First, trapped in a cage before him, surrounded on all sides by a wide stream of lava, stood his friends. Spinne, Dirk, Lästiges, Slick and Jiminy looked battered by whatever means had been used to bring them to this point, but they were all breathing and standing under their own power. Spinne cheered when she saw him.

The centre of the room, which led up to and past the captives, lay empty. Lizardmen in a vast variety of shapes and colours milled around the rest of the chamber, but the centre was clear.

The path that Dunk skidded on led straight up to the throne, situated on the far side of the chamber. On this throne sat a monstrously large, wide and morbidly obese creature that resembled nothing more than a slimy bullfrog gone to seed. While the creatures around it were mostly painted in hues of greens, yellows, and blues, this squatting beast's slick, greasy skin was a dark, bloody red.

The beast opened a mouth wide enough to swallow Dunk whole and croaked something loud and unintelligible at the thrower as he skidded uncontrollably towards it. The language difference, if the thing spoke a language, would have been enough to stop the conversation right there, but Dunk couldn't hear much at all over the horrible screech his disc made as it skittered along the rough stone floor.

The lizardmen in the room all turned towards Dunk, and most of them reached for their weapons. Others, which resembled something more akin to lizard-lions, spat fire in his direction, although none of them were close enough to even singe the speeding thrower.

Dunk had no idea what to do about any of this or how to handle the tremendous number of threats coming at him from every direction. His sense of terror had long since overloaded on his careening trip down the stairs, and, now that he was here, he found the only thing he wanted to do was stop.

Dunk jumped to his feet and found that he could stand on the disc, riding it like a wild beast that refused to be chained with bit or yoke. Still, this did nothing to stop his progress and only made him a better target to all of the lizardmen hoisting spears to hurl in his direction. Dunk decided that the ride had come to an end and it was time to get off.

He stomped down on the back of the disc with his heel and then leapt high into the air behind it. The disc bucked up like a wild bull trying to throw its rider, which was just what Dunk wanted to see happen. He went tumbling back into the air and hit the stone floor in a tight ball, rolling with the impact and the horrendous momentum he and the disc had built up after such a long, terrifying slide.

With the experience born of being tossed around countless times on the Astrogranite, Dunk sprang to his feet as his momentum finally slowed. He found himself in the centre of the room, spitting distance from the cage that held his friends, bouncing on the balls of his feet and ready to take on the entire lizardman army.

At that moment, he heard a voice in his head that was not his own, a psychic voice that could only have come from the massive beast that sat on the scaly throne on the other side of the lava-filled moat. 'Oh, no,' it said. 'Not like th–'

Dunk heard a sickening sound, like a cleaver through a sack of rotten meat, followed by a mighty clang that he could feel in his bones. Such a sound should have been reserved for the battle at the end of the world, when the swords of the gods met in the final conflict. Instead, it had come from the disc he'd ridden into this strange and horrid temple.

He looked up and gawked at the destruction the disc had caused. When he'd leapt from it, he'd felt it spring into the air, and he'd guided it forward with his feet until it left him behind. From there, it had caught the air and sailed through it, gaining altitude until it had been able to scud straight across the moat of lava and slam straight into the monstrous creature on his wide, low throne.

The tremendous creature sat there, its bulk quivering around the carnage the disc had left behind it. The disc had sailed straight through the creature's flesh, severing everything in its path, sending flesh, blood, and fat flying through the room, spattering everyone within several yards of the mortally wounded beast. Blood gushed from the wound and cascaded down the creature's front like a waterfall of gore.

The lizardmen in the chamber all gawked at their leader for a moment. As they did, Dunk walked over towards the cage and called to Spinne across the lava moat that separated them.

'I can't believe you're alive,' she said to him, tears welling in her eyes. 'I thought we'd lost you for sure.'

'I knew I'd find you,' said Dunk. 'I never doubted it.' He paused. 'Okay, I doubted I might live, but I knew that if I lived I'd find you.'

'Hold that thought,' she said, staring at something over his shoulder. 'Let's hope it lasts.'

Dunk looked behind him to see the lizardmen tending to their murdered leader. The space that had been cleared through the centre of the room had started to disappear as the lizardmen milled around, many of them unsure of what to do. At the moment, none of them seemed interested in killing him, which is what would have worried him most, but many of them held their weapons before them as they faced him, hoping to defend themselves if he somehow managed to produce another deadly flying disc, or series of them, with which to kill them all.

Dunk turned back to the cage that held his friends. 'How do we get you out of here?'

Slick slipped out between the bars, which were spaced too widely to hold him, and pointed at a long, black board over which Dunk had nearly tripped. 'They use that as a gangplank, son. It took two of them to move it.'

Dunk turned to snatch up the plank, but as he did, he saw a phalanx of lizardmen moving to intercept him. He reached to his side, but his sword wasn't there and hadn't been for a long time. All he had were his fists, and he put them up, determined to make the best use of them.

Before Dunk could even throw his first punch, though, the lizardmen closest to him fell to their knees. The ones behind them followed suit, and so on, as if a wave of worship worked its way outward through them, sparing none in its path. Within moments, everyone in the room but Dunk and his friends lay face down on the hot, stone floor.

Dunk stared around the chamber. The corpse of the monstrous creature he'd killed still sat against the far wall, leaking blood that hissed and sputtered as it ran into the lava. Yet, the creatures that had served it had turned on it in an instant.

'You have to be kidding me,' he said, louder than he had intended.

'My friend,' Jiminy said, impressed, 'you sure know how to make an entrance.'

A large lizardman, who'd been standing next to the gigantic toadman when Dunk came in, sprang to his feet and hollered something in a hissing and twisting tongue. The creatures all around him murmured in reverent tones, but stayed where they were, prostrate on the stone floor.

'Intruder,' the lizardman who'd spoken to the others finally said, in words that Dunk could understand. 'You have committed a grave and foul murder. For thisss I should make you pay.'

'But you won't,' said Dunk. He wasn't clear on what the lizardman's game was, but he knew he had to figure large in it.

The lizardman crept from the dais upon which the dead toad-god's corpse lay, already turning putrid. Perhaps its body had long been that way. The lizardman leapt across the glowing moat the way that Dunk might have jumped over a puddle in the street. Then he loped up to Dunk and crouched before him on his powerful haunches.

The lizardman wore crimson robes over scales the colour of the bluest sky. These bore gold and silver embroidery that depicted a figure much like the one that had sat on the wide, low throne, a fat, ugly beast that somehow rated the awe of this army of cold-blooded creatures.

The lizardman fixed a pair of slit pupil eyes on Dunk and spoke in a low, sinister voice.

'You have ssslain our god-massster, He Who Rules Over Usss All, in an inssstant, without any warning or challenge. Your might is great, and our people recognise your power.'

'Excellent,' Dunk said with a smile. 'In that case, let's get started with my list of demands.'

'Not ssso fasssst,' the lizardman said. Transparent eyelids blinked over the creature's large, yellow eyes. 'I am the Reverend Ssstallwell, the high priessst of our ssslann god. For years I have brought that foul creature's will to my people.'

Slick understood immediately what it was Stallwell wanted. 'And you're willing to do the same thing for us.'

'You are a wise and undersssstanding morsssel,' Stallwell said. He bared his full mouth of long, sharp teeth. Dunk couldn't tell if this was meant to be a threat or a smile. Either way, it spelled trouble.

'We have no designs on your people or your power over them,' Dunk said. 'We just want to leave here, unharmed.'

Stallwell bobbed his head up and down and rubbed his front claws together. 'I am sssure that can be arranged.'

Then Dirk piped up. 'What about what we came here for in the first place?'

'To get away from the zombies?' Dunk asked.

'I think your brother's talking about the Lizard's Claw,' Jiminy said.

'Right,' said Dunk. He looked at Stallwell, hoping to be able to read the creature's response. He hadn't had too much experience with lizards in the Old World, not enough for him to get any vibe from the beastman that didn't seem alien. 'So?'

'Of course,' Stallwell said. He clapped his hands, and a lizardman in robes similar to his own leapt to his feet and appeared at the priest's side.

Stallwell hissed something into the other priest's ears, and watched the creature leap off to do his bidding. None of the other lizardmen had moved an inch as far as Dunk could tell.

'No one else here can understand a word I'm saying,' Dunk said. 'Can they?'

Stallwell shook his head. 'I have found it ussseful to pick up many languages in my line of work.'

'Which is?'

'Ruling my people and bilking them for everything I can get.'

Dunk blinked. 'They don't mind?'

'For years, I was the only one who could protect them from the insane rantings of our slann "god". They owe me for that.'

'How did you manage that?' Lästiges asked. She sounded like she was interviewing a player at a game.

Dunk glanced over his shoulder and saw the camra hovering there still, taking in everything. He'd forgotten it was there.

'Yesss. Your deviccce there helped me convinccce the others that you are in fact a messsenger of the gods, sent down to remove the twisted soul of Rat Ssslobersssston from our midssst. The ssspectacular murder would have been enough, but the floating, burning globe put the heat in the blood.'

'Uh, great,' said Dunk.

'How did you protect your people from their god?' Lästiges asked again.

The lizardman snorted through his four nostrils. 'Poison,' he said, 'just a little bit every day, enough to keep Ssslobertssson ill and dependent upon me to maintain his rule for him.'

'You fed Slobertson poison?'

Stallwell opened his mouth, and a set of fangs popped down from behind his upper row of teeth. These dripped a green and viscous substance that made Dunk ill to look at it. The priest folded his fangs back and flicked his tongue in amusement at the reactions of Dunk and the people in the cage.

'A little nip, where no one would noticcce it, onccce per day.'

'Where?' Lästiges asked. Dunk squirmed in his boots, not wanting to know the answer.

'Sssquare in his monsssstrousss asss.' Stallwell put a claw on Dunk's arm. 'And thanksss to you, myssssteriousss ssstranger, I will never have to do that again.'

The second priest arrived with the Lizard's Claw. He knelt before Dunk and presented it to him as if it were the hand of a dead god being given to a living deity. It looked like it had been severed from a gigantic lizardman centuries ago, and Dunk feared to touch it in case it crumbled to dust in his hands. When he accepted it, though, it felt indestructibly hard and far heavier than he would have guessed. It also smelled of failure and rot. It seemed a fitting gift for the bokor who had demanded it.

Stallwell hissed another set of orders to the second priest. He sprang to his feet and tapped a number of other lizardmen on their tails to come and help him with his latest task. They immediately set about brining the scorched ramp into place and releasing the prisoners from their cell.

'You don't want this?' Dunk said, holding the Lizard's Claw between him and Stallwell.

'It is an artefact of untold and uncontrollable power,' Stallwell said. 'I have no need for sssuch a thing and would prefer it be taken away ssso that it could not be used againssst me. I will tell my people that thisss is what you came for and is the priccce for their lives.'

'What else will you tell them?'

'That you are leaving me in charge and will return if they do not obey my every word.'

Dunk surveyed the lizardmen once more. Scores of them filled the chamber, mostly as immobile as statues. Those that moved did so with inhuman strength and speed. He had no doubt that if Stallwell could rally their courage they would be able to tear every warm-blooded creature in the room to meaty shreds in a matter of seconds, and there would be little that could be done to stop them.

'Sounds like a deal to me,' Dunk said.

26

THE SUNLIGHT FELT like magic as Dunk stepped from the temple through the secret door to which Stallwell and his minions had led their warm-blooded guests. After the cold, clammy constriction of the tunnels under the temple, the sensation of being outside, with a warm breeze on his skin, delighted Dunk. He pulled Spinne to him, and they grinned at the day.

Then they wrinkled their noses at the stench that assaulted their nostrils. Behind them, Slick gagged at the smell, and the others complained loudly of the stink. None of the lizardmen with them said a thing.

Dunk knew the source of the smell, and a moment later a patrol of zombies confirmed it. The walking corpses surrounded the lizardmen and warm-bloods, shambling out of the jungle shadows to form a densely packed semicircle around the temple's exit.

Stallwell stepped up, ready to order either an attack or a retreat. Dunk stayed the priest with a gesture, raising his hand for everyone to wait. The zombies maintained a respectful distance, waiting with the patience of the dead as others thrashed through the undergrowth behind them.

Baron Somebody emerged from the thicket a moment later, an entourage of comparatively well-preserved zombies arranged around him. He bore a look of extreme surprise and delight, and his voice boomed louder than ever when he spoke.

'Strangers! I did not hope to see you again, much less so soon! I had decided to spend the day collecting food for myself. My zombie friends are terrible cooks.'

'We have your claw,' Dunk said, holding the mummified lizardman's hand before him like a trophy.

'That you do! Thank you so much, strangers.' The fat man put out his hand for the artefact. A thin line of drool ran down his chin. His time living with nothing but zombies had destroyed any self-respect he might once have had.

Dunk hesitated for a moment. He considered using the Lizard's Claw himself. With it, he might be able to destroy not only Baron Somebody and his zombies, but also Stallwell and his lizardmen too.

He felt the claw twitch in his hand. It wanted him to use it. It called to him, and images of unbridled power surged through his head.

Dunk pushed the thoughts aside. Such promises triggered suspicion in him, not greed. He didn't trust the claw and wanted nothing to do with it.

He didn't mind giving it to Baron Somebody though. He pitched the bokor the claw with an underhand motion. The fat man bobbled the claw in midair and dropped it on the ground. He tackled it with his entire bulk, making sure that it could not somehow crawl away on its fingers or find its way into the possession of someone else.

Baron Somebody pushed to his knees and held his prize aloft in triumph. The talons on the claw sparkled in the tropical sun, glinting as if thirsty for blood.

'Foolish strangers! You had the means of escape in your hands! Now you have handed me the means of my triumph!'

'Way to go,' Dirk said to Dunk, who never took his eyes off the zombie master.

'We had a deal,' Dunk said to Baron Somebody. 'We got you your claw. Now let us go.'

'Bwah-ha-ha-ha-ha! You idiots! Now that I have the Lizard's Claw, there is nowhere to go, nowhere that is safe. The entire world is mine!'

'Really?' said Jiminy, stepping forward. 'And just how is one brittle, old, lizard's hand going to pull off something like that?'

'Right,' Spinne said, catching on. 'Just how is some fat, ugly, old excuse for a second-rate priest for a third-rate religion going to manage ruling the world? If your prayers haven't been answered yet, I don't see how that's going to do it.'

Lästiges pointed at the man's belly and snickered. 'Perhaps he talks so loudly to make up for other, ah, inadequacies.'

Dunk smirked, and he saw Baron Somebody's features contort with rage. The last thing the bokor had expected on the verge of achieving his wildest dreams was to be mocked.

'You do not understand the powers you trifle with. I will grind this entire world under my boot, and all will tremble with fear at the mention of my name! Finally, everyone will know the name of Somebody!'

Jiminy couldn't help but laugh. 'That's mighty ambitious for someone who's been a real nobody. I've lived around these parts for years, and I've never heard your name except as part of a joke.'

'The joke is on you now,' said the bokor, 'you and all your breathing friends. I will suck the life out of this world and swallow it whole!'

Spinne giggled, pointing at the man's belly again. 'It looks to me like you've already got a good start on that.'

'I have had enough!' Baron Somebody held the Lizard's Claw high in his hand. 'I wish for the ultimate power over death!'

As the words left the bokor's lips, Dunk winced. He didn't know what to expect, but he knew it wouldn't be good. After a moment of painful waiting, though, he began to relax. He stared at Baron Somebody, who stood smacking and shaking the claw in an effort to make something happen.

'Are you sure that thing's on?' Dunk asked.

Baron Somebody turned and shook the claw at Dunk like a mother scolding a child, with a dead hand. 'This is the claw of the great wizard lizard Wecna Lecna! The ancient lich-ard invested various parts of his corpse unspeakable powers! His head, his tail, his claw! These are the unholy trilogy of his might!'

'Guess he wasn't using any of those,' said Jiminy, 'especially and particularly his head.'

'You fools! You will pay for your... Bah! This thing is useless! Wecna Lecna was useless, nothing more than a myth to frighten bad children.'

Baron Somebody hurled the Lizard's Claw to the ground, and it bounced away, almost as if it could flip through the air under its own power. As it crawled into the undergrowth, a shadow fell across the land. Dunk craned back his head to see a small, black storm cloud hovering overhead in the otherwise pristine sky.

'Oh!' The bokor's face fell, and his eyes hunted the ground for the dead hand he'd discarded. 'No!'

A bolt of bright blue lightning as wide as a building cracked into the ground, right where Baron Somebody stood. The blinding flash and the deafening crack of thunder that resulted from it dazzled Dunk for a moment. He blinked his eyes, but the only thing he could see was the silhouette of the fat bokor framed in the pillar of light.

When Dunk's vision and hearing finally cleared, he saw a pile of glowing ashes where Baron Somebody had stood. The Lizard's Claw had disappeared entirely, and the zombies that had stood all around them had collapsed to the ground like marionettes with snipped strings.

'I guess the moral here is to not mess with things you don't understand,' said Dirk.

'If that were true we'd have died a long time ago,' said Dunk.

'Look around,' said Dirk. 'How many of us do you see left from when we started out on this voyage?'

'I don't understand any of it,' said Lästiges. 'What just happened?'

Jiminy spoke up. 'The moral of the Lizard's Claw is, "Be careful what you ask for. You just might get it." I've been singing songs about it for years, and none of them ever seem to turn out right for the poor folks who end up with the damned thing.'

'I thought it had been stuck in the bottom of the Temple of Gloom forever,' Slick said as he trotted over from where he'd been hiding in the lush under-growth. 'How did you know about it?'

Jiminy grinned. 'Far as I know, it's been wandering around forever. Who knows? Shoot, could be there's two of them.' He eyed the lizardmen who'd come to the surface with Stallwell. 'Maybe four.'

Stallwell shook his head. 'There is only one, and we have not had it in our possession for long. It appeared in the sssack of a group of treasure hunters one day. They had wished for it to lead them to untold riches.'

'And did it?' asked Slick, his ears perking up.

Stallwell flicked his transparent eyelids open. 'The Temple of Gloom turns a tidy profit every year, mossstly trading in the goods ssstripped from the corpssses of those who attempt to raid our home. They found their riches. They alssso found their doom.'

'And you gave it to Rat Slobertson,' Dunk said, understanding dawning on him.

'Our fearlesss ssslann leader was getting on in years. He was ready to retire. He used his first wish to ask for sssomebody to be sssent to relieve him of his duties.'

Dunk glanced over at the steaming pile of ash. 'And Somebody did.'

'WHAT THE BLOODY hell kept you so long?' Edgar said
as Dunk, Spinne, Dirk, Lästiges, Slick and Jiminy
stumbled out of the jungle and onto the island's west-
ern beach. The treeman had been standing at the
water's edge, shading his eyes with his branches and
scanning the treeline.

'Hello to you too,' said Dunk. He could hear the
tone of relief in Edgar's voice, even if the treeman
would never admit to it.

At the sound of Dunk's voice, M'Grash, who'd been
soaking his feet in the water and moping about missing his friend, leapt up in sheer joy. The ogre dashed
across the beach, kicking up enough of it to start a
sandstorm. 'Dunkel!' he shouted. 'Dunkel safe!'

Dunk braced himself for what he knew was coming
next. M'Grash scooped both Spinne and him up in his

arms and gave them hugs that forced every ounce of
breath from them. When he finally set them down,
and both of them had hacked enough air back into
their lungs, they grinned up at the ogre, who apolo-
gised to them over and over, just as he did every time.
Being M'Grash's friend was normally wonderful, but it
wasn't always easy.

'All right!' Jiminy said, pointing to the little boat
floating next to Edgar. 'You went back and got the
boat and hauled it all the way over here.'

'Bloody right we did,' said Edgar. 'It's bad enough I
have to endure the humiliation of having the ogre
kick me from one island to another all around this
bloody continent of yours. I am not putting up with
being a bloody boat for the rest of you lot.'

Edgar narrowed his eyes at Dunk. 'You all seem
healthy for a crew of souls I last saw being chased by
a bloody mass of zombies.'

Slick and Jiminy gathered together with Edgar and
M'Grash and spun the tale of how they'd managed
their escape. They stopped long enough for Dunk to
finally describe to everyone just how he'd managed to
survive the death traps in the stairways of the Temple
of Gloom. By the time they finished, Edgar shook his
branches at them.

'Bloody amazing,' he said. 'I've never seen such a
lucky pack of liars.'

'Every word of that story's true,' Jiminy said. 'Well,
most parts anyhow. You've got to allow a storyteller
some room for embellishments, of course.'

'But all of the most amazing parts are true,' Slick
said, 'the traps, the lava, the slann mage-god.'

'You might have left out the part with the volcanic fishwomen who swam up through the lava just to fall in love with you,' said Spinne.

'Okay,' Jiminy said. 'Most of the best parts were true.' He considered this for a moment. 'Some of them, enough of them, for sure.'

'Never bloody mind,' Edgar said in disgust. 'It's already dark. We'll let you lot get some bloody sleep, and we can embark for Amazon Island at the first sign of dawn.'

'Embark?' Jiminy said. 'That's a treeman joke, right? I get it.'

'Shut up.'

With Edgar standing watch, there was no need for the others to stay awake. Soon each of them fell over exhausted in the encroaching darkness.

Dunk woke up once in the middle of the night with Spinne snuggled up tight against him for warmth. By the glow of starlight, he could see the whitecaps of the gentle surf crashing against the shore with its endless roar. Above, in the darkness, the stars sparkled and danced, and he wondered if his sister could be looking up at the same constellations. He hoped to find out soon.

Morning broke warm and early. They breakfasted on bananas and coconuts that M'Grash shook from the nearby trees, and set off soon after.

A long day's rowing and kicking brought them within bowshot of Amazon Island. It lay nestled at the very end of the Amaxon River delta, where the mighty river spilled into the sea. Unlike Xocibiki or Tobazco, Amazon Island bore no volcanoes or mountainous land. It seemed more like a giant sandbar with trees.

After some discussion, they decided that it would be best to land after dark. That way, they could enter the island unseen, hopefully slipping under the noses of any sentries.

'Maybe we should all dress up like Amazons to fit in,' Spinne said with a wink.

Dunk looked at Dirk and Jiminy. 'I don't think we could pass,' he said. 'Our chests are too hairy.'

'I don't know,' said Jiminy. 'Have you seen many Amazons in your time? They make most pirates seem soft and kind.'

'I thought they were a bunch of women who'd banded together to live alone on an island,' said Dirk. 'They can't be that tough.'

Lästiges smacked his arm with the back of her hand. 'They're a race of warriors,' she said, 'bred for the sword and bow, and trained to them from birth. You and your friends just run around and play with your balls.'

Dirk cringed. 'All right,' he said. 'Point taken.'

When night fell, they rowed and kicked ashore. As they hauled the boat onto the beach, Dunk turned to speak with Edgar and M'Grash.

'Don't tell me,' Edgar said. 'Sit here and guard the bloody boat.'

The treeman's words surprised Dunk. 'Yes,' he said, 'that's right.'

'You're going on a bloody scouting mission,' Edgar said. 'You don't need a pair of monsters like M'Grash and me crashing through the bloody woods with you.

You'll have a hard enough time on your own. If we come with you, you'll be spotted for bloody sure.'

Dunk clapped Edgar on his trunk. 'You're the smartest plant I've ever met.'

'You don't run in the same bloody circles as me.'

M'Grash sat down in the middle of the beach, right next to the boat, considerably more morose than Edgar. Dunk walked up to him and cocked his head to the side to look into the ogre's eyes. 'What's up?' he asked.

'Dunkel leaving again.'

'We'll be back,' Dunk said, 'soon. We just want to find my sister.'

'Hmph.'

Dunk raised an eyebrow at M'Grash. 'I miss her, buddy. She's my sister. I love her.'

'What about M'Grash?'

'You're my best pal. She's my sister. Two different things, see? One can't replace the other.' He put his hand on M'Grash's arm. 'Don't worry. She can't replace you. No one can.'

M'Grash clapped Dunk on the back and nearly sent him sprawling along the beach. 'Sorry!' the ogre said.

Dunk looked back and saw that M'Grash was grinning. He knew everything would be all right.

'We ready?' Dunk said as he approached the others.

Dirk nodded, as did Spinne. Lästiges frowned, and Slick looked away. Jiminy whistled a little tune.

'What?'

'Lästiges and I aren't coming, son,' Slick said. 'We'd just get in the way. We'll stay behind and make sure M'Grash and Edgar don't lose the boat.'

Dunk thought about this. 'You're part of the team. We need you.'

'Yes,' said Lästiges, 'but not right now. We each have our roles to play, and a reporter and an agent don't belong on a reconnaissance mission.'

'What about a singer?' Dunk said to Jiminy.

'As a singer, I have no right to come along with you. Truth be told, I'd rather not. The lady there wasn't kidding when she went on about the Amazons as a warrior tribe. Any one of those lovely ladies could kick my ass into the ocean. And after they got through with my donkey they could kick my butt too.'

Jiminy waited for a laugh but got none. 'Sorry about that. Trying too hard for the jokes again?'

'It's a little too true to be funny at the moment,' Slick said. 'Try it again when this is all done.'

'So you're staying here,' Dunk said to Jiminy.

'Afraid not,' the man said with a grimace. 'Seems I'm the closest thing to a guide around here you got. Me and the Moral Reefers have been out here a few times to entertain the ladies, and, ah, help them repopulate the island, if you know what I mean.'

'I thought men weren't allowed here,' said Spinne.

'They can't live here, but they can visit,' Jiminy said, 'some for longer than others. They raise their kids all the same. Once the boys hit puberty, though, they're on the first boat out of here.'

'What happens to them?' Lästiges asked. Her camra, which she'd finally taken back from Dunk, focused on the man, waiting for his answer.

'You're looking at an Amazon Island alumni,' he said.

'You? And all the Moral Reefers?'

'Where do you think guys like us come from around these parts? They don't fly us in from Altdorf for the rainy season.'

'So you know Amazon Island,' said Dunk.

'Like it was my home.' Jiminy winked. 'Exactly like that, in fact.'

'THAT'S IT,' JIMINY said in a soft voice, pointing at a clearing cut out of the jungle ahead. 'Home.'

Torches flickered in the clearing, illuminating the edges of huts and other structures scattered about the place. There weren't streets so much as spaces between the buildings. The land was nothing more than sand, after all, and Dunk hadn't seen or heard a single beast of burden on any of the islands they'd been on so far.

The Amazons got around the old-fashioned way, on foot. Dunk had only seen a few of them strolling along the sandy paths, and they'd all reminded him of Enojada: tall, muscular, tanned, and blonde. He hadn't seen any children at all, but he supposed they went to bed soon after dark or were at least called into their homes.

The huts had grass or bamboo sides and thatched roofs. Not one of them had a door on the entrance, and the windows all stood open too. The village stood close enough to the sea for a breeze to caress the place. It caressed the place steadily, keeping the biting insects away. With night having fallen, the temperatures had cooled to something reasonable. Perfect sleeping weather, as Dunk's mother would have called it.

'Now what?' Dunk said quietly. 'Where do we go from here?'

Jiminy pointed to the nearest hut. 'Why do you think I brought you all the way around here?'

'To avoid the guards?'

Jiminy smiled. 'The Amazons depend on their reputation more than their swords to protect this place. They haven't had an attempted invasion since long before I was born, and thieves and bandits are almost as rare.'

'What do they do to such people when they catch them?' Spinne asked.

Jiminy sucked at his teeth. 'They're almost always male, of course. Women don't come out to attack Amazon Island. Join, sure, but not attack.'

'What do they do?' Dirk asked, growing impatient.

'They take the men, hogtie them, and string them up by their genitals in the sun. Never seen anyone last for more than an hour that way.'

No one said anything.

Dunk sidled forward. 'Let's be sure not to get caught.'

'That's your sister's place right there,' Jiminy said, pointing at a large hut right in front of them. 'We should be able to slip in through the rear window.'

Dunk took a closer look at the place. While Kirta's hut was larger than most, it was made of the same materials as the rest. A torch on a stick flickered near the front corner, and somewhere inside the home several lamps burned, keeping back the night.

With a glance at Dirk, Dunk moved forward. He crept up to the edge of the wide window set in the rear of the hut and peered inside.

The room beyond the window lay in dimness, separated from the rest of the building not by walls but by translucent curtains. Through the fabric, Dunk could see a light burning at table height to the left and to the right. A third flickered a bit farther away, probably outside the hut's door.

Dirk, Spinne, and Jiminy crawled up beside Dunk and looked into the room too. They all waited for a long moment for something to happen. When nothing did, Dunk slipped over the window's edge and into the hut.

He was in a bedchamber. A four-poster bed that looked like it must have been imported from Altdorf stood to one side, and a massive wardrobe loomed to the other. The floor was nothing more than hard-packed sand.

Dunk heard something scratching in the outer room. After listening for a moment, he realised it was the sound of a pen on paper. Encouraged by this, he reached back and helped the others through the window and into the room.

When they were all inside, Dunk realised that the scratching had stopped. He held his hand up for the others to remain silent. They had to somehow figure

out if Kirta was alone. If so, they had to reveal themselves to her in a way that wouldn't surprise her so
much that she started screaming for help right away.

Dunk crept closer to the curtain, walking on the
balls of his feet to minimise even the tiniest noises
on the sand. As he neared the edge of the curtain
that separated the bedchamber from the rest of the
hut, he reached out for it slowly. He saw that there
were actually two curtains that met in the middle,
and he meant to part them with his hand and peek
through.

He did so, and saw the simple chamber beyond. It
contained a small table and chairs for dining, a writ-
ing desk and chair covered with ink-spattered papers,
a hammock strung near a window in the opposite
wall, and a door next to that. A pair of cabinets stood
against the wall to the left, and a rack filled with
weaponry sat on the ground to the right.

No one was there.

Dunk pulled the curtain apart a little farther. 'Kirta,'
he whispered. 'Kirta?'

A blade sliced towards Dunk from the left. He
ducked to avoid it and threw himself backward, bowl-
ing over the others in the path of the sword. It cut a
neat slit through the curtain, which then sagged away
from the top of the fabric, separated partially, but not
detached.

A face appeared in the hole. It belonged to a beautiful young woman with bronzed skin and black hair.
Her eyes flashed with anger, and she brought the
sword back up to strike again.

'Kirta!' Dunk said. 'Kirta! It's us!'

The woman froze. Then her sword moved through the air in three quick cuts, and the rest of the curtain fell to the ground. She backed off, unwilling to step into a darkened room.

'Come out here where I can see you,' she said. 'If this is some kind of trick, you can be sure you'll pay with your lives.'

Her voice was lower than Dunk remembered, and it featured a harder edge. He hoped the years had been kind to her. He wondered if she'd think they'd been kind to him.

Dunk stepped out into the light, his hands held palm out before him. Spinne came in on his left, while Dirk joined them on his right.

Kirta, the woman, not the girl that Dunk had thought dead for so many years, took a stunned step back and dropped her sword. 'Y-you made it,' she said.

Her voice cracked as she spoke, and tears welled in her eyes. A moment later, she launched herself at Dunk and Dirk and gathered them into a rib-cracking three-way embrace. She held them that way for a long time, and her brothers returned her grasp just as tightly.

'I thought I might never see you again,' she said, her voice barely a whisper. 'Even after spotting you in the Blood Bowl championship, I never thought I'd find a way to, to…'

Just as hard as she'd come at them, Kirta shoved her brothers away. 'You have to leave,' she said, her voice and hands trembling with fear. 'You have to leave now.'

Dunk and Dirk glanced at each other, and then turned to their sister. 'But we just got here,' Dunk said. 'There's so much we want to ask you about.'

'No time for that now,' Kirta said, her fear transforming into resolve. 'You must leave. You're putting us all in horrible danger! I'll see you at the tournament. It will have to wait until then.'

'We can't wait that long,' said Dunk. 'We want to talk with you now.'

Kirta groaned. 'The tournament starts tomorrow evening. You can't hold out that long?'

'Tomorrow?' Dunk said. 'But I thought we had plenty of time.'

'The volcano's ready,' Kirta said. 'The games start. You need to go.'

'But wait!' Dirk said. 'We're not just going to turn around and leave without some sort of explanation.'

'I think you owe them that,' Jiminy said, stepping from the darkness.

Kirta's jaw dropped at the sight of the singer. 'You! What are you doing here? With them?'

'Now, darling–'

'Darling?' Dunk and Dirk spoke in unison as their heads snapped around to stare at Jiminy, and then at their sister, and each other.

'Darling,' Jiminy said again, 'we all just want to see how you're doing.'

Kirta stepped forward and punched Jiminy in the shoulder. The singer yelped and pranced away. 'You should know better,' she said. 'You do know better. Get them out of here, now!'

As she spoke the last word, the lights in Kirta's home all went out at once. A chill breeze blew through the place, cutting into their skins like frozen knives.

'Too late,' Kirta said with a moan. 'Too damned late.'

'What's going on?' Dunk said. He reached for Spinne with one hand and for Kirta with the other.

'She's here,' Kirta said.

To punctuate that, someone let loose with a howling scream of agony that Dunk thought might freeze the blood in his veins.

'Who?' Dunk said. It was the only question he could think to ask. His brain urged him to stop talking and leave the damned place, but his feet didn't seem to want to move.

'It's Mother,' Kirta said, 'she's come home.'

'Who dares intrude upon the home of my daughter?'

Although the lights in the hut had all been snuffed out, Dunk could still see the apparition swirling in the air under Kirta's high, thatched roof. The pale, translucent figure glowed softly in the dark as it circled overhead, extenuated by its movements, but still recognisably his mother.

At least her face looked the same. She clearly wasn't herself any longer. Only her spirit must have survived that fateful night in Altdorf. She was nothing more, or less, than a ghost.

'Mother?' Dirk said, sounding very much like a little, lost boy.

Dunk cringed. First, he feared how his mother would react at seeing them, even if she had been alive. She had always been notoriously protective of them throughout their childhood, and she hadn't had the luxury of seeing them grow into strong, confident, Blood Bowl hardened men.

Second, whatever was swirling over their heads wasn't really their mother as they knew her. It was a ghost. Dunk didn't want to get into the metaphysical questions about whether or not it was his mother's spirit or some strange creature that happened to be around at the moment of his mother's death, and had imprinted upon her strongly enough at that most intense moment for it to believe it was his mother's spirit. In the end, a ghost could be nothing but trouble.

The ghost swung high into the peaked ceiling and glared down at the people in the hut. She seemed like she could see straight through each of them, but she'd been that way in life as well. Not liking what she saw, she threw back her head and shrieked.

Dunk and the others clapped their hands to their ears in a vain attempt to protect themselves from the painful noise. They fell to their knees, their eyes watering as they begged for it to stop. Somewhere, glasses shattered, dogs howled, bats fell from the sky, and babies wept.

'Stop it, Mother!' Dunk shouted. 'Knock it off!'

The screeching stopped as if someone had turned off a tap. Dunk's ears rang so loud from the racket that for a moment he didn't notice what had happened. When he finally opened his eyes and looked up, he saw his mother's ghost staring down at him.

'Dunkel?' she said in a soft, stunned howl. 'Dirk? Boys? Is it really you?'

Dunk stood up, and Dirk joined him, just a half-step behind. Both of them stood shaky on their feet.

'Yes, Mother,' Dunk said.

For a ghost, Greta Hoffnung seemed fairly calm and stable. Not that she'd been either of those things in life. Dunk had spent a good deal of his childhood trying to worm out from under her oppressive ways. The rest of the time he'd spent being punished every time he was caught, which was more often than he cared to think about.

'Oh, my boys, my precious boys!' Greta swooped down and tried to take Dunk and Dirk in her arms, but she only managed to sweep right through them instead. To Dunk, it felt like walking through a freezing breeze.

Greta swung around behind them and back to the spot where she'd been hovering before. 'Oh, the humanity!' she said with a horrifying moan. 'The cruelty that we should be reunited, finally, and I not be able to hold you in my arms. How could the gods be so petty and mean?'

Dunk shrugged, pretty sure that the gods hadn't had anything to do with this. Greta had always been strictly religious, which is perhaps what had turned Dunk off from the various churches she attended to appease all the different gods in the human pantheon. He wondered how death had affected that in her, especially since she hadn't found herself hauled into the heavens for the just rewards a righteous woman deserved.

'Oh, you've never given the gods the respect they deserve,' she said grimly. 'Why should you start now? After all, you have me as such a horrible example.'

Greta broke down entirely, and sobbed uncontrollably. Despite her nature, Dunk wanted to reach out and hold her, to pat her on the back and comfort her. For all the differences they'd had over the years, she was still his mother, and Dunk still loved her.

At the moment, Dunk felt no sadness for his mother, and he wondered why that would be. He supposed he'd mourned both her and Kirta years ago, when he'd first thought they were dead, and he'd used all his tears up then. The fact that Kirta was alive and in the same room with Dirk and him thrilled him to no end, but the fact that their mother's ghost hovered over them gave him chills.

'What happened?' Dunk asked Kirta. He hoped he might get Greta's mind off of the present by talking about the past, plus, he really wanted to know. 'I thought you were killed the night the mob stormed the keep in Altdorf.'

Kirta didn't answer. She was too busy staring up at Greta's ghost with a look of mingled disgust and fear on her face. Dirk gave her an elbow in the ribs and jerked his head at Dunk. Startled, she finally turned to Dunk and spoke loudly to be audible over Greta's wailing.

'That creep Lehrer brought us down to the keep's front gate. He told us that Father had sent him to bring us to safety. At the time, I didn't realise that he'd had a thing with Mother. I just thought he was doing his job.

'I trusted him.'

Greta paused to collect her thoughts. The memories of that fateful night clearly still troubled her. Dunk wondered if she might sometimes dream about it on the darkest nights of the year, much like he did.

'When we got to the gate, Lehrer revealed his plot. He told us that he'd arranged it so that we could go away together and leave you and Father. He tried to spin some pack of lies about Father being involved with the Blood God.'

Dunk squirmed in his boots until Kirta stopped and stared at him. 'That's not true is it? Tell me that's not true.'

'I'd love to. I really would.'

Kirta folded her arms across her chest. 'Who told you? Was it Lehrer? You can't believe a word he says.'

'Father told me.'

'He confessed his sins to you as he died that day? How noble!'

Dunk grimaced. 'We found out about it last year when Father resurfaced. I lost track of him after the riot. I thought everyone was dead but me, and Dirk, of course, but he'd left years before that.'

'I was the smart one,' said Dirk. He stared uneasily at the sobbing ghost. Her tears flowed away from her like wisps of mist, dissolving into nothing before they hit the ground.

'Hey!' Dunk and Kirta said together.

'You two stuck around with a domineering woman and a man who sold us all to a Lord of Chaos. You tell me who was the wiser.'

'We didn't know.'

'You didn't want to know. You didn't want to admit that something was wrong, but I knew it. I knew it from when I was a kid. That's why I got out when I did.'

'And left us behind.' Kirta smacked Dirk in the shoulder. Her eyes flared at him. 'Thanks for nothing!

If you were so sure, why'd you just leave us to the dragons?'

'I didn't know for sure,' Dirk said, raising his arms as a shield.

'You were sure enough to leave home. Wait!' She turned to Dunk. 'Father's alive?'

Dunk frowned. 'He was, right up until the Blood Bowl tournament last year. He played with us, for the Hackers. Lehrer played for the Chaos All-Stars. I would have thought you'd seen the highlights.'

Kirta clutched at her chest. 'I didn't see the actual game. We only have one crystal ball here on the island, and the elders use it for the big games. We just get the reports.'

She looked down at the ground. 'That's why it took me so long to realise that Dunk was playing Blood Bowl.' She shot Dirk a dirty look. 'I'd have figured out about you earlier if you hadn't changed your name.'

'Dunk knew about my new name.'

'Well, I didn't. Our parents sheltered me from such things. I think they thought I might be too delicate to handle the horrors of the real world.' She looked up at Greta's ghost. 'We can all see how well that worked out.'

'How DID YOU survive that day?' Dunk was determined to keep pressing her on this until he got an answer.

'Mother refused Lehrer's advances, and he threw open the gate to the keep. 'There they are!' he shouted to the mob. He ran away while they rushed us and tried to tear us to bits.'

Greta stopped, choking up, but forced herself to go on. 'Mother saved me. She threw herself over me to protect me from the mob, and they killed her almost instantly. She had such a death grip on me I could barely breathe. By the time the rioters pried her fingers off of me, her ghost had already come back to haunt them.'

Dunk's jaw dropped.

'I suppose when eternal vengeance wants to get started it wants to get started right away,' said Jiminy.

'We escaped down the Reik. Well, I did, and Mother's ghost shadowed every step of my voyage. In Marienburg, I tried to get away from her by slipping aboard a ship that set sail at dawn, but she found me.

'Unfortunately, I hadn't figured out where the ship was heading, and by the time the crew found me it was too late for them to drop me somewhere else. We were heading for the Scorpion Coast, where the captain of the ship auctioned me off on the slave block. Fortunately, the Lusties purchased the rights to me rather than some of the more unsavoury types in Tlaxtlan.'

She allowed a faint smile to cross her face as she looked up at her brothers. 'And that's how I ended up here.'

'And a fine thing that you did too,' Greta's ghost said. 'If you'd just listened to me instead of always doing the exact opposite of whatever I say, only out of spite, you never would have had to face such tribulations.'

The ghost had stopped sobbing. She seemed collected and rational, but Dunk knew it had to be a façade. He hoped that she'd been wailing too loud to hear everything they'd been talking about, but she soon shattered his hopes on that count.

'When I heard your father had survived the incident, I was thrilled,' the ghost said. 'The news of his death disappoints me more than anything your sister has done since I died, and let me tell you that is a high mark to have to top.'

Kirta rolled her eyes. Then she leaned in close to her brothers and whispered to them, 'Get ready to run.'

Dunk and Dirk shot her confused looks, but she ignored them to listen to whatever their mother was ranting about.

'I said, 'I wish I could have seen him one last time.''

'Why is that, Mother?' Dunk asked.

'So I could take my revenge on that multiply-damned son of a bitch!'

The ghost seemed to grow with her rage, expanding to fill the whole of the space under Kirta's ceiling. Dunk had seen this before, back when his mother had been breathing. She was only moments away from a full and complete meltdown, and there was little that he or anyone else could do to stop it.

Back when Greta had been alive, Lügner, Dunk's father, had always had some kind of extraordinary power over her. No matter how wound up or psychotic she got, he could always talk her down from the edge. With him gone, though, she'd have lost any sense of restraint.

'He never meant to hurt you,' Dunk said. 'He never meant to hurt any of us.'

'Well, he blew that all to hell then, didn't he?' Greta's voice became more shrill with every syllable.

'Why are you defending him?' Dirk said. 'You're only making her mad.'

'Don't take her side. You always took her side.'

'Somebody had to. Between you and Father, she never had a chance.'

'She didn't deserve one!'

Dunk stopped. He hadn't realised he still had such strong feelings about his mother. He thought he'd buried all that when she'd died, but seeing her ghost brought it all surging back.

'Father died a hero,' Dunk said, trying to scramble back from the edge. 'You were there. You saw him.'

Dirk nodded. 'He lived like a villain though. That's what drove me out of our home. You were just blind to it. You didn't want to see it.'

Dunk clenched his fist. This was how it had always started with them when they were kids. They'd start talking and end up shouting. Then one of them would take a swing at the other, and they'd wind up in a brawl that would shake down the walls.

The last time Dunk and Dirk had a knock-down, drag-out fight, they'd thrown each other out of the window of a dwarf tavern set in the side of a cliff face, a hundred feet above the sea. That sobering experience had put a check on their future arguments, cutting them short at mere bickering.

Now, though, Dunk could feel that restriction slipping away.

'If you folks would pardon me for getting involved in a family feud, I think I might be able to help,' Jiminy said.

All eyes snapped to focus on the singer.

'Now I don't know most of you all that well. Some of you I know better than I'd like, and others I'm sure I'd like better if I knew you more... I think.'

Kirta gave Jiminy a hand signal to hurry up whatever he had to say. He cleared his throat and started again.

'Y'all love each other and should be happy that you're all back together again. Think about how much you missed each other all those years you were apart. Then you'll realise how petty you're being.'

With each of the singer's words, Dunk's anger faded. He blushed with shame at his words and his actions, and he wanted nothing more than to ask for forgiveness for his stupidity. Before he could say anything, though, Greta's ghost spoke.

'What is *he* doing here?'

She punched the word 'he' as if she could drive the man through the back wall of the hut with the force of the pronoun alone.

Jiminy put up his hands in a placating gesture. 'Now, Mrs Hoffnung, I'm just trying to help. I brought your sons here to see you, and I figured you'd enjoy that. Believe me, I have nothing but the most honourable intentions with regard to your daughter.'

Dunk gaped at Jiminy and then Kirta. 'You two know each other,' Spinne said. 'That's how you knew just which hut to go to. You grew up here, but you left years ago, long before Kirta wound up here.'

'And he has been banned from this hut,' the ghost said, 'forbidden from ever returning!'

'Run!' Kirta said to the men, not bothering to whisper any longer. 'Run!'

'There can only be one penalty for such poor behaviour,' Greta's ghost said. 'Death! Death! Death!'

'You'll pardon my saying so, ma'am,' Jiminy said as he backed towards the open window behind him, 'but that sounds like three penalties.'

Dunk grabbed Spinne by the hand and dashed for the window. Dirk came hot on their heels, with Jiminy right behind him. As they moved, the air behind them turned as cold and biting as a blizzard.

Dunk put his hands down to form a cradle, and Spinne used them to vault out through the open window. Dirk did the same, any beef he had with his brother long forgotten. Jiminy made the leap without Dunk's help, vaulting over the windowsill with an ease that could only come from many chances to practise.

As Jiminy cleared the window, Dunk looked to Kirta. 'Go!' she screamed at him. 'She'll stay with me. She never leaves.'

Dunk blew her a quick kiss, much as they used to do when they were kids, and then dived through the window. As he did, the ghost's hands closed around one of his ankles, and he felt it begin to freeze solid. The colder it grew, the more solid the fingers felt, and he knew if he could not get away fast he would be trapped there for what little might be left of his life.

Dunk drew back his good foot and lashed out with it. His boot swished right through his mother's face, disrupting it as if it were made of smoke. It re-formed a moment later, and the ghost screeched at him.

'Dunkel! You've been a very bad boy!'

'Mother!' Dunk spun in her grasp, but she wouldn't let go. Her grip grew stronger by the moment, and Dunk knew that he only had seconds until she froze his leg solid, and perhaps the rest of him as well.

'Mother!' He shouted at her, needing her attention. As enraged as she was, he didn't know if she'd even hear him. 'You're killing me!'

He felt hands on him, and he looked back to see that Spinne and Dirk had come back for him, each of them grabbing one of his arms. They pulled as hard as they could, but they could not yank him free of the ghost's grasp.

Dunk knew what he had to do, as distasteful as it might be. He couldn't harm his mother's ghost with his hands or feet, and she was too strong for him at any rate. All he had left were words.

'Greta!' He shouted her name until she looked him in the eyes, until he could be sure she would hear what he had to say. 'Mother! I have always hated you! You were a terrible mother, and I! Always! Hated! You!'

Shocked at Dunk's venom, the ghost recoiled, releasing his foot as she went. Dirk and Spinne hauled him out through the hut's window and half-carried him into the jungle beyond as fast as they could.

As Dunk tried to get his frozen foot back beneath him, Dirk and Spinne each got under one of his arms and hustled him along. When it was clear that the ghost had not followed them into the jungle, nor any Amazons either, Dunk heard Dirk giggling like a little boy.

'What is so damned funny?' Dunk said. The feeling had started to return to his foot, and it tingled so hard it hurt.

'I'm just so jealous,' Dirk said as he squashed his laughter.

'Of having our mother's ghost try to rip my leg off?'

Dirk shook his head, still smiling. 'Of what you said. I've wanted to tell her that for years.'

When they reached the beach, Dunk decided that they should leave the island right away. 'With all the screeching from Mother's ghost, half the island has to

be looking for us by now. I'd like to be halfway back
to Columbo's Island before they reach this beach.'

'Don't you worry about that,' Jiminy said. He'd got
to the beach first and scouted it out to make sure no
one was waiting there for them, besides Edgar, Slick,
Lästiges and M'Grash, of course.

'I think he has a point,' said Slick. 'I could hear that
racket from here.'

Jiminy shook his head. 'Sad to say, but no one who
lives on the island is going to pay any attention to
that. We hear it all far too often.'

'You're kidding,' Dunk said. His mother's shrieks
still rang in his ears. 'I'd have thought they'd have run
Kirta out of town by now if that was true.'

Jiminy winced. 'There's been a lot of talk about that
for sure, but anytime someone even approaches Kirta
about it, Greta comes out and scares them away.
Kirta's talked about leaving, but the owners of the
Lusties don't want to let her out of her contract. She's
the best catcher they've ever had.'

'Blood Bowl must run in the family,' Slick said, smiling at Dunk.

The thought was little comfort to Dunk. He took
pride in doing well anything he put his mind to, but
playing Blood Bowl had always made him more
than a little uncomfortable. Besides the physical
injuries he sustained, the fact that he made his living in such a violent way bothered him. He
sometimes dreamed of giving it all up, retiring to
the family keep, or perhaps a secluded island off the
coast of Magritta, and settling down with Spinne to
raise a pack of kids.

Seeing his mother again reminded him that his own childhood had not been a particularly happy one. His parents had provided for him, Dirk and Kirta. The Hoffnungs had long been one of the wealthiest noble families in Altdorf, after all, but Lügner and Greta had always had a relationship with their children that was distant, even at its best.

As much as Dunk hated to admit it, the words he'd shouted at his mother's ghost had more than a little truth to them. Lügner had sold his family to Khorne, the Blood God, and Dunk was certain his mother had to have known something about it. At the very least, she was guilty of living in denial about something that had endangered every one of their lives.

'Let's hope not,' Dunk said quietly to Slick.

'All right,' Dunk said to the group. 'We'll camp here tonight. It's too dark to try to row out of here, unless we're being chased, and as hard as it is for me to believe it, I haven't heard anyone crashing through the jungle after us yet. We'll stay the night on the beach, close to the boat in case we need to make a quick get-away.'

He looked to Edgar. 'Are you all right with taking the watch again?'

'Aren't I bloody always?' the treeman said. He made a half-hearted attempt at a grumble, but Dunk could tell that Edgar was happy to have something useful to do.

'We'll have to get you going first thing in the morning to reach Tobazco in time for the first game,' Jiminy said as he built a fire from driftwood for the crew to gather around.

'You think Big Richard will make good on his pledge to have the rest of the team there?' Dunk asked as he settled down next to Spinne.

'I'd bet on it,' said Slick. 'The pygmy halflings want to win a game more than they want another meal. They probably already have the others there and registered.'

'Let's hope they're sweating bullets about us not being there yet,' said Dirk. 'Given the chance, I'm going to stomp all over our new team-mates, accidentally, of course.'

'That's not much of a fair fight,' said Dunk.

'Who said anything about a fair fight? This is Blood Bowl.'

The others all laughed, but Dunk stayed silent. After a long moment, when they'd all laid down to sleep, he spoke.

'If playing Blood Bowl means stomping on people the size of small children, I'm not so sure I'm interested in playing.'

'It was a joke, Dunk,' said Dirk. 'Don't take it so seriously.'

'Blood Bowl's always been a joke to you,' said Dunk. 'Maybe it should be more than that.'

'How?' said Lästiges. 'It a game. It's the greatest game in the world, but it's still only a game.'

'Only a game?' said Slick, sitting up, indignant. 'Tell me I'm not hearing you right. There is nothing better than Blood Bowl, nothing!'

'What about peace?' Dunk asked. 'What about going to work each day and not wondering if you'll be killed, or if you'll have to kill someone else?'

'Have to?' said Dirk. 'You mean "get to".'

The laughter from the others was more uneasy this time.

'What are you going to do?' Dirk asked. 'Quit? You're a star player on the world championship team. Slick's cut one hell of a deal for you. That's not the kind of thing you walk away from.'

'Why not?' asked Dunk. 'We have the family fortune back, such as it is, and I have my earnings from the last three years. If I wanted, I would never have to work again, much less pick up a football. Same goes for you, Spinne, Edgar, and M'Grash too.'

Silence fell over the crew so hard that Dunk thought he could hear the twinkling of the stars.

'I like playing Blood Bowl.'

It took Dunk a moment to realise that the words had come from Spinne's mouth. He got up on his side to look at her as she lay next to him in the sand.

'I enjoy it. Sure, there's the gold and the glory and the fame that goes with all that, but I honestly love the game.'

Dunk tried to swallow this, but found it went down hard. 'You enjoy murdering people?'

Spinne smacked him lightly on the arm to tell him to stop being silly. 'That's only one part of the game, and not the main one. I enjoy the athleticism, the competition, the sensation you feel when you slip past the defence to snag a pass in the end zone. That's all very real to me and has nothing to do with killing anyone.'

'Check her stats, son,' said Slick. 'Her kills-per-game ratio is lower than yours.'

Dunk considered this for a moment. 'I don't try to kill anyone when I play,' said Dunk. 'It just happens.'

Dunk could almost hear Dirk rolling his eyes in the darkness. 'Are you the guy who just bought part of a team?' Dirk said. 'I think that makes you more complicit than any of us. You're supporting a pack of killers. You help pay their salaries.'

'I did that so we could come here to find our sister.'

'You could have just sailed here on your own. You didn't need to bring everybody else.'

'Pegleg held my contract over me–'

'Please,' said Lästiges. 'Isn't that what you pay Slick for? Are you saying he couldn't have got you out of your contract, at least for a little while?'

Slick cleared his throat. 'Perhaps, perhaps, perhaps, but this was the cleanest route to travel. When you're one of the team's owners, people ask a lot fewer uncomfortable questions.'

'I play this game because I have to,' Dunk said. 'I was flat broke when I started.'

'But you aren't now,' said Lästiges, 'and that's not what I asked.'

'I-I don't know,' Dunk said. He fell silent, and no one else said a word.

One by one, everyone but Edgar fell asleep, their snores forming a shore side symphony that overpowered the sound of the surf. Dunk lay awake for a long time, thinking about what they'd said.

30

'WELCOME TO THE Tobazco Bowl, Blood Bowl fans, for what is being billed as the first true word championship in Blood Bowl history! The best teams of the New World are set to face off against the Bad Bay Hackers, the best of the Old, in a battle for bragging rights the world over. Isn't that right, Bob?'

'So right I'm turning in that direction, Jim! I haven't seen this kind of hype for a four-team tournament since the NAF disbanded. Commissioner Roze-El really knew how to whip the fans into a frenzy, and it looks like the teams of Lustria do too!'

'I understand that's mostly thanks to the Lustrian Lusties, the Amazon team, and their ace promoter Enojada. Without her advances, the Hackers would never have even known about this tournament, much less agreed to take part in it!'

'Do we have to listen to this dreck?' Dunk asked.

Pegleg glared at him and at the rest of the Hackers who'd been squirming in their seats since before the Cabalvision broadcast had begun. 'Because of you and your damned, miniature "sponsors", Mr Hoffnung, we haven't had any time to scout out our opponents, so yes, we will sit here and suffer through this entire pre-game show.'

'What about a pep talk?' asked Dirk. 'We always get a lot out of those. Won't this cut into your quality ranting time?'

Pegleg stared at Dirk as if he thought keelhauling him through a lake of sewage might be too good for him. 'You remember the speech I gave before the Blood Bowl tournament championship game?'

Dirk, silenced by Pegleg's menace, nodded. So did everyone else in the room.

'Mull that over in your head while we watch these idiots, Mr Heldmann, and keep your mouth shut.'

Every pair of eyes turned towards the large crystal ball that took up most of one side of the room.

'After the disastrous Dungeonbowl fiasco this year, Blood Bowl fans are hungry for a special treat!' said Bob.

Jim nodded along. 'I've never seen the College of Wizards so angry! I suppose that's what happens when the Oldheim Ogres decide to destroy the entire underground stadium as soon as they go up by a touchdown!'

'From their point of view, it was a flawless strategy,' said Bob. 'Start to win, end the game. If you can't play any longer, then the team in the lead must be the winner!'

'It all fell apart when they broke into the VIP box and devoured all the Verifiably Insane Panderers! Without that cabal of advertising agents, financial support for the event collapsed! We can only hope they'll manage to pull everything back together in time for next year's major.'

'There's an excellent chance of that. Even before the dust settled over the stadium, the PAs, Pandering Assistants, were making plans to move out of their cubicles and into their bosses' offices. Once the succession wars are over, we should have the right people in place to make sure that next year's Dungeonbowl goes off without a hitch!'

'I don't think they'll invite the Oldheim Ogres back to play again though!'

'I wouldn't say that! The footage of their demise is the most watched show on BooTube, the new ghost-run aggregation of shows too short and silly to show on a real Cabalvision network!'

'I thought that was only for goblin-stompers and other go-to-sleep aids!'

'Our boss here on the Wolf Network, Ruprect Murdark, just bought the Ghost Writers behind BooTube for several dozen sets of polished gold chains with Advanced Rattling Technology, so you can expect to see a lot more of *Funniest Horrible Accidents* rejects soon on a crystal ball near you!'

'Thankfully, we have a hot series of games here for you this weekend to make up for the astonishing lack in our schedule that old clips on BooTube can't begin to fill.'

'First up,' Bob Bifford said in his ogrish way, 'it's the Hackers, under the auspices of their local sponsors the

Sacrifice Flies, versus the all-lizardman team, the Ssservants of the Ssslann!'

'Isn't their name just Servants of the Slann? Or are you trying to mimic the local accent again?'

'No, look! It's written on the copy just like that!'

'Who taught you how to read? Or how to pronounce auspices? I thought you'd been forbidden from lessons after having your last tutor for dinner.'

'True, but she was delicious! Wolf Sports put me into an intense language camp, with wizards enchanting the words directly into my brain with little machines with glowing screens!'

'Still, how did they get anything to stick in that mind of yours when everything else failed?'

'Torture! Every time I got a word wrong, they removed one of my fingers!'

Bob held up his hand. All the fingers were there, but they'd been reattached at the wrong angles, often with the joints twisted in the wrong directions.

'Good thing they had an apothecary on the premises!' said Jim.

'I'll say! I went through each hand and foot at least six times!'

'I thought you were walking a little funny… er, than usual!'

'Anyhow, after the prime match-up, which is being played early to accommodate our viewers back in the Old World, we'll have the second part of our double-header: the lovely ladies of the Lustrian Lusties pitted against the Skaven Scab-Eaters.'

'I hear the Lusties are heavily favoured in that game,' said Jim. 'Word is that the skaven captain chewed off his right arm after a date with a particularly ugly cheerleader last night, and it has yet to grow back!'

'That seems like it should set up a final confrontation between the Hacker-Flies and the Lusties tomorrow!'

'Tell me, Bob, why do they play the games so close together?'

'For the answer to that, let's go to our roving reporter, Lästiges Weibchen! Lästiges?'

The scene shifted to show Lästiges standing on the edge of a field outlined in the bowl of an active volcano. Lava glowed along one side of the pitch and showed in cracks throughout the entire playing surface.

'Thanks, Bob!' said Lästiges. 'I'm here with Madre Caliente, the groundskeeper for the Lusties, who claim the Tobazco Bowl as their home field. Tell me Madre, what is it about this playing surface that makes it so special?'

The camra swivelled to focus on a woman whom Dunk had no doubt had once had men chasing after her for as long as they could manage to avoid slipping in each others' drool. Her skin had seen so many seasons of tan, though, that it had become as wrinkled as a shepherd's jacket. The only exception to this was her face, on which her skin had been pulled back so tightly that it looked like her features had been drawn on the outside of a baby-smooth football. She wore a bright yellow bikini that offered precious little protection from the sunlight that had ravaged her so regularly over the years. Her smile, though, seemed natural, except for how blindingly white it stood out against her bronzed skin.

'Well, Lassie, you don't mind if I call you that, do you?'

'Actually–'

'As I was saying, Lassie, this volcano explodes, like, once a year, you know? Right about this same time, kinda like a cute little clock, except, of course, it's big and deadly.'

'Why would anyone want to play Blood Bowl on such a deadly surface? Are the Lusties all crazy?'

'Like the hot, little foxes they are! The pitch is so hot, you know, that you can barely wear armour at all. That's why our girls wear bikinis on the field instead of all that stifling, restricting stuff. Those silly people who refuse to loosen up usually end up passing out from heat stroke before halftime. We even saw a tree-man burst into flames once!'

Edgar yowled in sympathy from the back of the room.

'What did you do?'

'Well, thankfully, I always keep a fresh supply of marshmallows in the dugout. We just broke off some of his branches – they were so dry, you know, I don't think he knew anything about a proper moisturising regimen, and then we had ourselves a tasty little roast right there on the field. After the Lusties scored, of course. Go, Lusties!'

'But why now? Certainly there are better times to play a match than just before an eruption.'

'You'd think so, wouldn't you?' Caliente winked at the camra. 'If you were a bunch of wussies! It's just a little lava. What's a second degree burn? That's how I keep my skin looking so young and fresh!'

'But isn't there a danger that the field will explode while the players are on it?'

'Oh, sure! Happens all the time.'

'But that's not a concern?'

'Oh, honey, a volcano's just like a man. It rumbles a lot and gets really steamed sometimes, but once it does its burning-hot business, it calms right down again.

'The key is to know when to get out of the way. We almost never lose a whole team, usually just a player or two, mostly catchers for some reason.' She scratched her head, and her scalp wiggled back and forth.

'Until then, though, that soft, hot surface is the best thing in the world to play on, you know. I love it so much I sometimes lay down on it and roll around on it. I rub my whole body on it until I feel toasty warm, inside and out!'

'There you have it!' Lästiges said to the camra. 'A playing surface that's deadly when toyed with, um, improperly. Hope the team apothecaries have vats of burn ointment lined up. They're going to need them! Back to you, Bob!'

Pegleg shut the crystal ball off. All eyes in the room turned to Dr Pill.

'What?' the cranky, old apothecary said. Like the rest of the team, he seemed no worse the wear for his time with the pygmy halflings. In fact, he seemed more relaxed than Dunk had ever seen him. That hadn't blunted his attitude though. 'Suck it up, you pansies.'

'You have to be kidding me, coach,' Dunk said as he stood in the dugout dressed in nothing but his helmet, boots, and shorts. 'We'll get killed.'

The other players on the team grumbled in agreement. None of them liked this arrangement.

'I feel naked,' said Spinne, who at least got to wear a short shirt in addition to her shorts.

'I can help you out of those last bits, baby,' Getrunken said. He was intoxicated again, although Dunk couldn't say for sure on what. His eyes looked like they'd been open for days, and he stank of some kind of burnt weed.

'Aren't you going to defend her honour?' Hernd asked Dunk.

Dunk looked at her like she was insane. 'Have you met Spinne?' he asked. 'She doesn't need my help. More to the point, she doesn't want it. I used to try to help her out with things like this.'

'And?'

'Watch.'

Getrunken draped a long, lazy arm around Spinne's shoulders and let his hand rest on her breast. 'Come on, baby, we've still got a few minutes before the game.'

In the blink of an eye, Spinne moved, and Getrunken dropped to the ground, clutching his crotch and moaning in a high-pitched voice that sounded like that of a little girl.

'Coach,' Guillermo said, looking down at his fallen team-mate, 'I'm going to have to insist on being able to wear a cup.'

All of the male players shot up their hands to call for one too.

A line formed at the equipment cage, and Cavre handed each of the players some additional pieces of armour. These included elbow pads and kneepads, each of which bore vicious gold spikes against the Hacker green. Each of the men received a codpiece, and this had a spike on it too.

'Isn't this a little, um, you know,' Dunk said to Spinne.

'Small for you?' She laughed. 'Get used to it, big guy.'

Dunk blushed. 'No, I mean it's ridiculous. Am I supposed to hurt someone with this?'

'It's extra protection,' Spiel said. 'Somebody would think, ah, long and hard before kicking you there.'

'Point taken,' Dunk said, being careful not to injure himself as he put the spiked codpiece on.

'Here,' Dr Pill said, as he wheeled a huge vat out into the centre of the room, 'be sure to cover all of your exposed skin with this too.'

Big Richard came walking in behind the apothecary, dressed in a tiny Hackers uniform. The few pieces of armour he wore were Hacker green, but the paint on them was so fresh it had rubbed off on to his skin in places. Someone had glued a label with a Hacker logo on it on the side of the helmet, but it had already fallen askew.

Five others just like him followed on his heels. With their oversized helmets on, Dunk couldn't tell them apart.

'That's an awful lot of burn ointment,' Big Richard said with a grin. 'Let's hope we need it.'

'You want to get burnt?' said Slick.

The pygmy halfling grinned. 'We usually get carried off the field before we have a chance to get singed. This should make for a nice change of pace. Right, fellas?'

The other five pygmy halflings answered as one. 'Right!'

'What are they doing in here?' asked Dirk. 'The kids locker room is around the corner.'

'Are you usually so unkind to your new team-mates, Mr Hoffnung?' Pegleg said.

'We agreed to play for them, not with them.' Dirk scowled at the six little Hackers in their makeshift uniforms.

'In case you hadn't noticed, we're a little short-handed at the moment.' If Pegleg noticed his shot at a joke there, he gave no indication of it. He always took his Blood Bowl deadly serious. 'Given how preoccupied we all were for various reasons before the game, we didn't have time to set up any tryouts. We had to do with what we had.'

'You could have picked a pack of dwarfs from the stands,' Dirk said.

'Did someone ask for a pack of whores?' Getrunken said as he staggered for the door. 'I'm on it!'

Cavre stepped in front of the lineman and stopped him with a hand on his chest. He turned Getrunken around and pointed him in the direction of Dr Pill.

'No one else wanted to play with a team associated with the Sacrifice Flies,' Cavre said. 'They have the stink of failure about them, and the superstitious folk around here fear that it may have rubbed off on us.

'The upside of this is, we only need to win by a single touchdown to beat the spread. Before the Flies joined us, we were favoured by five scores.'

'How comforting,' Dirk said, scowling at the newcomers.

'So, what is this stuff?' Dunk asked Dr Pill, eager to change the subject. He stuck a finger in the white goop in the vat. It felt greasy.

'Heatblock,' the old elf said. 'Like sunblock only better. It'll keep the sun off your skin and even offer a bit of protection from the lava. Any direct immersion in the hot stuff, and you're a goner, of course, but this can help with anything else.'

'What do you need bloody sunblock for?' Edgar asked, rustling his leaves against the locker room's ceiling. 'Sounds like deadly poison.'

'When skin gets overexposed to the sun, it burns, not like a vampire, but bad enough. The sun's rays are stronger here, closer to the equator. Even those of us with some kind of tan can get scorched in the course of an hour.'

'Okay so far,' M'Grash said, holding up his arm with a big grin. His skin had turned a bright pink since they'd landed in Lustria.

Dr Pill came over and slapped the ogre on the arm. M'Grash yelped and tried to squirm away.

'Thankfully, you're the worst of this lot of morons,' Dr Pill said. 'Mostly you've all had the good sense to stay out of the direct sun as much as you can. Out there on the pitch, though, there's no place to hide. Put on the heatblock.'

Dunk and the others all moved to comply. Only Edgar and the pygmy halflings didn't bother. Getrunken tried to drink the lotion, but Dr Pill stopped him by pushing his head into the vat.

When they were done with all their preparations, they only had a few minutes until game time. Pegleg cleared his throat.

'I suppose you bastards expect me to give you the pep talk of your lives. After all, this is a big game, huge. Technically, it's the first step towards establishing ourselves as the undisputed champions of the world. It's bigger than the Blood Bowl tournament in that respect.

'But I'm not going to bother. Those of you who are left from those who started this journey with me know better than to get fooled by such hype. You've been through big games before.

'Every game is always the biggest game ever if you listen to the announcers and promoters. That's the story they tell the fans to get them all worked up, so they buy tickets to the game or extend their Cabalvision subscriptions, or buy our hats and T-shirts.

'We know better. We're the players, the professionals.

'This isn't just a game for us. This is our job. This is our life.'

He paused for a moment and took off his hat.

'It's been a long journey. One I didn't want to take, but we're here now, and we're going to do our jobs.

'Before we do, I want to remember the people who set out with us who didn't make it to the journey's end.

'Anfäger. Anima. Roja. Bereit. Ciotola. Linson.

'They were good players, every damn one of them. They deserved the chance to die with their cleats on. They didn't get that.

'I'm dedicating this game to their memory. When you're out there on the field, or sitting on the bench, look around you. Remember where your friends used to play. Think about what it's like without them.

'Then hope that when your time comes, we remember you so well.'

Pegleg put his yellow, tricorn hat back on his head and stared at every one of his players all at once.

'You're professionals, and you're good at your jobs, maybe the best ever. It's time to get out there and do them. Make me proud. May Nuffle favour us, and may the other gods help those who dare to get in our way.'

Getrunken whooped at the top of his lungs, and the rest of the team-mates leapt to their feet. Filled with grim determination, they filed out of the locker room towards the volcanic field beyond, ready to get to work.

'Oh!' Bob's voice reverberated across the crater atop the Tobazco Volcano. 'Have you ever seen a hit like that?'

Dunk had to agree that he hadn't encountered anything like that in a game before. The match against the Ssservants of the Ssslann had been going well. The Hackers had scored the first touchdown just a few minutes into the game. Then all hell had broken loose.

The lizardmen had come out onto the field dressed in nothing at all, not even a loincloth. The only thing they wore was a leather harness emblazoned with the vibrant, jungle-green logo of the Ssservants: a fat, ugly slann. Dunk wondered if there were any other kind.

Of course, they didn't need any armour. Their scales served that function just fine, and the sharp crests along their backs and the backs of their limbs worked just as well as the spikes on a traditional suit of game armour. They swung their massive tails all around, using them almost as a set of separate blockers, clearing paths wide enough for any lizardman with the ball to race through.

One of the lizardmen, a particularly blue one called Sssam Gaash, grabbed the ball from a team-mate Spinne was tackling, and then turned and found daylight. He spun past Guillermo and Spiel, and leapt straight over Big Richard.

Then he tried to get past M'Grash. He stiff-armed the ogre, but that only partially deflected M'Grash's efforts to bring the lizardman down. The ogre's grasp missed Gaash's waist and came down around his tail.

Happy to have his hands on any part of a foe, M'Grash planted his feet and held on. Dunk had seen him do this before. If he managed to stop Gaash, he'd swing the creature around and hurl him back towards the Hacker end zone. The landing would knock the air clean out of him and make him easy prey for the Hackers' attacks.

Instead, when M'Grash gave Gaash's tail a yank, the whole thing came off in his hands. The ogre fell back on his rump, stunned, and when he sat back up he had the whole of Gaash's tail wriggling in his hands. He screamed like a halfling girl.

'I think K'Thragsh is going to be having nightmares for weeks!' Bob said.

'I might have them myself!' said Jim. 'Hey, you think he's going to eat that? If not, I'm planning a barbeque after the game, and that would look great on the spit!'

'I thought you said it scared you!'

'Most of what I eat scares me! I don't let that make me go hungry!'

Terrified, M'Grash flung the tail off, and then got up and stomped up and down on the fleshy thing until it had turned into a red and blue paste.

'Well, if Gaash was hoping to get that back, I think he's out of luck!' said Bob.

'It's no problem!' said Jim. 'He's a lizard! He can grow a new one!'

'Touchdown, Ssservants!'

The crowd went nuts to see one of the local teams take the legendary Hackers down a notch.

'Amazing!' Bob said. 'I had money on Hackers goose-egging the Ssservants, and I'm shocked to see how wrong I was. This could be a real game!'

'If the Ssservants are counting on the Hackers to fall for that trick every time, they may be out of luck. They only have so many tails to go around! Those things take some time to grow back!'

Dunk came over and collected M'Grash as he finished up with his gruesome work. The ogre still shivered with disgust, something Dunk had never seen. He suspected the surprise of finding a squirming limb in his hands might have put M'Grash over the edge. After all, it wasn't the first time he'd dismembered someone by accident.

At halftime, the Hackers went into their locker room with the score tied 2-2 and their heads hung low. Peg-leg was so disappointed in them that none of them could meet his eyes.

'At least no one got hurt,' Dunk said as he filed past the coach.

'No one got hurt, Mr Hoffnung?' The captain's voice strained with amazement. 'And that's a good thing? How in Nuffle's name did I ever let you on my team? What kind of attitude is that?'

'I meant none of us, coach. Isn't that a good thing?'

Pegleg scowled. 'If you're worried about people getting hurt, perhaps we should all go to the temple instead? Or perhaps you'd like to just lie on the beach?'

'That's not what I meant, coach.'

'I thought we were here to play in a tournament, Mr Hoffnung, not lie around on some half-arsed vacation.'

'We are, coach.' Dunk felt his determination growing. 'We're not just here to play. We're here to win.'

Pegleg slapped Dunk on the back with the blunt side of his hook. 'I'm glad to hear that, Mr Hoffnung. Now, let's see what we can do to make that happen.'

The Hackers burst out of the locker room as if Pegleg had dropped hot coals in their shorts. They kicked the ball off to the Ssservants, but instead of concentrating on the ball, they spent the next few minutes tearing off any tail they could get their hands on. Edgar even removed the tail of one Lizardman fan who'd sat a little too close to the field.

'Nuffle's salty nuts!' Bob said. 'Have you ever seen such carnage? Have you ever seen so many players grabbing so much tail?'

'To answer both your questions at once: Not since last year's Chaos All-Star cheerleader tryouts!' said Jim. 'This is awesome!'

The lizardmen scored in the middle of the Hackers' dismemberment efforts, but with the Ssservants' only real edge blunted, Dunk had high hopes that this wouldn't last long.

'Look,' Cavre said to Dunk as they awaited the kick-off. 'The Ssservants' coach is trying to get some of the lizardmen players to come in off the bench, but they're refusing to go.'

Dunk shaded his eyes and stared into the opposing dugout. The suited-up lizardmen each held his tail wrapped around him as if it might disappear in a painful puff of smoke.

With the Ssservants more concerned about their hides than the pigskin, Spinne was able to run through and score behind some solid blocking from Dirk and M'Grash. That tied the score, which put the lizardman coach Kill Parssselsmouth into a tail whipping frenzy. After he slaughtered his starting blitzer and tried to swallow his severed head whole, his players were more afraid of him than the Hackers, and Pegleg's players had a game on their hands once more.

Late in the game, the lizardmen barrelled down at Edgar who had the ball. The treeman tried to fake left and move right, but treemen don't jink that well. He ended up going left and not fooling anyone.

Three lizardmen crashed into Edgar. One grabbed his left leg, another grabbed the right, and the third scrambled straight up him like a cat chasing a bird.

Edgar spun around and hurled something down-field. The lizardman clambering up his branches leapt after it, and the two creatures clinging to his legs pushed off and chased after their team-mate, hoping to help him out or provide him with some blocks.

Dunk had been racing up behind Edgar to lend him a hand with the lizardmen, and found his targets racing away faster than he could follow. He stopped for a moment to check on Edgar, and the treeman looked down at him, rustling his upper branches.

The ball dropped out into Dunk's hands.

Dunk stared at it for a moment before he realised what he had. Then, without bothering to ask what Edgar had thrown away, turned and sprinted down the field.

'Look at that!' Jim's voice said. 'Hoffnung has the ball!'

'If that's the case, then what's Brew Dreesss swallowed whole down at the other end of the field?'

'I don't know, but it seems to me that's a rotten way to carry a ball down the field! Most players don't have the stomach for it!'

'Not Dreesss! He's on a swallow-them-wholesome diet! Whoa! It looks like he's coughed up Big Richard!'

'All but his helmet! I can see its spikes sticking out through the front of his neck! That's gotta smart!'

'Smart's not the word I'd use there, Jim!'

While most of the players watched the Jumboball that sat over the middle of the eastern side of the field, if only to see the replay of Big Richard being regurgitated, Dunk had a clear shot at the end zone. Just as he was about to hit it, though, a silvery mist enveloped the end of the field, and he felt a horrible, biting chill cut through him to the bone.

Dunk kept running towards the end zone, although every bit of his heart told him to turn around and sprint in the other direction. Winning the game meant something to him, though, and he wasn't about to let anything stop him, not even her.

Dunk heard Greta's high, piercing wail before he saw her face coalesce out of the mists. It rose over the roar of the crowd, which fast transformed into shrieks of sheer terror. 'Dunkel and Dirk Hoffnung!' she cried. 'You've been very naughty boys!'

Dunk skidded to a halt just short of the goal line and goggled at his mother's ghost as it loomed high over him, blocking all view of the end zone and the stands beyond. In his worst nightmares, he hadn't come up with something as awful and outright embarrassing as this. He felt like his mother had just reached over and adjusted his jock strap in front of an audience of millions of fans across the entire planet.

'Why did you run off like that?' she asked. 'A mother only wants the best for her boys, to give them all the advantages she's had.'

Still stunned, Dunk almost jumped out of his skin when Dirk put his hand on his shoulder. 'I always said she was crazy,' Dirk said, 'but I never imagined something like this.'

Coming back to himself, Dunk realised he was still standing on a Blood Bowl field in the middle of a ball game. Standing as still as he was, he could expect to be torn to pieces any moment. He swung his helmeted head around, willing to bet that it might be torn off before he even saw who was going to hit him.

Dunk spotted half the Ssservantsss team, less the poor player still choking on Big Richard's helmet, charging down the field, and he closed his eyes and braced for impact. When, after a moment, it didn't come, he screwed his eyes open again to see why. The lizardmen were still there. For some reason, though, they just hadn't got much closer, but why?

Bob and Jim provided the answer.

'The Hoffnung family matriarch seems to have had an unforeseen effect upon their foes! Tell me, Bob, what do you get when you mix freezing cold with cold-blooded creatures?'

'I'm no rocket scientist, but I'm guessing a bunch of sssluggish Ssservantsss! This is one reason why I always advocate for a little diversity on team rosters. When everyone on the team suffers from the same weakness, you're just asking for trouble!'

'I know what you mean! I used to play on an all-vampire team called the Arterial Jets. We lost every game we played against any Tilean teams. Those people sure do love to cook with garlic!'

Dunk glanced up at the clock ticking loudly under the Jumboball. With just over a minute left in the game, he could make this work for him. All he had to do was avoid a bunch of slow-motion lizards and an insane ghost-mother.

'Have you boys heard a word I've been saying to you?' Greta's ghost shrieked. 'You ungrateful little bastards! I can't believe I gave up nine months of my life to bear you! Each! And I don't even warrant a few moments of conversation in the middle of a "game". I can see just where your priorities lie, and let me tell you boys it's an ugly picture!'

'I don't know how long I can take this,' said Dirk. He shook like a pygmy halfling in a hurricane. 'If she wasn't already dead, I think I'd kill her.'

'That's our mother you're talking about!'

Dirk raised his eyebrows at Dunk and shrugged.

'All right,' Dunk admitted. 'You have a point.' He pump faked the ball at Dirk. 'Go down and out.'

Dirk nodded and took off.

'And just where do you think you're going?' Greta shrieked at Dirk. The younger brother skidded to a stop as a grey tendril swirled out of the mist to cut him off. 'You show your mother some respect, young man, or else!'

'Or else what, Mother?' said Dirk. 'I was dead to you for years before you died. You have nothing over me.'

The mists froze for a moment, as did the ghost. The crazy thought that perhaps Dirk had pierced the ghost's ego so badly that it would have to leave flitted through Dunk's brain, but Greta soon snuffed that hope out.

'I refuse to let you take that tone with me, young man! Even if I'm dead, I'm still your mother, and you will listen to me!'

'Sod off,' said Dirk.

Before Dunk could blink, a score of tendrils shot from the mists and enveloped his brother in a tangle of grey mists. The chill felt palpable and painful, even to Dunk, who stood a good fifteen yards from Dirk.

Dirk fell to the ground, growling in pain. He writhed against the tendrils, and they proved to be as insubstantial as the air. However, try as he might, he could not work his way free of them, and soon he lacked the strength to try.

Warm blood only provided some protection against violent temperature changes. Given enough time, that defence could be worn down to nothing, and Dirk had been pushed to that point in record time.

Dunk rushed over to help his brother. 'Let him go, Mother! You're killing him!'

The ghost swung around in front of Dunk, sweeping between him and Dirk and stopping him cold. 'That's the point, I'm afraid. If you boys won't respect me in life, then perhaps you'll give me my due in death!'

All thoughts of the game disappeared from Dunk's head as he dived away from the mists that stretched out for him, along with his mother's bitter tones. Scrambling beneath them, he tucked the football under his arm reflexively, and rolled when he hit the ground. The mists sailed over his head, and then curled up and back for another shot at him.

'Dunkel!' This time, the voice was deep and resonant, but no less strained. M'Grash scooped Dunk up off the ground and into his arms. 'Bad lady no hurt you!'

'Bad lady?' Greta said. 'Bad lady? You oaf of an ogre. How dare you question how I choose to raise my sons!'

The tendrils came straight for M'Grash this time, and the ogre did not even attempt to avoid them. Instead, he inhaled as deeply as he could, and then blew with all his might.

The mists parted before the ogre's mighty lungs, but only for a moment. It was like trying to push back the ocean by splashing through it. Even a creature as powerful as M'Grash had to concede the battle to the stronger power.

As the mists came rushing back at M'Grash, the ogre dropped Dunk and fled. The chill grey shot over Dunk's head and enveloped the entire field for as far as Dunk could see. He had to admit that this wasn't more than a few feet though.

'Can you see what's going on down there, Jim?'

'Not a thing, Bob. I've heard of freak fogs before, but this is ridiculous! That's thicker than my last wife's skull!'

Dunk could hear his friends calling his name. He wanted to call back to them, but the fog had come down close to his feet, and he could no longer see who was close to him. If he said something to give himself away, a lizardman might appear out of the mists and tear his head off. Or, worse yet, his mother might find him.

'Either way, something had better happen quickly, or we'll be going into overtime! The clock's just about to run out, and we have a tied score!'

At that moment, Dunk felt something tugging against his leg. He yanked his foot away, sure that he'd find a set of long, lizard teeth attached to it. Instead, he spotted Big Richard waving up at him from the floor of the volcano, which Dunk now realised was steaming from exposure to his mother's chilliness.

At first, Dunk just stared at the Sacrifice Fly. Then he knew just what he had to do. He scooped Big Richard up in one arm and stuffed the ball into the pygmy halfling's hands with the other.

'Which way is the end zone?' Dunk asked.

'That way,' Big Richard said, pointing over Dunk's shoulder. 'But why?'

Dunk slung the halfling down low and gave him three big swings. 'When you hit the ground,' Dunk said, 'keep running until you see daylight.'

'No,' Big Richard said as he tried to squirm from Dunk's grasp. 'No, wait!'

But it was too late. The man in the little Hackers uniform went sailing off into the mist and disappeared.

32

'DIRK!' DUNK SHOUTED. 'Mother! What have you done with Dirk!' He clawed his way through the mists, praying he would find his brother before their mother froze him to death.

A low moan wafted from downfield, and Dunk charged towards it. 'Dunkel!' the ghost's voice called. 'I'm almost through with your little brother. You're next!'

Dunk felt his way towards the ghost by following the freezing temperatures emanating from her. Dirk's groans got louder as he went, confirming he was on the right path.

'Mother!' he shouted. 'You're just as cold-hearted in death as you ever were in life! It must be a real treat for you to finally be able to do more than pluck at our heels with your disapproval.'

'You ungrateful brat!' Greta's ghost wailed. 'After all I did for you, this is how you repay me!'

'You let Lehrer and our nannies raise us. They were our parents, not you.'

The mists rose from the field, gathered up as if caught in an oncoming tornado. As they coalesced back into something Dunk could recognise as having once been his mother, they lifted from the floor of the volcano's centre, revealing the pitch and the people gathered around and on it. Most of these souls gasped in relief, pleased to have emerged from the freezing fog and to be able to bask in the tropical sunlight once more.

One tiny man crowed in triumph. A moment later, the horn sounded to signal the end of regulation time in the game.

'Nuffle's blessed balls!' Bob's voice said. 'That's the end of the game, but it's not over yet!'

'I thought it was already over!' Jim's voice said. 'Called on account of haunting!'

'The referees may have fled from the field, but they left the clock running! And look who's standing in the Ssservants' end zone with the ball!'

All eyes in the stadium turned to see Big Richard standing, holding the ball, which was almost as large as he was, over his head and jumping up and down in ecstatic joy.

'Touchdown, Hackers!' said Bob. 'Hackers win!'

Normally Dunk would have cheered for this along with everyone else and then joined his team for the post-game celebration. At the moment, though, he had a more urgent matter on his hands.

'You unbelievable bastard!' Greta's ghost screamed down at Dunk as she towered over him.

'Gosh, Mother,' Dunk said as he glanced towards Dirk, 'are you telling me you and Father weren't married?'

Dirk lay on the crater's floor, right about the Hacker's 40-yard line, curled into a ball. For an instant, Dunk thought perhaps he'd been too slow, moved too late to save his brother, as Dirk seemed still as death. Then Dunk saw him trembling from the extreme cold he'd endured, and hope surged in Dunk's heart.

Greta's ghost dived down from her vantage point high above the field, straight at Dunk. Knowing he couldn't do anything to harm her, at least not directly, Dunk spun on his heel and sprinted away. A blast of mist splashed down right where he'd been standing, followed by an unearthly wail that made Dunk wish he'd been born deaf.

Having achieved his goal, which was to lure the ghost from hurting Dirk, Dunk had no idea what to do next. It felt like the tiger had him by the tail, and all he could do was run, and hope he could somehow outlast the dead.

Dunk knew that his mother knew next to nothing about Blood Bowl or anything else athletic. She'd spent her days involved in the high society of Altdorf, unwilling to show interest in her husband's work and refusing to sully her hands with something as base as child-rearing. He knew he could avoid her attacks by jinking back and forth all day long, and he did just that.

Greta telegraphed her attacks long before they came crashing down, and Dunk easily danced around them, spinning and slicing across the field with the same skills that helped him avoid opposing players during a game. Every so often, he would nearly step on a lizardman from the Ssservantsss who'd just started to come out of the cold-induced torpor caused by the mists that had blanketed the field. Rather than trying to attack him, these creatures slunk off the field as fast as their sluggish limbs would carry them, not wishing to have anything to do with the Hackers and their ghostly family feud.

Dunk started to tire. He'd already played a full game, and while avoiding Greta's attacks was easy enough, he couldn't keep it up forever.

That's when he spotted Kirta. She stormed out of the stands and raced right for him, a murderous scowl on her face.

Staying away from Greta was one thing. Kirta was a trained athlete and fresh to the field. He might dodge her tackles a few times, but eventually she'd get a hand on him and would slow him down just enough for their mother to finish him off.

Dunk considered his options. If he beat Kirta to the ground, he might have a chance, but he knew he couldn't bring himself to do it. He'd come so far and risked so much to see his sister again. He couldn't hurt her, not now.

Dunk put his hands up before him to show he wanted to talk, but Kirta ignored him. Instead, she threw back her head and screamed out, 'Mother! You are embarrassing me!'

The ghost froze in mid-strike. She turned around, twisting on her smoky pillar of a waist to face Kirta.

'Kirta, darling, you know I never meant to do anything to hurt you. I only wanted to put an end to your brothers' shenanigans, and they absolutely refuse to be reasonable. Now they've done the worst thing possible!'

Out of the corner of his eye, Dunk watched Spinne haul Dirk to his feet and hustle him off the field into Lästiges's waiting arms. He avoided moving his head to look at them for fear of alerting Greta's ghost to the fact that Dirk was getting away.

That just left Kirta and him out in the open with their mother's crazed ghost.

'What are you talking about?' Kirta said. She seemed to have the situation far better in hand than Dunk did, so he began to sidle off the field.

None of the fans in the stands had left the stadium. They all wanted to see what would happen, despite the peril. They regularly sat up as close as possible to the mayhem of a standard Blood Bowl game. Dunk supposed getting a ringside seat to a fight with a ghost had to be just as compelling to them.

'They won their game!' Greta's ghost moaned. 'They won, and now you're going to win, like you always do, and they're going to end up playing you in the finals. I just can't stand it!'

'But, Mother, that's what we do for a living. Dunk and Dirk have played against each other, lots of times!'

Dunk winced as Kirta mentioned his name, and then froze as the ghost focused her attention back on him. 'Is this true?' she asked him. 'You willingly put yourself in a situation in which you might kill your brother?'

Dunk cringed at the question. 'No one got hurt, Mother.'

'Well, that's not exactly true now is it, Bob?' Jim said.

'Absolutely not! The Hoffnung-Heldmann brothers have two of the highest HOG ratios on any team!'

Dunk grimaced and promised himself to have a word with Bob and Jim once this was over with. He'd never met the two announcers in person. Few players had, as they had a habit of treating any Blood Bowl player who approached them as a lethal threat. A couple of rookies died every year before the point was made, but the veterans always gave the pair a wide berth.

'What?' the ghost said, aghast. 'What exactly is a HOG ratio, Dunkel?'

'Hurt Other Guy, Mother, but that's not important.' He put up his hands and waved down her protests. 'What matters is that Dirk and I survived all that, and we play on the same team now. There's no chance of us killing each other!' At least not on the field, he added mentally.

'You know,' Greta's ghost said, 'I have a perfectly reasonable solution to this problem.'

Dunk blinked, and then swallowed hard and folded his hands in front of him while he waited for her to continue. He felt just like a little boy back in the keep, waiting for his mother to hand down some ridiculous punishment for Dirk, Kirta, and him for having broken some rule or ignored some bit of etiquette about which they'd known not a thing. To interrupt her at this point would invite another bout of insane ranting. It was always better to wait her out rather than give her another reason to go mad.

'Death,' she said sweetly, just as if she'd suggested they all sit down to eat cake. 'Once we're all dead, we can enjoy eternity together, never without each other's company again.'

Dunk didn't know what to say. Fortunately, Kirta came up and put an arm around his shoulders. 'Can we get back to you on that, Mother?' she said with as much innocence as she could muster.

Dunk nodded along with his sister. 'That's right, Mother. Kirta has a big game to play right after this, and that's a big decision to make. I promise, we'll sit down afterwards and come up with a solution to all this.'

The ghost beamed down at them, her thundercloud grey colour turning to a cheery silver. 'Oh, of course! I was just so excited about my idea that I couldn't wait to share it with you. But I can be patient, at least until tomorrow's game.'

'We'll have it all sorted out before then, Mother.' Dunk looked down at his little sister and realised he couldn't tell which of them was trembling. 'I promise.'

THAT EVENING, WHEN Kirta walked out of the Lusties' locker room, leaving the post-game victory celebration behind, Dunk, Dirk, and Pegleg were waiting for her. 'Is there somewhere we can talk?' Dunk asked.

Kirta nodded and led them away from the volcanic stadium and into the jungle beyond. They strode down a long, well-worn path, lit by torches, until they came to a beachside shack with a thatched roof framed up among a stand of coconut palms right on the edge of the sand.

'Few people come here after the games,' Kirta explained. 'If they want a drink, there are plenty of places closer in. If they're going to walk this far, they're usually on their way home to one of the other islands.'

Kirta spotted a slim and lanky lizardman as they approached, and signalled for a round of drinks. The brownish creature dashed away into a walled hut that stood under a small portion of the thatched roof, the rest of which sat open to the refreshing sea breeze.

The four of them sat in wicker chairs around a bamboo table and stared out at the pounding surf and twinkling stars. The full moon had just risen, and it hung low and wide in the sky, its reflected glory sparkling across the water.

The lizardman appeared at the side of the table and slid four icy beers in transparent bottles onto it. As he did, Dunk noticed his fingers had become the same golden colour as the drinks, and then slipped back to the colour of the table as soon as the lizardman released them.

Without a word, the four each grabbed a beer, and then raised them and clinked them against each other in a wordless toast. After a quick drink each, Kirta spoke.

'So,' she said, 'what do you have in mind?'

Dunk nodded at Pegleg. The ex-pirate doffed his hat and then leaned in and put his elbows on the table as he spoke. His golden teeth glittered in the light of the torches burning near the place's kitchen.

'Come play for us,' he said.

Kirta smiled, and then giggled. Her jaw fell as she realised that it wasn't a joke.

'You can't be serious.'

'Think about it,' Dunk said. 'It solves our problem with Mother perfectly. Dirk and I are on the same team and so can't hurt each other.'

'On the field,' said Dirk, 'on purpose.'

'If you're on the same team as us, we can't hurt you either.'

'On the field,' said Dirk, 'on purpose.'

'Perfect,' said Dunk.

'But what if I don't want to play for the Hackers?'

Dunk froze. He'd anticipated a lot of arguments against his plan, but not this one. He nodded at Pegleg to give him some time.

The coach leaned back and used his hook to tick off a number of points on his fleshy hand. 'We offer excellent pay. We have full benefits, including a full-time apothecary on staff. We are the defending Blood Bowl tournament champions. Any other player would kill for a deal like this, and you are insane if you turn it down.'

Kirta narrowed her eyes at Pegleg. 'How do I know you're not going to screw around with my contract?'

'Your brother Dunk is a co-owner of the team. He's had his agent, Slick Fullbelly, look over your contract.' Pegleg produced a scroll from inside his coat and unfurled it on the table. 'It's a better offer than I would have given you, but my partners insisted on it.'

Kirta sat back in her chair and took another pull on her beer.

'I don't get it,' Dunk said. 'Why wouldn't you want to join the Hackers?'

'It's not the Hackers I'm worried about,' Kirta said, pointing her bottle into the air for emphasis. 'It's you and you.' The bottle punched at Dunk and Dirk.

Dunk's jaw dropped. 'What?' That was all he could get out.

'I spent most of my life being nothing more than a little sister to you two. I'm not sure I want to go back to that.'

'You'd prefer to live with and work for a team that purchased you as a slave?'

'I've paid off my contract and then some,' Kirta said, folding her arms across her chest. 'They treat me as an honoured guest.'

Dirk nodded. 'But never one of them.'

Kirta stiffened.

'I know what it's like, Kirta,' said Dirk. 'I left home voluntarily to get away from all the craziness. Everywhere I went though, I was never part of a family, not even one as broken and insane as ours.'

Kirta nodded and stayed silent. Dirk realised that she was fighting back tears.

'You have no idea what it's like,' she said. 'I was chased from my home by an angry mob, with my mother's ghost hounding me every step of the way. When I was sold as a slave, I was... I was relieved! Finally, I thought, I might have disappointed Mother enough for her to leave me alone for good. You should have heard her harangue me over that.

'When I got to Amazon Island, they treated me nothing like a slave. They gave me respect. They trained me to be an athlete and a fighter, to find self-respect. I have that now. I fought for it, and I earned it. I don't want to give it up.'

Dunk reached out a hand to Kirta, but she pulled away. 'It won't be like that,' he said. 'We're not kids any more. Our parents aren't around any more.'

'Mother's more around than ever. I used to wish she'd pay attention to me when she was alive. Now I wish she'd just go away.'

'This is the first step towards making that happen,' said Dunk. He scooted up in his chair. 'I understand your fears. None of us want to go back to our child-hood. It's not worth revisiting. But Dirk and I are back in the old keep, and we have the means to fix it up, to treat it right, and to make it a real home, not just the place where our parents warehoused us.'

'We'll keep out of your hair,' said Dirk. 'Spinne and Lästiges will see to that.'

Kirta smiled and let out a little laugh, and Dunk knew that it would be all right. Then she gasped and put a hand to her mouth.

'But I can't leave now,' she said. 'We have the finals tomorrow. There are rules about making trades in the middle of a tournament.'

'True,' Pegleg said. 'Teams at any level of a tourna-ment aren't allowed to make trades outside of the tournament. In fact, they can't make trades at all, with one exception: they can trade players with the next team on their schedule.'

Dunk nodded. 'If the two teams agree on it, it must be fair, because otherwise they wouldn't go for it.'

'Couldn't someone buy a victory like that?' Kirta asked. 'A wealthier team could buy all of a poorer team's best players and make it impossible for the poorer team to win.'

'True, except for two things: first, there are far eas-ier ways for a team to buy its way through a game. You can bribe the refs, pay for a team wizard to cast curses, or even give the players enough gold to make them throw the game. None of that involves making a public trade or having to take on the obligation of taking on a long-term contract with new players.

'Second, teams are restricted to the number of players they can have on their roster. To gain a new player, they must give up one of their current players in the trade. Most teams aren't willing to trade away valuable personnel in exchange for anyone else, particularly in the middle of a tournament.'

'But you have?'

Dunk nodded. 'Believe it or not, Rotes Hernd volunteered. She wants to play for the Lusties.'

'Why?'

'She watched your team play tonight. She thinks she's better than your starting thrower, Dayton No-Manning.'

Kirta nodded. 'She's tired of riding the bench behind you and wants her shot at being the starting thrower on another team.'

Dirk smirked. 'For a long time, she thought she might have a shot at unseating Dunk.'

Dunk shot his brother a look.

'What? It's not like people don't get hurt in this game. Anyhow, she gave up on that after he bought into the team. She figured even if Dunk was half-dead he could still push Pegleg into sending him onto the field, so she's been on the lookout for a better gig ever since.'

'But we've been away from the Old World since that happened,' said Dunk. 'This is her first chance to jump ship, so to speak, and she's eager to take it.' He glared at Dirk. 'For whatever reason.'

Dirk shrugged and grinned.

'So,' Pegleg said to Kirta, 'what do you think, Miss Hoffnung? I promise you that I will be your coach, not these jokers. I will work you as hard as anyone else, teach you what I can, and make you earn every minute you play on the field and every coin I pay you.

'I watched you play. You're an excellent catcher. Blood Bowl seems to run in the Hoffnung veins, and you are a proud example of that.

'Even if these two weren't pressuring me, I'd be happy to make you an offer. You'll be an asset to the Hackers, and I'll be proud to have you on my team.'

He pushed the contract towards her and produced a pen and a bottle of ink from another pocket in his long coat. 'So,' he said, 'what will it be?'

34

'WHERE'S KIRTA?' PEGLEG demanded for what seemed like the hundredth time, as Dunk tightened the straps on the few bits of armour he was permitted to wear. 'I trusted you on this, Mr Hoffnung. I offered her a sweetheart deal, and now your "innocent little sister" has taken off like a scared rabbit.'

'She's not afraid of anything,' Dunk said. 'She grew up with Dirk and me as her brothers and Lügner and Greta as her parents. She's as tough as they come.'

'Like a thief in the night, then, or a ship at high tide, or a cheap dress!'

'Watch it, coach,' Dirk said from the other corner of the locker room.

'The point, Mr Hoffnung and Mr Heldmann, is that the game is about to start in two minutes, the battle to determine which is the best Blood Bowl team the world over, and we are shy a key player! If she doesn't show up soon, I'll have to start another one of those pygmy halflings in her place.'

'We look forward to the opportunity!' Big Richard called from a corner of the room in which he stood huddled with the other Sacrifice Flies. The five other pygmy halflings nearly knocked each other out as they scrambled to hide underneath the nearest bench.

'Then today's your lucky day, Mr Richard!'

'Actually, Richard is my first name. Big is the surname. On the Island of Sacrifices, we do things a bit backward from your culture.'

'Right! Mr Big it is. I can't tell any of you apart in those helmets, and given the size differential with our foes, I don't suppose it matters. Pick one of your fellows to join us, Mr Big. We take to the field in one minute!'

'I really thought she'd be here,' Dunk said to Spinne and Slick. 'Last night she actually seemed eager.'

'And now we have to take the field without Rotes, who will be playing for the Amazons instead,' said Spinne. She shook her head in sympathy. 'I never would have guessed it.'

'Maybe she ran off with that Jiminy fellow,' Slick said. 'Have you tried checking with him?'

'No need to impugn my good name behind my back,' the singer said as he burst into the room. 'You can do it to my face if you like.'

'Where's Kirta?' Dunk asked.

Jiminy froze, concern etched on his face. 'She's not here? I last saw her after breakfast, and she left me to go to the stadium. I just came by to wish her good luck.'

'Was she mad about anything?' Spinne asked.

Jiminy shook his head, clearly confused. 'Not a bit. When I first saw her this morning, she seemed a little shellshocked about the new deal you'd offered her, but as we talked, she seemed to warm right up to it.'

'You didn't spend the night with her?' Dunk asked.

Jiminy stepped back in momentary horror. 'No, of course not!' Then he realised who he was talking to. 'Well, the honest truth is, I would have if I could have. I'd have married that woman a dozen times over.'

'And why haven't you?' Spinne asked. For some reason, Dunk felt her eyes burning at him.

'It's not for a lack of wanting on my part or hers, I can tell you that. Greta, though, she puts her... well, not her foot, her tendrils down, I suppose, every time.'

'Is she always with Kirta?' Dr Pill asked.

Jiminy nodded. The old elf scratched at his eye patch and sniffed. 'Clearly trying to live her life through her daughter. Classic substitution complex in which the parent tries to control every aspect of the same-sex child's life in an effort to make sure that it's as "perfect" as possible, from the parent's self-interested point of view, of course.'

Dunk pursed his lips at the apothecary. 'Care to translate that into plain speech for the rest of us.'

Dr Pill almost choked on his disdain as he tried to scoff and roll his eyes at the request at the same time. When he recovered, he said, 'Your mother won't take kindly to any major changes in your sister's life that she didn't instigate herself, especially if it means taking Kirta away from her, and especially if it comes from you and your brother, whom she identifies with your father, whom she hates with a burning passion and blames directly for her own death.'

Everyone stared at Dr Pill with blank looks.

'Remind me to buy a dictionary for the voyage home and make all of you read it. Let me try again.

'Your mother doesn't like you. She likes your sister too much. She wants you all dead because she thinks she'll have ironclad control over you then.

'Bringing Kirta into the Hackers is the opposite of what your mother wants. You are a threat to her. Taking her daughter under your protection makes the threat real. She will react in an irrational, but predictable way.'

Dunk nodded at the end of every sentence, proving he was following along. Everyone else in the room did too, even M'Grash.

'Which is?' Dunk asked.

'Your mother has probably kidnapped your sister to keep her from going through with your deal. She will kill her to cement their relationship. The only question is whether she's already done that or will wait until she can kill all three of you at once.'

A horrified murmur ran through the locker room. As everyone stood shocked, Carve, who had been out on the field, waiting for the signal to bring the Hackers out, poked his nose back into the locker room through the tunnel that led to the pitch. 'Dunk, Dirk, captain?'

'We have to go after her?' Dunk said.

Dirk nodded. 'We have to find her, right now.'

Pegleg stamped down on the stone floor with his wooden leg. 'You will do no such thing! The game is starting. You cannot leave me short three of my best players.'

'But, coach...' Dirk and Dunk started.

Before they could get going, Cavre cut them off with a shrill whistle that threatened to break their eardrums.

'Come with me,' he said, beckoning them towards the tunnel. He waved down their protests and pointed once again towards the exit. 'No comments. No questions. You want to see this. Trust me.'

In all the time Dunk had known Cavre, he'd never known the man to steer him wrong. Still, he had to know how important it was for them to find Kirta, before Greta's ghost could do something horrible to her. He had to know.

A ball of ice formed in Dunk's gut.

'Trust me,' Cavre said again. 'Come with me.'

The players filed out of the locker room, Dunk following right after Cavre, who was in the lead. As they emerged from the tunnel that led out into the back of the Hackers' dugout, the stench of sulphur and a wall of oppressive heat struck Dunk at the same time.

It felt, for a moment, like he'd been transported back to the Realms of Chaos in which the Hackers had been forced to play Blood Bowl against the Blood God last year, and for a moment he hesitated, not wanting to face something so horrible again. Barely breaking stride, Dunk steeled his nerve for whatever lay ahead.

As Cavre stepped out of the dugout, the crowd began to cheer, and the roar only grew louder as Dunk and the others strode onto the field after him.

'Blood Bowl fans,' Jim's voice said, echoing off every wall of the volcanic bowl, 'please welcome the current reigning champions of the Blood Bowl Tournament, the Bad Bay Hackers!'

'Kill! The! Hack! Ers!

'Kill! The! Hack! Ers!

'Kill! The! Hack! Ers!'

'Seems like the crowd's really behind their hometown favourites, the Lustria Lusties,' Bob said. 'And who can blame them? Power, speed, and killer bods! How can you beat that?'

Dunk heard the words, but they didn't mean anything to him. He was too busy gazing at what Cavre had brought them here to see.

The field, if it could still be called that, had devolved since last night. The volcano, it seemed, had not enjoyed the beating it had taken and had determined to fight back. Large cracks ran along the edges of the pitch and through it, like the ice thawing on a frozen bay. Instead of chill water peeking through, red-hot lava glowed up from below.

'No, no, no!' M'Grash said. 'No play! Ouch! Burn!'

Dunk clapped his large pal on the elbow. 'Can't say I disagree with you. This is insane.'

'Quit your whining, you lubbers!' Pegleg said. He pointed at the Lusties, who'd already taken the far end of the field. 'Are you going to let a bunch of little girls show you up for the cowards you are?'

Spinne took two steps towards the ex-pirate, who threw up his hand and hook at the sight of her. 'My apologies, Miss Schönheit. You're a clear example of how brave the women around here are. Looking out at the terrified faces of the *men* on my team, I'm appalled on behalf of my entire gender!'

'Wow, coach,' Dirk said, 'I'm astonished.'

'That I'd call you lot a bunch of cowardly pansies?'

'No, that you could make proper use of the word "gender". With all those long coats, tight breeches, and ruffled shirts you pirates wear I always wondered if you might be confused about that. Gender, you know.'

Dunk steeled himself for an eruption from Pegleg, but the coach surprised him with how well he'd taken Dirk's insult.

Pegleg glared at Dirk, who looked ready to either fight or flee. 'You think I'm going to let some second-rate blitzer who's only on my team at his brother's behest upset me with comments about my sexuality and my clothes? At least I'm not the one who brings his mother issues onto the field!'

'Hey,' Dunk said, leaping to Dirk's defence, although he wasn't sure why. Perhaps because he knew his brother's mother issues were also his own. 'That was only for that one game.'

'Oh, really, Mr Hoffnung?' Pegleg swung his hook out towards the field. 'Then what do you call that?'

Every one of the Hackers spun to look over at the Lusties' end zone, the one they needed to reach to score a touchdown. Dunk immediately recognised the grey mists curling over the place, forming a wall there: his mother's ghost.

'I'd call that a good reason to enter therapy,' Dr Pill said. 'I'll start with you both on the ride home.'

'What about right now?' asked Guillermo. 'She's blocking off the end zone. How are we supposed to score?'

'She's a ghost,' Spinne said. 'She can't touch you.'

'But she can make us wish we were dead,' said Big Richard. 'I'm from the islands. I can't take the cold!'

The other pygmy halflings clustered around him, nodding in agreement as they clung to each other and shivered. Whether they did so from terror, anticipation of the ghost's cold touch, or both, Dunk could not tell.

Cavre shaded his eyes with his hand and stared down at the fog wreathed end zone. 'This may work to our advantage, Hackers,' he said. 'The ghost seems to have chilled the lava flows beneath the end zone. Perhaps her touch and that of the volcano have balanced each other out.'

'You're trying to tell us that the safest place on the field may be in the end zone?' Getrunken said, slurring his words.

Cavre nodded.

'And that's because it's trapped between an angry ghost and a lava flow from an active volcano?'

Cavre nodded again.

Getrunken let loose a monstrous belch, and then pounded his chest to make sure he'd let all the gas out. 'All right,' he said with a drunken grin, 'just checking.'

Pegleg stepped in front of the team and shouted at them as the crowd roared louder. He doffed his yellow tricorn hat and brushed back his sweat slicked curls. His chin thrust forward in determination.

'Blood Bowl isn't about being safe! It's never been about being safe, not for the fans, not for the coaches, and certainly not for you.

'This is a deadly sport, and you take your life in your hands every time you step out onto the pitch. If a troll doesn't crush you, or a wizard doesn't zap you to death, you might trip in a hole and break your neck. There are no guarantees here, and that's what makes it worth doing!

'You think I pay you people so much money because I like you? Or because you're good at what you do? Some of you are, don't get me wrong, and I do appreciate that.

'What you get from me is hazard pay! Only so many people are brave, murderous, or dumb enough to put themselves directly in harm's way by joining a Blood Bowl team, much less actually playing on the field. Half the time you win the game just by surviving it!

'So don't pay any attention to that ghost in the end zone! At least not any more than you do to the Amazons between you and her.

'You're here to risk your lives, play Blood Bowl, and win the game! You are the Bad Bay Hackers, and you are winners! You are champions! And no one and nothing can stop you!'

Getrunken thrust his helmet in the air in agreement. 'We can do this!' he said. 'We can win this game. Let's do it! Who's with me?'

With that, Getrunken turned and sprinted out onto the field, screaming at the top of his lungs. The others stood and watched him go.

'No,' Pegleg said, 'watch out for the–'

But it was too late, ten yards out onto the field, Getrunken staggered towards a crack in the pitch and jammed his foot into it. An instant later, he leapt into the air and screamed, his boot ablaze, and sprinted back towards the Hackers' dugout at top speed.

Dunk had never seen the man move so fast, not even in a game. Getrunken dashed straight for the big cask of GatorMaim tucked into a corner of the dugout and kicked it open with his burning boot. The liquid turned to steam as soon as it touched his foot, enveloping Getrunken and the entire dugout.

Pegleg slapped the blunt end of his hook against his head. 'So much for a great speech.' He hung his head, defeated. 'Just get out there and try not to embarrass me too much.'

Pegleg turned to Big Richard. 'We're short two players, no pun intended. Pick two of yours and bring them in.'

The five Sacrifice Flies trembled in fear. 'Don't worry,' Pegleg said, 'you can't disappoint me any more than I've already been.'

Dunk and the rest of the Hackers slunk out on to the field, taking great care not to repeat Getrunken's error. Dunk knew he was supposed to line up in the Hackers' half, but he went straight for the mist-covered patch of earth instead.

'What's this?' Bob said. 'It looks like Hoffnung's decided to defect to the Lusties!'

'Does that require a sex change operation?' Jim said.

'I don't know, but I'd bet some of the Lusties would be happy to help him with that, right there on the field!'

For the most part, the Lusties ignored him. Each and every one of them was tall, statuesque, and beautiful, all cut from the same cloth. At first glance, Dunk could barely tell them apart, other than by the differing colours and styles of the long hair that flowed out of the backs of their helmets.

They all reminded Dunk of Enojada. He craned his neck around to peer into the Lusties' dugout and spotted the promoter standing there next to the team's coach, Lovie Jones. She waved back at him with a dazzling smile and seemed honestly happy to see him. He supposed that this game represented the culmination of months of hard work for her, and now she'd finally pulled it off. While Dunk being there might have thrilled her, though, she'd kept her distance from the Hackers since the start of the tournament. The rest of the Lusties clearly didn't share her glee.

They all glared at him hungrily, as if sizing him up for a meal. Dunk had no doubt that any one of them would try to take him out given half a chance, but he kept his guard up, unwilling to leave them even that much.

Only Hernd stopped him as he got closer to his goal. 'Come to take a look at the end zone, Dunk?' she said. 'It's the last time you'll see it today.'

'Just glad to see you finally got your chance to start as a thrower, Rotes,' he said, 'and I didn't have to get hurt for it to happen.'

'There's still time for that,' she said. He thought he detected a hint of a grin under her helmet, but that might just have been her baring her teeth.

'Mother!' Dunk called as he reached the end zone. 'What are you doing?'

The ghost's face swirled out of the mists at him. 'I just wanted to get a good seat to watch my boys play their last game,' she said. 'Isn't that what a good mother should do?'

'We came up with a solution to your problem,' Dunk said. 'We hired Kirta to become a Hacker. Now you don't have to worry about us hurting each other.'

The ghost's head bobbed up and down, and Dunk realised she was nodding. 'I appreciate your efforts, Dunkel. I really do. You're a good son.'

Dunk felt a smile tug at the corner of his mouth, despite himself.

'But that's just not going to be enough,' the ghost said.

Dunk's stomach felt like it toppled out of his belly and into one of the lava-lit crevasses. He'd worked hard to set up this deal, pushing Pegleg on it and strong arming the Lusties' coach, Lovie Jones, into agreeing to it. It had cost the Hackers a great deal of money to boot. And his mother had dismissed it all with a casual comment.

'Why not, Mother?' he asked, letting the irritation in his voice show. 'What more could you possibly want from us?'

'Why, don't you know, dear?' Greta's ghost covered her mouth in surprise. 'I want us all to be together for all eternity, and there's only one sure way for that to happen.

'I want you all dead.'

AT THAT MOMENT, Dunk knew just where Kirta had gone. She hadn't got cold feet at playing with the Hackers or against the Lusties. She hadn't decided to run off with Jiminy instead of facing her problems. She was somewhere nearby. He just hoped she was still alive.

'Mother,' Dunk said, 'what have you done with Kirta?'

'She's safe,' Greta's ghost said, 'for now. She's done with her team, I understand, thank you for that, Dunkel, and I didn't want her hurt.'

'Just dead?'

The ghost looked offended. 'Suicide is painless, they say, although that's just a horrible myth.'

'She's not committing… Wait. Didn't you get killed by the mob?'

'Wh-why would you say that, dear?'

Dunk gasped. 'When that mob stormed the keep, they didn't kill you, did they? You never gave them a chance.'

'I-I don't know what you're talking about.'

'You took the coward's way out.'

The ghost seemed to grow larger as she let her rage show. 'Is it cowardly to refuse to let a pack of peasants tear you limb from limb? To not let them violate and murder you? To rob them of their so-called revenge on you?'

Dunk waited for the ghost to finish, and then spat on the ground before her. 'Yes,' he said. 'Yes, it is.'

A roar went up from the crowd, and Dunk glanced up at the Jumboball perched over the stadium. He saw Jim and Bob's ugly faces leering out at him.

'It's game time, game fans! Listen to that Lustrian crowd howl!'

Dunk shot a piteous look at his mother's ghost. 'I have to go,' he said, 'but this isn't over.'

As he turned and started trotting back to the Hackers' side of the field, he heard the ghost say. 'Of course not, dear, but it will be soon.'

Dunk glanced up at the crowd in the stadium as he picked his way across the hot and treacherous pitch. A group of Amazons cheered directly behind the Lusties' dugout, but they were among the few humans in the stadium. A contingent of Norscans had arrived, too – Dunk could tell from their horned helmets, some of which had been retrofitted to allow them to sip from two attached steins of ale at once.

The fans who'd survived the journey on the *Fanatic* stood up behind the Hackers' dugout and made the most noise of any section in the stadium, bar none. The hardcore Blood Bowl aficionados had made it all the way across the ocean to see the game, and they were determined to make the most of it. Each and every one of them wore Hackers colours. Most of them had painted their faces and wore yellow tricorn hats in honour of Coach Haken.

Together, the *Fanatic* fans were loud enough to be heard over those rooting for the Lusties.

'What's that they're saying?' Spinne said.

'I don't know,' said Dunk. 'It sounds like "Fug the Lusties!"'

Spinne grinned. 'I don't think "fug" is the word you're looking for.'

'Then what could it– Oh!'

Getrunken leaned in with a leer. 'I wouldn't mind some of that action myself!' Then he joined in with the fans, waving his arm to lead them like a conductor.

The humans were notable for the fact that the lizardmen in the audience outnumbered them at least five to one. These creatures came in a wide rainbow of hues, from glowing blue to scarlet red, and everything in between. Some of them spat fire into the air as they cheered, and a number of terradons circled high above the stadium, riding the updrafts formed by the heat from the volcano's crater.

The lizardmen didn't cheer like regular crowds. They hissed their approval instead, flicking their tongues everywhere, flinging their saliva all around. Dunk gave thanks, not for the first time, that the Hackers' dugout had a roof.

Out on the field, of course, such things meant nothing. Dunk could not allow anything to distract him from the matter at hand. To do otherwise would be to invite death.

'Now that Hoffnung's finally decided which team he wants to play for, it's time for the kickoff!' Bob said.

'This one's for all the teeth,' Jim said. 'The winner not only takes home the Tobazco Bowl trophy, but gets bragging rights as the undisputed Blood Bowl champion of the entire planet!'

'Which should last until at least the next morning!' said Bob.

The crowd's roar rose to a crescendo, and the game was on. The Hackers had lost the coin toss and had to kick off. As soon as Edgar's trunk connected with the ball and booted it downfield, Dunk raced forward, ready to join in the play.

Within seconds, a number of Amazons broke through the Hackers' front line and surrounded Dunk on all sides. They'd made the most of the mismatches with the Sacrifice Flies and stomped two of them into the nearest crevasses. Dunk could still hear one of them squealing from the double hotfoot the lava was giving him.

Then the ball appeared in the sky, having been hurled downfield by Rotes. With four Amazons in the backfield and only Dunk and Cavre to defend against them, Dunk knew he'd have to move fast.

As much as Rotes thought Dunk had held on to his position out of some twisted sense of loyalty she believed Pegleg felt for him, the fact was he was a much better thrower than her. On her end of the field,

M'Grash had nearly tackled her, and she had thrown the ball up as far as she could in a dead panic. While this had got the ball, and the ogre, away from her, the barely controlled throw meant the football was up for grabs.

Everyone on Dunk's end of the field went for the ball. As an experienced thrower, Dunk had a good idea where it would land. He'd spent many hours watching Rotes throw the ball and sometimes even coaching her, although she always seemed to resent his advice. He knew she'd throw it too long. Even in practice she'd do this so that no one would rib her for having a weak arm. Here, in a game against her former team-mates, she'd have a lot more to prove.

Dunk faded back, all the way until he was in the Hackers' end zone. The others gathered around the 20-yard line and the ball sailed high over their heads. Dunk plucked it out of the air to the amazed roar of the crowd.

Of course, that put him in the end zone with the ball, with four Lusties nearby and only Cavre to lend him a hand. Dunk suspected that would be enough.

A veteran of more Blood Bowl seasons than Dunk ever hoped to play, Cavre had already knocked down two of the Lusties before the ball reached Dunk's hands. While the Amazons had been playing the ball, Cavre had been playing them.

That left two Lusties turning to take on Dunk. He cut to the left, towards Cavre, and the veteran blitzer took out another Lusty with a sharp block from behind. The other had been too wary to get drawn closer to Cavre, and she went straight for Dunk.

Dunk gave the Lusty a quick jink. She hesitated, buying him the instant he needed to sweep back to the right and look for blockers and a target downfield. He pump-faked the ball back to the left, and the Lusty leapt into the air, hoping to block the pass. As she recovered from her jump, he spotted Edgar wide open in the middle of the field.

The treeman made for such a large and easy target, it almost felt like cheating to throw him the ball. As Pegleg and Slick constantly reminded him, though, there was no shame in making the easy play. Even cheating wasn't a problem in Blood Bowl. The only crime in the game was getting caught.

The ball sailed through the air, and Edgar caught it in his upper branches, high up enough so that no Lusty ever had a chance to touch the ball. With a lumbering spin, the treeman pitched the ball forward again, straight towards Spinne.

She leapt up between a pair of Lusties and snagged the ball out of the air. Unfortunately, she had to move forward to get the pass from Edgar, who despite all his branches didn't have much of an arm. This put her out of the end zone, with the two Lusty defenders doing their best to pull her down.

Spinne spied M'Grash thundering her way and tossed the ball to him in an underhand arc. He gathered it up in his hands like Dunk might hold an apple, and charged straight for the end zone.

Three Lusties bravely stood in his way. Despite his ogrish heritage and his love for the game of Blood Bowl, M'Grash didn't like to kill unless forced to. He took three huge, bouncing strides and then leapt straight over the Lusties' heads. He came down in the end zone with a thump, holding the ball high in triumph.

'Touchdown, Hackers!' Bob said.

Dunk cheered at the top of his lungs. Despite the problems with his mother, despite his worries about his sister, despite the fact that most of the fans in the stadium wanted the Hackers to lose, they were playing well, and they were going to win. He could feel it.

Then the end zone exploded.

'Um, we may want to check the instant replay on that, Bob!'

Dunk raced forward, keeping half one eye on the cracked field, which seemed to have become even more rugged with the blast. The other he kept on the Jumboball, watching the scene in the end zone play back in slow motion.

M'Grash leapt forward into the end zone. As he did, the ghost swirled in underneath him, the ground below her growing so cold that frost rimed its ridges. When M'Grash came down, he passed right through the ghost and hit the cracked ground.

M'Grash landed so hard that he shattered the crust that the ghost's chill had caused to form over the top of the lava. The liquid rocks below had built up a tremendous amount of pressure, as the ghost's cold mist in the end zone had essentially created a large cap over the lava. When M'Grash cracked the cap open, the pressure below finally had a means to escape, and it did so, violently.

The force of the blast sent a glowing pillar of lava high into the air, fountaining out over the end zone and sending the players nearby scrambling. It threw M'Grash about like a child's doll, sending him high into the air. The camra followed his progress, and Dunk watched him come down on an end-zone section of the stands filled with pinkish lizardmen.

The lizardmen scattered as the ogre came hurtling down at them, but not all of them were as fast as they needed to be. The ogre's great bulk smashed them flat, along with the benches in their part of the stadium.

Dunk held his breath as he continued to watch the Jumboball. Although he'd made it almost all the way down the entire length of the field, he still couldn't see past the cloud of smoke, steam, and ash that filled the end zone. M'Grash had crashed down somewhere past all that, but Dunk had no way to reach him.

He decided to cut to the right and take his chances in the crowd. Most times Dunk had found himself in the stands during a game had turned out terribly. In his first game, the fans had body-passed him up to the stadium's top edge and tossed him over.

Blood Bowl's best fans, the ones who took the time and paid the money to come to an actual game, were as tough as they came, harder and meaner than the players sometimes. They often saw a player in the stands as a source of the best souvenirs a fan could have: body parts. These could go for hundreds or even thousands of gold coins on the black market or on one of the magical auctioneering programs like eVilBay.

Dunk knew of the danger of entering the stands, but he had to risk it to make sure M'Grash was all right. He turned and charged towards the sidelines. Before he could reach the low wall that kept the fans off the field, for the most part, a pair of hands grabbed him from behind and hauled him back.

'Forget it!' Dirk said. 'You can't help him!'

Dunk spun around and tore out of his brother's grasp. 'I have to try! I can't just leave him there!'

'No one is stupid enough to try to tear apart an ogre unless he's dead! And what could you do for him either way? He's too big to carry!'

Spinne rushed up behind Dirk. 'He's right,' she said. 'I love M'Grash too, but it's madness to try!'

'Then it's madness!' Dunk said. 'I wouldn't leave either of you lying in the stands, and neither would M'Grash, and you both know it!'

Dirk scowled at Spinne, who gave him an equally angry and frustrated look. 'All right,' Spinne said to Dunk, 'but we're going in together!'

Dunk nodded, clapped them on their shoulders, and gave Spinne a passionate kiss. Then he turned and led the way into the stands.

Some of the fans reached for them as they entered, but Dunk smacked down anyone that came close to him. He took point while Dirk and Spinne covered the flanks, and they waded through the mass of people between them and their friends.

The crowd had already thinned out a bit after the explosion. While Blood Bowl fans always knew there was some threat of death just from sitting in the stands, when faced with an eruption from an active volcano, even a comparatively small burst like this, most of them would decide imminent death wasn't worth seeing a game they could watch on Cabalvision at their local tavern.

Dunk, Dirk and Spinne fought their way through the crowd, but it was slow going. The fans, mostly lizardmen, sometimes froze when they saw them coming, and they had to be bodily shoved out of the way for the players to get by.

Eventually, they reached M'Grash. He'd created something of a small crater where he'd landed, and blood trickled out under him in at least three different spots. Dunk could not tell if any of it belonged to the ogre.

The fans had cleared out the area around M'Grash, with a few exceptions. A couple of small, greenish lizardmen were pulling on the ogre's golden nose ring as Dunk and the others arrived.

'Get away from him, you vultures!' Dunk shouted at them.

The creatures looked over their shoulders and spied Dunk, Dirk, and Spinne, looking like spirits of vengeance bearing down on them. They weren't particularly smart, otherwise they wouldn't have tried to rob an ogre, and seeing the players coming their way only encouraged them to tug harder on the nose ring.

Dirk stepped up and punted one of the little lizardmen high into the air. Before the first lizardman even came down to a rough landing amidst a bunch of salamander-men who'd run out of snacks to roast during the game, Dunk snarled at the other one, who finally decided he'd had enough and dashed away at top speed, climbing up the front of a nearby spectator and then sprinting away over the heads of others.

'How is he?' Dunk asked Spinne, who'd gone straight to M'Grash.

She looked up from where she'd laid her head against the ogre's chest. 'Still breathing, but he's not in good shape. We need to get him to the locker room right now.'

Dunk looked into the end zone, which was still filled with steam and smoke. They'd had a hard enough time getting here going through the stands. He didn't see how they could make it back that way while carrying M'Grash, who had to be at least 500 pounds of dead weight.

'We'll have to go through the end zone,' he said.

'No way,' said Dirk. 'We can't even pick him up, not the three of us. We'd need five at least, ten would be better.'

'How about twenty?' a man said as he raced down the aisle.

Dunk looked up at the man, a hefty fan decked out in Hacker gear from head to toe. A score of others dressed just like him pushed straight down the aisle, shoving aside any of the lizardmen who dared to approach them.

'We're here to help,' the man said. 'What can we do?'

Dunk recognised the man. 'You were on the *Fanatic*.'

'We all were. We really grew to respect you guys on the voyage, and we're ready to do whatever we can to help out.'

Dunk bit his lip. He didn't want to trust his best friend's fate to a pack of Blood Bowl fans, but he clearly didn't have a choice. 'All right,' he said, 'let's get everyone around M'Grash. We lift and carry him as one, and it shouldn't be too bad.'

'I couldn't blame you for thinking that,' said Dirk. He pointed over Dunk's shoulder, 'but I think maybe you forgot about her.'

Dunk turned around and saw his mother's ghost looming over him. The smoke and steam curled around her, making it impossible to tell where she ended and the disaster in the end zone began.

'Dunkel,' Greta's ghost said, 'I think this has gone on long enough.'

'I couldn't agree more, Mother,' he said as he stepped towards her. 'It's time to end this.'

'I DON'T THINK you quite understand, Dunkel,' the ghost said. 'I want you to shape up. Don't spend what little time you have left worrying about the fate of an ogre. Enjoy your last few hours among the living, or I'll kill you right now.'

'Gosh, Mother, you always know how to say the sweetest things. It's a good thing you were such a concerned, involved parent when you were alive, or I might think you were desperately trying to make up for something you failed at in your life.'

The ghost let loose a shriek that made everyone in the stadium cover their ears. 'Dunkel Hoffnung! I am still your mother, and you will talk to me with the respect I deserve!'

As Dunk spoke, he saw Dirk and Spinne leading the *Fanatic* fans down to the far side of the end zone, away from him and the ghost. He knew that he had to keep her busy until they managed to get through the dangerous section. Not only would they have to contend with the brittle crust over the lava, which might explode if broken, but also with the fact that the ghost might spot them and come after them at any moment. If they dropped M'Grash there, Dunk knew they'd never get him out of there alive.

'First of all,' Dunk said, 'you're not my mother.' He spoke slowly and let his voice drip with cockiness. 'You're nothing more than a collection of spirit-stuff that happened to be around when my mother died. You just think you're Greta Hoffnung, but the truth is she's dead and gone.'

'How dare you say that? I gave birth to you! I raised you from an infant! I turned you into the strong and able man you are today!'

'Second of all, you, and by you, I mean the woman you pretend to be, may have birthed me, but you never raised me. You were too busy with your social schedule and your gossip about the noble class to burden yourself with anything as inconvenient and messy as child rearing.'

'That's not true!' she said. 'I saw you every day! I took most of my meals with you!'

'How kind,' Dunk said mockingly. 'Maybe if you'd been around more, Dirk wouldn't have decided that he couldn't stand you so much that he had to run away.'

Dunk winced as he spoke Dirk's name. It felt good to get all of this off of his chest, but he hadn't planned on saying his brother's name. If Greta's ghost decided to look for Dirk to confront him on any point that

Dunk raised, she'd see them hauling away M'Grash, and all would be lost.

'That's not true! That was your father's fault! I-I would have spent more time with you if not for him. I… When Dirk ran away, I was heartbroken. You know that!'

Dunk remembered all too well. Greta had refused to come out of her chambers for over a week. Dunk had heard screaming matches between her and his father, but he'd never dared to get close enough to learn exactly what they were about.

'Sure, Father brought the Blood God into our lives. That's what drove Dirk away, but you knew about it, and you didn't stop him!'

'Oh, don't get so high and mighty with me, Dunkel. You knew about it too. Oh, sure, perhaps you didn't know about the daemons, but anyone living in that house had to know he was up to no good. You could have said something as easily as me, but you never did.'

'I was supposed to be getting married! I spent as little time in the house as I could!'

'Yes, but your father sold us out to Khorne years before that. You had your whole childhood to figure it out, and I know that you paid attention to your father when you were younger. You idolised him for a while.'

Dunk turned grim at these thoughts. 'That was a long time ago.'

'I supposed that goes for all the feelings you once had for me as well. I know I wasn't much of a mother to you and Dirk and Kirta, Dunkel, but I promise to make it up to you throughout eternity.'

The ghost's sheer madness staggered Dunk to the point that he didn't know how to respond to it. Still, he had to keep her distracted just a little bit longer.

He snuck a quick peek, and saw that the crew hauling M'Grash out through the end zone had just about made it. He wanted to give them plenty of time to get clear, though, perhaps even all the way back to the dugout.

When he looked over his shoulder to the crew's goal, he spied Slick racing towards him, as fast as his little legs could carry him. Dunk didn't know what sort of insane thoughts could have propelled his agent on to the field, especially with a ghost occupying the end zone, but he already had too much craziness on his hands to deal with it right now. To turn around to chase Slick back to safety would alert Greta's ghost for sure.

'What makes you think that eternity will treat us any better than our lives in Altdorf?' Dunk asked. 'You were a miserable mother then, and I can't imagine you've improved upon your parenting skills while terrorising poor Kirta over the past few years.'

'I saved your sister! Without my help, she'd have been dead a dozen times over!'

'Saved her for a life of slavery and then to be sold into the most lethal sport in history? Well done, Mother. Gold stars for you!'

Tendrils shot out of the swirling mists from beneath the ghost's face, lashing towards Dunk. He dived to the right, away from the others carting M'Grash off the field, and rolled away. As he touched the ground with his bare hands, he cried out in surprise and pain at the heat emanating from it.

As intent as Dunk had been on his mother's ghost, he hadn't realised that the cracks in the field had started to widen. He felt like he was rolling about on a giant's griddle. He sprang to his feet as soon as he could, if only to put his boots under him again and keep his bare skin from blistering.

The chilling mists that had sailed over his head came curling after him. He looked past them to see Slick guiding the crew bearing M'Grash into the dugout. The crowd cheered on their efforts, showing that even if they didn't care much for the Hackers, they hated Dunk's mother even more.

'You hear that, Mother?' Dunk said. 'Everyone in the stadium hates you. They think I'm right and you're wrong.'

'The people here, if you can call them that, are little more than barbarians, cold-blooded freaks who have to restrain themselves from eating their young, something at which they rarely succeed!'

The crowd turned ugly at the attention focused on it. The people in the stands began to hurl things into the end zone: Bloodweiser, Killer Genuine Draft, *Spike! Magazine*'s Hard Lemonade (which came frozen solid as a brick), bleachers, skinks-on-sticks, smaller spectators, and more.

All of these things passed right through the mists, of course, doing the ghost not a bit of harm. Despite this, she grew furious. 'Don't!' she said, turning to screech at the crowd. 'Stop!'

'Would you look at that?' Bob said. 'It seems like the Undead Mother of the Year doesn't like people polluting her pure and virtuous mists.'

'That's amazing, Bob! Truly amazing! How do you think a proper stadium of Blood Bowl fans might react to that?'

The crowd roared and began to hurl more and more things into the end zone. Dunk wondered how long it would take them to run out of things to throw, and if the end zone would look like a landfill or an incinerator when it was all done.

The ghost unleashed an ear-splitting screech that forced everyone in the stadium to cover their ears. Those who were standing fell to their knees in pain. Those who were sitting wished that they'd been standing so that the pain of falling to their knees might distract them from just how much their ears hurt.

Through it all, Dunk thought he could make out some kind of words, but it wasn't until his ears stopped ringing that he could figure out what they were. 'Stop it! You're killing her!'

Once the echoes from the horrible scream faded away, Bob's voice came out over the Preternatural Announcement system.

'I think after all this we can see how the Hoffnungs all became tough enough to become Blood Bowl players!'

'Sure thing!' said Jim. 'Between their father's performance in the Blood Bowl championship game last year and their mother's appearance here, my only question is why didn't they get into the game earlier?'

'Too true! After all, their home life must have made playing Blood Bowl seem like a picnic in paradise!'

Dunk pulled himself back to his feet and dusted off his knees, which glowed red from getting too close to the lava beneath the stadium's floor. He knew what his mother had meant with her scream, and why she'd screamed so loud. In his gut, he knew.

'What did you do with her, Mother?' he asked, trying to peer past her into the roiling bank of mists that still covered the Lusties' end zone.

'You were my favourite, Dunkel,' Greta's ghost said. 'You were my first, my special little boy. I loved Dirk when he came along too, but I'd already had a little boy. When Kirta entered my life, though, she stole my heart away.'

'Where is she, Mother?'

'I knew what your father had done, and I couldn't live with the thought that you would all someday be sacrificed to the Blood God. I hardened my heart against you all, perhaps against Kirta the most.'

Dunk tried to peer through the mists. The ghost seemed to be coalescing in front of him, gathering the low bank of steam over the end zone into herself. He thought he could finally see something in there, something besides all the things the fans had thrown into the place.

'When it all went bad, when that mob stormed our castle, I decided I would do the right thing. I'd protect my daughter and keep her safe, even if I couldn't do the same for Dirk and you.'

'Thanks for nothing, Mother.' Dunk could not keep the bitterness from his voice.

The ghost sobbed with grief, slim wisps trailing down from her eyes where tears should have formed.

'When it came down to it, when the moment arrived for me to do what I had to do, I couldn't manage it. I-I...'

Dunk eyed the ghost suspiciously. A sense of dread began to grow in him, and he felt the hairs on the back of his neck rise up. 'Couldn't manage what, Mother?'

'I had the dagger in my hand.' The mists around the ghost's hand formed into the shape of a long, curved knife. 'When Lehrer abandoned us, when I refused him, I-I never thought he'd just leave us like that, but he did. So I drew out my dagger and prepared to use it.'

'Mother,' Dunk asked, knowing he didn't want to hear the answer, 'what did you do?'

'I raised the blade over Kirta and steadied my hand to plunge it into her back. I would kill her and then myself to prevent the mob from getting us, from handing us over to Khorne, from meeting justice at his blood-soaked hands.'

Dunk stared at his mother's ghost, his jaw dropping low in horror. The mists behind her parted finally, and he saw Kirta lying unconscious in the end zone.

One of the first bleachers tossed onto the field had fallen near and then toppled over onto her. While it had pressed her to the searing floor, it had also shielded her from many of the other things the fans had thrown into the ghostly mists. However, a large, glowing hole had appeared in the end zone, right where M'Grash had landed and then been blown back, and Kirta's body lay perilously close to it. Dunk could see that her armour and hair were starting to smoulder. If he could not deal with Greta's ghost soon, poor Kirta would burst into flames.

'But you couldn't do it, could you?' Dunk said.

The ghost had swirled around on its ethereal tail to look down at Kirta. Greta shook her head back and forth, unable to say a word. She leaned in close to caress the unmoving girl's cheek, and the proximity of her chill to the lava's heat caused a new burst of mist to billow up around Kirta's body.

'She's alive, and you're not. The mob didn't kill either one of you, did it, Mother?'

The ghost angled back to face Dunk again. She shook her head. 'No. I couldn't do it. I didn't have the courage to keep my angel safe from harm.'

'You turned the knife on yourself.'

The ghost held up the misty blade in her hand, and it melted away in the sunlight. She nodded.

'I saved myself instead.'

'And that's why you came back as a ghost.' Now Dunk finally understood. 'You did have unfinished business to take care of: protecting Kirta.'

'Which proved nearly impossible,' Greta's ghost said with a moan. 'I can scare people. I can scream at them all I want, but I can't touch them.'

'You nearly froze Dirk to death.'

'As I said, if we could not be together properly in life, then I'll be happy to gather us all together for eternity in death.'

Dunk rolled his eyes. 'Given your stellar track record, what makes you think it's going to work any better this time?'

'Because it will! It has to! And you cannot stop me!'

Dunk heard footsteps thundering up behind him, and he spun around to see Dirk and Spinne rushing to help. Spinne held Slick in her arms, cradling him like a small child.

'No!' the ghost said. She unleashed another screech that brought everyone in earshot down once more. Dirk and Spinne fell to their knees, and Slick slipped to the ground, still clutching something to his chest.

The ghost hurled herself at Dunk once more, and he ducked nimbly under her attack. Once he rolled back to his feet, he realised that Greta hadn't been aiming for him, this time, but for the people just beyond.

Spinne saw the ghost coming at her, and she managed to shove Slick out of the way. Dirk moved to protect her from Greta's ghost, but this proved impossible. If the ghost had been substantial, he would have kept her from harming Spinne, but as it was Greta simply enveloped them both.

Even from where he stood, yards away, the ghost's chill felt like a wintry blast straight off the Sea of Claws. Dirk howled in pain, and Spinne screamed.

Dunk glanced over his shoulder and saw the lava inching closer and closer to Kirta's unconscious frame. Flames licked the bench that lay on top of her, and it would only be a matter of moments before both it and she would be engulfed.

Dunk knew this might be his only chance to rescue his sister, but to do so might cost his brother and his lover their lives.

Dunk froze for a moment. The choice was just too hard for him to make, but if he didn't do something soon all three of the most important people in his life would die.

Spinne cried out, and Dunk knew that he had to go to her. No matter what happened to Dirk and Kirta, he loved this woman and wanted to build a new family with her, one that wouldn't be cursed with the madness that had affected the family in which he'd grown up.

He only hoped that Kirta might hold on a little longer and that, if she didn't, Dirk could forgive him. He hoped he could forgive himself.

Just as Dunk was set to charge at the ghost and do his worst to her, whatever that might involve when trying to fight an insubstantial spirit, Slick stood up and held something over his head.

'Son,' he shouted at the top of his lungs, 'I have the answer right here!'

Dunk stared at the halfling in disbelief. In his upraised hand he held the Lizard's Claw.

'How in the world did you end up with that?' Dunk wanted to ask, but there was no time. Instead, he held out his hands and shouted, 'Throw it here.'

Slick swung it back for an underhand pitch. As he did, he shouted again. 'Remember, you can use it to wish for anything you want. Anything at all! Just be careful.'

Greta's ghost spun around at these words and focused on the halfling. Dunk silently cursed his agent for having such a big mouth. 'Just throw it!' he said.

Slick swung the claw back once more and then tossed it high into the air. Dunk never would have guessed that the halfling had such a strong arm, but the Lizard's Claw sailed up and over his head. He leapt for it, but it was just out of his reach.

Dunk glanced at the ghost, saw the desperate hunger in her eyes, and then turned and charged after the Lizard's Claw.

'THAT WILL BE MINE!' the ghost screeched as she jetted past Dunk to fall onto the magical severed hand.

Dunk's legs pistoned as he strove to reach the Lizard's Claw first, but he could not outrun the ghost's unearthly speed. She fell on top of it, curling her icy mists tightly around it, so thickly that Dunk could no longer see the claw beneath her.

He knew, though, that she could not pick the claw up, no matter how thick the mists might get. That didn't mean she couldn't use it. Maybe she could just by touching it, and maybe she couldn't. He didn't want to debate the issue, just get the damned thing away from her.

Dunk dived into the mists and swept his arms and hands in wide arcs. At first, all he could feel was the fast-cooling lava forming a brittle shell beneath him.

He made a mental note to be as careful as he could so that he wouldn't suffer the same fate as M'Grash.

Even so, he worried more about getting a hold of the claw than avoiding a painful death. If his mother's ghost managed to somehow use it, he could bet that nothing good would come of it.

'I wish–' Greta's ghost began, just as Dunk's fingers brushed against the claw. His hand clamped down on it in triumph, even as he began to lose the feeling in his fingers and toes from the cold that surrounded him.

'Forget it,' Dunk said. 'I won't let you kill us all!'

The ghost wailed once more. With the Lizard's Claw held tightly in his hands, Dunk could not cover his ears, and his head rang with the ghost's anguish.

'Your sister is about to die!' the ghost said. 'You can still save her if you let go of the claw, now!'

'No!' Dunk said. 'I w-w-wish…' He tried to say more, to finish the wish that would activate the Lizard's Claw, but his teeth were chattering too hard, and his lips felt like they'd frozen together. He felt the skin on them tear as he pried them apart and tried again.

'I w-w-wish.'

The ghost screeched louder than ever before, and Dunk found that he could not go on. He knew, though, that if he could just hold on a little bit longer he might be able to catch enough of a break to spit out his wish.

In his head, Dunk damned his mother for being so horrible. He damned himself for not being stronger, and he damned Slick for opening his mouth. He'd always thought of his agent as smarter than that, much smarter.

The ghost's screaming stopped, and Dunk realised that he'd been screaming right along with her. He pulled back his lips to expose his teeth and took one last frozen breath so he could spit out his terrible wish. He wondered, for a moment, what terrible price the Lizard's Claw would make him pay, and then he damned that as well. If it meant saving his brother, his sister, and his love, the price could not be too high to pay.

Then Dunk realised he'd been going about this all wrong.

'Don't touch me!' he said. 'You can't touch me! You can't hurt me! Not anymore!'

Dunk dragged himself back on his haunches. The cold had forced every bit of air out of lungs, and he could not catch his breath. The world began to spin and grow dark around the edges. He fell backward, and the Lizard's Claw spilled from his hand.

'Yes!' the ghost shouted.

Dunk's head hit the encrusted lava, and he felt it crack. The pressure building beneath threatened to blast him back to his feet, although perhaps without his skull. He rolled onto his side and felt a pair of hands grab his shoulders and haul him back from the freezing mists that still curled around his feet.

'I'll stop her,' Spinne said once Dunk was clear, but Dunk knew it was already too late. He grabbed her arm and held her back. He looked around for Dirk and spotted him hauling Kirta from under the burning bleacher. She looked like she might still be alive.

The ghost's upper body spiralled into the sky while her swirling, ethereal tail enveloped the Lizard's Claw. She had something to say, and she wanted everyone to hear it.

'I wish,' she said, louder than even the PA system, 'that I could be solid enough to hold my children one more time, and strangle them to death!'

'You have got to be kidding me,' Spinne said as she stared up at Greta's ghost in awe. 'I see now why you never talked about your mother.'

'Move it!' Dunk said. He grabbed Spinne's hand and began to pull her away. Slick had already raced off ahead of them and had made it halfway back to the dugout. 'Run!'

Dunk glanced back over his shoulder. In the distance, he saw that Dirk had tossed Kirta over his back and was climbing into the stands. A few of the *Fanatic*'s fans still standing there helped to pull the two of them to safety. Almost everyone else had found the good sense to run off.

Greta's ghost began to coalesce in mid-air. As it did, it changed in both shape and hue, becoming less grey and more solid. Soon it formed into an all-too familiar figure that Dunk had known since his birth. His mother hung there in the crisp sky, hovering over the smouldering field for a long moment.

'Yes!' she said. 'Now, I will finally be able to bring us all together! To unite my children! To–'

Gravity kicked in, and pulled the solid creature back to the earth. As she plummeted towards the frozen crust of lava below her, she screamed. This time, she sounded all too human.

As Greta, or her ghost, or some other strange cross between the living and the dead, hit the field, the crust below her broke, and the lava trapped beneath it geysered into the sky, enveloping and incinerating her in a lethal instant.

Spinne, who'd long ago seen enough, pulled hard on Dunk's arm. He whispered a silent goodbye to his mother, and then turned his attention to chasing after his love as fast as he could.

The burst that had opened up beneath M'Grash had destabilised the field, and Dunk guessed that once that happened it wouldn't be too much longer before the entire crater erupted again. The blast that had destroyed Greta must have been the tipping point. It set off a chain reaction of other bursts throughout the pitch, which rocked the ground so hard that Dunk found it difficult to stay on his feet.

'To the dugout!' Spinne said.

Dunk glanced there and saw Cavre gathering up Slick and pulling him inside. Otherwise, the place was almost empty, everyone else having already raced down the tunnel to the locker room at the first sign of the eruption. Only Pegleg still stood there, waving Dunk and Spinne in by windmilling his hook.

Dunk looked back and saw Dirk, Kirta, and the last of the *Fanatic* fans charging up the stairs in the stands to reach the exit. He hoped they would make it in time. He hoped they all would.

Hissing steam and burning ash burst into the sky all around Dunk and Spinne. A blast from a large crack in front of them shot lava thirty feet into the sky and forced them to change course to circumnavigate it.

With a final burst of speed, Dunk and Spinne reached the dugout and dived through the door. Pegleg swung in right behind them and slammed the iron-plated door shut. The torches that had once been lit inside the tunnel had gone out, but Dunk could see well enough by the reddish glow the metallic door began to give off as the lava outside roiled against it.

Dunk pulled Spinne into his arms and gave her a passionate kiss. If the door wouldn't hold against the lava, he wanted to die in her arms, and if it did, there still wasn't anywhere else he wanted to be.

After a moment, when it became clear they would not die, at least not right away, Pegleg cleared his throat. Dunk and Spinne broke off their embrace and looked at him, blushing just a little and giggling in relief.

'I'll say one thing for you, partner,' the ex-pirate said. 'You always think of the important things first.'

Dunk grinned like a fool. He didn't understand what the man meant, but at the moment he was too happy to be alive to care.

Spinne, who had still managed to keep her wits about her, said, 'What do you mean, coach? He just blew up the entire stadium.'

Pegleg turned the pair of them to face back down the tunnel and put a hand and a hook on their shoulders as he guided them back towards safety and light. 'True. The game is over, and the tournament is done, but Dunk did one thing right before it all went straight to hell.'

'What's that, coach?' Dunk asked.

'You ran the play that let us score first.'

38

'Will you marry me?'

Down on one knee, Dunk looked up at Spinne, a beautiful ring set with a rose-red gem held up to her in his hands. He'd been planning this since the end of the game against the Lusties, and he'd worked nearly every moment since then to set it up just right. He'd arranged for a delicious and private, candlelit dinner in the captain's luxurious quarters aboard the *Fanatic*. He'd picked up a bottle of the finest wine he could find on Amazon Island, and he'd been on his best behaviour ever since they'd survived his mother's self-destruction.

Spinne looked down at him, tears welling up in her eyes, and said, 'What, now?'

'Yes,' said Dunk, a little taken aback. He'd hoped for a 'yes,' dreaded a 'no,' and had not at all considered any strange tangents such as this. 'Is that all right?'

Spinne bared her teeth as she squirmed in her chair. 'How… how soon do you want an answer?'

Dunk's heart fell. He felt it bounce through the boards of each deck and emerge in the dark waters of the night-black sea, into which it continued to sink until he could feel it no longer.

'The sooner the better,' he said, offering up a weak smile to go along with the ring. This was not going nearly as well as he'd hoped. She hadn't hurled him out of the wide window at the aft of the ship, which had been his worst-case scenario, but this was almost worse. That he could understand, at least.

Dunk put the ring down on the table next to them and put his hands next to Spinne's in her lap. 'What's wrong?' he asked. 'I thought you wanted this too.'

'I do,' she said, looking at him with shining eyes, her voice raw as a fresh bruise. 'I did. I… I don't know.'

'You did?' Dunk sat back in his chair, his shoulders slumped. Something had gone wrong. He'd had his chance, his window of opportunity, and somehow he'd missed it. 'What happened?'

Spinne wrung her fingers together. 'I don't know. It… When we were in your keep in Altdorf, after we won the Blood Bowl championship and saved the Empire from the wrath of the Blood God, I knew then that I wanted to marry you, that I wanted to be with you forever.'

'And?'

'And you never asked. I waited, I hoped, I even tried a prayer or two to Nuffle, but nothing. I thought maybe something would happen in Magritta. After all, that's where we first met, right?'

'But I didn't do anything.'

'Right, and I figured I'd bring it up when we got back to Bad Bay. I'm not some damsel in distress who needs rescuing and then a proper wedding before bedding, as you well know.'

Dunk nodded.

'But then we got sidetracked. We wound up going to Lustria to find your sister, and then we got wound up in this disaster with your mother, and you got so focused on everything else that I wondered if you wanted to marry me.'

'But I do!'

Spinne looked straight into him. Most of the time, he loved it when she did that, but now it terrified him. 'You say that, but you haven't been acting like it. For much of this trip, you haven't paid much attention to me at all. I wondered sometimes if you knew I was around or if you just thought of me as another one of your friends on the team.'

'But...' Dunk desperately searched his memory for something to contradict her claims, some evidence that her concerns had no foundation. 'What about that night on Columbo's Island?'

Spinne gave him a wistful smile. 'That was wonderful. You were sweet and romantic and full of life. But the next morning, when it turned out everyone else was gone, kidnapped by the pygmy halflings, so was the Dunk I'd spent the night with.'

'I... I had a lot on my mind,' he said. 'You're right. I'm sorry. I didn't spend enough time thinking about you.

'I don't think I realised it until my mother's ghost almost killed us out on that field. When I had to choose to save you or my sister, I chose you. You meant the most to me of anyone. You still do.'

He reached out and took her hands again. 'I don't ever want to lose you.'

Spinne smiled at him, and his heart leapt with hope. 'What about Dirk? Didn't he figure into that at all? Two lives instead of one?'

Dunk arched an eyebrow at her. 'Dirk? Dirk who?'

They both laughed, and the tension between them flowed out of the room.

'I do want to marry you, Dunkel Hoffnung,' she said, holding his hands again, 'but can we make it a long engagement?'

'How long?'

She winced gamely. 'At least until we get back home?'

Dunk nodded. 'Does that mean yes?'

Spinne jumped up and hauled Dunk into a tight, passionate embrace. 'Yes!'

Dunk's heart rocketed up from the depths of the oceans and zoomed right past him on its way towards the stars. He had never been so happy in all his days. He slid the ring on her finger, and she admired it, both of them wearing the grins of lovestruck fools.

Then Dunk looked to the door. 'Oh, ah, I need to, um, say something to the, ah–'

'How many people do you have waiting outside to hear about this?'

Dunk flushed as he hemmed and hawed before spitting it out. 'The whole crew.'

'The whole team?' Spinne's eyes flew wide in astonishment.

Dunk winced. 'Plus everyone else on the ship.'

'And what do they think is going to happen?'

Dunk rubbed his neck. 'Well, the plan calls for me sweeping you up in my arms and then carrying you up to the top of the forecastle where Pegleg would marry us.'

Spinne stuck out her bottom lip and appraised Dunk in a new light. 'Amazing.'

'Any chance you'd change your mind?' he asked. 'Not on my behalf, of course. Think of M'Grash. He'll cry like a baby.'

Spinne caressed his cheek and kissed him softly on the lips. 'You're a good man and a great friend. Someday you'll make a wonderful husband.'

'Someday soon?'

Spinne nodded. 'But not today.'

Dunk put an arm around her waist. 'All right,' he said, 'but we have to tell everyone together.'

Spinne grinned as they walked to the door. 'Of course.'

The door opened to a massive cheer. Everyone aboard the ship had turned out on the deck to learn the results of Dunk's proposal. They were all there: the fans, the crew, Dirk, Slick, Lästiges (her camra still over her shoulder and recording every moment), Cavre, M'Grash, Guillermo, Spiel, Getrunken (who couldn't seem to stop whooping), Edgar, and Pegleg, and even Kirta, and Jiminy who'd decided to sail back with them to the Old World.

The ship had been decorated from one end to the other with lanterns flickering in the wind. A white runner stretched the length of the ship, right up the forecastle's steps. Kirta held a beautiful bouquet of flowers ready to hand to the bride-to-be, and from somewhere on the foredeck the scent of a delicious feast wafted towards Dunk's nose. Everything was just as he had planned it.

Dunk held out both hands and waited for the crowd to quieten down. When the only sound was that of the ship cutting through the waves, he spoke. 'I have good news, and I have bad news. The bad news is that there will be no wedding tonight.'

A collective 'awwwww' ran through the assembled crowd. Before it could die out, though, Spinne stepped forward and held her hand in the air, the ring sparkling on it. 'But we will be married soon!'

The crowd went from crushed to jubilant in an instant. Well-wishers rushed in to offer congratulations and embraces all around, and this went on long enough for Dunk's face to hurt from smiling so hard.

Eventually, Kirta made her way through the crowd and wrapped her arms around both Spinne and Dunk in a huge hug. 'I can't wait to finally have a sister,' she said, kissing them both on their cheeks.

Jiminy stepped up behind her and offered his hand in congratulations. 'I wonder if I might make a request of you,' he said to Dunk and Spinne. He gave them a bashful grin.

'Anything,' Dunk said.

Jiminy looked around the ship. 'Well, it seems like an awful waste, a crime if you will, to let this amazing spread go to waste.' He took Kirta's hand in his. 'Since you've gone to all the trouble to come up with the perfect shipboard wedding, that is. If you wouldn't mind,

I'd like your permission to ask Miss Kirta if she'd be amicable to–'

'Yes!' Kirta said, leaping into Jiminy's arms. 'Yes! Yes! Yes!'

The crowd sent up a cheer that rocked the *Fanatic* from one end to the other. Although it was clear his sister didn't need anyone's blessing, Dunk and Dirk both stepped forward and gave it freely. Tears welled up in many an eye as Kirta tossed Spinne the bouquet, and then scooped up Jiminy and carried him straight to where Pegleg awaited them atop the forecastle.

Dunk held Spinne close as they watched his sister dash off to her wedding, the wedding that could have been theirs. Spinne held the bouquet up to her nose and gave it a tender sniff. 'It smells wonderful,' she said. 'You thought of everything.'

'Kirta helped,' Dunk said. 'Actually, she managed most of it. She knew where to get everything on Amazon Island, and she tackled it as if it was her own day about to happen.' He smiled. 'Now I guess it is.'

Spinne leaned in close and gave him a kiss. 'I won't make you wait too long,' she said, 'just long enough for us both to be sure.'

'We're going to be on this ship for a while,' Dunk said, squeezing her tight, 'and the instant you change your mind, I think I know where I can find a captain.'

ABOUT THE AUTHOR

Matt Forbeck has worked full-time in the adventure games industry since 1989. He has designed collectible card games, roleplaying games, miniatures games and board games, and has written short fiction, comic books, novels and computer games. For more details about him and his work, please visit *www.forbeck.com*.

A GUIDE TO BLOOD BOWL

Being a volume of instruction for rookies and beginners of Nuffle's sacred game.

(Translated by Andreas Halle of Middenheim)

NUFFLE'S SACRED NUMBER

Let's start with the basics. To play Blood Bowl you need two warrior sects each led by a priest. In the more commonly used Blood Bowl terminology this means you need two teams of fearless psychotics (we also call them 'players') led by a coach, who is quite often a hoary old ex-player more psychotic than all of his players put together.

The teams face each other on a ritualised battlefield known as a pitch or field. The field is marked out in white chalk lines into several different areas. One line separates the pitch in two through the middle dividing the field into each team's 'half'. The line itself is known as the 'line of scrimmage' and is often the scene of some brutal fighting, especially at the beginning and halfway points of the game. At the back of each team's half of the field is a further dividing line that separates the backfield from the end zone. The end zone is where an opposing team can score a 'touchdown' - more on that later.

Teams generally consist of between twelve to sixteen players. However, as first extolled by Roze-el, Nuffle's sacred number is eleven, which means only a maximum of eleven players from each team may be on the field at the same time. It's worth noting that many teams have tried to break this sacred convention in the past, particularly goblin teams (orcs too, but that's usually because they can't count rather than any malevolent intent), but Nuffle has always seen fit to punish those who do.

TOUCHDOWNS AND ALL THAT MALARKEY

The aim of the game is to carry, throw, kick and generally move an inflated animal bladder coated in leather and - quite often - spikes, across the field into the opposing team's end zone. Of course, the other team is trying to do the same thing. Once the inflated bladder, also known as the ball, has been carried into or caught in the opposing team's end zone, a 'touchdown' has been scored. Traditionally the crowd then goes wild, though the reactions of the fans vary from celebration if it was their team that just scored, to anger, if their team have conceded. The player who has scored will also have his moment of jubilation and much celebratory hugging with fellow team-mates will ensue, although a bear hug from an ogre, even if his intention is that of mutual happiness, is best avoided! The team that scores the most touchdowns within the allotted timeframe is deemed the winner.

The game lasts about two hours and is split into two segments unsurprisingly called 'the first half' and 'the second half'. The first half starts after both teams have walked onto the pitch and taken their positions, usually accompanied by

much fanfare and cheering from the fans. The team captains
meet in the centre of the pitch with the 'ref' (more on him
later) to perform the start-of-the-game ritual known as 'the
toss'. A coin is flipped in the air and one of the captains will
call 'orcs' or 'eagles'. Whoever wins the toss gets the choice
of 'kicking' or 'receiving'. Kicking teams will kick the ball
to the receiving teams. Once the ball has been kicked the
whistle is blown and the first half will begin. The second
half begins in much the same way except that the kicking
team at the beginning of the first half will now become the
receiving team and vice-versa.

Violence is encouraged to gain possession, keep and move
the ball, although different races and teams will try different
methods and varying degrees of hostility. The fey elves, for
instance, will often try pure speed to collect the ball and
avoid the other team's players. Orc and Chaos teams will take
a more direct route of overpowering the opposing team and
trundling down the centre of the field almost daring their
opponents to stop them.

Rookies reading this may be confused as to why I haven't
mentioned the use of weapons yet. This is because in Blood
Bowl Nuffle decreed that one's own body is the only weapon
one needs to play the game. Over the years this hasn't stopped
teams using this admittedly rather loose wording to maximum
effect and is the reason why a player's armour is more likely
than not covered in sharp protruding spikes with blades and large
knuckle-dusters attached to gauntlets. Other races and teams
often 'forget' about this basic principle and just ignore Roze-el's
teachings on the matter. Dwarfs and goblins (yes, them again)
are the usual suspects, although this is not exclusively their
domain. The history of Blood Bowl is littered with the illegal
use of weapons and the many devious contraptions brought
forward by the dwarfs and goblins, ranging from monstrous

machines such as the dwarf death-roller to the no-less-dangerous chainsaw.

THE PSYCHOS... I MEAN PLAYERS

As I've already mentioned, there are many ways to get the ball from one end of the field to the other. Equally, there are as many ways to stop the ball from moving towards a team's end zone. A Blood Bowl player, to an extent, needs to be a jack-of-all-trades – as equally quick on the offensive as well as being able to defend. This doesn't mean that there aren't any specialists in the sport, far from it – a Blood Bowl player needs to specialise in one of the many positions if he wishes to rise above the humble lineman. Let's look at the more common positions:

Blitzers: These highly skilled players are usually the stars of the game, combining strength and skill with great speed and flexibility. All the most glamorous Blood Bowl players are blitzers, since they are always at the heart of the action and doing very impressive things! Their usual job is to burst a hole through their opponents' lines, and then run with the ball to score. Team captains are usually blitzers, and all of them, without exception, have egos the size of a halfling's appetite.

Throwers: There is more to Blood Bowl than just grabbing the ball and charging full tilt at the other side (though this has worked for most teams at one time or another). If you can get a player on the other side of your opponents' line, why not simply toss the ball to him and cut out all that unnecessary bloodshed? This, of course, is where the special thrower comes in! These guys are usually lightly armoured (preferring to dodge a tackle rather than be flattened by it).

Throwers of certain races have also been known to launch other things than just the ball. For decades now, an accepted tactic of orc, goblin and even halfling teams is to throw their team-mates downfield. This is usually done by the larger members of said teams such as ogres, trolls and in the case of the halflings, treemen. Of course this tactic is not without risk. Whilst the bigger players are strong it doesn't necessarily mean they are accurate. As regular fans know, goblins make a reassuring 'splat' sound as they hit the ground or stadium wall head-first - much to the joy of the crowd! Trolls are notoriously stupid with memory spans that would shame a goldfish. So a goblin or snotling about to be hurtled across the pitch by his trollish team mate will often find itself heading for the troll's gaping maw instead as the monster forgets what he's holding and decides to have a snack!

Catchers: And of course if you are throwing the ball, it would be nice if there was someone at the other end to catch it! This is where the specialist catcher comes in. Lightly armoured for speed, they are adept at dodging around slower opponents and heading for the open field ready for a long pass to arrive. The best catcher of all time is generally reckoned to be the legendary Tarsh Surehands of the otherwise fairly repulsive skaven team, the Skavenblight Scramblers. With his two heads and four arms, the mutant ratman plainly had something of an advantage.

Blockers: If one side is trying to bash its way through the opposing team's lines, you will often see the latter's blockers come into action to stop them. These lumbering giants are often slow and dim-witted, but they have the size and power to stop show-off blitzers from getting any further up the field! Black orcs, ogres and trolls make especially good blockers, but this fact has hampered the chances of teams like the Oldheim Ogres, who, with nothing but blockers and linemen in their team, have great trouble actually scoring a touchdown!

Linemen: While a good deal of attention is paid to the various specialist players, every true Blood Bowl fan would agree that the players who do most of the hard work are the ordinary linemen. These are the guys who get bashed out of the way while trying to stop a hulking great ogre from sacking their thrower, who are pushed out of the way when their flashy blitzer sets his sights on the end zone, or who get beaten and bruised by the linemen of the opposite side while the more gifted players skip about scoring touchdowns. 'Moaning like a lineman' is a common phrase in Blood Bowl circles for a bad complainer, but if it wasn't for the linemen whingeing about their flashier team-mates, the newspapers would often have nothing to fill their sports pages with!

DA REFS

Blood Bowl has often been described, as 'nearly organised chaos' by its many critics. Blood Bowl's admirers emphatically agree with the critics then again they don't like to play up the 'nearly organised' bit, in fact some quite happily just describe it as 'chaos'. However, it is widely accepted that you do need someone in charge of the game's proceedings and to enforce the games rules or else it wouldn't be Blood Bowl at all. Again, this point is often lost on some fans who would quite happily just come and spectate/participate in a big fight. In any case, the person and/or creature in charge of a game is known as 'the ref'. The ref, in his traditional kit of zebra furs, has a very difficult job to do. You have to ask yourself what kind of mind accepts this sort of responsibility especially when the general Blood Bowl viewing public rate refs far below tax collectors, traffic wardens and sewer inspectors in their estimation.

Of course some refs revile in the notoriety and are as psychopathic as the players themselves. Max 'Kneecap' Mittleman would never issue a yellow or red card but simply disembowel the offending player. It is also fair to say that most (if not all) refs are not the bastions of honesty and independence they would have you believe. In fact the Referees and Allied Rulekeepers Guild has strict bribery procedures and union established rates. Although teams may not always want to bribe a ref – especially when sheer intimidation can be far cheaper.

THAT'S THE BASICS

Now I've covered the rudimentary points of how to play Blood Bowl it's worth going over some of the basic plays you'll see in most games of one variation or another. Remember, it's not just about the fighting; you have to score at some point as well!

The Cage: Probably the most basic play in the game yet it's the one halfling teams still can't get right. This involves surrounding the ball carrier with bodyguards and then moving the whole possession up field. Once within yards of the team's end zone the ball carrier will explode from his protective cocoon and sprint across the line. Not always good against elf teams who have an annoying knack of dodging into the cage and stealing the ball away, still you should see the crowd's rapture when an elf mis-steps and he's clothes-lined to the floor by a sneering orc.

The Chuck: The second most basic play, although it does require the use of a semi-competent thrower, which rules a large proportion of teams out from the start. Blockers on the 'line of scrimmage' will open a gap for the team's receivers to run through, and once they are in the opposing team's back field the thrower will lob the ball to them. Provided one of the catchers can catch it, all that remains is a short run into the opposing end zone for a touchdown. The survival rate of a lone catcher in the enemy's half is obviously not great so it's important to get as many catchers upfield as possible. The more catchers a team employs, the more chances at least one of them will remain standing to complete the pass.

The Chain: A particular favourite of blitzers everywhere. Players position themselves at different stages upfield. The ball is then quickly passed from player to player in a series of short passes until the blitzer on the end of the chain can wave to the crowd and gallop into the end zone. A broken link in the chain can balls this up (excuse the pun), giving the opposing team an opportunity to intercept the ball.

The Kill-em-all!: Favoured by dwarf teams and those that lack a certain finesse. It works on the principle that if there isn't anyone left in the opposing team, then who's going to stop you from scoring? The receiving team simply hides the ball in its half and proceeds to maul, break and kill the opposition. Chaos teams are particularly good at this. When there is less than a third of the opposing team left, the ball will slowly make its way upfield. The downside is that some teams can get so engrossed in the maiming they simply run out of time to score. Nevertheless, it's a fan favourite and is here to stay.